UP
JIM
RIVER

MICHAEL FLYNN

A TOM DOHERTY ASSOCIATES BOOK
NEW YORK

UP JIM RIVER

Copyright © 2010 by Michael Flynn

All rights reserved.

A Tor Book
Published by Tom Doherty Associates, LLC
175 Fifth Avenue
New York, NY 10010

www.tor-forge.com

Tor® is a registered trademark of Tom Doherty Associates, LLC.

ISBN 978-0-7653-6282-7

First Edition: April 2010
First Mass Market Edition: February 2011

Printed in the United States of America

0 9 8 7 6 5 4 3 2 1

acknowledgments

It's a big Spiral Arm and the human stew has been thoroughly mixed. Languages have changed and blended along with the cultures they once supported. I would like to thank Basheer Alawamleh for help with Arabic words, Kathleen Wong for some Chinese advice, and Rohit Ramaswamy, Geetha Rao, and Raj Nanduri for terms and usages of the Tamil language. Naturally, pronunciations (and grammars) have changed a bit over the centuries, and I have deliberately altered them to suit my purposes.

chapters

those of name

Lucia D. Thompson	d.b.a. Méarana, a harper, daughter of Bridget ban
Donovan (the scarred man)	d.b.a. The Fudir, sometime agent of the CCW
Cerberus	receptionist at the Kennel
Zorba de la Susa	retired Hound, Bridget ban's mentor
Graceful Bintsaif	journeyman Hound assigned to the Academy
Johnny Barcelona	d.b.a. Resilient Services, emperor of the Morning Dew
Morgan Cheng-li	Grand Secretary of the Morning Dew sheen
The Bwana	Chairman of the Terran Brotherhood on Thistlewaite
Boo Sad mac Sorli *and* Enwelumokwu Tottenheim	commercial jawharries on Harpaloon
Greystroke	a Hound
Little Hugh O'Carroll	his Pup, d.b.a. Rinty
Billy Chins	a Terran khitmutgar and actuary on Harpaloon

Shmon van Rwengasira y Gasdro	Director of the Dancing Vrouw Tissue Bank
Dame Teffna bint Howard	a tourista from Angletar
Teodorq Nagarajan	a Wildman
Judge Trayza Dorrajenfer	a prosecuting magistrate on Boldly Go
Cheng-bob Smerdrov	an import-exporter on Gatmander
Debly Jean Sofwari	a science-wallah from Kàuntusulfalúghy
Maggie Barnes	captain of the trade ship *Blankets and Beads*
Dalapathi Zitharthan ad-Din	"D.Z.," her first officer
Mart Pepper, "Wild Bill" Hallahan, et al.	crew of *Blankets and Beads*
Paulie o' the Hawks	a second Wildman
Zhawn Sloofy	a translator from Nuxrjes'r
Djamos Tul	a translator from Rajiloor

Bartenders, sliders, Terrans, flunkies, movers, 'Loons, merchant princes, cab drivers, news faces, Amazons, Gats, Residents, Dūqs, sundry wildmen, and the Princess of the Farther Spaces

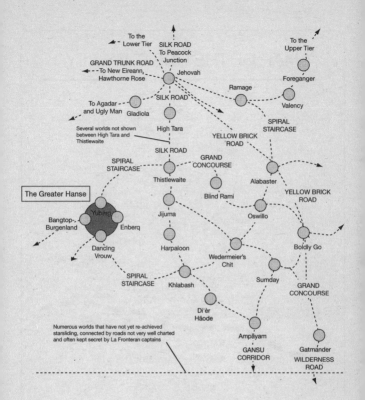

To the
Lower Tier

SILK ROAD
To Peacock
Junction

GRAND TRUNK ROAD
To New Eireann,
Hawthorne Rose

Jehovah

To the
Upper Tier

Foreganger

Ramage

Valency

To Agadar
and Ugly Man

Gladiola

SILK ROAD

SPIRAL
STAIRCASE

High Tara

YELLOW BRICK
ROAD

Several worlds not shown
between High Tara and
Thistlewaite

SILK ROAD

GRAND
CONCOURSE

SPIRAL
STAIRCASE

Thistlewaite

Alabaster

Blind Rami

YELLOW BRICK
ROAD

The Greater Hanse

Jijuma

Oswillo

Bangtop-
Burgenland

Yuberg

Enberq

Dancing
Vrouw

Harpaloon

Boldly Go

Wedermeier's
Chit

SPIRAL
STAIRCASE

Khlabash

Sumday

GRAND
CONCOURSE

Di'èr
Häode

Numerous worlds that have not yet re-achieved
starsliding, connected by roads not very well charted
and often kept secret by La Fronteran captains

Ampäyam

GANSU
CORRIDOR

Gatmander

WILDERNESS
ROAD

THE WILD

THE RIM

Map of Lafrontera District
of the Periphery

*Planar projection of Lafrontera District, ULP. View is from Galactic
North. Not all intervening worlds are shown along the main roads.
Worlds are not all on the same plane.*

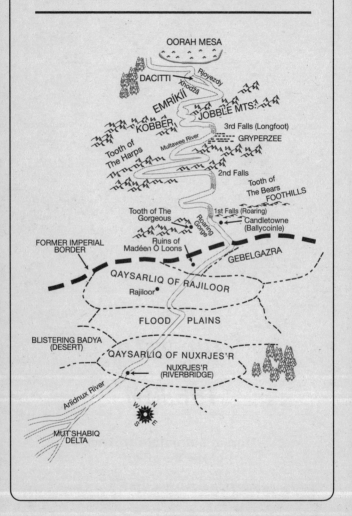

MAP OF THE GREAT VALLEY

OORAH MESA

Rjoyezdy

DACITTI

Xhodża

EMRÍKÍI

JOBBLE MTS.

3rd Falls (Longfoot)

KOBBER

GRYPERZEE

Tooth of
The Harps

Multawee River

2nd Falls

Tooth of
The Bears

FOOTHILLS

Tooth of The
Gorgeous

Roaring
Gorge

1st Falls (Roaring)

Candletowne
(Ballycoinle)

Ruins of
Madéen O Loons

GEBELGAZRA

FORMER IMPERIAL
BORDER

QAYSARLIQ OF RAJILOOR

Rajiloor

FLOOD PLAINS

BLISTERING BADYA
(DESERT)

QAYSARLIQ OF NUXRJES'R

NUXRJES'R
(RIVERBRIDGE)

Arîdnux River

MUT SHABIQ
DELTA

UP
JIM
RIVER

ALAP (VILAMBIT)

*T*his is *her* song, but she will not sing it, and so that task must fall to lesser lips.

There is a river on Dangchao Waypoint, a small world appertaining to Die Bold. It is a longish river as such things go, with a multitude of bayous and rapids and waterfalls, and it runs through many a strange and hostile country. Going up it, you can lose everything. Going up it, you can find anything.

A truism in the less-than-United League of the Periphery holds that every story begins on Jehovah or ends on Jehovah. This is one of those that begin there. It is a story of love and loss and finding—and other such curses.

What makes the saying a truism is that Jehovah's sun—the Eye of Allah—is a major nexus on Electric Avenue, that great network of superluminal highways that binds the stars together. More roads converge there than anywhere else in the South Central sector, and so the probabilities favor—or the Fates pronounce—that sooner or later everyone passes through.

And when they do, they come to the Bar of Jehovah, for unless your pleasures run to such wildness as hymn-singing—and what can be so wild as that?—there is no other place on the planet so congenial. The hymn-singing is good and surprisingly affective, but many of those who wash up on Jehovah seek to anesthetize the memory of the past, and not to anticipate the glories of the future. For many of the patrons, there is no future, and there is not even the memory that there may once have been one.

In a Spiral Arm where "the strong take what they can and the weak suffer what they must," Jehovah is the pearl without price, she whose worth is measured in rubies; for she is too valuable a prize to be taken. "A hundred hands desire it," the saying runs, "and ninety-nine will keep the one from seizing it." And so it is a refuge of sorts for many, and a cash cow for the Elders. And if cash cows remind one of golden calves, that can be overlooked at round-up time.

And so colorful and cryptic Chettinad merchants rub shoulders with their rivals from the Greater Hanse; the crews of tramp freighters with Interstellar Cargo; with Gladiola seed ships, and League marshals and colonists and trekkers; with touristas, too: those starsliders who come in on the great Hadley liners for their quick blick and then *off again*! to stars worth longer visits.

And so also, with the detritus of the Spiral Arm: those who tramp from star to star, one step ahead of a creditor or a spouse or a League marshal; those whose lives and dreams have become to dream their lives away.

One of these is the scarred man. He has a name, or he has many names, but that one will do for now. It is no longer clear, even to him, which of his names are real, or if any of them are. He has sat so long in his niche that he is very nearly a fixture of the Bar, an ornament like the great gilt-worked chandelier mobile that casts an uncertain and ever-changing light upon a patronage equally changing and uncertain. He has become, for a small and self-selected group of connoisseurs, something of a tourist attraction himself. He has come because his past is too heavy to bear, and here he may slide down his load and rest. Recently, certain elements of that past have come to press upon him . . .

. . . But this is not his story; or it is not quite his story.

And lastly—and these are most rare—come those who are not driven by their past, but drawn by their future. It might seem odd that the path to the future would pass through the Bar of Jehovah; but the path to heaven is said to wind through purgatory.

As, too, the path to hell.

I DOG GONE

And so the story begins, if it did not begin else-where and at another time. The scarred man sits in his accustomed place in the Bar, robed in shadows in a niche cut into the wall. The other niche-seats are favored by lov-ers seeking shadows—but there is no love here. Or love only of the most abrasive sort.

The early morning is a somber and introspective time, and the scarred man's visage is nothing if not somber and introspective. He owns a gaunt and hollow look, as if he has been suctioned out, and not even a soul remains. He is all skin and skull, and his mouth sags across the saddle of his hooked chin. He has been known to smile, but not very often and never is it comforting to see. He is weathered, his skin almost translucent. His hair is snow-white, but not the white of purity, for that has been a long time lost. A checkerboard of scars breaks the hair into tufts like a woodland violated by streets and winding roads. Those scars and a sad story have kept him fed and reasonably drunk for a long time. He has changed the story from time

*to time just to keep it fresh; but his eyes are never still and
the true story may have never been told.*

Although it was early morning, the Bar was full. There are
those for whom the night is day, and these have slipped in
one by one to escape the unconcealing sun, discuss their
nocturnal ramblings, and divide the take. Longshoremen
have trudged up Greaseline Street from the Spaceport Yards
to celebrate the end of their shift. There were sliders and
touristas, too, since liners and freighters tocked to shipboard times and it was only by wildest chance that these
ever coincided with the Bar's own meridian. Sliders were
as likely to come weary with the dawn as bright-eyed with
the eve.

And they talked, all of them. They told tales, aired griev-
ances, warbled songs. They muttered darkly, and whispered
intrigues as intricate and Byzantine as their states of intoxication allowed. It all merged into a hum that rose and
fell with numbers and furtiveness but which never ceased
entirely. It was a joke among the regular patrons that there
were conversations still ongoing long after the originators
had died; and what jest is ever purely a lie? There are docu-
mented cases of ship captains returning after long absences
and resuming the self-same discussion.

The scarred man sat to his breakfast and his breakfast was
one of daal, and baked beans and sautéed mushrooms, with
scrambled eggs and cold, fatty bacon. He ate in a silence
punctuated by occasional mumbles and subvocalizations, as
if he himself embodied in small the chattering crowd around
him. Some thought him a little mad because of this, although
they were wrong, for there was nothing little about his
madness.

Above, a door closed, and the scarred man's eyes flicked
upward for just a moment before he dipped his daal into the
beans and lifted the dripping mass to his mouth. Footsteps

followed on the wooden staircase, and still the scarred man did not move. Then *she* was with him, pulling out a seat opposite, and directing a sneer at his noisome breakfast. She herself had only a cup of black coffee—or something that had coffee in its ancestry. (The human diaspora was millennia old, and genes had been tinkered with on this planet or that. The bean went by many names—caff, chick, moke, joe—but even when it bore the same name, it was never quite the same drink.)

"She" was the harper, and that name, too, will serve for now. She had come to him a metric week ago and pricked from his teeth the tale of January's Dancer, in the process unearthing in him old and hurtful memories. And he saw in the backlit dawn of the thrown-wide shutters that she intended to hurt him further. For she had walked with purpose in her stride, and purpose meant motion, and, as an ancient sage had once said, "With the motion of creatures, time began to run its course." And time was the one thing the scarred man had not measured for all these many years.

Her eyes were the hard, sharp glass-green of flint, and her hair was a great flame of red, but her skin was dark gold. The bhisti science-wallahs who had touched the genes of coffee had not forborne to touch the genes of men, and what they had done had wrought wonders and horrors; and it was just as well that their art had been forgotten, for the world can bear only so much wonder.

The harper waited in silence. It was a talent she had, as great a talent as her harping; for silence is a vacuum that sucks words from the throats of men. She lifted the coffee to her lips; set it upon the table; adjusted the cup slightly.

Minutes died.

But the scarred man, too, knew the art of silence, and had had many more years of practice.

Finally, she looked up, halting for a moment his restless

eyes. "I'll be leaving today," she announced, but in an uncertain voice that indicated an unsettled purpose.

The scarred man smiled—because he had won a small victory in the art of waiting. A part of him wished to bid her adieu, but another part wished her to stay. "Where away?" he said, serving a neutral response.

"To find my mother."

The scarred man nodded slowly. He could see the mother in the child; should have seen it earlier; should have seen it in the moment the harper had first strode through the Bar like the Queen of High Tara. The harper was not quite so striking, not quite so wild in her look as had been Bridget ban; but neither was she quite so hardened. For Bridget ban had practiced the art of seduction, and nothing quite so coarsens the soul as to use too roughly a tool so soft. The harper preserved something deep within herself that in her mother had grown rigid and worn.

"Your mother was a witch," he said. "A harlot queen. She is best left unsought."

He had hoped for some reaction from the harper, but the young woman only dipped her head. "I understand your hurt. You loved her once and lost her; but I knew a different woman."

"Don't be so sure you did," the scarred man responded. "A leopard does not change her spots. It was not my idea to love her, but hers. It is not in any man to resist her if she but chooses that he not. She played me like you play your harp, until I sang her tune. What chance does a child have against such snares as *she* could lay?"

"I think you are too bitter. You made your own choices. It was *you* who left *her*."

"I *escaped*." The scarred man remembered an early morning in the slums of Chel'veckistad, on Old 'Saken: stealing from the bed of Bridget ban, cold-cocking Hugh, and heading off to secure the Dancer for himself.

Of all the hard things he had done in his life, those three had been the hardest.

"How long has she been gone?" he asked grudgingly. A part of him wanted to know. A part of him was curious.

"Three years. She left when I was sixteen metric."

"And only now you've come looking?"

"Don't think you were easy to find. I followed clues, rumors. They led here."

"They shouldn't have. No slip of a girl should have tracked me down."

"Mother is a Hound. She taught me things."

The Hounds of the Ardry were resourceful agents—skilled in arts politic and martial; without pity or remorse when what had to be done had to be done. They could be many things, and any thing: messenger, scout, spy, ambassador, saboteur, assassin, savior, planetary manager. Child-rearing was not beyond the multitudinous talents of Bridget ban.

He pushed his breakfast aside. "And what makes you, a harper, think you can find a Hound if she does not wish the finding? A Hound may be years on a case. She may be on her way back even now."

"Gwillgi came to see me on Dangchao, on our family's ranch."

"Gwillgi!"

"He was searching for Mother and thought I might know something, some small detail. That's how I knew she'd gone missing and was not simply a long time on her task."

"All the more reason not to get involved. I've met enough of the Ardry's Hounds to be wishful of meeting no more; Gwillgi least among them."

"He did seem an . . . intense little man."

"He could kill you with a flip of his wrist."

"You know how thinly the Kennel is spread. There are always more missions than Hounds to take them. They cannot neglect their other missions." She reached out and seized the scarred man's wrist. "Fudir, *they've called off the search.*"

"And did you?"

"Did I what?"

"Know one small detail."

The harper thought for a moment, fingering a medallion that hung on a silver chain around her neck. "I . . . don't know. Mother had been conducting disaster relief on Thistlewaite. She came home, took a fortnight's home leave, then she was gone." The harper's voice hardened just a little bit at this, and the scarred man gave her a sharp look.

"And she didn't tell you where she was headed."

The harper gave him a look. "If she had," she snapped, "I'd nae be searching! She ne'er told me aforehand. Hound's business . . . It was nae for me tae know!"

Irritation washed across the scarred man's face and he grimaced. "All right," he said, as if to himself. "I'll ask." Then, addressing the harper: "How did she seem to you while she was home?"

"Like . . . Mother. We had dinner. She attended one of my concerts. She spent a lot of time in her office, reading, writing her reports. She gave me this." The harper took the medallion from around her neck and held it out to him.

The scarred man reached out and seized it: a simple black ceramic disk with a diamond set in its center. Below the diamond, a sinuous ruby sliver zigzagged to the rim. "It's broken off at the tip," he pointed out. "It used to extend beyond the rim. How like her to bestow a defective gift."

"It's only a memento from Thistlewaite. She often did that when she came home from a mission. But it's her whence, not her whither."

"Except this isn't thistlework. They don't shape jewels in quite this way. They prefer the gaudy and elaborate." He handed it back to her, and the harper tucked it once more between her breasts. "Trade goods," he said. "You'd get two, maybe two-fifty shekels in the Jehovah market. Less, if you dealt with the Bourse."

"I showed it to jewelers in Dangchao City. I even took it over to Die Bold herself, to the Mercantile Loop in Port Èlfiuji. No one recognized the style."

A shrug. "It's a big Spiral Arm." He dipped his bread once more into the beans and swirled it around. Then, with a gesture of disgust he threw the bread into the bowl. "Happy? Sad?"

"What?"

"Your mother! Did she act happy, sad, depressed, the week she was home? Afraid? Maybe she was running from something, and that's why she didn't tell you where she was going."

"Mother, afraid? I wouldn't even know what that looked like. She seemed . . . excited, I suppose. I asked her what, and she only said that it was something so outrageous and so wonderful that it could not possibly be true. But if it *was* . . . If it was, we need no longer fear the Confederation."

The scarred man looked up sharply. He himself had been, at one time, an agent of the Confederation of Central Worlds, though one insufficiently devout—as the scars on his scalp testified. Her rulers were cold and ruthless—beside them the Hounds were eager puppy dogs—and he knew a moment's unease. If the daughter had been asking around, the words she had just spoken had been dropping into any number of ears, and it was as certain as death that Those of Name would hear them eventually and take an interest. They did not believe that there should ever be anyone who did not fear Them.

The harper held out a slip of notepaper. "She left nothing but this note."

The scarred man reacted with genuine anger and snatched

the slip of paper from the young woman's hand. "I'm no harp, girl. I don't like being played." He unfolded it, saw it was handwritten, and succeeded in astonishing himself. All these years flown past, and he could still recognize her handwriting.

Out on the edge, it read. *Fire from the sky. Back soon.*

"Fudir, what does it mean?"

The harper had again used one of his names—or he thought she had. He chose to believe that she had not called him something else. *Go ahead, "Fudir," a part of him jibed, tell her what it means.*

"What do *you* think it means?" he asked her.

"I don't know. 'Out on the edge.' Perhaps she went into the Rift, or out to the Rim, or perhaps to the edge of settled space, past Krinth or Gatmander, or to the unsettled worlds of the Galactic East."

The Fudir grunted. "Which pretty much brackets the Periphery." He gave her back the note, and it, too, vanished into her clothing. "But it might not mean that sort of edge. It might have meant the challenge would drive her to the edge of her talents." He waved his hand to get the Bartender's attention and pointed to his table. The Bartender, a Jehovan who went by the office name of Praisegod Barebones, understood. Like cock's crow, the scarred man's first drink heralded the new day. He brought a bowl of uiscebaugh to the table and set it before him.

"I don't know that she has an edge to her abilities," the harper said, "or that any challenge could push her to them."

"The more fool, she."

"Otherwise, why write 'back soon'? She thought this would be a simple task. But months became years. And then Gwillgi came. His visit frightened me."

"A visit from Gwillgi would frighten anyone."

"No. I mean, it is a big Spiral Arm, like everyone says, and it's often weeks and weeks between stars. But she's been gone too long now, and no one knows where, or why, or what happened to her. I thought . . ." And the hesitation in the harper's voice drew his attention from the uisce bowl.

"What?"

"I thought that you would help me find her. You're clever. You can see things."

The scarred man stared into the bowl, from the amber reflection of whose contents he stared back. "I'm too old to travel," he said. "Too old for adventure." He ran a hand across the table. "But she hasn't gone into the Rift. That far, I can conjure her meaning. If she had gone there, she would have said 'in,' not 'out.' Any Leaguesman would. It's the Confederates who say '*out* to the Rift.' And now I will tell you, being as how I am so very clever, why you should not chase after her, and should leave the search to the Hounds."

The harper leaned across the table, and the scarred man knew that whatever reason he would give this young woman would serve only to whet, not to weaken her resolve. Yet he could not let her go without a warning. "A Hound keeps in touch with the Kennel," he said. "Always. Message drones. Swift-boats and packets. Now the Ourobouros Circuit, on those worlds with a station. Even if she'd had to entrust a message to some tramp captain streaming toward High Tara, there's been more than enough time for that message to reach the Kennel—even from Gatmander or Krinth. And that can only mean that she *can't* send a message; and that can only mean that she's . . ."

"No, she isn't. I would know it if she were."

The scarred man said nothing for a moment. "At the very least," he suggested, "it means she's in an exceptionally dangerous situation. Gwillgi might go in with some chance of coming out. Not you."

"That's why I need you with me," the harper insisted. "You're a Terran. You've got the . . . the . . ."

"Stritsmats," said the scarred man. "An old Terran word."

"And you're an old Terran. I could . . . I could pay you."

"If I wouldn't do it for love, why would you think I'd do it for money?"

The harper pushed away from the table and stood. "You're right. I don't. I thought you loved her. I thought you *owed* her for walking out the way you did . . ."

"You think too much," the scarred man told her.

The harper made no answer, but only looked at him. She was a young woman, but those were an old woman's eyes.

"There was a matter . . ." the scarred man said. "I failed the Secret Name. We were punished. A new style of paraperception."

"Paraperception can be useful. To see independently with each eye; hear with each ear . . ."

"No! You don't understand. The operation was botched. Or maybe it was deliberate. They tried to give him complete personalities. Each of us was to be a specialist—an entire team in one mind. But we're not. It's all turmoil up here." He tapped his head with their finger. "Half the time we're not even sure who I am. You need someone single-minded to help you; and the one thing we are not is single-minded."

"They 'diced and sliced' your mind, you told me," the harper said slowly. "Fudir and Donovan and . . . how many others?"

"We're not entirely certain. Six. Maybe seven."

"Good," said the harper. "Then there will be more of us."

II A MAN OF PARTS

The scarred man's breakfast had gone as cold as his heart, but he mopped up the last of the beans, chewed down the last strip of fatty bacon, and washed it all down with an acrid gulp of uiscebeatha. He had sent the harper off with his refusal in her ears, and yet, quantum-like, it entangled also on his tongue, so that he could taste nothing of his meal. Praisegod always served the worst whiskies first, in the hope that it would drive clients off the creature, but this morning the fire lit the scarred man's throat and belly almost as an afterthought.

"That was a terrible thing to do," he said.

A Gladiola ark-master passing by the niche turned startled eyes toward him. The voice had seemed to come disembodied out of the shadows. Perhaps he wondered what terrible thing it was that he had done, and who it was who had caught him out at last.

"What did she expect us to do?" Donovan answered. "Drop everything and run off on a goose chase across the whole Spiral Arm?"

"Drop everything?" the Fudir answered in a slightly different voice, and gestured around the table, as if to encompass the "everything" that they would have to drop.

The goose is of high value, a part of him said. There are those who would be grateful for the finding of her.

And the puzzle is a pretty one, the Sleuth commented.

"The answer is 'out on the edge,' " Donovan said. "We're safe here in the center."

There is such a thing as honor. Honor has some value.

"Great value," said the Fudir, "it being rare." The Fudir seldom heard that silky, seductive voice. He wondered how many others were lurking. Somewhere in the back of his mind there was a rustling, as of dried leaves in the winds of autumn.

I'm bored. Do one thing or the other; but *decide*.

That voice, he did recognize. He and Donovan called him the Brute. In their artful carvings of Donovan's psyche, Those of Name had thought physical prowess would be as useful as cleverness and reason and seduction.

"Go back to sleep," Donovan told the Brute. "Later, we'll go out and cruise the Corner."

I liked her. She was taking *action*.

Foolish action.

And so?

You owe it to her.

"We owe no one," said Donovan. "It's the rest of them that owe *us* everything."

Praisegod had come by with a fresh bowl of uiscebeatha. "You owe *me*," he said offhandedly, "and that's for certain. You run a tab."

The Fudir laughed. "They all think we're crazy."

"Are they wrong?" said Praisegod. He gathered up the empty bowls and left, chuckling to himself.

"I don't know why we're even discussing this," Donovan said. "Think about it. You, too, Brute, if you can. In all the Spiral Arm, who has the nuts to make a Hound disappear?"

That entrained an uncomfortable silence, broken only by the gentle hissing of an unheard wind. The Fudir shivered, as if the moon had passed behind a leafless tree.

And so what if it is *Those?* the Brute demanded, though with less bravado.

"If anyone beside the Confederacy has the skill to take on a Hound," Donovan insisted, "I'll be glad to hear." He waited a few beats, but his inner voices were silent. "Do you want to risk *Those* laying hands on us again?"

What more could they do to us? asked the Sleuth, attempting insouciance.

"Do you want to find out?"

The Brute laughed.

You all know why we should help her.

The Fudir turned a little in the niche so that he could stare at the wall and not at the milling crowd in the Barroom. "Maybe," he said. "Maybe not."

You loved her mother once.

"Once was enough. And, besides, that was nearly twenty years ago."

Yes. Exactly.

"That was *you* who slept with her," Donovan said. "I missed the whole thing."

"Don't complain. It was less a lark than it sounds."

"Why not complain? I've had an obligation laid on me without the pleasure of incurring it."

It would be, allowed the Sleuth, *something of a coup to rescue a Hound. Gratitude can loosen purses.*

Or loosen belts. Then you could have the pleasure you missed out on before.

The Fudir knew a sudden stab of jealousy. He could not have her again. There would be too many watching, too many participating.

<Don't go. I'm afraid.>

And the Fudir shivered in fear unadulterated, in terror unfiltered. The niche he sat in was suddenly a trap. There was no escape. The doors were far away.

Donovan sighed. "Holy Saint Freud, who woke Inner Child?"

Boo! said the Brute and laughed at the frisson of fear on the backwash.

Go to sleep, Child.

"I suppose," said Donovan, "that she's out in the Spaceport looking to charter a ship."

The logical course, said the Sleuth, *is to go to High Tara first. The Kennel must know from where she last reported.*

And they might know why she had gone out. Knowing why is the first clue to knowing where.

Gwillgi said nothing.

Would he have, if he knew? He was collecting information, not disbursing it.

The Fudir dropped his empty bowl to the table. "Big dhik, sahbs, but it's no use. Can you think of anyone else we could trust to help her?"

"I can't think of anyone," said Donovan, "let alone an 'else.' Whatever Bridget ban encountered, it would not likely be something from which the likes of *us* could save her."

Then how much less so her daughter alone? Would you send the harper out to deal with Confederate agents?

"The chances of two snowballs in hell are not appreciably greater than those of one."

"You can't hide here from the CCW forever," the Fudir reminded him.

"I'm not hiding. I'm bunkered up. Jehovah is the first place *Those* would look."

<It's been a long time. No one's come. Maybe they've forgotten.>

Donovan said nothing. Those of Name had forgotten many things, but he was certain they had not forgotten him. They had hobbled his mind for a reason. The Fudir nodded agreement. Years before, he had believed himself forgotten. But *Those* had summoned him at last. There had been an agent of theirs, a tall slim woman who had used the name Ravn Olafsdottr. She had come as back-up to awaken Donovan if the prime agent failed. The scarred man recalled as if in faded and colorless holograms old days spent with Greystroke and Little Hugh . . . and Bridget ban. Those had been . . . "interesting times."

More interesting than drinking all day, and running scrambles in the Corner at night.

Somewhere in his mind: a rumble of laughter like the onset of a distant storm.

He had met Olafsdottr only that one time, when they had both been enslaved by January's Dancer and the only escape lay in awakening the unaffected Donovan persona. *Your dooty then is yoor dooty now,* she had said in her hooting Alabaster accent. And Donovan had emerged and taken over and the Fudir had spent a long time afterward in the dark.

"Tough," said Donovan. "Think how many years *I* spent bundled away. I'm the prime, the original. The rest of you are only the pencil shavings of my mind."

"So you say," the Fudir told him. But the rejoinder sounded weak, even to himself.

The uisce's gone, the Brute pointed out. **What do we do, order more, or . . . ?**

"We'll go with her as far as High Tara," said the Fudir. "What risk in that?"

To all appearances the scarred man had frozen in place and muttered to himself for a few minutes. Those who knew him paid him no mind, and this had reassured those who did not. Now he pushed his bowl aside and rose from the table.

Praisegod looked his way and his eyebrows rose. "In the daylight?"

The scarred man wended his way through the milling throng. He had a way of moving—supple and balanced—that enabled him to slip through crowds with a minimum of delay and at a modest profit. When he reached the bar, he slapped someone's ten-shekel note down. "I'll need your prayers, friend Praisegod. I'm going aloft among the heathens."

"I'll pray for *them.* A decent heathen is hard to find."

The Fudir smiled through the scarred man's eyes and

bowed Terran-style over his folded hands. "Nandri, sahb. I go jildy now. You sell less-less whiskey me gone."

"You always leave," said the Bartender, "but you always come back." He touched his fingers to his temple with his palm facing out. "Sah!"

As the Fudir reached the door, Praisegod picked up the ten-shekel note and stuffed it in a shirt pocket, and he said softly, "And perhaps a prayer for you, as well." But the Fudir pretended not to hear him.

Outside, the harper waited, leaning against the building with her arms folded.

The Fudir grunted as she fell in step with him. "Don't look so smug."

AN AISTEAR

The scarred man and the harper booked passage on *Dragomir Pennymac*, out of Hadley Prime bound for Hanower and Dancing Vrouw by way of High Tara. She was the sort of liner called an "Eighteener," after her complement of alfven engines, and she bore three thousand souls, passengers and crew. She was pushed out of High Jehovan Orbit onto the crawl, and Space Traffic Control's network of magnetic particle beam projectors juggled her steadily upward, handing her off from this platform to that, building her velocity; hurtling her up past the orbit of Ashterath and into the arms of the giant projectors tapping off Shreesheeva, the superjovian in the outer reaches of Jehovah Roads. By that time, *Pennymac* had achieved a sizable fraction of light speed, and was homing for a hole in space.

The Fudir explained the process to the harper one

evening in the aft passenger lounge called Devi's Delight, a large room done up in a décor suitable for those impecunious enough to travel below Eight-Deck. Holograms of scenery on Beth Hadley surrounded them; but adjacent panels clashed and the overall impression was of an incompetent landscaper. The harper and the scarred man dined on plates of over-cooked vegetables and a filet of something that very much resembled the flesh of swine.

"The ancient god Shree Einstein," the Fudir explained, "decreed that nothing could move through space faster than the speed of light. He did this, so it is said, to imprison mankind on the Home World of Terra."

The harper was less interested in how they would get to High Tara than in what they would do once they got there; but the hunt for Bridget ban could not begin until then. She sighed. "And why would Shree Einstein do such a thing?"

"He foresaw, so it is said, the overthrow and degradation of Terra by her colonies and thought to prevent that by preventing star travel itself."

" 'So it is said . . .' " She allowed skepticism to show.

The Fudir shrugged. "Shree Einstein spoke with such gravity that the very nature of matter responded. But the trickster god, Shree Maxwell, set loose his demons. Unlike the word of Shree Einstein, which is univocal and lovingly draws everything toward ultimate unity, the words of Shree Maxwell are bipolar, and may repel or attract. Plasmas ran from star to star at his command, creasing the very fabric of space into superluminal folds when the universe was a cosmic egg, no bigger than my hand might hold. And it was through these roads that mankind spread across the Spiral Arm."

The crook of the harper's mouth expressed her skepticism. "But Shree Einstein decreed that nothing could move faster than light. Can one god then overrule another? If so, what sort of mewling half-gods can they be?"

The Fudir bobbed his head from side to side in the Terran *yes*. "And so it was. But Shree Einstein also decreed that space cannot exist without matter; and so space itself is no 'thing.' And 'no thing' *can* travel faster than light. It is what we Terrans call a 'loophole.' The plasma loops create holes in space itself, and these deceive Shree Einstein, since what falls into the creases cannot be seen from the Newtonian flats. Thus, we escape his ire by escaping his notice. Within the creases, ships like *Pennymac* must still move more slowly than light, but ship and light alike are carried along by the speed of space."

"Awa' wi' your parables." The harper turned her attention to the meal, but it was not such a meal as to merit much attention; and so after a moment she said, "I'm not one for theology, but my mother was skeptical. She believed there could be at most one god, and all the others were but wise men of the past who had been ordered and guided by the Divine Wisdom. She liked to cite the ancient prophet Ockham, who said you should not worship more gods than necessary; and one was quite enough, thank you."

The scarred man began to laugh, only to stiffen with the smile half-formed. He held this terrible rictus for a moment before he shuddered and his features took on a sharper and more vulpine look. The edges of his lips pulled away from his teeth in a manner not at all comforting. It was not the smile that he had started to make.

"You will have to forgive friend Fudir," he said. "He was a chartsman himself in the long ago and thinks everyone finds the theology of superluminal travel as fascinating as he does."

"Ah . . ." The harper sat back and stared at her companion. She had seen these sudden mood shifts before. Now she understood what lay beneath them. "You must be Donovan."

The smile was cold. "Yes. The others 'may' be, but I am the one who 'must' be. I am the *hule prote*, the prime matter from which all of them were formed. But let me tell you: the Fudir will dance three ways around the Bar before he gets through the door, so I have taken the tongue from him to explain something that he will not; namely, that you are on a fool's errand, and your search will end in failure."

"Well," said the harper, "aren't *you* the little bluebird of happiness."

"Mock on, harper. Optimism is the child of ignorance."

"I'd wish my harp with me. There is a goltraí coming on and my fingers itch to play you."

"Oh, what a cacophony that would be! In which mode might we seven harmonize? Pay attention. The Spiral Arm is home to only two sorts of men: those who have paid attention and those who are dead. Your mother was a Hound, sought diligently by other Hounds. Do you suppose that your flailing can succeed where their craft has failed?"

"Perhaps." The harper pushed the remains of her meal away from her. "And for two reasons. The first is that a daughter may know her mother more thoroughly than any colleague, and so see her where other eyes have failed."

"But she vanished on a Hound's business, not a mother's. If she has contacted neither you nor the Kennel, it means she *cannot*; and where a Hound is concerned, 'cannot' means she is dead. Accept that."

"No."

"Your denial is insufficient refutation. I cannot see your mother falling to any mere quotidian disaster. There are very few things in the Spiral Arm that can effect the disappearance of a Hound, and one of them is a Confederate courier."

"And the second reason," the harper continued unperturbed, "is that her colleagues have abandoned the hunt.

Were there even a hint of 'Federal involvement, can you doubt they would have pressed matters to the limit?"

"Can you be so sure they have not? Do not discount Those of Name. Their ears are keen, their arms are long. Do you know the Weapon of the Long Knife? They may strike from stars whose very light has yet to reach us. They may strike with no more than a word spoken into the right ear or a coin dropped in the right palm. But the Fudir is a sentimental fool. Somewhere in the cockle of his heart rests a mustard seed of affection; and you have watered it, a little, over the past few days. Like a stone embedded in a pane of glass, it is a weak point. It is *there* he can break, and we with him. The nostalgia you awakened for your mother has turned his head. And that is a mistake, for a man looking backward can blunder into unpleasant surprises before him. And as little as I care for him, his well-being is tied inextricably to mine. We will take you so far as the Kennel. On that we have agreed. There, the Hounds will also explain how hopeless a task you have undertaken. If after that you insist on pressing the chase, you will do so without our help." Donovan scowled and shook his head vigorously. "Without our help," he said again.

The scarred man stilled briefly. His smile faded like the embers of a fire, and the cast of his features changed once more. Where Donovan might be called "cold," the Fudir seemed merely "devious," a mien almost friendly in comparison. He was a fox to Donovan's wolf. But there was no humor now in the set of his mouth or eyes.

"I hate him."

The harper did not ask who he meant. "He's afraid. I understand why."

"No. You don't. You can't understand, unless *you* have a mind like shattered glass—and had endured the shattering."

She looked into his ever-shifting eyes. "You're afraid, too."

"You're a fool. We all are. Except Brute, who's not smart enough to be afraid."

"Yet, you wanted to help me."

He shrugged. "It's not like some of us could stay home."

III GUARD DOGS

In the far-flung fiction that is the United League of the Periphery, High Tara is the invented capital of an imaginary realm. This is neither as arbitrary nor as futile as it sounds. Everything must have a center; and everything real started sometime as a dream. The dream may come at the end or even after the end, or it may come at the beginning. High Tara is a dream that came at the beginning. It might fairly be said that there was a United League only because, once upon a time, certain men and women had imagined that there might be.

The ancient god Planck once decreed that even dead matter requires first that it be observed. What can be more dreamlike than that? If even the fact of being depends upon a wish, how much more so constructions of becoming erected upon those facts?

But neither should a fiction become too real. A dream must be perfect, but reality is always flawed. So when the serpent Planck observed the quantum state and brought order from the chaos, he did reality no great favor.

High Tara, seen from orbit, seemed one great forest. Something in her soils had proven remarkably receptive to the ancient seed ships. Where New Eireann had started with little more than basalt, High Tara had possessed a substratum of prokaryotic raw materials. It had been a world almost alive, depending on how far one stretched the fictions of life.

The original colonists had been the usual amalgam of late Commonwealth times: Vraddies and Murkans, Zhōgwó and Roomies, and they had spoken the Taṇṭamiž *lingua franca* of that era. It had been a Romantic age, as all dangerous and interesting times are. No one crosses the stars for a decimal point, but they may for a dream. Contrived anachronisms from the Terran past had been all the fashion; and thus—"so it is said"—a mere dozen or so Irish had managed, quantum-like, to impress their own imagined and somewhat eccentric past onto the colony. But across so many years, ancestry was a collective thing and every Finn was a Bantu beside. Most people no longer had any clear idea whence their re-created culture had come. *I'm a 'Cocker,* they might say; or *I'm from Die Bold,* or *A Gatmander, me.* And other names, older names, names like Polynesia or Britain or Roosiya, brought now little more than a puzzled stare. And so it was that the colorful and kilted throngs of High Tara were as likely as not to braid their hair in queues or hide it under turbans, and to own skins of gold and bronze and cinnabar—and call themselves Gaels in spite of all.

The Green Gawain was a broad, manicured park in the center of Bally Oakley. Hedgerows were mazes, colorful gardens spilled out into patches of wildflowers. Forgotten writers and artists postured on plinth and pedestal. Fountains murmured theatrically and benches gave respite to lovers or the weary. Ornamentation was everywhere: floral arrangements blossomed into pictures when seen from a distance; serpents twisted up lampposts; intricate geometries rimmed pools and walkways, breaking out of their borders here and there into fanciful flowers and more fanciful beasts, into lotus blossoms, swastikas, or taijis, or simply into ornate capitals in the ancient Taṇṭamiž script. It was a peaceful refuge, where one could relax or take a pleasant and conversational stroll with an old friend, and there were secluded groves where you could forget you were in the midst of a great city.

Yet there was something artful in the artlessness of the Green Gawain, something careful about its casualness. Despite the wildflowers and the broken symmetries, it was a bit too well-manicured, a little too obviously contrived. Perhaps the hedge maze was its true heart: a place a bit devious, in the embrace of which one might get lost.

The harper and the scarred man hurried through this restful arbor to the sprawling compound of muted grey stone at its eastern end. Occasional couples demurely holding hands on the benches would turn their heads as if whipsawed by the wind of their passage. But the harper was anxious to get started, and the Fudir anxious to finish.

The Kennel's main building, facing the public ways along the Green, was dwarfed by its neighbors, a shy architectural maid between her more brazen sisters. No murals, no statues. The Kennel bore beside its plain black doors only a brass plaque reading AN SHERIVESH ÁWRIHAY, "The Particular Service."

There was an unobtrusive scanner just beside the door, placed so that visitors could affect no notice of it. The Fudir framed it with his hands. "It's an old-style facemaker," he said. "It scans two dozen dimensions on the face—features immune to the surgeon's art, like the distance between the eye sockets." His forefinger and least-finger made a gauge with which he indicated his two eyes. "Scales you against the eigenfaces in their files." He stared directly into the scanner and pulled his mouth open with his two forefingers.

"Should you do that?" the harper asked uncertainly.

"Ah, it can only improve my beauty. If *my* face isn't in their records, it's not worth their mounting a scanner by the door." He squinted at the lenticel. "In the old Terran Commonwealth, it would be HDTV."

"Ah, the lost glories of Olde Terra. What was HDTV?"

"Oh missy. In old Murkan language, it stand for *Hostile Detection Technique Visual*. They use-then '*real-time, non-invasive automated sensor technologies to detect culturally independent, multimodal indicators of hostile intent.*' "

The harper frowned. "You mean the Terrans had a *machine* to tell them if someone were acting suspiciously."

"Oh, yes, memsahb. No budmash man kamin, if 'AI' say 'he big dhik.' Such machine, much wonderful."

"Though more wonderful not to need them. What sort of age was it that they must *automate* the identification of hostiles?"

But the harper was spared another tale of the wonders of the Terran Commonwealth by the clack of the bolt unlatching. The Fudir pushed the door open and they walked down a short hallway into a broad, marble-floored lobby possessing a single desk at its far end. At the desk sat a small, dark, wrinkled man with baggy jowls and a pug nose, a race of men known as "sharpies." He gave the impression that his skull had been exchanged at some point for one of a smaller size, so that the skin wrapping it now hung in folds. He looked up at their arrival and pushed a pair of spectacles back up a nose barely large enough to hold them.

"An affectation, the glasses," the Fudir said. "The Hounds do nothing without intent."

"Be quiet," Donovan told himself.

"Since they can nae have the wonder-machines of the Commonwealth," the harper said with sly humor, "they can nae be certain of screening all assassins. Yet, they put only a single elderly clark in the foyer."

"Look over your shoulder," said Donovan without turning.

The harper's glance was swift and she made no visible response to the sight of the machine-gun nest over the doorway or the two Pups who sat within the enclosure. "How did you . . . ?"

"A 'murder hole.' It's what I would do. There are other eyes in this room, too. Depend on it. Nor would I discount the old clerk. I think he lies with that harmless mien of his. Remember the maze in the park. This is a world of twists and turns."

The room was oval in shape, with the hallway opening at one focus and the desk at the other. Small onyx statues backlit in yellow stood in niches along the walls. Donovan guessed that these might be great Hounds of the past and noted that several niches were empty. A nice touch. There would be greatness to come, the empty niches said.

As they approached the clerk's desk, Donovan realized that it was placed just a little off-focus and that the niches varied slightly in size. To an intruder standing in the other focal point, the perspective would be slightly off, as would be (were he so foolish as to bring a gun) his aim. This was definitely a room designed to kill any hostiles who entered.

The clerk's spectacles flickered with transient lights and the scarred man recognized them as infogoggles. Donovan's life had surely flashed before the man's eyes. Different files on each pane of the goggles, he was certain. If the receptionist was not paraperceptic, able to read independently with each eye, the Kennel had missed a bet; and the Kennel never missed a bet.

The receptionist gave the harper a quizzical look and the Sleuth interrupted Donovan's thoughts to suggest that the harper's face may not quite match what they have on file. *The one thing that can fudge the eigenfaces is bone growth,* he explained with annoying delight. *So if the data-face has only a childhood portrait of her—*

Shaddap, suggested the Brute.

Quiet, all of you!

Shaddap some more.

"Can I help you?" said the receptionist Hound. His tone of voice suggested that it was not very likely that he could, but a slim possibility must be allowed for. He was dressed in a black, tight-fitting short-sleeved shirt, and the slack in his face did not extend to the muscles of his chest and arms. Around his neck, he wore the white collar of a Hound. "Duty blacks" did not present a very prepossessing uniform; but among the strutting, kilted, colorful throng that infested High Tara, the Hounds of the Ardry had nothing to prove. His desk placard gave him the office-name of Cerberus.

The Pedant roused himself. 𝔠𝔢𝔯𝔟𝔢𝔯𝔲𝔰. 𝔗𝔥𝔢 𝔱𝔥𝔯𝔢𝔢-𝔥𝔢𝔞𝔡𝔢𝔡 𝔤𝔲𝔞𝔯𝔡 𝔡𝔬𝔤 𝔬𝔣 𝔥𝔢𝔩𝔩.

The Sleuth cried, *Ah! His paraperception is likely tripartite.*

"Then he's not half the man we are," the Fudir muttered.

The harper glanced at him, but Donovan remained mute while he gathered his scattered thoughts. "We need to see Himself," she said in the momentary silence. "The Little One." This was the title of the Master of Hounds, the Ardry's right hand.

Cerberus raised his eyebrows, an impressive movement given how low they hung on the loose folds of his face. "Do ye now?" he asked. "One day, a visitor will come wanting to see some underling, and not the Big Dog; but that day is not today, I see. Well, ye can fill out a wee request form—'tis on the public network—and we'll process it. Himself has an opening come Michealmas Eid."

Neither the Fudir nor the harper was familiar with local

holidays, but it did not sound to the Fudir as if that day were fast approaching.

"We need to see him today," the harper said.

"Oh, and wouldn't we all? What business would that be, if ye don't mind my asking?" He subvocalized as he talked. Paraperception often included the ability to speak out of both sides of the mouth. Donovan, who had finally silenced his inner cacophony, was certain that Cerberus was alerting others within the Kennel. He glanced at the distance to the door, at the guard dogs in the murder hole above it.

"We're looking for Bridget ban," the harper said, "and we thought the Little One could tell us where she'd gone."

"A Hound's business is not for the vulgarly curious."

The harper's cheeks colored. "'Tis more than vulgar curiosity," she said with some heat; but the Fudir interrupted before she could turn things into an argument.

"Is Greystroke in?" he asked. "He'll vouch for me."

Pages of files flashed across Cerberus's eye-screens. "Are ye sure, Donovan, that he would give ye a favorable report?"

A card on the table, that. But Donovan had been certain from the get-go that Cerberus had held it. "Is the Pup at Headquarters or not?"

"Greystroke is a Hound now," Cerberus continued. "He has a Pup of his own; but he's not here."

The Fudir grunted. "How would you know it if he was?"

Something almost like a smile created a fold in the sharpy's face. Greystroke's ability to come and go unnoticed was legendary. "And why would ye expect us to be telling ye anything, you being a Confederate agent, and all?"

"I'm retired," Donovan grunted. "The Names and I had a falling out, and I'm rather broken up over it."

The Hound shrugged. He subvocalized and his glasses flickered as a record was updated. "The request forms are in the public network," he said. "FOI 39584 dash XC."

The Fudir turned to the harper. "It wasn't wise to bring us along. They'll never tell you anything as long as we're with you. I should return to Jehovah. Or at least, step outside."

The harper pushed to the fore. "What of Gwillgi? *He* came to *me* on Dangchao Waypoint, so I know your people were looking for my mother. I need to know what you've learned, so I can start looking myself."

Cerberus nodded, a suspicion confirmed. He updated his files. *This* is what Bridget ban's daughter looks like today. "And your name would be . . . ?"

The harper stood up straighter. "Méarana of Dangchao."

Cerberus grunted. "Harper, are you." In Gaelactic, *méar* could mean by a shift of inflection either "swift" or "finger." In this case, it was a pun and meant both.

"An ollamh," the harper corrected him.

The guard dog tried not to look impressed. Master harpers were two-a-penny, his hangdog look said, no matter at how young an age. " 'Swift-fingers' is an office name. I need your base name."

"Her name is Lucia D. Thompson," a new voice announced, high and reedy, but with subsonic echoes. "I knew her before she was knee-high." Harper and Fudir both turned, and Donovan's first thought was to wonder how someone so large could have walked so softly.

His second thought was that "knee-high" for this one was not all that small.

He was long and gangly, with prominent joints and a lugubrious expression. His legs were enclosed in power walkers and his eyes had the quality of a basset hound, save that they bulged slightly. His black T-shirt and shorts were devoid of any ornamentation—unless that darker patch against the raven cloth was the Badge of Night.

The newcomer was as wizened as an old corn stalk. In his prime he would have been taller, but now he bent ever so slightly at the shoulders from the weight of the years on him.

The Fudir leaned to the harper. "Be wary of this one," he whispered.

"Don't be silly. I've known him since I was bread-and-buttered. Hello, Uncle Zorba." And she stood a-toe and kissed him somewhere south of his chin.

Zorba de la Susa, the greatest Hound of them all. Old? He should have been dust. That the harper—that Lucia—had known him from childhood and called him uncle was small comfort. On Appalachia's Bangalore, children kept cobras as pets, and smiled at tigers. That didn't pull the fangs or blunt the claws.

The Tall Hound looked at the Fudir. "What are you doing in this man's company," Zorba said. "Do you know who he is?"

"Aye. Maybe more so than does he."

The Hound's laughter was like the first notes from a bagpipe. "Then, do you know *what* he is? You are safe here, if he's abducted you."

"It was I who abducted him, Uncle."

"Ha! That may be a story worth telling. Cerberus?"

"Yes, Cu."

"Did we ever catch that 'fed agent? The one who called herself Olafsdottr?"

"One moment . . ." His goggles flickered. "No, there's no record of it."

"Well, that was years ago. She may have been sent off to fry bigger fish." Zorba laughed again, but gave the Fudir a significant look.

Donovan was moved to protest. "I was quite happy where I was, but your . . . niece . . . was ready to hare off across the Spiral Arm after her mother. I convinced her to come here instead. I thought you people would talk sense to her. When you're finished, I plan to go right back to Jehovah."

"Right back to the bowl. Oh, don't look away. The Ouro-bouros Circuit is a wonderful thing. We can get the answers to our queries in hardly any time at all."

"My mother . . . ," said Méarana.

"Aye." Zorba turned to Cerberus. "Have Bridget ban's trip reports collated and sent to my office. You two, come with me."

"Cu," said Cerberus, "you don't have an office. You are Status Inactive."

De la Susa stopped in his tracks. "Am I? Don't be a cow's calf. Arrange it. And have someone make reservations at The Three Hens for dinner. My usual table."

Cerberus gave the Fudir a doubtful look. "For two? We can question this one while you and your protégé's daughter dine."

Zorba laughed. "What do you suppose he can know after all this time? Nothing is more useless than an agent past his expiration date. What say you, Donovan? Have you any tales worth the telling that the Kennel ought to hear?"

Careful . . . , said one of his voices.

It's a test, said the Sleuth.

Of course, it's a test. But a test of what?

The Brute began to clench a fist. Zorba's eyes narrowed. Cerberus reached under his desk.

The Fudir seized control. "Sure, I've made my living as a seanachy these past uncounted years. A teller of tales. Why should I not tell tales here, as well? My fees are modest."

The two Hounds relaxed just the smallest amount. Donovan heard the distant click of safety catches being re-engaged. Yes. Was erstwhile Confederate agent Donovan as erstwhile as he seemed? His willingness to be debriefed was the test.

———

Cerberus found an empty office that de la Susa could use. It contained a barren desk of opaque metaloceramic, a comfortable chair, and little else. De la Susa took the chair. The Fudir searched nearby offices and returned with two more. They sat around the desk and waited. The Tall Hound worked his lips for a few moments with a distant look on his face. A part of the Fudir wondered if the old cripple had lost the train of his thought.

Zorba smiled at them and wheezed, "Well. Bridget ban's daughter, and a master harper, no less. Just as well. Just as well." He nodded. "Her mother's trade was not for her."

The Fudir was uncertain how to respond to that and, from the tentative look in Méarana's eyes, he guessed the harper was not sure, either. This was not the Uncle Zorba she remembered.

"Perhaps I should begin that debriefing you wanted," he suggested, starting to rise. "There's no need for me to listen to this. I agreed to accompany the harper this far; but I'm for Jehovah by the next ship out."

But neither Hound nor harper was listening. De la Susa passed a hand over his face, rubbed his cheeks. "Ah, she was ever too close-lipped for her own good, your mother was. We love one another like brothers here, but there is a certain amount of jealousy in the Kennel. Oh, yes. I'm sorry to say it, but it's true. A certain jealousy. Brothers and sisters . . . But family rivalries can be mean. If she was on the trail of something big, she might keep it quiet lest others beat her to it. Some of us would, you know. And if the trail proves false, one doesn't look as foolish. Better to scout things out alone."

The Fudir sat slowly. "In Terran, we call people like that '*lone rangers*.'"

"Do you? What's that in Gaelactic? Never mind. My earwig is a little slow. Maor aonarach, is it? Hah, that's good." His jowls shook as he chuckled. "Maor aonarach . . ." Then he sobered. "I don't remember it that way when I was Status Active. A band of brothers back then. Though back before the Circuit, we mostly *were* on our own, now that I think on't. So it may just be habit. 'Lone ranger . . .' Hah! But we only remember the best parts, eh? The best parts. No, Donovan, I want you to stay and hear this. No need to rush back to *that* place. Yes, Graceful Bintsaif, thank you."

A whippet-thin woman in powder-blue undress uniform and black choke-collar had entered with a pocket brain, which she handed over. A glance captured the room and all that was in it. "Ochone, sèan-Cu," she said in a deferential voice. "This room has no armillary."

De la Susa shook as he chuckled. "Yes, that was Cerberus's little joke. He will receive a riposte in the ripeness of time. He is jealous, I think. 'Old Three-Head' doesn't care for me hanging around the Kennel. I'm some sort of relic, a ghost at the banquet. He and I once . . . Ah, but those are times long gone."

"Cu," said Graceful Bintsaif, "you are a treasure."

"Yes. A buried one. Ha-hah! Cerberus thinks I should be off on Peacock Junction shooting inoffensive ducks and drinking abominably flavored teas on some tropical verandah."

"I don't like it here," said Graceful Bintsaif. "There's a meanness to this infighting. I wish I were back at the Rift."

The Old Hound grinned. "Not all duties are so easy as *that* one, eh? I suppose you have prepared an armillary for me."

The younger Hound bowed from the shoulder. "Aye, Cu. Games are not in me."

De la Susa grunted. "They should be. Your time here would pass more quickly." He rose and gestured to Méarana with a sweep of the arm. "If you would follow Ban-Cu Bintsaif . . . ? You, too, Donovan."

In the hallway, the harper leaned close to the Fudir and whispered, "*This* is the famous Kennel?"

Donovan answered, "Don't be deceived, harper. They show us a feckless face; but look in their eyes. The eyes are as hard as stones."

"But why the façade?"

"A man's greatest weapon is his opponent's underestimation."

"But we're come for their help. We have the same objective. How are we opponents?"

"They like to keep in practice." But if Donovan had understood the old man aright, there were those in the Kennel who were more interested in finding what Bridget ban had been up to than in finding the woman herself.

The armillary was in a conference room. Graceful Bintsaif had activated it earlier and it now displayed a three-dimensional projection of the Spiral Arm, centered by ancient convention on Old 'Saken. The projection would have been impossible to read had all the stars of the Arm been displayed; but only those connected by Electric Avenue were shown, and even so it was a dazzling display of diamonds and golden threads. The young Hound-instructor took the brain from de la Susa and inserted it into the armillary.

De la Susa spoke into a phone. "From insert>Files>Sent from>Display."

Immediately, several nodes on the network brightened, while others dimmed.

"Add>Subordinate coordinates." He turned to the harper. "These are worlds she mentioned having visited in her reports." He leaned over the phone again. "By 'Send Date'>Sequence."

Light ran through the display like a river, flowing from

star to star. It rose from Dangchao Waypoint, through Die Bold and out the Peacock Shortway to the Junction. From Peacock Junction, Bridget ban had traveled the Silk Road through the great interchange at Jehovah and all the way to Harpaloon. After that, she had zigzagged across the Lafrontera District: down the Spiral Staircase to Dancing Vrouw and Bangtop-Burgenland; along the Grand Concourse to Siggy O'Hara and Boldly Go; out Gorky Prospect to Sumday and Wiedermeier's Chit.

"And the Chit is where she was last heard from?" asked the Fudir, in spite of himself. He gave the Sleuth a mental elbow in the ribs. The Sleuth did not have control of the tongue, but sometimes Donovan or the Fudir accidentally verbalized his thoughts.

De la Susa sighed. "No, she returned to Siggy O'Hara. After that, we never heard from her. Most of Lafrontera is outside the Circuit, so at first we thought she had come back to Siggy O'Hara to use the Ourobouros station there, and we awaited the late arrival of drones or messages entrusted to passing ships; but . . . none came. It's possible she sent a message by a ship that was lost through mishap."

That would be two mishaps at roughly the same time, the Sleuth pointed out. *A Hound gone missing* and *her last message lost. The probability of that is . . .*

"Quiet," said Donovan. "No one cares what the probability is."

The other three in the room turned to look at him, and Méarana said, "Don't worry. He talks to himself sometimes." Why this might be a reason not to worry, she did not say.

The Fudir was sorry the witch was missing. After all these years, the anger no longer flamed. But the ashes were bitter and he was not about to spend his life looking for her.

It's obvious where we have to start, said the Sleuth.

"Where the harper has to start," Donovan muttered sotto voce. "It's Jehovah for us."

You can't be thinking of sending Méarana out there alone?

"And why not?" he whispered.

You know why not.

It suddenly seemed very cold to him, and he shuddered like a drunk caught thin-shirted under a Harvest-month sky.

"Are you all right, Fudir?" the harper asked.

"Just old and decrepit," he said. "Zorba, can you give her the reports of the Hounds who followed up on her mother's disappearance?"

"Ah, child," the old man said to the harper. "How can you hope to find her where we have failed—even with this wreck of a man to help you."

"I'm not helping her," Donovan protested once again.

" 'Tis not so much 'this wreck of a man' but 'the wreck of this man.' "

The Tall Hound nodded. "Ah . . . I can see where that might matter."

"And I thought that—if we followed Mother's itinerary—we may see things the others missed," said Méarana. "I am her daughter, after all."

Zorba looked at her with sadder eyes. "A slim hope."

"When hope is all there is, it is enough."

The Aged Hound nodded, as if to himself. Then he said, "Graceful Bintsaif."

"Yes, Cu?"

"Give them the redacted reports that Greystroke and the others filed."

"Is that wise, Cu?"

"Ask, 'Is it useful?' " He turned to Donovan and the harper and extended the pocket brain. "Do not suppose we have neglected to visit these places."

"Yes . . ." Donovan accepted the brain and gave it to

Méarana. ". . . but your reports can at least tell her which trails *not* to follow. And maybe they can convince her by the thoroughness of your harvest that there is little point to her gleaning."

The Old Hound rubbed his cheeks again with his hand. He glanced at Graceful Bintsaif. "You'll tell Himself everything, of course."

"Of course." The junior Hound bowed slightly from the shoulders.

"Ochone! She's the Little One's spy, you know," he added aside to the harper. "Oh, the old man is garrulous. He talks too much. So she is my second shadow. Well, I will tell you this much. Bridget ban had picked up rumors. She never said where. But she was hunting something big. She said it could shield the League against the Confederation for aye. Or it could destroy us."

"In the wrong hands . . . ," said Donovan slowly.

"Oh, aye. But consider it a warning. If such a power exists, it proved too much for a Hound. It would make short work of a harper and a drunk."

"You're a blunt one," said the Fudir.

"Is it wise, Sèan-Cu," said Graceful Bintsaif, "to lay such temptations before . . . layfolk?"

The Fudir cackled. "No worries, sahb. I haven't laid hands on absolute power in almost twenty years."

The restaurant called The Three Hens sits on a narrow side street just west of An Caislinn. It is entered by three short steps down into a small barroom and then through an archway into a larger dining room where the tables sit within vast wine barrels. The ceiling is vaulted stone, suggesting that this was once the cellar of a larger building and these had been its storage rooms.

The restaurant takes its name from three clone-lines of

poultry that, to this very day, have been nurtured and pruned for their flesh. What grows in the vats is not exactly alive, nor does it resemble much the images of hens that decorate the dining room. How long the lines will yield their harvests no one can say. Legend holds that they were started by Commonwealth "scientists" and will last forever. Yet there are aged and nearly unreadable images at the Taran Archives in which, in the background, one can make out a sign: The Four Hens. Nothing lasts forever.

The meal is tasty, the smack of the poultry accented by subtle sauces, and the staff is attentive to de la Susa and his party.

Donovan has told the Kennel what happened to the Dancer and a portion of what the Names had done to him afterward. He has said only that his ill-treatment had left him "disoriented."

Over Hunter's Hen, fenneled potatoes, and glasses of Gehpari Mountain White, the scarred man does his best to forget the memories roiled by the debriefing. So he lets the Fudir tell of some scrambles in the Terran Corner of Jehovah. The Old Hound finds great amusement in the account of the rescue of Little Hugh O'Carroll. In return, he tells of his liberation of Hector Lamoy, the "Friend of Truth," who had been sentenced to death on Chamberlain for a poem satirizing the Alish Bo Wanameer, the People's Hope.

"He wasn't happy with me," the Hound concludes with a reedy chuckle. "His martyrdom was to signal the Insurrection. He'd been looking forward to it. But his fanatics were no better than the PeopHope thugs, and I saw no reason to bring the one down so the other could rise up."

The host of the restaurant comes to their table and whispers in the harper's ear.

"Of course, I will," Méarana answers and reaches for her harp case. She follows the man to a stage area, which is hastily prepared for her.

Donovan had seen Zorba signal to the host, so he knows that Méarana has been removed from their table by design. He waits to hear the nature of that design. In the performance space, the harper begins a plaintive love song—a cliché, but suitable for this comfortable and satisfied audience.

"Lucia D. Thompson," says the Hound.

The scarred man waits for elaboration on this point. But when none is forthcoming, he says, "An odd name; but her mother is of Die Bold and they name folk strangely there."

"The Pashlik of Redoubt." The Hound adds precision to the birthplace of Bridget ban. "But she had sought political asylum in the Kingdom before I met her. I trained her, you know. Bridget ban."

The scarred man nods. He had known.

"She was my prize. My dearest one. A daughter to me." A tear escapes his ancient eye and trembles on the edge of his withered cheek. "And I much fear she is dead now."

The Fudir knows a sharp pain in his chest. "It is likely so."

In the performance space, the harper has shifted to a more lively tune, and the Fudir recognizes it with a start. It is the theme she had developed on Jehovah. The Rescue in Amir Naith's Gulli. The very tale the scarred man had spun during dinner. It conjures again for him the stinking radhi piles, the fetid pools of waste water, the assassin, the death of Sweeney the Red, Little Hugh desperately trying to pry loose the grating barring his escape. And he, the Fudir, climbing down from the rooftops to confront the assassin.

"I would rather she . . ." He would rather what? He

does not dare explore that; not yet, not now. "But I fear you're right."

Zorba's breath leaves him like a deflating bagpipe. "Bridget ban . . . Her base name was—"

"Francine Thompson. Yes, I know. It's their custom to pass the mother's name to the daughter, and the father's to the son."

"Ah, Frannie. Frannie. It wasn't easy for her. When she defected in the Kingdom, she was cut off from her . . . No, not her family. The Pashlik thought families reactionary. But from her dormitory. From her age-mates. And Lucia . . . I was at her name-day ceremony. In the Kingdom, they had the custom of naming a child by pouring water on its head. I stood by her for that, what they call a 'goodfellow.' I held her while they poured the water."

The scarred man holds his breath.

"And Lucia's mother was away a lot. Frannie was. A Hound expects that. A Hound's daughter, maybe, does not. What do disasters and negotiations and assassinations and rescues mean to a child? She was raised by Drake and Mari Tenbottles, the ranch foreman and his wife. And now and then her mother would come home with wonderful presents and still more wonderful stories."

"Cu," says the scarred man with sudden fear. The harper is playing out the masquerade in the hills by the Dalhousie estate, when he and Bridget ban had fooled Lady Cargo's security staff. She maintains a tremolo while the deceit lies in doubt and breaks into a jaunty geantraí at the end. "Cu," he says again, "why are you telling me this?" That the Old Hound has a reason for his rambling he takes as granted.

The head turns and the eyes catch him, and they are the same iron-hard eyes as before. There is something yet inside that aging body. "I've lost my Frannie, I'll not lose my Lucy. I held her while they poured water on her; I'll

*not hold her while they pour dirt. I think I see where this
may go, and that is into dangerous territory."*

"Tell her not to go."

" 'Tell the wind to cease/Tell the tide to ease,' " *he sings.
"But don't tell Lucia D. Thompson not to seek her mother.
She's been doing that her whole life and old habits are
hard to break. I would not look kindly on the man who lost
me my Lucy."*

"Cu, I—"

"I would go with her myself, but my legs will not take
me there. You saw them. But you . . ."

"I'm returning to Jehovah."

*The Hound's face turns entirely toward him then, and
there is something of Gwillgi's deadliness in his mild-
eyed, basset-hound glance. "Well, no," he says, "you're
not."*

A part of the scarred man thinks, Arrogant bastard! *And
Inner Child whimpers. The Brute says,* He's old. We could
take him down. He's tall, but they only fall farther. *The scarred
man grabs his skull with both hands to silence the cacophony.*

"No," *he says. "You can't ask me that. Send someone
else. Send Greystroke. Or Grimpen. Or . . . It's been years
since I . . ."*

*But the Hound shakes his head. "Nineteen metric years.
I can count. I've enough fingers and toes for that. Which
means this is something* you *must do. How much more
abandonment do you think she can take? You're a Confederate. You know the Weapon of the Long Knife. Do you
think only* Those *know how to wield it? 'It's a big Spiral
Arm,' they say. But if you fail in this, it is not big enough to
hide you. Do we understand each other?"*

*The scarred man knows misery. "You don't know what
you're asking."*

"I think I do."

"No. The Names . . . My mind . . ."

The Hound's head dips, rises again. "I saw the neuroscanner results, the emorái. That will make your task more . . . challenging."

"If you employ a defective tool and it fails—"

"Then I discard the tool. But it is better that you fail than that another succeed."

In the performance space, the harper is playing Bridget ban's Theme and the scarred man curses her under his breath, for she, too, is forcing him into this role. Pushed by Zorba's threats, pulled by Méarana's music, what other possible course is left him?

"We'll both die," he groans.

"That would be better for you," says Zorba de la Susa, "than if only she does."

AN AISTEAR

Curling Dawn was not a Hadley liner, but she was going in the right direction, and so the harper and the scarred man bought passage on her as far as Harpaloon. It gave Donovan sullen pleasure to use the chit that the Kennel had given him. If he was to be forced to tramp the Periphery, he may as well do so at Kennel expense.

The Grand Star ship was a throughliner, a flyer-by. She came out the Silk Road from Jehovah at just under Newton's-c and crossed the coopers of High Tara toward the Rimward Extension on a two-day transit. She would not stop or descend to the capital. Rather, the bumboat *Cormac Dhu* had been boosted up the crawl to match trajectories with her as she passed through. A high-v match in the coopers was never entirely routine, and the scarred man, still nettled at Zorba's threats, took some pleasure in describing to the more nervous passengers with whom he shared the bumboat all those things that could go wrong.

"If the rendevoo manoover is soo dangeroos," a scowling businessman from Alabaster said, "why doo soo many use it?" Like most people from his region, he heightened his back and central vowels, a favorite trope for comics on a score of other worlds.

"Shortens trip for most," said another passenger; this one, an elderly woman from the Jen-jen. "Imagine if throughliners must crawl down to planet, then crawl up again! Why— longest leg of trip is Newton's crawl! Such time-waste!" She gave the scarred man a sidelong look. "Even if some exaggerate risk."

The bumboat latched onto the throughliner with much clanging and hissing before the airlock doors pulled open from the connecting gangways. Disembarking passengers from *Curling Dawn* entered through the rear doors and embarking passengers left *Cormac Dhu* through the front. The liner and the boat had so synchronized their gravity grids that almost no one stumbled as they passed through the shipways. But even with the stewards shepherding people along, embarkation was a confusion.

The scarred man fell back until he stood at the rear of the throng, and when he reached the threshold, he hesitated. It was a small step to cross it, but a bigger one than he had taken on leaving the Bar of Jehovah. Then, he had offered to escort Méarana only to High Tara, intending to return once the Kennel had talked her out of her foolishness. But far from discouraging her, the Kennel had given her tools by which to pursue her doomed quest. Donovan had half a mind to step back, allow the air locks to close, and catch the next ship to Jehovah.

The problem was that the other half urged him forward.

Let's go. It's something to do, said the Brute with what was for him irrefutable logic.

We owe her our help. What if she encounters some danger on the Roads?

"If she does," Donovan said with acid in his voice, "we'll hold another debate like this one—which may not prove much help to owe her. Damn it, we can't even go through a door without a lot of bickering."

This is our last chance to turn back. Once we board, we're committed.

Tell me something I don't know.

<Remember Zorba's promise,> Inner Child cautioned them. <There's no safety in turning back, either.>

But what finally brought the scarred man aboard the throughliner was not the Brute's boredom, nor the fear of the Inner Child, nor the idealism of the Silky Voice, nor even the Fudir's nostalgia, but his realization that the harper, too, had hesitated, just for a moment, at the brink.

That sort of unspoken doubt deserved support.

Although the Kennel had deep pockets and the chit would have enabled them to travel in first class, Donovan had booked them into third. He and the harper found their adjoining cabins on H-deck, where the hum of the idling alfven engines gave the gray walls a mild shiver, as if the ship were a living thing trembling with anticipation. The section steward—a Terran—delivered their trunks shortly after, and the Fudir tipped him generously in Gladiola Bills of Exchange and whispered certain instructions in his ear. After that, he waited for the harper to complain.

Which she did soon enough. She strode through the connecting door and threw herself onto the day couch in Donovan's room. "Was this the best you could do?"

"Be memsahb so accustomed to luxury? Much sorry no satin pillows, no silk sheets."

"No taste, either. I don't mind cheap so much as tacky."

The room was done up in tired colors, and the bunks and bureaus might be called Spartan had the Spartans been a less festive and sprightly folk. The Fudir shrugged.

"This be best ship in Grand Star Lines, missy."

"The best ship of a second-rate line."

"What of it? It's not like second-rate is the worst there is. How many lines are of the first water?" He looked around the cabin. "This isn't so bad, actually," he assured her. "Donovan and I, we've traveled in accommodations far less splendid."

"You haven't seen *my* cabin. But I wasn't talking about the accommodations."

"I'll switch with you, if you like. Besides," he added as the harper made a gesture that meant *nichevo*, "there's a certain freedom in traveling third. For one thing, you meet a better class of people. And there are fewer obligations. If we'd gone first class, we'd be expected at the Captain's Dinner, assigned to one of the deck officers' tables."

"Oh, the horror!"

"Yes. 'Better to live unnoticed.' A Terran in first class is bound to excite interest, and never of a proper kind. Half the sliders will go out of their way to snub me; the other half will go out of their way to prove how oh-so-tolerant they are. Either way, I would stand out. Throw in an ollamh of the clairseach and tongues will wag from stem to stern. That could prove a nuisance when the time comes."

"I was complaining about her speed," the harper said. "She's only a niner."

Donovan chose to misunderstand her. "She's fast enough to outrun most pirates, and well enough armed to give the rest pause."

"That wasn't what I meant. It means slower going to

Harpaloon. If we had pushed it, we could have caught *Joan Hadley* before she left. She's not only a faster ship but slides nonstop to Harpaloon."

"But I don't expect pirates along the old Silk Road," the Fudir continued unperturbed. "Not this close to High Tara. Pirates may not respect much, but the High Taran Navy is one of them. Did you read the witch's reports to the Kennel?"

"Stop calling my mother a witch. There'll be plenty of time for that. It's three weeks to Harpaloon. Oh, wait. *Four* weeks on this slogger."

"Such a hurry!" the scarred man said, waving his hands in the air. "Rush, rush, rush. Hurry too fast and you only reach disappointment sooner. Beside, we're getting off at Thistlewaite."

"Thistlewaite!"

"Ya. That's why I picked this bucket. *Joan Hadley* isn't scheduled to rendezvous with any bumboats there. That's why I picked third class, too. If we showed up missing at the Captain's Dinner after Thistlewaite, everyone would know where we'd gotten off. Down here . . . Well, no one notices the cattle."

"But . . . *why?* Mother went to Harpaloon."

"Yes, but *before* that she had gone to Thistlewaite."

"That was to organize disaster relief after the earthquakes . . ."

"I read about it. It was in all the newsfeeds. She was there for two years, wasn't she?"

"Yes, but . . ."

"Yes, 'but' she came home excited, you told me, and spent most of her leave reading and searching the Die Bold libraries."

"She's always reading. She has to keep up with . . ."

"Stay with me. The Hounds have been working from an unexamined assumption: that Bridget ban received intelligence of some sort during her home leave and it set her off on a quest. But I think she learned that something on This- tlewaite. She came home to plan and then set out on the trail."

The harper leaned forward on the couch, her eyes sud- denly bright. "Are you certain?"

"Certain? Which Spiral Arm do *you* live in? The Sleuth is certain, but he can read things between the lines that aren't actually there. But look: Your mother left Dangchao in her mobile field office on the fourteenth of Tenmonth, Taran Green Time, but she arrived in Harpaloon seven met- ric weeks later. A Hound's field office should have made the transit in five and a half. The Sleuth thinks she spent the extra week on Thistlewaite."

"It needn't have been to do with her quest. Wrap-up work on her assignment there . . ."

"She would have filed a Supplement to her final report, and Uncle Zorba would have told us. Remember the map he showed us? None of her reports mentioned a stopover on Thistlewaite. Why conceal the visit?"

The harper fell silent for a moment. She stroked the pil- low on the sofa, then looked up. "What do you think?"

"We don't think. We take votes."

Méarana leapt to her feet and clapped her hands. "But it's something new, at least. It's something none of the others have looked into! Oh, F—Fudir! I knew it was the right thing to bring you along!" She threw her arms around the scarred man's neck, and he could not back off in time to evade them. "We'll find her. I know we will."

Donovan carefully disengaged from her embrace and stepped back. "No, we won't. If we're lucky, we'll find out what sent her off on her last quest. If we are luckier still, we'll find the thing she was hunting for. If we are luckiest of all, we won't."

"You're a horrible man."

"Whatever killed your mother would make short work

of us. It's one thing to learn what it was; another to get anywhere near it."

"If we find it," she said confidently, "we'll find Mother."

The scarred man looked at her bleakly, but he said nothing and after a moment he turned away. "I want you to place an Ourobouros call to your home on Dangchao. Is there someone there you can trust? Do you have a secure code?"

"It was Mother's code. And yes, Hang Tenbottles has been with the family for ages, and his father practically raised me. He's segundo on the ranch—runs it, really—and he's been like an older brother to me."

"All right, all right. You can trust this Tenbottles. Can he access the household gods?"

"The lares or the penates?"

"The penates. I don't think the home security system would tell us anything useful. Unless someone's been nosing around your place . . . ?"

"Only Gwillgi, and he came openly."

"You wouldn't have known it if he hadn't. Gwillgi doesn't show up on ordinary home security systems."

"Mother is a Hound. There is nothing ordinary about our security system."

Donovan grunted. "Fine. What I want you to do is encrypt a message to this Tenbottles; have him check the household database and find out what your mother was reading during her home leave."

"But Gwillgi already—"

"Something may seem more significant after we've nosed around on Thistlewaite. Go to the ship's Passenger Comm Center tomorrow and give them the message so they can put it in the squirt queue for the next system we pass through with an Ourobouros station. Khlaphalon, I think. Tell Tenbottles to send the reply in care of the Plough and Stars on Harpaloon. We'll catch up with it there."

"Why not send it to us on Thistlewaite?"

"Because I don't want anything on record that puts us on Thistlewaite. The Kennel may be monitoring transmissions in and out of Dangchao."

The harper frowned and bit her lip. "You want to keep the Kennel in the dark? But aren't we working *with* the Kennel? They gave us a chit, and letters of transit . . ."

The scarred man crossed his arms. "Let's find out what Bridget ban thought she had before we lead the Hounds—or anyone else—to it."

IV ON RICKETY THISTLEWAITE

There is an ancient Terran word: rickety. *It is not clear to scholars what this word meant exactly, but that it applied to Thistlewaite was undoubted. "Rickety Thistlewaite" had been its appellation from the beginning, from the days before even the First Ships set down. At least, if you can depend on their legends, which like everything else there, are shaky. The planet's nature can be seen in its propensity to earthquakes. Somebody had forgotten to caulk the seams of her plates and they slip and slide with greasier abandon than they do on more gritty worlds. "As sturdy as a Thistlewaite skyscraper" is a proverb on half the planets of the South Central Periphery. The Thistles are not so mad as to build skyscrapers—and so the proverb does double-duty. What can be more sturdy than something left unbuilt, runs a Thistlean joke. A building never erected can never fall down. Ha, ha. But the Thistles have developed a keen sense of balance along with their mordant wit, and a fatalistic conviction that nothing can ever be done that will not eventually fail.*

They have contrived no fewer than fourteen states in the tropic belt between the Mountains Acreeping and the River

Everwinding, for their political structures are no more permanent than their architectural ones. There had once upon a time been a single state—an Empire, in a modest Thistlean fashion—but it, too, had collapsed.

"In the days of the gods, the seedships came," begins an ancient story of theirs, the first of the Cautionary Books. Most of the Periphery takes the gods only half seriously, but on Thistlewaite they are taken wholly so. Of course, the gods are real—and they are absentminded and fumblethumbed. How else to account for matters? Only the great sky gods—Einstein, Planck, Alfven—are steady and reliable. And who can blame them? The starry heavens above have alone not come crashing down upon them.

The harper and the scarred man disembarked the throughliner without exciting interest, and here the money that the Fudir had cast upon the steward—as well as a *certain grip* exchanged in the hand clasp—returned value a hundredfold. The steward had agreed to slip them into the exit queue as smoothly as the Fudir had slipped the buckshish into his palm; maintain otherwise the fiction that they were still aboard ship; and on arrival off Harpaloon see that their trunks were delivered to the *Phundaugh* Plough and Stars. Terrans would do anything for buck' and sometimes even for Brotherhood.

It was three days down from *Curling Dawn* to Floating Hyacinth Platform in stationary station above Hifocal Big Town, the once-upon-a-time imperial capital. The bumboats and platform were operated by House of Chan, which contracted for port operations on any number of worlds. From Floating Hyacinth, ferries rose and fell to each of the Fourteen States.

Bridget ban had supervised the relief work from Jenlùshy, in Morning Dew sheen, where most of the devastation had occurred. "Sheens" were what the Thistles called their states, and Morning Dew was the literal translation of Jenlùshy. "Everything means something," Méarana said, "if you dig deeply enough."

Donovan believed that if you dug even more deeply, all meaning would vanish; but he did not share this thought with his companion, nor was he single-minded about it. The scarred man was said to be most disagreeable; but most of his disagreements were with himself.

They took the "high speed line" from the shuttle port into Jenlùshy. The train was slow when judged against those of less rickety worlds. There is a limit to the velocities one gambles when the land may ripple the monorail in surprising and undesired ways. On the other hand, there was a sense that the faster the trip, the less likely that a quake would catch the train along the way. Hence the motto of the Thistlewaite Bullet: "Hasten slowly."

Jenlùshy had sat on the epicenter of the great thistlequake and two-thirds of the sheen had been knocked about like jackstraws and flinders. This in itself was no great thing. Many of the poorer buildings were routinely constructed of little more than paper reinforced by 'boo-poles. But the Palace had been made of sterner stuff, and the One Man, the Grand Secretary, and five of the Six Ministers had perished in its collapse. Across the countryside collapsing province-towns, mountain landslides, floods, and fires had swallowed two-thirds of the District Commissioners, along with half the dough-riders. In a state as highly centralized as the Jenlùshy sheen, that was the equivalent of a frontal lobotomy.

Some Administrative Commissions kicked like pithed frogs, but every decision a Jenlùshy official made required ratification by an official higher up—and most of the high-ups had been laid low. The praefect of the Eastern Marshes, on her own initiative, traveled to Hifocal Big Town in the next sheen over to ask for League help over the Ourobouros Circuit. She was publicly caned by the Eastern Marshes Surveillance Commission for this breach of filial subservience—it didn't matter that there had been no superiors to be subservient to—but Bridget ban had arrived shortly after, took matters well in hand, and for nearly two years was, for all practical purposes, Empress of the Morning Dew.

She had overseen the restoration of sanitation, of water and utilities, of housing and roads, of public order, and did this primarily by providing in her own person an authority figure to whom the surviving Commissioners could give their devotion. The entire society was based on the Family writ large. The Eastern Marshes praefect had, in effect, gone looking for a mommy or daddy to kiss the hurt—and had been soundly spanked.

The late Emperor had clearly lost "the approval of the sky." What more proof was needed beyond the descent of his replacement *from that very sky*? (Thistles knew that Bridget ban had arrived by ship in the normal fashion, but they read meaning into every concatenation.) A change of dynasty was called for, and Bridget ban chose Jimmy Barcelona, who had been Chief of Capital District Public Works Unit. At her suggestion, he selected the office name of Resilient Services and for his regnal theme, "a robust and reliable infrastructure." It rang less glamorously than most regnal themes, but was surely apropos, all things considered.

The surviving Minister held a different opinion, but when he and three of the imperial censors opened debate by opening fire, he discovered that where a Hound was concerned the decorative could also be deadly. The vote was four to one against Jimmy, but Bridget ban had the one vote, and so he was installed and the others cremated.

No one could do business in Jenlùshy without the emperor's permission. Certainly, no one could go about making a nosy nuisance of himself without what the Terrans called a "heads-up." Normally, obtaining an audience with a Thistlewaite emperor was a long, laborious, and expensive affair. The recovery from the 'quake was still in its final stages, and Resilient Services had better things to do than put on a show for Peripheral touristas. Donovan had counted on this as yet another delay to the harper's journey, although he had by then given up on dissuading her entirely.

But if the visitor was the daughter of the very Hound who had placed the emperor on the Ivy Throne, doors swung open with disconcerting ease.

The Grand Secretary did insist that protocol be observed. A certain formality of dress was required, although the sumptuary details differed for folk from different worlds. Happily, the harper had brought with her several bolts of Megranomic anycloth, so the morning of the audience, she consulted *Benet's Sumptuary Guide to the Spiral Arm* and programmed the material to assume the chosen color, cut, and texture.

The Fudir watched. "Technically," he said, "we don't need the One Man's permission to enter the Corner." There was a Terran Corner in most major cities across the Spiral Arm. Having been deprived of their home world, Terrans had found no home anywhere, and so could be found everywhere.

Méarana looked up from her 'face. "'We.' Do you mean us, Terrans in general, or the mob inside your head?" Donovan's use of the first-person plural was idiosyncratic.

"Oh, Terrans, memsahb." The Fudir dropped into the patois that he sometimes affected. "Thistle see no manyfolk-one-folk, but for Terries."

She rolled her eyes. "Speak Gaelactic, Fudir. I can't follow the jibber-jabber half the time."

"You aren't meant to, half the time. Corporate bodies, I

mean. There are none here. No universities, no cities, no guilds, no medical societies."

The harper inserted the datathread into the port and ran the program. The cloth began to ripple. "Dinna be silly. They have universities and doctors; and if this be nae a city we're in, what is it?"

"A department of the imperial court. It takes more than a lot of people living close together to make a 'city.' Jenlùshy Town doesn't govern itself. It isn't recognized at law as an entity. The same goes for Imperial College: it's a Department of the Grand Secretariat under the Third Minister. And doctors are employees of the Second Minister. It's the Minister who sets rules and regulations, not a 'medical society.' The Terran Corners are the only places on the planet recognized as self-governing corporate bodies."

"You sound proud of that." She detached her clothing from the 'face and made way for the Fudir to sit down. "You want me to do your clothing for this afternoon?"

"You don't think I can achieve 'the appropriate level of formality'? Of course, I'm proud of it. It means that when I go to the Palace *as a Terran*, I have certain rights and liberties. So does a citizen-rancher from Dangchao."

"I don't get it, then. If we're legally outside the imperial system, why the fancy getups for—what did they call the audience? High Tea?"

The Fudir grunted. "There's law and there's custom, and custom is the stronger. They may lack legal recourse if we dress uncouthly—but that doesn't mean they have no recourse at all."

The harper wore a *leine* of pure white linen with fitted sleeves, and intricate red geometric embroidery at the neck, cuffs, and hem. It was pulled up and bloused though a leather *crios* at the waist, in the pouches of which were placed the

tools of the harper's trade. Over this she had thrown a
woolen *brat* in bright green with gold borders. She wore it
like a shawl fastened at the right shoulder by a large golden
brooch showing a snake entwining a rose. She walked un-
shod and the nails of her feet and hands matched the color
of the embroidery of her *leine*. Her red hair fell free, to
indicate her unwed status, but she wore a silver ollamh's
circlet at her brow.

The scarred man wore Terran garb, and if fewer eyes
caressed him than caressed the harper, it was because he
was a moon to her sun. He dressed in a dark yellow *sher-
wani* over embroidered *jutti* and matching *kurta paijamas*.
His sandals were plain and of brown leather with golden
crescents on the straps. The scars on his head were de-
cently covered by a skullcap, and across his shoulder he
had thrown a *gharchola* stole. Gold lac-bangles adorned
his wrists and ankles, and rouge had reddened his cheeks.
When he wanted to, the Fudir could cut a figure.

In the anteroom to the audience chamber, the Fudir bowed
to the Grand Secretary, and said, in a croak resembling
Thistletalk, "This miserable worm prays that these poor
rags do not find disfavor in the eyes of noble Grand Secretary."

That worthy went by the name of Morgan Cheng-li and
was known therefore among the backroom staff as "Jingly"
in a play on both his name and the sound of the coins that
so often crossed his palm. He had that air of self-importance
often found among underlings. His frog-like mien—pigeon-
chested, eyes bulged, cheeks blown out—gave the impression that he had been holding his breath for a very long
time.

The Fudir had learned from the Terrans in palace maintenance that Jingly fancied himself a calligrapher, and so he
produced a Gladiola Bill of significant denomination. "Per-

haps," he said, ducking his head by an appropriate amount, "most-accomplished-one might give this humble servant educated opinion on engraving of this wretched bill?"

The Grand Secretary made a motion with his hands, and an underling's underling scurried over, took the bill between her fingertips, and held it before Jingly's eyes. "Barbarian work," the latter said after a moment, using the local term for off-worlders. He placed a loupe in his right eye. "Not without merit, but lacking . . ." A wave of the hand. ". . . panache. Perhaps," he added distastefully, "designed on computer."

"Your eminence is wise."

"Pfaugh. Child see such flaws. Observe portrait visage. Where serenity? Where balance?"

"Perhaps expert hand may attempt improvement. Perhaps, use this bill as model."

"Pfaugh, again. Work for apprentice draftsman. No great skill. But one may essay task as étude." A nod to the underling caused the bill to disappear into a fold of her gown before she scuttled back to her station.

At the appointed time, the Grand Secretary directed the Assistant Palace Undersecretary of Off-World Affairs to escort them into the throne room. "Rags?" the harper whispered in Gaelactic as they proceeded down the hallway. "After all the work I put into this wardrobe?"

"Self-deprecation is mandatory here," Donovan answered curtly. The Fudir added, "You should see officials defer for places at a banquet table."

"Och. Mother and I hold to a faith that values humility, but that sort of servility smacks of unseemly pride. And I thought off-worlders were exempt from the rules on bribes . . ."

"Do you tip service workers? A bribe is simply a tip offered before the service. Besides, I only asked his opinion on the calligraphy of a Gladiola Bill." Donovan interrupted and said, "Hush, both of you. And remember what we told you. Don't mention that your mother has vanished. She came from the sky; and if she's vanished into the sky—"

"Then she's lost the Approval of the Sky," the harper returned wearily. "I know. I know."

Donovan turned to her. "And through her, the emperor she appointed. Tell them your mother's gone missing and it's tantamount to a call for revolution. And don't think old Frog-Face back there won't lead it, either."

At the Assistant Undersecretary's nod, White Rod knocked on the Golden Doors with the head of a mace. These doors ran floor-to-ceiling and were made of intricately carved rosewood displaying in each panel scenes from the life of Morning Dew. The whole was painted over with a golden lacquer. Méarana admired the attention to fine detail: the studied indifference of the scholar at his terminal, the boredom on the face of a bhisti shuttle-pilot. There would not be the like of these doors anywhere in the Spiral Arm.

The doors swung open on a broad room. The throne on which Resilient Services perched was fashioned of solid gold. The stiles had been molded in the form of climbing ivy and from them on threadlike wires hung leaves of artfully tarnished copper. This gave them a greenish cast and, when movement caused them to sway, they tinkled like wind chimes. Under the throne, for some age-long and forgotten reason, rested a large stone. The high back rearing above the yellow-robed emperor, bore four ideograms: the motto of the sheen. "Behold the August Presence," the Voice of the Sheen cried out. "Behold the Resilient Services Reign, who provides the sheen with robust and reliable infrastructure!"

Now *there's* a battle cry to rally the troops, said the Brute.

It works for them. The earthquake destroyed so much. Why not make its restoration a quasi-sacred duty?

The Fudir scolded them. "Quiet. We're not here to mock their customs."

"Who," the Voice demanded, "approaches the August Presence?"

The Fudir bowed, sweeping his arm to the right and holding his left over his heart. "I hight Donovan buigh of Jehovah, special emissary of the Particular Service to the Court of the Morning Dew. My companion is the ollamh Méarana of Dangchao, master of the *clairseach*."

The emperor had gone, first pale, then flushed. "Ah. So," he said. "You much resemble my illustrious predecessor, and I had thought . . . Ah, I had thought she had returned to resume her duties." He clapped his hands and a flunky struck a hanging gong. "Bring forth the crumpets and scones!"

Underlings and flunkies scurried about in what appeared to be absolute confusion, but from which in short order emerged a table in the center of the hall, dressed with cloth, napkins, and fine bone-china cups. Three soft-backed chairs were arranged around it, and a silver tea service wheeled into place. A tray of biscuits, ceremoniously escorted, was placed on the table, and the visitors were shown to their seats. The emperor stood and descended from the Ivy Throne, unhooking his yellow robes of state and handing them to the Assistant Deputy Undersecretary, Count Wardrobe, who bundled, folded, and scurried off with an economy of motion.

Beneath his robes, the emperor had been wearing a simple day suit: a cutaway cloth coat of dark blue possessed of brass buttons over a plain buff waistcoat and matching pantaloons. His feet were shod in riding boots with golden spurs; and at his throat was gathered a stiffly starched cravat. He took the seat at the head of the table and, with a flick of his wrist, dismissed his ministers and staff. These scurried to the walls, where they stood in various poses pretending to converse with one another, but watching always for a summons from the Presence.

"Tea?" the Presence said, holding a cup under the samovar.

He proceeded through the ceremony with meticulous detail. One lump or two? Cream? Scone? Jam? Each motion practiced; each stir a precise radius and number of revolutions.

The Fudir supposed this was the Thistlean equivalent to the Terran ceremony of bread and salt. More elaborate, of course, in that mad and fussy Thistlean fashion.

When all had been served by the emperor's own hand, Resilient Services intoned formally, "We shall now make small talk."

The harper was uncertain how to begin; but the Fudir said easily, "How do matters stand since the great thistle-quake, your imperial majesty? Recovery proceeding apace, I hope?"

"Oh, yes. Quite, thank you," the emperor responded. "And for duration of Tea, you call me 'Jimmy.' Port Tsienchester not yet fully operational; but perhaps by end of sixmonth. You." He pointed at the harper. "I mistake you for another. She, too, from Kennel. She give mandate to rule. How I curse that day."

"Bridget ban can be very persuasive," said the Fudir.

"Ah. You know her."

"She is my mother," said the harper.

"And I have been charged to escort the daughter to her."

The emperor cocked his head. "And where that?"

"I regret, ah, Jimmy, that the information is privileged. You know the ways of the Kennel."

"Why do you curse the day my mother made you emperor?" the harper interjected. "She made you emperor of one of the Fourteen States."

"That curse." Jimmy turned a little in his seat. "See sigils over throne? Love-heaven. Person. Protect. Heaven-below. In ancient tongue: Low tyen chay, pow tyen-sha. It say that man who love heaven-sky will protect empire. But heaven perfect. Never fail, never fall. Heaven-below, Sheen Jen-lùshy, should be imitate that perfection. Never does. But if emperor love heaven good enough, everything fine below, too. Never fail, never fall. One Man must be regular as sky, must be never-changing. I move in orbit, like planet. Go here, go there. All same ceremony, all same word. All pest black-fly ministers buzz round me. Buzz, buzz, buzz. Do this, do that. All 'veddy propah.' No mistake. Mistake in heaven-below cause mistake in heaven-above. Very bad. Calf stillborn. My fault. Did not recite sunrise prayer proper. Bandit rob exchequer in Bristol-fu. My fault. Did not make proper ablution. All universe connected through dough. Everything affect everything. Mountainslide in Northumberchow Shan . . ."

"Your fault," said the Fudir. "We get it. I can see cosmic oneness has its drawbacks. If you forget to clip your toenails, who knows what horrors might be unleashed? I can see why none of the Fourteen States wants to conquer the others. Considering what can go wrong in one day in any one sheen, being emperor of the whole kit and kaboodle must have been hell on wheels."

Jimmy frowned. "Please?"

"Never mind him," said the harper. "He's a Terran."

The emperor shook his head. "Only here in tea ceremony, two three other times, is emperor become Jimmy again." He turned abruptly to the harper. "Tell me of home world, Mistress Harp."

"Dangchao Waypoint? It's a small world, a dependency of Die Bold. Mostly open prairies on Great Stretch continent, where we raise Nolan's Beasts. A few big towns. When we go to Die Bold, we say we're going to 'The City.' May I have one of those finger sandwiches? What is the spread?"

"Pimento and Devonchao cream. Made in Praefecture of Wild Violets. I hear of planet in Wild, out in the Burnt-Over District. They talk of 'The City.'" He waved an imperial wrist. "Out past Ampāyam and Gatmander. Somewhere."

"The 'Burnt-Over District,'" the harper suggested.

"Traveler tales. Suns go nova now and then. Burn up cities."

"If their suns went nova periodically," the Fudir said, "it would burn up more than their cities. There'd be no one left to spread travelers' tales."

"The Wild," said the harper, "is a region of romance. Anything can happen there."

"Even romance," the Fudir replied. "But what usually happens out there is death or bankruptcy. Or both. Most of the worlds are uncivilized. A few have spaceflight; none have rediscovered sliding. Their cities are smelly and dirty, and you'd be lucky not to come away diseased. Romance," he concluded, "is best considered from a distance."

"You have harp with you, mistress? Of course. Ollamh never far from instrument. You bring with tomorrow. Play songs of your Dangchao, so far away."

Méarana put her cup carefully on its saucer. "Well . . . Donovan and I have some business to conduct . . ."

"Oh, no," said Resilient Services. "I must insist."

And there was something hard in the way he said it that caused the harper to hesitate and glance at her companion.

"I had planned to visit the Corner," the Fudir said. "You can entertain the emperor while I do that."

"Yes," agreed the emperor of the Morning Dew. "You do that."

The next morning, as Méarana prepared for her command performance at the palace, the Fudir prepared to enter the Corner of Jenlùshy. For this, he did not dress as he had for the palace. Indeed, he barely dressed at all. Around his waist he tied a simple blue-and-white checkered dhoti. On his feet, sandals. His upper body he oiled.

"Easier to slip out of someone's grip," he said with a leer. Save for secreting various weapons in unlikely places, that completed his toilet.

The harper looked him over before he departed. "That's no more than a long towel wrapped around you," she said, pointing to the dhoti. "How do you bend over in that thing?"

"Very carefully. Be sure to keep the emperor happy. I think he's a little taken with you. But remember: no hint of anything wrong 'up in the skies.'"

"How many times will you tell me that, old man? Just be careful in the Corner. The concierge told me it's a dangerous place."

"Full of Terrans. You be careful, too. There aren't any Terrans in the palace, but that doesn't mean it isn't dangerous."

He slipped out the service entrance of the hotel and followed the Street of the Tin Smiths to the Street of the Plastic Injection Molders, where he turned left and entered the Corner.

He had never been to the Corner of Jenlùshy, but he knew it when he was in it. Thistlewaite buildings tended toward the ramshackle, even without the help of a 'quake, but as he proceeded farther along Beggars' Lane they grew positively sketchy. Many did not bother with such vanities as walls. What could a wall ever do except collapse? If curtains and tapestries did not exactly bar entry to the burglar, neither did they hurt as much when they fell on you. And what might be within such hovels as to tempt a burglar?

Granted, this was no more than an accommodation to the geophysical realities, but by Alfven! A Terran ought not care if walls came down on him! Compared to the expulsion of their ancestors from Olde Earth, what harm could a few bricks and beams do? Nor ought they ape the dress of the Thistles quite so closely, nor speak that unadorned dialect of Gaelactic favored here. On Jehovah, the Terrans of the Corner spoke the old patois among themselves, and spoke it proudly.

The directions he had obtained from the Assistant Underwasherman in the hotel's laundry brought him as far as the Tibbly Fountain, which formed the social center of the Corner, and there he found the women filling their water jugs. The Great 'Quake had wrecked the water distribution and one of the prices of independence was that you went to the end of the line when it came to restoration of services. The more he had seen of the Morning Dew, the more he had realized how unfinished Bridget ban had left things. What had she learned here that had sent her off elsewhere?

The Fudir found himself an overhang sheltering an outdoor moka shop and he leaned against the pole while he admired the sight and studied the crowd.

His home Corner on Jehovah was larger than this and its folk more bustling. There was a kind of unhurry to the crowd around him, leaving time for a bit of sport among the younger water-women, who splashed one another and laughed. This dampened their colorful sorries in often delightful ways.

He also noted the mama-sans watching from doorways and balconies, and the gonifs and grifters lounging about. Not one of them had failed to mark his presence.

Well, it was a small Corner as these things went, and a stranger stood out. The Fudir considered whom he might approach, and finally decided on a small, rat-faced man who squatted on his heels on the other side of the square, engaged in no apparent vocation. In any crowd of this sort, the Committee of Seven would have its eyes and ears, and the savvy man learned to recognize them.

But the Fudir hesitated. The rat-faced man was surely

armed, and just as surely unfriendly to strangers. And who knew how the Seven would receive him after all these years? Did the Corner of Jenlùshy have anything like those Dunkle Street ghats that made the Corner of Jehovah so perilous for intruders? His own skills with knife and tongue must had rusted during his long inaction. If he failed here, what would become of Méarana?

What sort of piss-ant cowardice is this, the Brute demanded. One of the Fudir's legs twitched, as if trying to step forth on its own.

He who hesitates is lost. And never more so than he who hesitates in a Terran Corner.

Comrades? I suggest we get off the pot, said the Sleuth.

<No,> said Inner Child. <No no no no no . . . >

"Donovan?" the Fudir whispered. "Help me out here."

"All in favor of remaining a sitting duck," said Donovan, "say aye."

Well, a moving target is harder to hit . . .

The Fudir crossed to the fountain with only a slight hesitancy in his step. It could have been a limp. The chatter and gaiety continued, but he was tracked by two dozen pairs of eyes.

The die is cast, the Sleuth announced. *Or as Caesar said,* alea iacta est.

𝔄𝔠𝔱𝔲𝔞𝔩𝔩𝔶, 𝔆𝔞𝔢𝔰𝔞𝔯 𝔰𝔞𝔦𝔡 𝔦𝔱 𝔦𝔫 𝔊𝔯𝔢𝔢𝔨. 𝔍𝔱 𝔴𝔞𝔰 𝔞 𝔮𝔲𝔬𝔱𝔢 𝔣𝔯𝔬𝔪 𝔞 𝔭𝔩𝔞𝔶 𝔟𝔶 𝔐𝔢𝔫𝔞𝔫𝔡𝔢𝔯: Ἀνερρίφθω κύβος. That was the Pedant. It could not possibly be anyone else.

<Shut up. Shut up shut up shut up . . . >

At the fountain, the Fudir stared into the waters. The rat-faced man affected not to notice him and continued to do nothing with great concentration. When the Fudir had once more gotten a hold of himself, he stretched and, in doing so, made a sign with his right hand.

The rat-faced man had been twirling a stick with one

hand. Now he dropped it and, in picking it up, made the answering gesture.

The Terran Brotherhood was not outlawed within the League of the Periphery, as it was within the Confederation, but neither did it like to draw attention to itself. For one thing, Confederate agents were ofttimes about, and willing to freelance an assassination or two, and some Terrans were genuinely sympathetic to the Confederation, if for no better reason than that Olde Earth was their hostage. For another, League governments would sometimes decide that détente was the order of the day and move to suppress the Brotherhood to curry favor with the 'Feds.

Two others in the square had noticed the by-play and one of the water-women pursed her lips in disapproval. There was a third faction among the Terrans, and by no means a small one, that believed that what was lost was lost. They still believed in Terra—else they would cease to be Terrans at all—but they believed in the Ideal Terra, Terra-of-the-Dream, the "City-on-the-Hill" toward which one must always strive, and to which one would be transported after death. The idea of one day returning en masse and in the flesh to a physical Terra struck them as somehow sinful. To them, the Confederation was neither friend nor foe, but an irrelevancy.

The rat-faced man stood and walked toward the southern end of the square, where he ducked between a one-story wattle hut selling hand-phones and an open shed where a naked man with a welding mask was repairing a truck. After a decent interval, the Fudir followed him.

But as he turned into the alley behind the phone shop, rough arms grabbed him and a canvas hood was pulled down over his head.

The Silky Voice whimpered and Inner Child cried out in alarm. The Brute, for just a moment, seized control of the scarred man's limbs and began to struggle; but the

Fudir took them back and relaxed. If they had meant him harm, the darkness would have been permanent and not a mere hoodwink. They intended to take him somewhere and did not wish him to know where. He was still in grave danger; but the danger would come when the hoodwink was removed and he was in a comfortable room with smiling people.

"I long to see fruited plains of your home world," the emperor said after Méarana had played a set of Dangchao songs from the Eastern Plains. "To ride like wind chasing Nolan's Beasts with lasso and bolo. To drive herd to market in—how you say? Port Qis-i-nao? No, Port Kitch-e-ner." He pronounced the alien sounds with great care. "Oh, life of Beastie boys, live free under stars."

Sometimes Méarana wanted to slap the emperor of the Morning Dew. He confused song with life. You didn't *chase* Nolan's Beasts. That would run the meat off them. And life on the plains, under the stars, driving the herd to the knocking plants for shipment to Die Bold, was dirty, tiring, bone-breaking labor that stole sleep and health and even life itself. Beastie boys fared better in song than on the plains.

"Play again song of Dusty Shiv Sharma," said the emperor over cups of Peacock's Rose tea; and he warbled with a bad accent, " 'Best Beastie boy o'er alla High Plain.' "

Dusty Sharma had been a real "beast-puncher" a hundred and fifty metric years ago; but he had been called "Shiv" because he carried a hide-out knife in his knee boot. Historians said he would not have been a pleasant man to meet, even when sober; but he had been so encrusted with legend that the real man was unrecognizable.

And so she played a geantraí, a jaunty tune that evoked what the Dangchao beast-punchers called the Out-in-back. Of "the splendor o' the mountains, a-rearin' toward the

sky, cloud-shaker, avalanche maker, cool an' dry an' high."
Of such things as these at least there could be no musty
historians' doubts.

When they pulled the hoodwink from him, the Fudir
blinked at the light and found himself facing seven men
and women sitting on cushions behind a broad, low "kaffé"
table, and not one smile to share among the lot of them.
The Fudir was puzzled at first, since at every meeting of
the Seven of Jehovah that he had ever attended there would
be at least one or two that were "in the wind" due to mis-
understandings with the Jehovan rectors. But then Terrans
on Jehovah lived an edgier life than here, where a certain
amount of segregation kept the Terrans more to themselves.
He did not doubt that Jenlùshy Terrans ran their share of
scrambles, but fewer of them seemed to intersect with the
folk of the sheen.

The man in the center—pale-skinned, tow-haired, beak-
nosed—was the one they called Bwana. He was bare-chested
and wore buckskin pantaloons with fringed seams. His
cushions were larger and done up in elaborate green, black,
and red patterns. To the extent the Corner had a government
and had a president, these were them and he was it.

"Ah, Bwana," the Fudir said, bowing over his folded
hands. "May I introduce my humble self."

But the Bwana replied in the patois, so thick that it
seemed almost the old Taṇṭamiž *lingua franca* itself. Even
the Fudir had to call upon his earwig to thin it out.

"Thou art known to us, o Fudir, as a man of promise.
Thou *promised* Memsahb Jehovah, thou *promised* Fendy
Die Bold, thou *promised* to give us back the Earth. Those
wert thy words. This promise, he run jildy from corner to
corner, in whispers. Hutt, hutt, 'from Gatmander to the
Lesser Hanse.' But many years die since and . . ." He
spread his hands in entreaty. ". . . no Earth."

The Fudir marveled that, the farther from the promise the rumor had run, the more fervently it seemed to have been embraced. The Memsahb and the Fendy had not taken either his promise or his failure to heart. The key to success was low expectations.

"The tool I had hoped to use," he suggested, "proved too dangerous to employ. Big dhik, sahbs. A dagger with two blades may be showed back on the one who holds it. So my hope was false all along, and none wept greater tears than I to learn so."

"And there are more stories still," Bwana continued. "That thou art an agent of our enemy, the Great Shittin, the Confederation that oppresses Olde Earth. Deny this."

"Bwana, I do not, save that that was past and no longer true. Many a Terran has worked for Those of Name—*because* they hold Olde Earth hostage. A man named Donovan 'took their nickel' long ago; and I was once that man. He passed on to them certain information regarding the League—and what do you or I owe the League? We are in it, but not of it—but never did he inform on the Brotherhood, or harm the interests of Terrans. And then, after a time, the Names put him to sleep, to be called upon as needed. And in that time he forgot them; though not they him."

Donovan intervened then and prevented the Fudir from saying any more. The Fudir agreed that this was not for the ears of others, but resented Donovan's high handedness. A bit of trust was not uncalled for. But Donovan laughed, for he had not lasted this long by over much trusting, even of himself.

To Bwana, it appeared as if the Fudir had choked for a moment. He drummed the table with his fingertips, looked left and right at his committee, gathered in their verdicts, bobbed his head side-to-side. Then he clapped his hands, twice.

"Bread and salt!" he cried out. "Bread and salt for our guest!"

The Fudir let out the breath he had been holding. Deep within, Inner Child wept for joy, while the Brute felt keen disappointment at the lost prospect of danger and combat. Donovan and the Sleuth were amused by their reaction, and the others grew angry. Relief, joy, disappointment, amusement, anger. Enzymes and hormones warred and the contending emotions sent a wave of dizziness through the scarred man that nearly overcame him. Bwana frowned and asked if he were ill, but the Fudir waved him off.

The servants came then with silver salvers of steaming flatbreads fresh from the tandoors and small bowls with ground sea salt. A pot of kaffé accompanied them, and Bwana gravely served the scarred man with his own hands.

When all had eaten and the Fudir was once more closeted with the Seven, Bwana relaxed in his cushions and said, "Tell us then, Fudir, why thou hast sought the Brotherhood out. By what right doest thou call upon Terra?"

"I seek very little, Bwana. As little as this: the readiness of lips to speak of matters that befell here on Thistlewaite. As you know the ears of Terrans are large, but their mouths are small."

"As befitteth folk in our station. And thou swearest this toucheth not on Holy Terra?"

"Save only that some have said it may discomfit the Confederation; but this is nothing more than the whisper of a supposition."

"And we all know what is worth a suppository! Haha! What matters are these?"

"They are matters that touch upon the Kennel, Bwana, and are not to be spoken of."

The Bwana's face hardened and his cheeks grew red. "There is the small matter of trust, Fudir. If the Kennel be neither foe nor friend, neither are they Terrans. Doest thou value them more than thou valuest your own blood?"

Danger had once more raised its red-rimmed eyes. The Brotherhood would not harm him, not after offering bread and salt; but there were more Terrans in the Corner than belonged to the Brotherhood, and a disingenuous word spoken here or there could make his departure problematical. "I will tell ye so much as is safe for ye to know, brothers. But ye must swear a mighty oath to contain these words only within these walls. I wish to know of the doings of the Hound, Bridget ban, during her sojourn here. The Folk must speak to me with open hearts."

Bwana studied him, and the Fudir could see the wheels turning behind his eyes. Then he clapped his hands again and cried out. "The Book!"

The others of the Seven looked uncomfortably at one another. One rose and murmured, "Perhaps I would not hear this." Bwana flicked his fingers at her and she and two others rose, bowed over their folded hands to both the Bwana and the Fudir, and departed swiftly.

Shortly, a book was brought in. It was a thick volume, bound in the ancient style and inscribed on its binding with the curlicues of the old Taṇṭamiž script. The printing was badly worn and a dull brown stain covered some of it. Of its title, the Fudir could make out only *Guest is God,* but on the reading of those words his heart went hollow. It was in the old script and its spelling was antique. *Athtithi Dhevo Bhava,* instead of *Adidi Dyefo Vapha.* The author's name was not visible, but he wondered. Could this volume be that written by Saint Shanthanand Saraswathi himself? *How old was it?* It was encased in a plastic block—destroyed and preserved in one act—and so its age had ceased. It might have come from Lost Terra herself, lovingly cradled and carried from the Home World to the Old Planets and from there to come to rest finally on rickety Thistle-waite.

The Fudir, who fancied himself an unsentimental man, was surprised to find himself on his knees before the book, his cheeks hot with tears; but whether for the ancient, half-legendary swami-ji, or for everything lost that had once been, he did not know. He placed his hand on the block along with the Bwana and the others of the Committee who had stayed, their fingertips touching one another: pallid, ebony, dun, and sallow. The colors of Olde Earth.

> *"By the blue skies and the green hills*
> *By all that was and all that yet might be,*
> *By the Taj and the Wall and the Mount of Many*
> * Faces,*
> *We swear that what we say will be said only here and*
> * only now.*
> *May we never see Green Terra if we lie."*

After the words were spoken, the Fudir rocked back on his heels. His fingers lingered on the Book, maintaining contact, as if he could feel the binding and the covers and the pages preserved forever unreadable within the plastic. He had spoken many oaths in his lifetime, and some he had even kept. This was the first he had ever taken that he had felt was holy.

And so he told them that the harper's mother had vanished and that the daughter had set forth on a hopeless quest to find her, and that he had come with her as her guide and protector. As Terrans, his hosts knew all about hopeless quests, and so were inclined to sympathy. They gave their leave to make inquiries in the Corner.

Nor did it hurt that the Fudir would pay for information from the deep pockets of the Kennel.

"And this," he said, pulling from his scrip the necklace

he had borrowed from Méarana. "It may mean nothing; it may mean everything. The Hound bought it here on Thistlewaite, or received it as a gift. Somewhere there is a merchant or a dealer in curiosities who remembers it, and perhaps remembers whence it came."

Bwana and his councilors studied it in turn. "It is unfamiliar to me," said the chairman. "If it be thistlework, it must be of a far-off sheen. Yet, we see imports in our bazaars from even Fire Over Water, which is the farthest of the Fourteen States, and I have never seen its like. See thou Mwere Ng as thou departest, and she will prepare whole-grams of it. I will have its likeness circulated among jewelcrafters and importers and may fortune reward thy curiosity."

And so matters ran for several days. Méarana would play songs of the Periphery and engage in "small-talk" with the emperor, and the Fudir would nose around the Terran Corner and other eddies of the city asking after the activities of Bridget ban and the provenance of the medallion. The journey of a thousand leagues begins with a single step, but it seemed to the harper that neither she nor Donovan were advancing the search for her mother by so much as even that single step. The sense of being stuck in a dreamland crept over her. The days were distinguished only by the particular songs she sang, and the precise lack of information with which the Fudir returned each evening.

Now and then, simply to remind them where they were, the world shrugged his shoulders and the land trembled. Once, Méarana was shaken awake in the night and she lay awake a long time thereafter before sleep reclaimed her, and in the morning she found that a great tree had come down on Great Heaven Street.

Because Resilient Services had discovered the relaxing properties of her harp, he had bid her remain for his afternoon

Council and play gentle suantraís while he reviewed the reports the dough-riders had brought in from the distant shau, prefecture, and county officials. And so her day at the palace expanded from command performances at High Tea, to "muzaq" at staff meetings.

No decision in Sheen Jenlùshy was ever final until ratified by the emperor: not the death sentence to a murderer meted out in Wustershau, not the mei-pōl festival to be held in Xampstedshau, not the list of candidates proposed from the 7th Dough for the imperial examinations. Each must be reviewed with the Six Ministers, a decision rendered, and the triplicate copies apportioned.

The suantraí was supposed to induce drowsiness in its hearers. Méarana wondered why the emperor thought it necessary. The subject matter alone should induce coma.

While her fingers plucked long-mastered melodies from the strings, she learned that for each official there was a quota of decisions to be overturned. This number could be exceeded in the case of an especially inept official, but never shorted. "If all decisions stand," Morgan Cheng-li explained as he escorted her from the palace later, "official think above station, fixed by birth and examination. So, if no other cause, council overrule random cases, as lesson in humility."

Resilient Services himself overruled the Council on a few occasions, and Méarana supposed that this was for the same reason. In one case, the emperor denied "yin privilege" to the daughter of the Minister for All Things Natural Within the Realm. "Yin" was the privilege of bypassing the examination system to secure a place in the hierarchy. Apparently, this was sufficiently pro forma for the children of officials that the Minister's face twitched in irritation. The Grand Secretary noted this and snapped, "Five blows! Filial impiety!" The sergeant-at-arms, who stood by the wall with a long cane of slapstick, stood to attention; but Resilient Services, looking up from perusal of yet another report, said, "Belay that, please. Imperial grace."

"I was frightened," the harper later admitted to the Fudir, when that worthy had emerged from the Terran Corner slightly scathed and greatly enlightened. "At least, a little," she added. They had met in the Fudir's room at the Hotel Mountain Glowering. Méarana sat in the comfortable sofa while the scarred man examined his face in the mirror.

"What? Of our young emperor?" The Fudir applied a healing stick to the cut over his left eye, wincing slightly at the sting.

"Not so much *of* him as *for* him. His slightest whim is instantly obeyed. What does that do to a man's soul? And the others grovel before him. It can't be good for a man to have others grovel to him."

"Better perhaps," said Donovan, "than for the ones who must grovel."

"There was one set of reports . . . Did you know there is a second, independent hierarchy whose only purpose is to monitor the behavior of the regular officials and report any 'nonharmonious words or acts'?"

The Fudir dabbed at the other cuts he had suffered. "The Bureau of Shadows," he said. "It could be worse."

"Worse, how?"

"They could be shadowing the common people. If a government is going to snoop, they may as well restrict their snooping to one another. The system could be brought to perfection if the first set of officials were then restricted to monitoring the second. How soon can you break off these afternoon tête-à-têtes?"

Méarana sat up. Something in the Fudir's voice . . . "What did you discover?"

"Two things. First, the jewelmonger Hennessi fu-lin remembers your necklace. He bought it in pawn from a man of Harpaloon. The man never came back for it, so he sold it to your mother."

"Harpaloon. Mother's next stop. Was she following the necklace? What was the second thing?"

"The Terrans remember that she met several times with a man from Kàuntusulfalúghy who had been stranded here by the thistlequake. It isn't much, but it's the only activity of hers that I've heard about that wasn't tied directly to disaster relief."

"Who was it? What did he and Mother talk about?"

The Fudir held up a hand. "It may mean nothing at all. The Sleuth is always too eager to see patterns. The rest of us pointed that out and the Sleuth got huffy and left . . ."

"Fudir . . . The Sleuth is inside your head. Where could he *go*?"

"He's sulking; not communicating. That makes it hard for the rest of us to put things together. The Terrans claim that when your mother returned she asked after this Kauntling. Debly Jean Sofwari. He was a science-wallah, or impersonating one, because he wore the white robes they favor. The Terrans say that he was flitting all around the sheen swabbing people's mouths."

"He was *what*?"

The Fudir spread his hands, palms up. "Could I make up something like that?"

"That must be why Mother met with him. She wanted to learn if he was a madman."

"I bribed the log-keeper at Dewport Field, but Sofwari must have had his own ship. There's no record of him in the departure logs. The automatic system was wrecked in the 'quake and they were doing everything the hard way. I'll spend another day snooping after Sofwari, but if the Terrans had known anything more, I'd have some inkling. We don't know why your mother found him so interesting. He was too young for her bed."

Méarana stiffened. "Dinnae speak of Mother in such ways."

"Méarana . . . You must know that your mother's bed was not a restricted area. Little Hugh was there; I was there. Even Greystroke was there. So was a Die Bold businessman, the Peacock STC director, a—"

"Stop it!"

"And that was in the short time she and I were 'associated.' It's no use clapping your ears like that. You can hear the truth from your inner voice."

Méarana took her hands from her ears. "You didn't know her the way I did."

"I should hope not."

"She's not like that any more."

The scarred man forbore to answer. Proverbs about leopards and spots came to mind. But the argument continued despite Méarana's silence, with himself taking all sides. *Shut up!* he told himself. *Shut up! Shut up! Shut up!* Turning away from the harper, doubling over his clenched arms, he fell to his knees on the thick carpet of the sitting room and . . .

. . . suddenly, everything around him was unfamiliar, as if he had stepped off-stage. What was he doing here, in this comfortless room, so far from the consolations of Port Jehovah? He cursed Zorba de la Susa. He cursed Méarana Swiftfingers. Most of all, he cursed Bridget ban.

𝕭𝖚𝖙 𝖙𝖍𝖆𝖙 𝖜𝖆𝖘 𝖎𝖓 𝖆𝖓𝖔𝖙𝖍𝖊𝖗 𝖈𝖔𝖚𝖓𝖙𝖗𝖞, a part of him said. 𝕬𝖓𝖉 𝖇𝖊𝖘𝖎𝖉𝖊, 𝖙𝖍𝖊 𝖜𝖊𝖓𝖈𝖍 𝖎𝖘 𝖉𝖊𝖆𝖉.

Tears squeezed from his eyes. Though why should he mourn the death of Bridget ban? She had been dead to him for years.

Something subterranean rumbled with gigantic laughter, sending Inner Child scurrying in flight, silencing even the silent Donovan (for there is a silence more deep than mere quiet).

Each of him regarded himself to the extent that things unreal can regard anything. A fragment of an ancient poem brushed his mind too lightly for the words to alight; and a terrible foreboding took hold of him. An image of a shadow, slouching, at a distance, like a stranger seen under a lamp-post on a foggy night. *Dead,* he thought; or a part of him thought. *All tears are dust.*

And the word—*dust, dust, dust*—echoed down the drainpipe of his mind like a man falling into an endless cavern. He saw a party of people, small, as if viewed by an eagle from a distance, circling along a narrow ledge above an immense abyss. One of them pointed with a walking staff into the darkness below them. *There is something down there,* he said, *that cannot speak.*

When he came to himself once more, it was night. The room was dark, save for a reading lamp in the corner. He lay curled up upon the bed and, in the corner, the harper slept upright in a padded chair. Slowly, he straightened, careful lest he make a noise, but Méarana's eyes opened.

"You had a seizure," she said. "Worse than before."

The scarred man lay still for a while, then pushed himself erect and sat on the edge of the bed. He leaned his hands on his knees. "It was easier," he said, "when I thought I had forgotten."

The harper didn't ask him what he had thought forgotten. She said, "I brought a doctor in. He prescribed rest, and some herbs."

He laughed softly and without humor. "The famous herbalists of Thistlewaite. Did he stick pins in me? I've heard they do that here. Chicken soup?" He remembered being haunted by thoughts of death. But whose death? And whose thoughts?

There was something very wrong inside his head.

That elicited a second humorless laugh. It was more

pertinent to wonder if there was anything very right in that vandalized ruin.

How could such a kaleidoscope keep Méarana safe from harm? De la Susa had not known what he was asking of him.

The Thistles divided their daylight into twelve hours starting from the sunrise ceremony, but unlike folk on other worlds they did not number their hours. Instead, each had a name. Thus, the third hour after equatorial sunrise was Bravely Working Hour, presumably because by that time most people were at their jobs. The other hours were named in like manner after the rhythms of life, and in this wise the Thistles synchronized their activities. When at the Mid-day Snacking Hour one sat to a light meal of biscuits and cheeses, one experienced the harmony of knowing that everyone in the sheen was doing the very same. There might be some dissonance with other sheens, or even with those districts in the Eastern Marshes where dawn arrived before its appointed hour, but it was generally acknowledged that the Eastern Marshes were out of synch in more than their sunrise, and the folk of other sheens were odd beyond all credit.

There were no public clocks. The right of proclaiming the Hours was reserved to the emperor. Within the palace complex stood a single cesium clock of unimaginably ancient vintage. It did not match the Thistlean hours, having been calibrated long ago to the tock of a different world, but the Sages of the Clock would note the time displayed and perform a ritual called the Transposition of Times, and determine when each new local hour began. Uncounted people on uncounted worlds spent their workday "watching the clock," but on Thistlewaite there were workers actually paid to do so. The Voice of the Sheen would then, to trumpet blast and gongs, announce the Hour from the parapet of the imperial palace, and the cable channels would carry her word throughout the sheen.

Méarana heard the trumpets as she made her way down Poultry Street, a narrow lane whose coops and butchers had long given way to mobi stores and shopping arcades, leaving only subtle aromatic reminders of its original inhabitants. Méarana said a word equally pungent and quickened her pace, for the trumpet meant that she would be late for her command performance. She tolerated Donovan's eccentricities on most things, but the packing of her clothing was not among them and that had delayed her.

White Rod was as pale as his wand of office when Méarana finally appeared. Trembling, he led her into the throne room, where Resilient Services sat alone at High Tea, to all appearances sorely vexed. Méarana thought she would need a suantraí to sooth the man's palpable anxiety. She waited for White Rod's underling to pull her chair out for her. Instead, underlings hesitated, emperors rose, and guests sat in fits and starts. Apparently, custom required that He Who Serves the Tea was to sit last of all; but because the tea had already been poured before Méarana's entrance, harmony was now broken. She did not see why this mattered at all, least of all that it mattered so terribly, but she supposed that now there would be a two-headed calf born somewhere for which her lateness could be blamed. She was a Die Bolder, born and bred, and a devotee of causality. Concatenation struck her as absurd.

You would think that a harper would know all about harmony, the emperor told her when that quality had been restored. It was an elliptical rebuke, with a great deal of opprobrium in the ellipsis. "It is a terrible discourtesy with which to end my visit," she allowed.

The emperor of the Morning Dew sat back a little in his chair. Today he wore a dinner jacket of bright green, done up with contrasting red embroidery, with a ruffled cravat at his throat. On his head, he had placed a white powdered wig bearing a long pigtail down his back. "End visit," he said, as if examining the phrase for possible alternative meanings.

"Yes. Donovan and I leave on the evening shuttle to rendezvous with the throughliner *Srini Siddiqi*. My mother awaits me."

"Your mother. Yes. Play me," he said as he poured a second cup of tea and, using a silver tongs, dropped a lump of sugar in it, "song of your mother."

Hitherto, the emperor's requests had been for songs of adventure, of faraway planets, of romance and distance. The harper played Mother as a geantraí: a jaunty tune that conjured her in the moment in which Bridget ban strode across the decks of *Hot Gates* like the queen of High Tara— tall, magnificent, purposeful. Somehow, though, as her fingers wandered across the strings, a goltraí crept in: a keening lament as heartbreaking as all the losses of the world. By then, she had been transported by her own music, as sometimes befell when the harp took charge and the strings played her fingers rather than the proper way round.

The emperor's sob startled her from her trance and, realizing what she had done, she transformed the music once more into geantraí, pivoted by progressions out of the seventh mode and lessening his black bile with the eighth. It was intricate fingerwork, finding the right cadences so as to shift without dissonance. When she had finished, she laid her hand flat against the strings to still them; though it seemed to her that the strings still wanted plucking and vibrated softly even so.

"I did not mean to upset you, Jimmy," she said.

"No, no, quite all right. Chin-chin. Emperor *should* be upset now and then. Tedious business, remaining always in balance—always in harmony." A quick smile and with a nod toward the harp. "As you must know."

"Perhaps I can play a song of your own world. Thistle-waite. Something pleasant and hopeful."

"World hopeless. Keeps breaking."

"And yet you persist. My mother always said courage was one of the Four Great Strengths."

"You mother. Yes. What other three?"

"Prudence, justice, and moderation."

The emperor nodded. "Those good strengths for ruler."

"How does your First Cautionary Book begin? I could try to set it." Méarana's fingers poised ready to wrest a melody from her strings, and Jimmy began to recite in a singsong voice.

"In day of gods, seed-ships come.
Out of night eternal, to quicken life
And stir our olive seas. Oh, beam it down,
Oh, beam it down, brave captains say.
So yang from sky meet yin on ground.
Thrusting deep within. . . ."

Afterward, Méarana said, "This worm trembles that she must leave so soon." She did not sound much like a trembling worm, having had little practice in the art.

Jimmy laid a hand on her bare arm. "Do not go," he said with eyes as wide as sorrow. "How else I hear such distant places? Duty pin me forever to Jenlùshy like butterfly to board. You stay here. Be empress. Bring songs of places I never see."

Méarana slid her arm gently from his touch. She adjusted the green shawl around her shoulders. "I cannot. I would be a prisoner here."

"In chains of gold," he told her. "In velvet bands."

"Ochone! Are chains of gold chains no less? I must go. It is a *geasa* upon me."

The emperor of the Morning Dew slumped a little in his seat. "Obligation. Yes, I understand. You must find her."

She said nothing for a time, stroking the strings of her harp, but without striking them, so that they only murmured but did not speak. "How did you know?"

The emperor gestured elegantly toward the harp. "What else? Such sorrow come only from death or loss. And death not drive you to cross whole Spiral Arm."

Méarana closed her eyes. "No one has heard from her in three metric years. Many search, myself most of all."

Jimmy Barcelona lifted his teacup to his lips and his eyes searched the courtiers who lined the walls out of ear-shot, engaged in faux conversations. "Then," he said, dropping his voice, "I, too, search. I go with you . . ."

Méarana had expected the invitation to stay; but not the offer to go. "Ye . . . Ye cannae," she said, falling into her native accents. "Jenlùshy needs you. Mother selected you because of your expertise in infrastructure. You must stay here and rebuild the Morning Dew so that it can survive the next thistlequake."

But Jimmy dismissed that with a wave of the hand. "No build so strong but Thistlewaite stronger. This miserable worm, engineer. Lay pipe, calculate sewage by ancient rules. Estimate building loads and construction costs. Bridges . . . Was *happy* build bridges. Never ask for this."

The harper touched the strings of her harp. "No one ever does," she said quietly, running her fingers down the cords.

"I give orders. Modify systems; implement fault tolerancing and redundancy; increase reliability of infrastructure. Ministers . . . make up numbers to please me, and always build as always. Ancient rules. One day, all come down again. No. Better one seek Bridget ban across whole Spiral Arm. There, perhaps, success."

To maintain the harmony of heaven-below by trying to

impose the regularities of astronomy on the behavior of humans was very nearly the definition of madness. And yet mystics throughout the ages, from astrologers to computer modelers, had sought it. They forgot that even the heavens held surprises.

Jimmy Barcelona at least could see the futility of his efforts, even if he was not quite clear on why they were futile. Méarana almost told him that her quest was no less so, but that was something she had not yet told even herself.

And so she spoke truth to power. "Ye maun seek Bridget ban for her sake, not because you want to shuck your own responsibilities."

Power didn't like to hear that; or else he knew she spoke truth, which was much the same thing. "If *purpose* same," whispered the emperor, "what matter, different *motives*? Keep smile. We pretend talk small nothings. Courtiers cannot hear. Listen. If Bridget ban now lost, approval of sky lost, too. So order in heaven-below, in Jenlùshy, not maintain, and all become chaos above."

"That's absurd, Jimmy! What happens in the Spiral Arm does *not* depend on how well you maintain the Morning Dew!"

"This Thistlewaite. Nothing absurd. You know Garden of Seven Delights?"

"What? But . . ." Was this a shift back to "small talk"? "Yes. Donovan and I have eaten there several times. The food is . . ."

"Listen. Garden have back door. I come tonight, at Domestic Entertainment Hour. I come in front, lock door on entourage, run out back. You wait by back door with fast flitter. Rent most fast in whole sheen. I come out back door, jump in, and you 'light a shuck for Texas,' as your friend say. Go so fast as possible to Hifocal Big Town in next sheen. We take shuttle. Once buy ticket . . ." At this point he relaxed and sat back in his chair. "Port Authority protect. Then you, me, your Donovan, we fly across sky, go . . . maybe Texas, maybe find Bridget ban."

The harper took her napkin and dabbed at her lips. High Tea was coming to an end and the servitors were gathering to take down the café table and set the throne room back to rights. "I must confer with my friend."

The emperor, too, glanced at the approaching staff. "No time. No confer. Decide."

Méarana took a deep breath, exhaled. "Second night hour. Behind the Garden of Seven Delights."

"With most fast flivver. Now," he rose from the table and raised his voice a bit so others could hear. "No need more play. Tomorrow, come back, sing of High Tara."

Méarana rose, showed leg in a graceful bow, and swept up her harp case. "Your worship commands; this worthless one obeys." And she slung the case across her shoulder and strode for the door.

She wondered what Donovan would say about this latest development; but she thought she could guess.

"Have you gone mad?" Donovan demanded.

The sleek Golden Eagle flivver floated up Double Moon Street on a cushion produced by the magnetic field in the paving. "You better hope not," the harper said. "I'm driving." To the west, the Kilworthy Hills had darkened, but their highest peaks still caught the un-set sun from over the horizon and flashed a brilliant white and gray.

"Kidnapping the emperor? Tell me that's sane."

"It's not a kidnapping. It's his idea."

"Then you don't know Thistlewaite. He may be the emperor, but 'custom is king of all.'"

"Donovan, listen to me. He may be subject to custom—that's what he wants to escape—but he's certainly capable of keeping the two of us here under lock and key and demanding I play escapist music for him every afternoon *for the rest of my freaking life*! And then how would I find my mother?"

"Uncle Zorba told me to keep you out of trouble. I guess he didn't think you'd be the one starting it."

"The emperor would let *you* go. You have no songs for him."

A part of the scarred man's mind flashed with anger and Donovan chuckled. *Was that you, Fudir? Insulted that she expects you to abandon her? I'm shocked.*

The Fudir told him what he could do with his shock.

<This is dangerous,> said Inner Child. <Kidnapping the emperor, even with his consent.>

We needn't smuggle Jimmy *off-world,* the Silky Voice suggested. *We need only spirit Méarana from the emperor's clutches.*

Ah, said the Brute. **You take the fun outta everything, sweetie.**

It would not need much, whispered another voice. *A slight tap on the temple and she'll wake up on the shuttle halfway to Harpaloon.*

<The emperor wouldn't like that,> Inner Child pointed out.

Donovan said nothing aloud. *Brute, do you think you can do it without injuring her?*

No problemo.

Yeah? Do you want to tell Uncle Zorba about it, or should I? said the Fudir. *If we stiff the emperor, he'll seal the borders. And even if we make it across somehow, Snowy Mountain would be happy to hand us back.*

Somehow? said Donovan. *Where was there ever a border you or I found uncrossable?*

Alone, and not with a naïf of a harper in tow.

And not, said the Sleuth, who had been silent until then, *with a pause for debate at every juncture.*

Méarana shook his shoulder. "Fudir. We're there."

The scarred man gathered his thoughts and looked around the service alleyway. The paving here was not magnetized and Méarana had switched over to ground effect, which blew the litter about in swirls. Cans clattered; paper whipped. The narrow lane was unlit, and what illumination spilled across the roofs from Gayway Street did little to lift the shadows. On the right, dustbins stood by each door along the back walls of the Gayway shops. On the left, a stone wall enclosed the residential lots. The emperor had made a good choice for his abduction. Except for the Garden, the other shops were closed up for the night. Blocked from the Garden, his entourage would be forced to run to the far ends of the block to reach the alley, by which time the flivver would be long gone.

"You're going to do it, aren't you?" said Donovan.

"Of course, I am," said Méarana. "It's our only way to get off this planet." Then, realizing that the question was not meant for her, she favored him with a searching look. "You don't have to do this, you know."

"Don't worry about me," said the Fudir. "I promised Zorba that I'd watch out for you."

"I'm not without resources. Mother taught me a trick or two."

"Actually, he said he'd hunt me down and kill me if anything happened to you."

Méarana laughed. "Uncle Zorba is a great kidder."

The Fudir said nothing. Zorba was not that great a kidder. He raised the flivver's gull-wing, and hopped into the alley. The ground effect was just enough to keep the chassis above the paving. "Keep the turbines at hover." Then he crossed to the utility door of the Garden of Seven Delights, ready to hustle the emperor into the waiting vehicle.

Where do you think they'll be? asked the Sleuth.

"Shut up," Donovan explained.

He heard the distant blast of the trumpets from the palace

walls, and pole-speakers about the city carried the Voice of the Sheen's announcement of Domestic Entertainment Hour. Clever timing, thought the Fudir. Most of Jenlùshy would be indoors with their visors active, watching the evening installments of their favorite shows.

Shortly after, he heard the whine of flivvers pulling into the restaurant's parking lot on the Gayway side of the building, followed by the hiss and chunk of doors rising and closing. "Get ready," he told Méarana.

He heard the front door slam, rapid footfalls approaching, then the utility door flew open and Jimmy Barcelona rushed out into the alley. The Fudir pushed a large dustbin in front of the door to impede pursuit and took the emperor by the elbow and hurried him toward the car.

At which point, a dozen men dressed in black rose from the surrounding shadows and leveled hand stingers at them.

Yes, said the Sleuth, *that's where I thought they'd be, too.*

The Fudir cast about for an escape route, torn between Inner Child's impulse to run and the Brute's impulse to fight. Donovan, who had been stung more than once in his career, raised the scarred man's hands. The Silky Voice wept over their failure. Pulled thus in half a dozen directions, the scarred man remained motionless at their average.

Inside the flivver, the harper sat with her hands clenched on the control yoke. Rage dueled with sudden relief in her features. Her hands moved a fraction and the turbine's pitch subtly increased. Donovan, who knew the capabilities of man and machine, thought it a desperate ploy, but one with a hairsbreadth chance of success. Cut losses, abandon allies.

It's what he would have done.

But the flivver's whine dropped into silence. Méarana

turned open-faced to the Fudir and the scarred man read her fears writ there.

Flivvers approached from either end of the alley and came to a rest, neatly boxing them in. The doors of the one facing them arched open and Morgan Cheng-li stepped forth, followed by White Rod bearing the Yellow Cope.

"Ah, Majesty," said the Grand Secretary. "This worm abases himself for interruption of such clever evening entertainment, but Monthly Tattoo waits August Presence on parade ground." He showed leg and, with a sweep of the arm, invited Resilient Services to enter the flivver.

Jimmy Barcelona slumped and he looked at Donovan, and then at Méarana. "What I say? This Thistlewaite. All plans fail."

Two of the Shadows led Resilient Services to the flivver where White Rod waited.

By this time, the harper had come to stand beside the scarred man. "Are you all right?" she asked him in a whisper.

The Fudir did not know what to tell her. That he had frozen when fast and decisive action might have been most necessary? That it was just as well that they had not escaped because he would not be reliable in a pinch? The sum of his parts was less than the whole he had once been. Donovan answered for him. "No worries," he said. "Hush, here comes Jingly."

The Grand Secretary bestowed a slight nod and sweep of the arm. "You should not have indulged him," he said in Gaelactic. "He is needed too much here."

"He threatened to hold me captive if I didn't," the harper said.

A wave of a jeweled hand. "That contrary to Treaty of Amity and Common Purpose. Fourteen States all signatories to League Treaty. You think we want Hounds come here, tear down prison to free you?"

Donovan did not know if The Particular Service would go that far; at least not for his sake. Though they might for Bridget ban's daughter.

"You spy on your own emperor?" he said.

Jingly looked surprised. "Of course! You know 'Shadows'? Provincial Surveillance Commissions duplicate Provincial Administrative Commissions. Yang, yin. Each official, each prefect, each dough-rider has shadow. Shadows report piety and harmony to Imperial Censor."

"Yes, I know that."

"So. Who need harmony more than emperor? All balance depend on him. I say 'balance,' but no word in Gaelactic mean same."

"I understand."

"No," said Jingly. "You *not* understand. Only Thistles understand. Our star, central star of whole universe. Microwave 'walls,' same distance, all direction. Heavy burden, balance whole universe on shoulders. No man have such strength. Often bend, sometimes break. Like today. No one man manage all. But all Morning Dew, all Thistlewaite unite in this. All share burden; all *help* emperor. Like today."

Behind him, White Rod placed the Yellow Cope on the emperor's shoulders and bowed him deferentially toward the waiting car.

"You go now," said Jingly. "You not come back Jenlùshy."

Méarana bowed and Donovan bowed and, rising, she saw behind the yellow-garbed August Presence, the trapped eyes of Jimmy Barcelona, who had wanted of all things only to build bridges.

AN AISTEAR

The throughliner Srini Siddiqi, *Megranome for* Harpaloon, *is by every measure a finer ship than* Curling Dawn, *but neither the harper nor the scarred man are in a position to appreciate it. Donovan does not want the trip to show on the Kennel's accounts, so they have paid their own way and have taken quarters in steerage; and from steerage, all liners look the same.*

"Just once," says Méarana when she has stowed her trunk into the locker provided on board, "I'd like to travel in a little luxury."

"It does seem a shame," the Fudir admits, "to be on the arm and not squeeze the most out of it."

The harper slams the locker closed with a little more force than required to latch it. "But a dormitory . . ."

"Think of it as an opportunity to make new friends. At least you don't have to share a bed. One time on a transit from Salàmapudra to Nigglesworth, I berthed on a tramp freighter and . . ."

"I don't want to hear this."

The dormitory is a large open area. The beds line the walls in racks of three and the gravity has been dialed down to half-standard to facilitate the luckless travelers in the top bunks. The center of the common area holds dining tables, game tables, and various other means to occupy one's up-time. The room is already crowded when they enter. Men and women and children occupy bunks and tables or run about the room laughing and causing the harper to dodge their career.

Several men spot the harper and call out to her. Children clap in anticipation. Emigrant families smile. Even those driven to the frontier by the ghosts of their pasts *emerge from their introspection and wonder if this might provide the balm their hearts require. There is something about the way she carries herself and carries her harp case that promises uncommon melodies. Troubadours are always welcome. Enemies will suspend their quarrels with knives already pressed to throats to gather like brothers at their feet.*

The swarm of men and women and children in the steerage dorms of Srini Siddiqi *are a mixed lot from across the Spiral Arm: Sharpies with sagging jowls, squat Jugurthans with wide, out-turned noses and pasty-white skin, ebony blonds from Alabaster, second sons of the High Taran aristocracy, fringe-cloaked Jehovans fingering their prayer beads, bored youngsters spurning the stodgy proprieties of the Old Planets, 'Cockers disinclined to mount their heads in the Halls of Remonstration. They hail from Abyalon and Megranome, from Ramage and Valency, from the Lesser Hanse and Gladiola, from New Eireann and Hawthorn Rose. More of them, indeed, than there are berths in the dorms, since, for a lesser fee, one may elect to share a berth and sleep on it in shifts.*

And all of them bound for Harpaloon, "the Gateway to Lafrontera."

The dormitory has self-organized into sections for single men, single women, and families. The harper and the scarred man claim berths in the appropriate sections and rejoin at one of the common tables. The harper has opened her case and her instrument sits upon her lap while she tunes its strings. It will not be long, Donovan supposes, before he loses her to this crowd.

It is a way to pass the time, says the Silky Voice.

<That's not why he's irritated,> suggests another.

Donovan scowls, waiting for the Fudir to chime in with his half-ducat's worth. But the scrambler says nothing, which irritates Donovan further still.

"A geantraí, I think," the harper says, brushing her nails across the strings, then tightening one or two of them with a key. "The music should reflect the hope in their hearts."

"That is called 'enabling,'" Donovan answers. "I think you should play them a goltraí. They may need the antidote more than the poison."

She looks to him and then to the passengers about the steerage dorm. "Hope is a poison?"

"All those who die of disappointment have first ingested hope."

"The hopeless are never disappointed. I will grant you that much. Unless things turn out well despite all. I suppose that would be a kind of disappointment."

"Which they never do. Turn out well, I mean." Donovan gestures to the dormitory and its inhabitants. "Look at them. They think the streets of Lafrontera are paved with platinum. But it isn't that way at all. They are paved with blood and tears."

"Really. I would have expected asphalt or magplast."

"Mockery sits ill on such cheerful features as yours. Later generations might call them heroic; but it seldom looks that way from steerage. A burning bridge flares more brightly at a distance than in the eyes of those crossing it. Some of your audience are bummerls. Their hope is really carelessness. Each is convinced his bad luck has been an accident of his place and not an essence of his character, and if only he can go some other place, he can 'start over.'"

"Some do."

"No, no, no. That's the great fallacy, don't you see? Everything is already started. It started with the midwife's slap, if not before. After that, there is no starting over."

Méarana's fingers dance over the strings, tossing off flower petals of music. "What of that family over there? A *young man and woman, their three children. They seem prosperous, well-fed. From Mfecanay, by their clothing. They are no bummerls, fleeing failure on old worlds. They are movers, seeking success on new ones. The frontier is hungry and they hope to make their fortune in Lafrontera."*

"If the frontier is hungry," the scarred man says, "it will devour them and all their hopes. And if they seek their fortune out there, it can only mean that they have not found it on Mfecanay, and so they, too, are failures, if of a more subtle sort than the bummerl. If a man has what it takes, he can 'make his fortune' anywhere. He needn't put it all to hazard on a strange raw world. One in three of your movers will break and go home."

"Then two in three will be tempered and make a home. What of those who simply yearn for new constellations to point their ways? For them, even Lafrontera may prove too tame, too settled. They'll go out into the Wild, perhaps even to the Rim itself."

"The more fool, they. What can a new sky offer that an old one cannot? New constellations mean strange gods, which is always a chancy thing. There are human worlds in the Wild that have not yet rediscovered starflight; and some indeed have rediscovered little more than grass huts and stone knives. Among such, a man might live as a god—or a saint. Or worse."

Méarana's fingers call out a jaunty, martial tune. "In they end, it does not matter whether the past drives or the future lures. Bummerl or mover or the merely restless . . . It is the going that matters. What sort of Spiral Arm would it be if men had never gone out from Terra herself?"

The scarred man grunts. "A less noisome one, I think."

"Is this your way of commenting on our quest?"

"Your *quest.* No. I remember what you told Zorba.

'When hope is all there is, it is enough.' But I'd not place such hope in hope. Of all the virtues, it is the greatest liar."

The harper laughs, but a little sadly. "I realize that I may never find her. If something has happened to her . . . I couldn't . . . I mustn't . . ." She pauses for a moment in search of her voice. "But I must learn what that something was. Do you understand that? Mother has vanished into the void, and I don't know where or how."

To this, the scarred man makes no answer.

Afterward, she goes off and plays cheerful music for the steerage, despite the ache in her heart; or perhaps because of it. A man has produced a fiddle, which he plays in the crook of his elbow. A woman has a tambourine; another, a guitar. Somehow, they sort things out in that spontaneous human way. Young men and women form lines and dance toward and away from each other, stamping the floor on the beat, so that the dorm becomes a drum.

How, the scarred man wonders, can a woman in such sorrow play with such joy; and he wishes he knew the secret of it for himself.

V HARPALOON OR BUST

Harpaloon is a rawboned world with a raucous flux of folk from all over the Spiral Arm. She is the oldest of the settled planets edging Lafrontera, and beneath the movers and the bummerls and the adventurers and the second sons settling down or passing through lies a substratum who claim descent from the aboriginal population. These folk occasionally celebrate odd holidays and conduct strange festivals. Every three hundred and forty

metric days, regardless of the season, they deck their hair
with three-leaf clovers and walk en masse onto the barren
Plains of the Jazz to drink green beer and throw rocks at a
sandstone pillar for reasons no one can provide.

During the Great Diaspora, humans had been scattered
far and wide, but few had been scattered as far as the
'Loons. After the Reconnection, when explorers from Cud-
dalore and New Shangdong discovered and partitioned
Harpaloon between them, they found little more than rus-
tic villages and market towns—and the brittle remnants of
ancient machines. Since then, other folks have swarmed to
the half-empty world, eventually outnumbering the natives
and even the old Cuddle-Dong aristocracy. This has not
gone unremarked by the 'Loons, who call the newcomers
"coffers" or "gulls" and nurse a resentment that at times
boils over into riot. To this, the coffers are largely oblivi-
ous, since life on Harpaloon is riotous even at the best of
times.

Harpaloon was not the only world that claimed the honor of
"gateway to Lafrontera." Siggy O'Hara had a fair claim, and
so did Dancing Vrouw and a number of others. The frontier
was a broad swath of stars and there was more than one road
into it. But Harpaloon lay at the end of the fabulous Silk
Road and if not all set forth from there, a substantial number
did. Ships crowded her parking orbits; and out in the libra-
tion points, enormous colony vessels awaited the settlement
companies that would fill them. Each of the great ships broadcast a marker for her shuttles: "TenBeck's World, Home on
this Beacon!" "Slufut Settlement Company! Departure immanent! Final Call!" "Stavronofsky's World, terraforming
90% complete! Openings available! Apply now!"

Openings indeed. The Great Hall on Folkinward Station
was lined with booths rented out to the various companies,
each under its own colorful banner, and it was to these that

the bulk of *Siddiqi*'s disembarking steerage swarmed. Why pass through Harpaloon Customs if you were only going somewhere else? The famous "Floating Dome" overarched lounges and restaurants, jugglers and magicians, venues for simulated, interactive, recorded, and live performances. A minstrel bowed a Keller's viol in a reasonable rendition of a recently popular tune. Here and there, someone famous (or infamous) had gathered a tail of followers—newsers, websters, admirers—much like a comet approaching its sun.

Above their heads, but below the springline of the dome, stretched the famed Harpaloon Murals, painted fifty years before by Hendrik Pak Gbǫnju. Bold, broad, bigger than life, they portrayed the great migrations of the mythic past. Thick-hewn men and resolute women moved west in ox-drawn "prairie schooners," Cossacks trudged east through S'birski snows, Zhōgwó families creaked in great two-wheeled carts up the Gansu Corridor, Magreebees home-steaded in the decaying suburbs of Yurp. Across the banks of the Great Fish River, Four-trekkers heading north greeted Mantu cattlemen heading south. Here, too, legendary figures posed: Jacinta Rosario peered across the rusty sands of Mars; Yang huang-ti pointed dramatically to the lichen-covered plains of Dao Chetty; Chettiwan Mahadevan, hands a-hip, stared at the crumpled ruins of the first-found prehuman city on New Mumbai.

It was all very improbably epic, the harper thought while standing on line for Inbound Customs. Gbǫnju's imagination had wrestled with history and had pinned history defeated to the mat. Most heroes didn't know at the time that they were, and seldom had occasion to strike dramatic poses. Rosario was certainly a myth, a storybook character; and the same was likely true of Yang. And while Mahadevan was known to history, his story was surely embellished beyond recognition.

The lander gate for Preeshdad Town was crowded: fellow passengers from *Srini Siddiqi*, private travelers, movers with time to kill before their ark departed, customs and immigration shift-workers returning home for their "down" time. The harper and the scarred man were among them, for it was from Preeshdad that Bridget ban had checked in with the Kennel.

Nearby, but a little apart, stood a hatchet-faced man and a wife with lips pulled as tight as harp strings, and two small children in nondescript clothes and terribly solemn faces. Méarana heard snippets of fierce, whispered conversation.

"I *told* you we'd be late. I *told* you."

"They said they'd hold our berth. How'd I know they would give it away?"

"You could've got us here on time. What do we do *now*?"

"There'll be a second voyage. They promised."

"Like they promised to hold our berths? What'll we *live* on until then? Those tickets took our last ducats. We *need* that money."

"Cash the tickets in, and you can kiss TenBeck's World good-bye. We'll never save up . . ."

Perhaps they noticed the harper, for they lowered their voices still further and moved off a distance, followed by their bewildered and silent children. Donovan chuckled.

"Behold, the noble pioneers!"

"Must everything be with you a bone of contention? When I set out to find you, I had expected a better man at the end of the hunt."

"Instead, you found only a man, more or less."

"Rather more than less." She tapped him on the forehead with her finger. "When do I meet these others that you carry with you?"

The scarred man backed away. "They come out when

the Fudir and I let them. He and I are the consuls of our little republic."

The harper glanced once more at the mover family. She was not so foolish as to confuse the particular with the general, and already she was limning the encounter in a goltraí, a lament for a lost world. What sadder fate than to lose your future?

Pwairt na Pree, the groundside shuttle field, lay in the Jazz plains, a few leagues east of the capital. It handled trans-global semi-ballistic shuttles as well as ground-orbit traffic, and most of the passengers who downsided with Donovan and Méarana swarmed off to their connecting gates, bound for newly-opened townships in what the locals called the Boonlands. Even so, the monorail platform outside the terminal was crowded with those eager to sample the city life of Preeshdad itself.

A warm, gritty wind tore at their clothing when they stepped out onto the platform. Cloaks billowed and hats fled the heads of those who wore them. The green banner of the planetary league snapped in the stiff breeze: a golden harp enfolded by a silver crescent moon.

𝕿𝖍𝖆𝖙 𝖋𝖑𝖆𝖌 𝖑𝖔𝖌𝖔 𝖗𝖊𝖒𝖎𝖓𝖉𝖘 𝖒𝖊 𝖔𝖋 𝖘𝖔𝖒𝖊𝖙𝖍𝖎𝖓𝖌, said the Pedant.

What doesn't? jeered the Sleuth.

The scarred man's head jerked here and there, as the desires of some of him to study the flag struggled with desires of others to watch their companions on the platform.

<There could be danger here,> said Inner Child.

"Are you ill?" A woman standing beside the scarred man reached out to him to steady him, but Inner Child cried out and pulled back.

"It's all right," Méarana assured the doubtful woman. "It's a muscle spasm. He gets them sometimes." She held tight to his arm.

The Fudir calmed his disparate mind and bowed to the woman. "Thankee, missy. You much kind this-man."

But the woman was not reassured. She, too, took a step back. "You're a Terry," she said and glanced half-consciously at the hand with which she had touched him. Waiting passengers, attracted by the by-play, reacted in various attitudes. One man scowled and stepped closer to the woman, fists clenched as if to defend her. Others, newly dropped from other worlds of the Periphery, pursed their lips or tsk'ed or simply turned away, but whether from distaste for the Terran or for his treatment by a local, the Fudir did not know.

"Watch ourself here," the Fudir warned himselves. "They don't seem well-disposed toward Terrans."

"Considering that nowhere are Peripherals well-disposed to Terrans," Donovan answered, "that is a considerable understatement."

That was why Donovan preferred Jehovah. Jehovans did not like Terrans, but Jehovans did not like anyone; and as long as they did not dislike Terrans more than anyone else, Donovan counted that as warm embrace.

The train was approaching from the city, slowing with a hum of its magnets into the station platform. "It's why we should have stayed there," he told the others. "Like I suggested."

The Fudir demurred. "Then who would ward our . . . our Méarana?"

Up until now, said the Sleuth, *I don't see that she's needed much warding.*

"Not yet. But you know where this is all heading," said the Fudir.

Of course, said the Sleuth. *I saw that back in de la Susa's office.*

Technically, it wasn't his office.

Shaddap, Pedant.

"What if she did have to lean on us?" the Fudir said. "We'd snap. We'd break."

"Yes," said Donovan. "Remember the alley in Jenlùshy, when the moment came for quick and decisive action."

If youse guys had let me take charge, like you shoulda . . .

"Quick and decisive, Brute. Not quick, decisive, and stupid."

Preeshdad was the capital of Cliff na Murph, the largest of the sovereign states of Harpaloon and by default the nominal capital of the planet. She was a middling town and as ramshackle as Jenlùshy. But where Jenlùshy was often shaken down, Preeshdad was shaken up. Her buildings had the indefinable patchwork irregularity of things thrown together in haste, as if the folk of Harpaloon had been in a tearing hurry to get on with something else.

The folk, too, had that same improvisational quality. They made life up as they went along. Rioting was the municipal sport; but a man was as apt to fight someone one day as stand him a drink the next. If on Thistlewaite all plans failed, on Harpaloon they barely got started before another overtook it.

The town had been built in a bowl valley on the western edge of the Jazz, hard by a natural harbor on the eastern shore of the Encircled Sea. For most of the local year, the sea breeze tempered the climate, keeping it cool and moist and escorting the occasional storm as the price; but twice each year the winds reversed and carried the dust off the grasslands. The hot-breathed, bale wind was called the *shrogo*, and during the season people doffed their waterproof tweed caps and donned instead the bright checkered head scarves known as *caephyas*. It was a bad time of year; for the warm, gritty breeze rubbed tempers raw, and even the meekest of men would grow irritable. The seasonal body count typically rose a bit in the good years, and spiked in the bad.

The few minutes on the train platform were all the convincing Méarana needed that the *shrogo* was in full career. Peddlers with mobile carts did a brisk business at the midtown rail terminal, selling headgear to touristas to protect hair and neck from the dust. Méarana bought a type of *caephya* called a *chabb*. Rimmed with tassels and woven of a light cloth known as *shoddy*, it wimpled her golden features in an emerald frame, so that her face, peering out as if from a window, seemed small and almost childlike. Lead slugs sewn into the hem allowed her to drape it to best effect and kept the fly ends from flapping in the stiff breeze.

Donovan she thought abrasive enough that the wind might need protection from his face. But he purchased a red-and-white checkered *caephya* and two pairs of protective goggles, called *gloyngo santas*.

They had noticed that some Harpaloon terms were strikingly similar to the Gaelactic, where *síoda* meant a kind of silk and *an gloiní cosanta* meant literally "the goggles protective." But *caephya* and *chabb* and other words were unknown and seemed peculiar to Harpaloon. The Pedant suggested that these terms had come from the aboriginal 'Loon tongue.

The *Phundaugh* Plough and Stars was a short walk from the terminal and the Fudir found that all had been arranged there to his instructions. Members of the Brotherhood, acting with that solidarity that persecution creates and bribery knits together, had even conjured the illusion of occupation. Beds were mussed, linens used, clothing left in disarray. Room service had been ordered. Surely, this was fellowship!

Or an opportunity to live high on another's expense. Donovan brushed away the tear of sentiment in the Fudir's eye. And a close inspection of the disarray revealed some small objects missing.

The harper regarded this with no little amusement. The Fudir's primary occupation on Jehovah had concerned small objects going missing. Not that she hadn't been pilfered, too; but nothing of terribly great value had walked away and, "It does make a fair compensation for their effort, doesn't it?"

"The Brotherhood was to have covered it," the Fudir grumbled, surveying the remnants of his luggage. "And I was to compensate the Brotherhood from the Kennel's chit."

"Perhaps *Curling Dawn*'s steward did not explain things so clearly to his groundside contacts."

"Perhaps *Curling Dawn*'s steward is wearing our second-best set of wrist bangles."

"He may be. But note: it was the *second*-best he took."

A sealed envelope bearing the tail-biting logo of the Ourobouros Circuit was waiting in the room: the reply from Hang Tenbottles to the request she had squirted en route. Méarana picked it up, but Donovan plucked it from her hands and inspected the envelope closely.

"It hasn't been opened," the harper said.

"Or it's been opened by an expert." He frowned some more over the cover, then handed it back to Méarana. "What does Tenbottles say?"

The harper broke the cover and pulled out the flimsy. "585.15, 575.02!" she read. "1041.07 937.20 + 407.11. 870.07 253.09."

Donovan grunted. "Well, *that's* informative."

"There's more," she said, gesturing to the sheet.

Donovan took it from her.

"It's in code." she told him.

"Really?"

"Your humor is heavy-handed. Everyone encodes Circuit messages. It saves face-time."

"All right. What's the basis for the code?"

"Weren't you once a spy or something?"

Donovan shrugged. "Why pick a lock if someone will hand you the key?"

I love this, said the Sleuth. *I can sink my teeth into this one.*

"If you had any teeth," Donovan told him. "I think the Brute owns those."

The better to bite you with, said the Brute, showing a rare flash of humor.

𝕷𝖊𝖙 𝖒𝖊 𝖘𝖊𝖊 𝖙𝖍𝖊 𝖒𝖊𝖘𝖘𝖆𝖌𝖊, said the Pedant. 𝕴 𝖓𝖊𝖛𝖊𝖗 𝖋𝖔𝖗𝖌𝖊𝖙 𝖆𝖓𝖞𝖙𝖍𝖎𝖓𝖌.

The response was a chorus: "We know."

Méarana scanned the message into her personal brain. She knew that Donovan was holding another of his internal debates and wished she could hear what the others were saying. Hearing half of a dialogue might enable one to tease out the whole thing; but hearing only two parts of a heptalogue was another matter entirely.

Hang had listed everything that Bridget ban had sent, received, or accessed during her home leave. Books, journals, correspondence, call logs . . . Some were local, or to and from Die Bold, and Méarana recognized many as dealing with ranch management. There was a Circuit call placed to the College of Scholars on Kàuntusulfalúghy, and a reply from the same source, but the contents had not been entered into the penátès.

"The College of Scholars," said Donovan. "She was probably checking the bona fides of that Debly Jean Sofwari."

"Sofwari was on her reading list, too," Méarana said.

"Here's a story in something called the *Kauntling Journal of Accumulated Facts*. '27th Eve: a genetic reconstruction of the Old Planets.' What does that mean?"

The scarred man shrugged. "It means Sofwari told your mother something hard to believe and she wanted to find out if he had the chops."

"Well, yes, I suppose; but I meant what does the title of his story mean?"

"Do I look like a scholar? OK, Pedant, you know all sorts of useless facts. What does . . . Well, what good are you, then? Of course. The rest of us will try to bear up under your silence. Fudir, what do you think you're . . . !"

Méarana looked away in embarrassment at the argument. When she had gone on her search for the scarred man, she had found more than she had bargained for.

"Donovan doesn't know how to wheedle," the Fudir told her. "He doesn't politick enough. Now we're going to be ignorant for a while until Pedant resurfaces all because Donovan buigh doesn't know how to kiss his own ass."

Méarana would not look at him. "Ignorant?" she said.

"Pedant has our long-term memory, or a big chunk of it, anyway. When he sulks, we forget things."

The harper looked at him, at the ever-mobile eyes. "You should try to get along."

"Get along? He's me."

"All the more reason."

The two of them fell silent then. A certain sort of propriety had been breached. The scarred man usually tried to keep his internal chaos from breaking surface; the harper usually refrained from mentioning it. Méarana took the decoded list and pretended to read it once more.

After a while, the Fudir said, "The Pedant doesn't know everything. He can only know what we've seen or heard or read. He never forgets, is all. But our memory is holographic;

so it's not like the rest of us know *nothing* when he's . . . in his tent. Genetics is an ancient dogma. It has something to do with Predestination. We should try to get a copy of the story. The witch went out of her way to read it, so it may mean something. What else did she read during home leave?"

Méarana cleared her throat and continued to look down at the list in her hands. "Uh, gazetteers of the Spiral Arm. Communications with hotels. Maybe reserving rooms planet-side. She read a book by Mani Latapoori called *Commonwealth Days: The Rise and Fall of Old Terra*. You ought to like that one, Fudir. A novel by Ngozi dan Witkin titled *The Greening of Hope*. I remember dan Witkin from school. We had to read ancient literature, but what we read was . . ."

"Abandonment," said the Fudir. "Everyone has to read that in forming school. It's the classic novel of the Diaspora, a memoir of her grandparents. I didn't even know she had written other books. Anything else?"

"Rimward Ho! The History of Lafrontera. And—these seem more scholarly—*Compendium of Charters of the Gladiola Terraforming Institute. Monstrous Regiment: The Constitution of Boldly Go.* Here's one we ought to find locally: *Customs of the 'Loon Tribes of Cliff na Mac Rebbe."*

"Ay-yi. How long was your mother at home?"

"She's a fast reader; and if she already knew what she was looking for, she could have search-functioned these texts and been done in a blink." Méarana unplugged her pocket memory. The Fudir nodded at the small box.

"The key to your code is in there?"

"Sure, but you'll never find it." She tossed it to him and he caught it one-handed. "So tell me that this has helped us find my mother."

"The clues are somewhere in those texts."

"You mean somewhere in the tens of thousands of screens that she read during her home leave. Yet, surely some of this—" She waved the hardcopy. "—maybe even *all* of this—was leisure reading. She did relax from time to time."

"Did she? We're not so certain of that. I don't believe she ever did anything without purpose. She was the most intentional person I ever knew." The scarred man consulted the clock. "Better lie down and get some rest. We're space-lagged. Ship-time noon was four hours earlier than Preesh-dad noon. I'll wake you when it's time to go on the prowl."

"To find the jeweler who sold the medallion."

"To go through the motions of finding him. The jewelist on Thistlewaite said only that the man who pawned it came from Harpaloon."

"You make it sound hopeless."

The scarred man grunted. "Good. I meant to."

Harpaloon jewelers, called *jawharries*, were scattered throughout the town. So Méarana and Donovan compiled a list of shops courtesy of the municipal office, the Kennel chit, and a bit of buckshish under the table; and splitting the list between them, spent several days going from one to another. Not that they expected to find the 'harry who had sold the trinket; but someone might remember that Bridget ban had come asking, and someone might recognize the style or workmanship. It was worth the shot, though Donovan rather hoped that the shot would miss and Méarana would give up her hopeless hunt before it led them to where he feared it would.

They quickly learned that Bridget ban had indeed been asking after the pendant's provenance. A few jawharries even mistook Méarana for her mother returned, remembering only the red hair and green eyes and the catlike grace in her step, and being greatly deceived on the number of years that underlay them. But they learned, too, only what she had learned then, which was nothing.

Until, as luck would have it, luck had them. Twice.

Or three times, depending on how one defined luck.

The first time was on the fourth day, when Donovan entered a small shop on Algebra Street. This tight-fit lane had been in Preeshdad's earliest days its central street. Addresses still pegged east and west from it, although the main business district had long since wandered off to the newer parts of town and Algebra Street now sported slapdash boarding houses and brothels, saloons and small shops. The district was called alternately "The Kasper" or "The Liberties." Donovan thought that in the dark of night the street might appear ominous, but in the bright afternoon it was merely shabby, and teeming with aimless humanity—ragged 'Loons, *soi-disant* Cuddle-Dong aristos, rough-trousered settlers in from the Boonlands, a sprinkling of more brightly-garbed touristas lured from the city center—all of them seeking bargains or thrills or forbidden pleasures, and hailed from all sides by the hawkers of each of them. The Kasper was strung out and tangled in a warren of streets: Aonsharad and Dhasharad to the east; Trickawall and Trickathanny to the west; but it seemed more crowded because the streets were tight and never straight for very long.

BOO SADD MAC SORLI, the sign announced in Gaelactic, FINE JEWELRY, PAWN, AND PRE-OWNED. Above this ran a line of gracefully curling symbols that might be a decorative border. Behind the shatterproof window sat displays of all the small, dispensable possessions of men and women who had found the need to dispense with them. Donovan wondered how many, driven to pawn such property, ever rebounded enough to redeem them.

"Donovan," said the Fudir, "let me bukh with this dukāndar."

A local, pushing by in the throng, gave him a startled look and hurried on.

The scarred man shrugged. "Have at him. I'm tired of all the chaffering. This is the fourteenth shop on our list. I don't think she'll ever give up."

We could simply tell her we'd gone to these places, the Sleuth pointed out. *Why waste our time just because she wastes hers?*

That would not be honorable.

You are in the wrong business for honor, Silky.

"We're not in that business anymore," Donovan reminded himselves.

Boo Sadd, summoned by the door chimes, proved to be a 'Loon: large nose, red hair, hazel eyes, and a dusky complexion against which freckles barely showed. If the approach of a possible customer pleased him, he concealed his joy admirably well. "*Shoran,* you wouldn't be off your orbit, coffer, now would you?"

The Fudir smiled and chose to use a Valencian accent. "Ain't no mover, me. Just a tourista. Got a question bout some jewelry, an' mebbe you kin help me widdit." He held out a hologram of Méarana's medallion. "Guy sold it to me on Thistlewaite, said it come from here, an' . . ."

The jeweler's eyes barely flicked to the image. "Ah, no, fendy," he said, making a fluttery wave of his hand. "As lush, flowing streams on the parched plains of the Jazz, are Thistles in my poor dook. No Harpaloon hand made this. I grieve that I cannot help you." His face revealed the depth of his grief.

The Fudir leaned on the edge of the counter. "You got a long mem'ry, friend, for such a quick answer. This woulda been a coupla years ago. If it ain't Harpy work, mebbe you know where it come from. Not too much to ask, innit?"

Valency had famously been ruled by a line of tyrants of

notable brutality and, consequently, most people felt an urge to cooperate when a Valencian asked politely in just *that* tone of voice.

The jawharry took the image in his hand and studied it. "Hard to tell, o best one, from such a poor reproduction. Do I know if the colors are true? No. May I proof the hardness? I cannot. I have seen work—kluzni, they call it—from the Cliff of Anne de Louis, far across the Jazz which . . . But . . . No. This is not Louisian work."

"But you seen stuff like it? Import ware?"

"I recall now a coffer woman half a handful of years past who asked after something much like this. I will share with you what I am after telling her. My dook does not handle coffer work. Such things are *harm*. But at times it comes into the hands of *assdikkas* and they bring it to me so as not to pollute their fingers. Allow me to check . . ." He whispered into a microphone, studied the result, and whispered a few more parameters. After a moment, he swiveled the viewing stage so the Fudir could see the resulting holo. "These pieces, I am thinking, are like in craftsmanship to yours."

Above the stage floated two rings and a man's bracelet. Each was inlaid with the same sort of pastel-colored stones, cleverly cut and fitted into impressionistic and abstract patterns.

"Pedant?" whispered the Fudir.

The jawharry misunderstood. "No, fendy. No pendants, only these rings and bracelet."

𝔚𝔥𝔞𝔱? said the Pedant. 𝔒𝔥. 𝔜𝔢𝔰. 𝔗𝔥𝔢𝔰𝔢 𝔭𝔦𝔢𝔠𝔢𝔰 𝔡𝔢𝔣𝔦𝔫𝔦𝔱𝔢𝔩𝔶 𝔞𝔯𝔬𝔰𝔢 𝔣𝔯𝔬𝔪 𝔱𝔥𝔢 𝔰𝔞𝔪𝔢 𝔞𝔯𝔱𝔦𝔰𝔱𝔦𝔠 𝔱𝔯𝔞𝔡𝔦𝔱𝔦𝔬𝔫.

Donovan's heart fell. The search, it appeared, would go on.

"Where'd dis stuff come from?" the Fudir asked.

The 'harry checked his records. "A man of the sook, who is called Boo Zed O'Culinane. He had them off a Wildman who was less than prudent of his purse."

"Ah. We learn by our mistakes."

"Then thanks to Boo Zed he departed Harpaloon a far wiser man."

The Fudir laughed. "If ya can't know the truth, ya better know yer errors. Which Wild-world did dis guy come from?"

"O best one! Who may number the grains of sand on the beach of Inch? So many are the worlds of the Wild. But few Wildmen come so far as Harpaloon, and so they are more clearly noted than other coffers . . ." The jawharry bowed slightly and struck his breast. "Begging your honor's pardon. I heard that he came from a world within the Burnt-Over District. The name of it was something like Ōram or Eḥku or Enjrun, but who can keep straight such heathen names?"

The back of the scarred man's scalp prickled. Enjrun, he did not know, but the other two sounded eerily of the old Taṇtamiž. Without thinking, he bowed over his folded hands, "Nandri, dukāndar. You have been . . ."

But the jawharry's eyes narrowed. "Am I looking like a *moose* to you, you farking coffer?" And he mimed spitting on the floor.

Inner Child started in fright and the Fudir said, "Dint mean no fence. Whassa moose?" He knew of two kinds of animals that were called by that name. One was a sort of giant elk on Bracka; another was a variety of rodent that had spread across several worlds in the Jen-jen Cluster.

"A Terry," said the jawharry, and this time the spitting was not mimed.

"Is there something wrong with . . . ," the Fudir began, but Donovan seized control. "Hey, no fence," he said, reasserting the Valencian accent. "But ya used a coupla words I heard from Terrans. Die Bold Terrans call their leader 'Fendy.' On Jehovah, dey call a shop a dukān; and you call yours a dook."

The 'harry touched his breast, lips, and forehead, and then each shoulder. "*Shoran,* they steal everything, even our tongues. They are worse than movers, seventy times seven. The Terries abandoned us after we had risked everything for them."

The man's voice has risen as he spoke and now took on a pitch close to cracking. But he suddenly stopped and visibly subsided into a dull rage. "I think you had better leave. You never call a 'Loon a moose. *Shoran,* that's a deadly insult. Darkness falls on Algebra Street, and I cannot answer for your safety once the light is fled. Go and, *inchla,* you find your way whole to your *Phundaugh.*"

The second piece of luck befell Méarana a little later that same day at Jawharry Chinwemma. Since this stood at Côndefer Park on the prairie east of Preeshdad, she took the air bus from Shdad-Center. The tourista rush was over, but a family of movers from Gladiola was aboard and their children shrieked most admirably when the bus left the launch rail and hit free fall. A trio of 'Loons twisted their faces at this, but aside from a muttered comment about coffers and spawning, they said nothing. The two young men wore their *caephyas* at a rakish angle and sported goatees. Their companion wore a gauze mask across her nose and mouth and her hair was caught up in a *tammershanner.* It was the garb of the "Young 'Loons," a youth movement gaining in popularity.

Below, the grasslands rolled sere and uninterrupted to the horizon. Just as the bus lost its ballistic lift, the rotors kicked in and they settled into powered flight. The children flocked to the windows and pointed and chattered as the cluster of steep hills came into view. Méarana had one quick glimpse before the bus descended toward the receiving platform, where it hooked onto the brake-rail with a minimum of jostling and squealing.

Jawharry Chinwemma proved to be a gift shop attached to the park. The harper saw immediately that it was a jawharry in name only. True, it sold jewelry, mostly of an inexpensive sort designed to advertise Côndefer Park, but that it might harbor a genuine jeweler seemed beyond chance. The sign above the entrance announced the establishment's name and asserted, curiously, that "God owns everything beautiful." Like most other signs on Harpaloon, it bore a row of decorative squiggles underneath.

Behind the counter a pale, flat-nosed woman smiled at the late afternoon traffic. She was thin and of middling height, a few metric years older than Méarana herself.

"Excuse me," Méarana said. "Are you Chinwemma? The jeweler . . . I mean, jawharry?"

The young woman's eyes sparkled. "You're from the Old Planets, aren't you? I could tell by your accent. Your Gaelactic doesn't have the lilt of High Tara, and you are *much* too direct."

"Um . . . I'm from Dangchao Waypoint."

"I would have guessed Die Bold. My, you are a long way from home." Her eyes dropped to Méarana's fingers, noted the nails. "And are ye after leaving yer harp behind ye?"

This last line was delivered with such a pitch-perfect impression of High Taran Gaelactic that Méarana laughed. "I'm afraid so. Is there a song out there on the plains?"

A half-smile. "There may be, but you'd best not sing it. Not until you've put parsex between yourself and Algebra Street."

"Umm, parsex?"

"A local term meaning 'a long distance.' This is sacred ground to the 'Loons. The spot where their ancestors touched down. They claim the 'Iron Cones' are the landers they came down in. And they do look like landers of a sort, though precious large ones if they are. They'd be the only boats from Diaspora Days to have lasted. Historians have always been twitchy to study them, but the 'Loons will not allow it. They'd not like you mocking them, either. No, my name's Enwelumokwu Tottenheim. Call me Enwii."

Méarana was grateful for the contraction as well as for the pause. "I'd not mock a sacred spot. Do you expect Chinwemma back today?"

"Oh, no, no, no, Chinwemma is the name of the shop. It was my mother's name. She told me it means 'God owns all things beautiful' in some ancient language. And I thought it would make a marvelous name for a jewelry shop."

Méarana heard nothing from her earwig and was forced to agree. There were languages so long forgotten that the translators knew not even their names. Scraps of family traditions were all that remained—personal names, place names, a few phrases embedded in the tongues of others. "And what of Enwel . . . Enwela . . . Your name. Does it mean something, too?"

"I have something to say."

Méarana waited, and then she realized that Enwii had answered her question, and she laughed again. "Don't we all. Now if we could only get someone to listen . . ."

"*Mehwíí*. Is there something . . . Excuse me. Thank you, sir. That will be five punts, four dinners . . . Gladiola Bills? Of course, we take them." Enwii checked the rate of exchange and made change for the man. She ran the little statuette through the packager, and handed it back to him. "Come again some day."

When he was gone, Enwii laughed. "A set of three featureless steel cones. But it's a replica of the Famous Iron Cones of Harpaloon. It says so on the base. The Cone of Momad, the Cone of Fìnmakūhl, and the Cone of Homer ben. Sells for just under five-and-a-half punts. I'll leave you to guess how much it costs Wimbley and Chatterji to make them."

"You're not trying very hard to sell me anything."

"Well, you didn't come here to buy anything, now did you?"

Méarana pulled the medallion from under her blouse. "Do ye recognize this? I mean the sort of work, not this particular piece."

Enwii took it and put it under the magnifying light. "Hmm. No, I can't say I do . . . Of course, I'm not a real jawharry; but I suppose you know that by now. Sadd!" She called to a young man standing by. "The sun is coming through the windows. Be a good boy and turn the shades?" As the lad shuffled off, Enwii whispered, "His father's a small-time 'harry in the Algebra Street Kasper. He prenticed him out here to give him a taste of the business—and maybe to keep an eye on the holy ground. I've lived on Harpaloon most my life, but to him I'm just a mover. My mother was Jugurthan and my father was a 'Cocker—if you can imagine so unlikely a couple!—so what does that make me? Sadd's a conscientious lad, but he's a 'Loon and you have to keep on him all the time or he'll . . . Oho! What's this! There's writing on the back side. Micro-relief. Sadd! Wait a minute before you roll down the shades. The light catches it . . . See here, ah . . ." Enwii straightened and blinked. "What *is* your name?"

"Lucy. Lucy Thompson."

"Funny name. No offense. Die Bold, right. What do they say there? 'Die Bold, Live Bolder!' There, do you see the lettering? Let me put it on the screen. The light has to catch it at just the right angle. There."

The back side of the medallion, which had hitherto seemed smooth and featureless gold, now sported the shadows of lettering.

"What does it say?" asked Méarana.

"I've no idea. I've never seen that script before."

"Can you capture an image of it? My partner knows some of the old languages."

Enwii touched the rim of the magnifier and a sheet slid out of the printer. "Thompson," she said, this time with a slight frown. "Rings a bell."

"Rings a . . . ? I'm sorry. I don't know the idiom."

"I mean, I've heard the name before . . ." The shop-keeper cocked her head. "About five years ago."

Méarana's heart leapt. "Did she have red hair, too?"

"Don't know. Never laid eyes on her."

"Never laid . . . ?"

"Never saw her. What was it, now . . . Excuse me. Oh, here they come. The tour must be over. Let me just . . ." She whispered into her throat mike, called something onto the touch board, and brushed it with her hand. "But no. It was a package left for a *Francine* Thompson. Five years ago. But you say your name is Lucy? I wonder if we still have it. Be right with you, mistress; I'm helping another cus-tomer right now."

"Five years? But Mother was on Thistlewaite then. She didn't reach Harpaloon until . . . Oh, local years! That would be more like two years, metric time, right? That fits. You can give it to me. I'm on my way to meet her."

"Francine Thompson was your mother? I suppose you can prove that. Maybe I threw the package out long ago. Wait here. I'll be right back."

Wait here? As if she were not welded to this very spot! *Oh, Donovan! We* will *find her! I know we will.* Méarana dug in her pouch, looking for identification. What if Enwii refused to hand it over? What if she had discarded it al-ready?

The shopkeeper returned from the back room with a small parcel in her hand. It was wrapped in plain brown paper, the cheapest sort and was about a palm in length and width. A printed label affixed to it read: FRANCINE THOMPSON. HOLD UNTIL CALLED FOR.

"I recalled the name only because it was so odd," Enwii

said, "May I see your identification? I suppose if I've held it so long, I really should make sure it goes to the right person."

Méarana handed her a photograph. "Will this do? It's from the *Dangchao City Elucidator*. That's me on the left after a concert; and that's Mother. Francine."

"I told you I never saw the woman; so this . . ." She stumbled to a halt. The holograph had been taken at a formal dinner at the Comchal Odeon on Dangchao Waypoint following one of Méarana's concerts. Bridget ban stood beside her daughter, wearing the beribboned mess jacket and slacks that the Hounds of the Service called "dress greens."

Enwii looked up from the holograph a bit more pale than when she had looked down. Méarana displayed the chit that Zorba had given her, holding it so that none other could see what was in her hand. It glowed a muted gold, which such sigils could do only in the hand of their rightful bearer.

"Take it," said Enwii, shoving the package across the counter. "I don't want it here."

"You're doing the right thing."

"It doesn't matter. Hound's business? That's a magnet for trouble. I don't want to be involved."

"I'll tell her you kept it faithfully for her."

"Tell her nothing. Here." She took a set of steel cones and sent them through the wrapper. "My gift to you. Just get that . . . package out of here. The air bus leaves in . . ." A glance at the wall clock. "In ten metric minutes."

Méarana thanked her again and turned to go. Enwii did not tell her to come back some time.

Ten metric minutes was a little under seven grossbeats in the dodeka time used in the Old Planets, or a little less than a "quarter hour" in Donovan's Terran time. That gave her time to stride over to the viewing platform, and a quick blick at the famous Iron Cones.

The sunset threw long, ruddy shadows across the prairie, casting the Cones into high relief. The lowest reaches were overgrown with grass and shrubbery, but the higher parts were clear so that the broken and corroded metallocene of the half-buried structures was revealed. They were gargantuan, towering as tall as the hills behind them. Enwii had been right. If those had once been landers, they were the largest landers she had ever heard of. Most of the worlds of the Periphery had stories about their First Ships, but she'd never heard them described as so enormous.

Landers or not, the Cones were undoubtedly the largest artifacts to have survived from ancient times; but they were more likely apartment buildings, or factories, or even the tombs of the first rulers. An ancient land on Old Earth, called Meesar, had buried its kings under great pyramids of stone. Likely, that is how each cone had gotten its name. Momad and Finmakūhl and Homer ben might be the names of ancient, now-forgotten kings. A line of fences surrounded the cones and a sign in Gaelactic warned touristas against closer approach. She supposed that the interior ruin and decay made entry hazardous. The ancients had built for the ages, but the ages had passed and only wreckage remained.

"Seen enough, gull?"

Méarana started at the sudden voice at her elbow. It was one of the 'Loons from the bus: a pleasant-faced young man with the swarthy complexion and blue eyes common to his breed. The hair was so darkly red as to be almost chocolate-brown. His manner of asking the question implied that she had certainly seen enough.

Méarana pulled her head back. "Is it any of your business?"

The man shrugged. "It could be." Casually, he pulled a

spring-knife from his pocket and used it to pare his nails. Méarana stared at the blade.

"I could help you with that," she said, and the 'Loon looked up with a puzzled squint.

"Help? How?"

Méarana shrugged and the quillion dagger she carried up her sleeve dropped into her hand. She held it horizontally in underfist position, a little to the side so that she could use it in a backhand slash or an overhand stab as opportunity presented itself. The blade was lively in her grip, almost alive. "I've manicured a few fingers here and there," she said.

The 'Loon studied the quillion and his own spring-knife, shrugged, and made the blade disappear into his handle. "Take your farkin picture, then, brasser. May the cat eat you and the shayten eat the cat." He stepped away with ill grace.

"Thank you," she said sweetly, and tucked the quillion back into its cache. Raising her imager, she hoped her hand would not shake too much. Half the advantage was projecting a mien of confidence. She wondered if she could have followed through on her implied threat. It was one thing to practice on dummies in Mother's gymnasium; another thing entirely to face a living man.

The sun was low, illuminating the west side of the Cones. One of the holes in the side of the largest cone— the one they called Momad—received the light directly, revealing a tangled mess of broken decking. Supposedly, there was a chamber deep inside called the *gáván gofthayin*, where the ruler was buried. A bird flew toward the hole, probably to a nest inside, and impulsively Méarana captured that image.

The backdrop was impressive, too. The irregular cluster of hills behind the Cones was also deeply shadowed by the setting sun, and in the dim light they looked almost as if they, too, were cones arrayed in serried ranks.

That was plain silly. An entire mountain range of these things?

Behind her, Méarana heard the warning hoot from the air bus platform and the hum as the magnets on the rail kicked in to receive the incoming bus. So she stuffed package and comm in the pockets of her jacket, pulled her *chabb* tight against the *shrogo* wind and hurried to the departure ramp. Glancing back, she saw the 'Loon genuflect on one knee toward the Cones and touch his breast, lips, forehead, and shoulders with the fingers of his right hand.

Despite his knife and his menace and his banty-cock threat, her heart went out to him. Did not everyone deserve something sacred?

She had agreed to meet Donovan at the Café Gwiyōm, and there Méarana discovered the scarred man already worrying two fingers of uiscebaugh. He was not drunk, but he was immersed in that morose frame of mind that soured his every word. Drunks at least were sometimes cheerful. Méarana hesitated at the threshold, for she had not seen him in such a state since leaving Jehovah.

She considered the possibility of going on without him. If she left him here, he would barely notice. He would sink into the Terran demimonde and into the prison of his past. But she had invested too much effort in the finding of him and could not bring herself to forgo the return on that investment. And if the Fudir had the prison of his past, did she not have the prison of her future? Growing up, she had learned the art of patience.

She had forgotten that the scarred man was a man of parts, and one part, keeping vigil through his right eye, saw her standing irresolute in the entry, and his arm waved her inside. So she gathered herself, her thoughts, and her excitement and hurried to the table.

It was a bright and open café, unlike the Bar on Jehovah:

spacious where the Bar was dense, well-lit where the Bar was dark, its clientele careless where the Bar's were more carefree. And yet the scarred man had contrived, like a tea ball steeping in hot water, to lend the facility some of the hue of his former estate.

As always, the table he had chosen nestled near the rear wall of the café with himself facing the room. *Never sit with your back to the room,* he had told her once. *You have to see them coming.* Fine advice, she had thought, from one already occupying the recommended seat. And to "see them coming" didn't you have to lift your gaze from the fascination of the whiskey?

She took the *siege perilous* opposite him, with her back defiantly to the room, and placed the package on the table. The scarred man did not lift his head, but she thought those restless eyes of his sought it out and found the name to which it had been addressed, for the grip of his hand on the tumbler tightened and his knuckles grew white.

"It's been waiting for her at Côndefer Park for two years metric," she told him. "It was all I could do on the air bus to keep from ripping it open; but . . . You know what it means? Whoever left the package would have notified her through the Circuit and . . . If we simply wait at the Park, eventually she will come to pick it up, or send a message to forward it . . ."

"We'd wait as long as the Cones, and the birds of the air would make their nests in our beards. And," this he said more forcefully, "if she hasn't come for it in two years, you will, sooner or later, have to face what that really means."

"It could be that she changed her itinerary and the message went to the wrong world; or it reached her hotel after she had left and the hotel didn't know where to forward it. Or she went to a world outside the Circuit. Or . . ."

The scarred man looked up from the table. *"Or she's*

dead! Whatever she had been looking for, she found it. Or it found her."

Méarana stuck her chin out. "Or the package meant less to her than it did to its sender."

"You think she left it behind on purpose?"

The harper hesitated, then looked away. "She leaves a great many things behind."

They fell silent, each with their own thoughts, and one with a multitude of them. "No one I spoke with knew anything about the medallion," she said finally. "Of course, this is a town with a high turnover, save for the 'Loons and the Terrans, and jawharries have come and gone since *she* passed through."

"Moosers," said the scarred man, staring into his whiskey. "They call us moosers here."

"I thought it was 'coffers.' "

"Everyone is a *coffer*—or a *gull*, they use the two terms interchangeably—but they have a special term just for Terrans. Because their holy books say we once abandoned them. A mooser is 'one who submits.' Submits to whom, and how that constitutes abandonment, no one will say."

"Their holy books . . ."

". . . are forbidden to others to read. The *Birakid Shee'us Nakopthayiní* and the *Asejáhn Robábinah*."

"The first one sounds almost like Gaelactic. The 'specklings down of the headmen.' "

"That's what most headmen do. Speckle down on the rest of us."

"The burial chamber of the king, out in the Cones, is called the *gáván gofthayin*. Sounds like it might be related."

" 'Loonie headmen. Kopthayini. Gofthayin. Capitàn. Who cares? Shaddap, Pedant." The Fudir gripped his head in both hands. "All these years, he's silent. Now he won't be quiet. Jabber, jabber, jabber. Yes, you!"

If Méarana understood the linguistic shifts that had

taken place, then *gáván* must have once been *kábán*, meaning a "hut." So, the burial chamber of the king was the "hut of the headman." But when she mentioned this pleasant deduction to the Fudir, he shook his head.

"Please, missy. This ples nogut by Terries. Very budmash. We go from here jildy." Then, dropping the patois, he added, "But I wouldn't mind getting my hands on a copy of their sacred books. Find out what drives these 'Loons crazy against my people."

"And yet they produce decent harpers," said the harper. "The 'Loons do. And they've learned the Auld Stuff. The aislings and the airs. I've heard them when I've gone by 'Loontown. No geantraí, though. I've heard no geantraí." She glanced at the placard above the servers bar—the harp and crescent moon—and wondered what it meant. "Have you ever seen the Cones?" she asked. "There was something in their appearance against the western sky, something ancient and forlorn."

"They were the ships of exile. Did you expect joy?"

"Donovan, I think . . . Look." She flipped open her comm into a holostage and showed him the image she had captured in the late afternoon sun. "Look at the Cones. Awesome enough to think they were tombs. But if they really were *landers* . . . Look at the hills. They have that same conical shape. Maybe . . ."

Donovan tore his gaze from the image. "What?"

"Maybe an entire fleet once set down there. And still rests there. I think the *shrogo* covered them in soil, and chance has disrobed only the southernmost three. There may be hundreds more of them buried out there."

But Donovan had no eye for the hills. He brushed a tear and took the imager from her. The Cones floated above the table, as if lifting off. "Ah, will you look at that, then."

"What? The bird?"

"No, on the bulkhead above the bird's nest." He upped

the zoom. "Do you see it? That is the Great Burst of the old Commonwealth of Suns. Tsol in the center and the Seven Colonies around it. Of course there were more than seven before the end. There may have been seven hundred. Ah, those were storybook times, indeed, when even their wreckage is magnificent."

"Magnificent? It's all burnt and rotted and corroded, but . . . If the 'Loonies' ancestors came in those ships, then they are Terrans, too."

"We all are. But what does ancestry matter if you don't remember—and persecute those who do?" Donovan's eyes closed and his lips moved silently. "Hundreds, you think? Well, you can't be the first to notice the resemblance, but no one is ever going to dig there until the movers and the moosers cut the throat of the last 'Loon. Sometimes, I think 'Saken had the right idea."

Méarana expressed surprise. "The 'Forsaken' dismantled their landers in the early days and used the material to build their settlements. They paved over First Field two hundred years ago and redeveloped it. Sentiment is not their forté. I thought you said the remembering mattered."

A certain ferociousness passed across the Fudir's face. "I'd rather see the past paved over than birds nest in it."

The harper refrained from extending the sympathetic hand that she knew would be rebuffed. "Sometimes," she said, "it's the ancestors who neglect the descendants."

The Fudir looked at her. "Do they."

"And what did you find, Donovan, out among the jawharries?"

The scarred man stared at his whiskey. After a time, he heard the silence and his head rose. "Donovan, he no got nothing."

Méarana's sigh was long and weary. "So the medallion

is a dead end. We must find Mother's trail some other way. Perhaps the package . . ."

The Fudir parted his lips as if to speak; but a voice called out, bluff and hearty: "Is this a private party or can anyone join?"

Méarana made the package disappear and the scarred man turned to snarl at the newcomer, but paused in shock and instead cried out, "Hugh!" And it seemed as if the wind had blown away the clouds of ten thousand years and the bright sun of delight shone through his face unfiltered.

It was only for a moment before the face closed in again; and though the smile remained, it was a sorry thing to that which it had come before. Yet the harper was glad to have seen it, if only just this once.

The man pumping hands with the Fudir was solidly built. He had a square jaw and dusty-red hair. His left cheek bore a scar now only faintly visible. "You must be Little Hugh O'Carroll," she said, extending her hand.

"I must be," said the Ghost of Ardow, bowing low and kissing the back of her hand, "for no one else wants the fookin job." He pulled out a seat on the left side of the table. This was the third time luck had had them, depending on how one counted luck. "An' how do ye fare, Fudir? Still keeping ahead of the law?"

"I've retired," said Donovan. "The law ran out of breath from the chasing of me."

"Ah, it's a sad thing, not to be wanted, even by the likes of the Jehovah proctors."

"Donovan has told me so much about you," the harper said.

Hugh grinned infectiously. "Nothing too bad, I hope." He pointed a finger at her. "An' you, if I had to guess, I'd say you are Little Lucy."

The harper covered her face. "Oh, no! No one's called me that for ages."

"Sure, not too many ages! Fudir," he said turning, "how can you drink that fuel oil? Let me buy you a porter." He twisted in his seat and signaled to the waitress with his fingers. "Fudir and I," he told Méarana, "used to 'pal' around in the old days. Did I say that right? 'Pal?' He must have told you about it? The last time I saw him, he cold-conked me and left me on the front stoop of a tenement in a Chel'veckistad slum. I haven't paid him back for that one yet."

"No charge," muttered the Fudir.

Hugh laughed. "You haven't changed."

A number of emotions chased themselves across Donovan's features. After a handful of beats and behind a faint smile, he said, "You've aged well. Run any guerillas lately?"

"Two. No, three." Hugh laughed at their reaction and, reaching inside his tunic, pulled out a badge. "All in a good cause," he said. "I'm a Hound's Pup now, and there are two tyrants and a pirate king who won't be breaking the Ardry's Peace now."

Donovan took the badge from him and the golden glow faded as it passed from Hugh's hands. He handed it to Méarana. "I left you in bad company. You've been corrupted."

"Oh, 't isn't so bad as all that. I was a little older starting than the Kennel liked; but my Oriel training in planetary management gave me a leg up on the admin skills, and the civil war on New Eireann gave me a leg up on, well, the operational skills. Beside which, I was motivated."

"How?"

"They promised me my first assignment would be to hunt you down."

The Fudir grunted. "If you find me, let me know."

At the jest, Méarana did lay a hand on his shoulder, but only briefly. "But you didn't," she said, passing the badge along. "You went on an adventure with my mother."

Hugh nodded and fell silent, fingering the scar on his cheek. "Aye, so I did. Into the Rift . . . By then, the betrayal no longer hurt as much. No, don't tell me it was all for the best, old friend. From what I hear, it was. But that doesn't really matter, now does it? Sometimes . . . I think about those days. Amir Naith's Gully, sliding with January and his crew—whatever happened to them, I wonder—or the Restoration of New Eireann, or . . . 'On to the Hadramoo!' " He pumped his fist. "Remember that?" He sighed. "Ah, but it can never be that way again, can it?" And there was something in his eyes that was sad and distant.

"I know," the Fudir said quietly. After a time, with something of his old spirit, he added, "And as long as you're not hunting for me, I wish you good luck. What's your office name? Not Little Hugh. You don't work for Clan na Oriel any more, so you can't use one of their names."

"I'll still be Hugh where you and I are concerned. But for Kennel work, I'm 'Rinty.' "

"Rinty. Who's your doggy?"

The waitress came by and set four mugs on the table. Hugh paid her. "Greystroke," he said.

"Greystroke!" The Fudir laughed and slapped the table. "There never was a man as good as he was at blending in. Where is he now?"

"Right here," said Greystroke, who sat at the table's fourth side. He handed the badge back to Hugh, picked up one of the mugs, and smiled at Donovan.

The scarred man shook his head. "I wish I knew how you did that." He took a drink of his own. "Did I not tell you, harper? He is so *ordinary* that no one notices him."

"Only when he wants it so," said Hugh. "Otherwise, he can be as obtrusive as . . . Well, as you."

"You make a good pair," admitted the Fudir. "The Ghost of Ardow was hard to find, too."

"It comes in handy," admitted Hugh.

"Speaking of which," said Greystroke, "Rinty and I have just finished a case on Khlabash and being in the neighborhood, thought we'd stop here and sift for information on Bridget ban." He looked from Donovan to Méarana and back, and smiled. "Imagine finding you two here! If I had to guess, you must be doing the same."

Evening had come on and they ordered dinner from the café. The waitresses brought special pillows for them to sit on and plates of beaten copper and small cups of turgid coffee. They ordered McLoob—boiled chicken and fried vegetables all cooked together with rice. It was sometimes called the "planetary dish" of Harpaloon, though it was popular only in the Cliff na Murph and neighboring countries.

The *craic* ran high. Inevitably, there were reminisces of the Dancer affair, and the Fudir had the opportunity to set straight what had happened in the endgame and his close brush with Ravn Olafsdottr. "Still on the loose, I hear," said Greystroke. "Hope she's not still hunting for you. There are signs that many of their agents have gone back. Some sort of trouble in the Confederation." The Hound and Hugh recounted some cases they had worked on, "as much as we can tell you." And Méarana talked of her music and promised to play for them the next day. When the Fudir told them, with almost proprietary pride, of her song cycle around the Dancer, Hugh said lightly, "Be sure to play the part where the Fudir knocked me cold."

They spoke, too, of Méarana's mother, praising her skills. But the Silky Voice saw in the cast of the harper's face the thought that one only eulogizes the departed.

"She was a woman easy to love," said Greystroke, "but at the same time, difficult."

"Aye," said Little Hugh. "Easy for her to be loved, less easy for her to love."

"She used her affections as a weapon," Greystroke said. He lifted his coffee toward his lips, but it never arrived, and after a while he returned the cup to its saucer. "It blunts them," he finished, "to use them so. She grew coarse, numb. She could not feel the caress of others."

The third person. The past tense.

"Translation," the Fudir said. "You wanted her to love you, and she would not."

"Or she could not," the Hound countered.

"All three of us wanted that," said Hugh. "Didn't we? We wanted her to love us; but she only wanted us to love her. I didn't mind that. I wasn't looking to be loved. Not then."

"No," said the Fudir. "She wanted control, not love. A bond becomes a leash when it fastens on only one end."

"Ah, bile yer haids," said Méarana with some heat. "Ye're havein' because ye got the fling from her. What else could she have done—*as a Hound?* To love someone, ye maun gi'e yourself awa'. And she could nae afford that. The tightest leash? She kept that on herself. At home, wi' me, 'twas different." At that, she turned away a little from the table and fell into silence.

The Fudir exchanged glances with the others. "The strange thing," he said finally in the quiet that had followed Méarana's outburst, "is what I remember most clearly about her."

"And what's that?" said Greystroke.

"You would think it would be the . . . the weapons she used on me," the Fudir said. "But what remains with me most clearly is the flair with which she did everything. The audacity. She was not always happy; but she was always full of cheer. With her, you always felt that things were possible." Méarana turned and half looked at him over her shoulder. Her left eye, the one he could see, glimmered and a tear trickled down her cheek.

"Ah, it was different with me," said Hugh. "It was more like exercise. She laid a trap for my heart, but I saw the trap and stepped into it willingly. So you might say we trapped each other."

"Then perhaps," said Greystroke, "she did love each of us, in a way, and if only a little."

The Fudir pursed his lips. "With Hugh, she may have enjoyed the sheer recreation. With me, she may have liked battling wits. But only the gods know what she saw in you, Greystroke. No offense, but she had flair and she had drama; and among your many fine qualities those are not to be numbered."

The Hound smiled. "Haven't you heard? Opposites attract."

The jibe irritated the Fudir almost as much as the chuckles he heard from the other voices in his head. "I, at least, was not snared," he told the others. "In the end, *I* walked out on *her*."

"She wasn't the only one you walked out on," said Hugh. "But, tell me: did you walk, or did you run?"

The Fudir flushed; and he shifted, suddenly uncomfortable, on his pillow.

"She was quite angry with you afterward," the Pup added, "and for a long time."

"And what greater anger," the Fudir said with a smile toward Greystroke, "than that of love spurned? She wasn't used to rejection."

Hugh grinned. "Greystroke was madder than any of us. Does that mean he loved you even more?"

The question caught the Fudir short and he saw in a momentary slip that it caught Greystroke, too. Then he blew the Hound a kiss and said, "Gray One! I didn't know you cared." They laughed more heartily than the joke had warranted, and Méarana rejoined the banter dry-eyed once more.

Dessert had come by then and, when they were enjoying the mango sherbets and the McMoul cookies, Greystroke said, "So, how goes the search? Zorba told us over the Circuit that we should cooperate if we happened to cross paths. Retired agents have no authority to issue orders, but you know how that goes . . ." He wagged his hand ulta-pulta. "Though the Friendly Ones alone know how you hope to succeed where we have failed."

The harper closed her eyes briefly. "I thought, being her daughter, I would notice something that you and your colleagues overlooked. No offense."

Greystroke pursed his lips. "None taken. What have you found?"

"Very little," Donovan said before the harper could speak. "They told me in the Corner that she met with some Terran and 'Loon leaders. Oh. And she was traveling as Francine Thompson—but that, you already knew."

Greystroke sighed. "There is so much else to learn," he ruminated. "What of her taste in jewelry, for example?"

Inner Child twitched and the scarred man's hand knocked over his coffee cup. Everyone pushed back from the table and the waiters swooped in to clean things up.

The scarred man apologized to everyone for the spill. He found Little Hugh staring at him with grave concern. "Are you all right, Fudir?"

"Me-fella *ṭhīk hai*. You no worry, sahb." If Greystroke noticed that the jewelry topic had been skipped, he was not so boorish as to point it out.

In the lift to their suite on the fifth floor, Méarana said, "I liked what you said about her."

The Fudir looked wary. "What I said? What was that?"

"You said, 'She was not always happy; but she was

always full of cheer.' And that, old man, is the essence of hope."

When they had reached their suite, the scarred man intimated to the harper by portents and signs that she should remain silent and change her clothing.

Méarana started to ask why, but he mimed silence again, and so, puzzled, she did as he wanted. While she changed, he chattered from the other room about past adventures with Hugh and Greystroke on Jehovah and New Eireann, and how pleased he had been to run into them like that. "Of all the cafés in all the worlds of the Spiral Arm," he said, "they walk into ours." Then he laughed, as if at some secret joke.

When she rejoined him in the common room he was dressed up in a *shawkéad fáwsuc*, what on Dangchao Waypoint was called a "bush jacket." Into one of its capacious pockets he slipped the package she had gotten at Chinwemma. "It must have been nice," she said as she watched him, "to see your old friends again."

"It was enlightening," he said. "That's always nice." He produced an audio player and set it on the table. "Did I ever tell you about my experience as an instrument tech on January's ship? Let me explain about astrogation." With that he activated the player, and Méarana heard a recording of a conversation they had had weeks before on *Dragomir Pennymac*. It picked up seamlessly from Donovan's question and while it chattered on about roads and the currents of space and holes in space, he led her quietly to the door.

Their *caephyas* hung on hooks by the door, but he waved her off. The door slid open soundlessly and they stepped into the hall. Méarana started to ask him what he was doing but Donovan covered her mouth briefly with his hand. His lips moved. No talking yet.

He took her to the far end of the hall and down the stairs

to a side exit, where they stepped out into the bitter night-time wind. It tore at her hair and filled her nose with grit. She coughed and brushed at her hair. "I'll be a week wash-ing this clean! Why did you make me leave my chabb be-hind?"

He leaned close to her ear. "Do you know what aimshi-fars are?"

"Microscopic *jeepyeses.* Shippers put them in packages to track their locations by satellite . . . Oh."

"Yes. 'Oh.' Of all the cafés in all the Spiral Arm? I don't believe in coincidences. 'Imagine finding you two here!' Come on. Not the hotel shops."

They crossed the darkened parking lot to a haberdash-ery on the other side of Comfort Street. Inside, they found a variety of headgear and bought themselves new hoods and dust goggles. "Greystroke is what we Terrans call a 'prick,'" Donovan explained. "But he isn't a *stupid* prick. That whole encounter in the café was carefully choreo-graphed. He wanted to find out what we knew about your mother. If he had half a brain—and if he doesn't, Little Hugh has the other half—he would have sprinkled some aimshifars onto our clothing sometime during that amia-ble dinner we had."

The dukāndar returned with the *caephyas,* and Méarana noted that they were styled very differently from the ones they had worn earlier. "Lost yours, hey?" the woman said. She had a Megranomic accent—a mover or the daughter of movers. "That happens a lot if'n yuh don't tie 'em down proper. Wind shifts and—hey!—off'n she goes liken a kite. That'll be fifteen punts, eight dinners."

As they left the shop, Donovan said, "I feel like a walk in the park."

"At night? What's there to see at night?"

The scarred man cackled. "You'd be surprised. At least—I hope you'd be. But me, night is my natural habitat."

They passed through a darkened neighborhood, where the only sound was the brush-like hiss of sand against the stones and, once, angry but unintelligible voices from behind one of the shaded windows. The Fudir paused and studied their backtrail. "Greystroke's talent is blending in," he said. "For that, he needs other people around. Open areas can defeat him."

"Then, we're . . ."

"Hugh's talent, on the other hand, is concealment. Give him a shadow, and he's in it."

"But . . . If they bugged our suite, they'll think we're still in it, talking about astrogation."

"We *hope* so. But we'd be a fool to depend on it."

They emerged onto Beachfront Highway. Normally busy, traffic had faded at this time of night into a few solitary autos and some trucks coming in from the townships with food for tomorrow's markets. There was no grid on such a raw frontier world, so the vehicles were all manually piloted.

𝔚𝔥𝔶 𝔡𝔬 𝔱𝔥𝔢𝔶 𝔠𝔞𝔩𝔩 𝔱𝔥𝔢𝔪 "𝔞𝔲𝔱𝔬𝔰," the Pedant wondered, if 𝔱𝔥𝔢𝔶 𝔞𝔯𝔢 𝔪𝔞𝔫𝔲𝔞𝔩𝔩𝔶 𝔠𝔬𝔫𝔱𝔯𝔬𝔩𝔩𝔢𝔡?

Wardalbahr Park stretched along the coast of the Encircled Sea. It encompassed a long beach called Inch Strand, several groves of trees, and a wildlife sanctuary on a rocky hook of land farther to the south. They crossed the pedestrian walkway over the highway and walked to the beach, where tired waves lapped against the land.

Harpaloon had a moon, but it was on the smallish side; so while the Encircled Sea had tides and breakers, they were modest and unassuming. Méarana watched them roll in for a while. It was rare to find terrestrial worlds with giant moons. Terra itself was said to have a companion more than a quarter of her own size, the result of a cosmic freak accident, and it was this freak gravitational ball mill

that had churned its oceans into tidal estuaries and provided self-organizing organic matter with an escalator
onto the land. Harpaloon had been less fortunate. Some
primordial collision had glanced across its face, creating
the great divot of the Encircled Sea and tossing the clot of
land aloft to become Gummar-Gyalack. A large moon, but
not quite large enough.

Only a little bigger, some Harpalooners had claimed,
and "Old G-G" might have stirred the seas to life here as
the Great Moon of Terra had done. Only a little bigger . . .
There was a harp tune there, a goltraí perhaps. A lament
for life that never was. But that was a lament so well-worn
that tears were no longer in it. No one assumed that a planet
would hold anything more than pseudo-living matter—
archaea, or bacteria, or protists—as likely to exchange
genes laterally as vertically. *Dough, but never kneaded,*
the great Alabaster poet, Shishaq sunna Pyoder, had once
written.

"Do you really think Greystroke is listening?" she asked
him. "Or is that only your paranoia? Inner Child, you
called him."

Donovan stood by her side facing seaward. His glance
was a question.

She pointed at the sea and its waves. "I understand. You
brought us here so the surf could mask our whispers—in
case he has microphones aimed at us, right?"

Donovan shrugged. "It's what I would do. He almost
surely installed listeners in our hotel room. He may have
followed us around—he knew we were canvassing jewelers, but he doesn't know why. By tomorrow, he will. I just
wish I knew how long we've been under his surveillance.
Damn him."

"You don't think he's standing *right behind us*, do you?"

Donovan started and turned. (She thought that was
Inner Child again.) He scowled at her. "Hey, you no tease

old Terry, right? Whoever bukkin, face ocean. Whoever harin watch beach. Here . . ." He pulled the package out of his pocket. "You open this."

She popped open the flaps and found beneath the wrappings a gift box from the Chinwemma jewelry store. Inside the box was a pocket brain of the standard sort. And a note.

"Read it," said Donovan, possibly the single most needless instruction he had ever given her.

Lady Hound [it read]. *It appears to the author that he has reached Harpaloon before you. The difficulties of coordinating travel along the roads. But a delightful half-doozy days in the Great Hall were spent and samples from all over the Spiral Arm were gathered and collated. A trove richer even than Jehovah. The range of the sampling domain was extended considerably and this updated dibby has been left for your pickup. Preliminary analysis indicates a most peculiar pattern, somewhat at odds with prior results. Further data are required to clarify the issue, possibly from Boldly Go, since the markers sought pass from mother to daughter. Your assistance will be necessary to access their information, as previously discussed.*

It is still unclear to the author how that silly old tale of the Treasure Fleet fits into this. Fire from the sky, indeed!

Méarana folded the message, then unfolded it and read it again. *Fire from the sky.* There was that phrase again. What did it mean? More than she had assumed at first. She handed the slip of paper to Donovan, who barely glanced at it and did not take his eyes from the shadows that surrounded them.

From just such shadows, his own hauntings told him, *the ninjas of Jenlùshy emerged.*

Bring 'em on.

<No!>

The scarred man shuddered and his eyes began to wander as all of him struggled for their possession.

"Who do you expect to leap from the shadows here?" the Fudir asked himself. "Hugh? Greystroke?"

Hugh would not attack us!

Would he not, then? asked the Sleuth.

"Men change," the Fudir whispered. "I knew him then; I don't know him now. And he was a *very* good assassin."

Méarana pulled the message from his fingers. She refolded it and returned it to the box along with the dibby. "What data?" she said to the whispering ocean waves.

"And who left it? said Donovan. "I see the quid, but where's the quo?" The sand beneath him seemed suddenly of the quicker sort and a sound that would have been laughter rippled through his mind. Inner Child started and the Brute clenched Donovan's fists.

Méarana touched his arm lightly. "Come, old man. We can't read the dibby here on the beach."

A moment longer the scarred man lingered. He turned his back on the shadows and stared out across the sluggish waters of the Encircled Sea. The curls hissed as they broke and rolled across the sands. An ochre moon hovered over the far horizon. Larger than Jehovah's Ashterath, larger than Old 'Saken's Jubilee Moon, far larger than "the moonlet fleet" of Peacock Junction; but smaller than the Moon he had never seen, the Moon toward which his blood was drawn like the ocean's tides. He sighed. He didn't know whether Hugh had turned against him. And the sorrow of it was not the turning, but that he didn't know.

The scarred man offered his arm to the harper. "787.09," he said, "161.26 228.15!"

Re-crossing the highway, Méarana noticed a knot of people congregated at the three-way intersection between them and the hotel. They numbered perhaps twenty and she recognized in their garb and goatees the demeanor of Young 'Loons. She pointed them out to Donovan and mentioned again her encounter at Côndefer Park. "The Young 'Loons," she said, "don't believe in the accommodationist tactics of their elders."

The scarred man looked on them with distaste. "I haven't found their elders all that accommodating."

"They want change."

"Changing things is never a problem. Changing them for the better is."

They had reached the stairs leading back down to street level. Méarana hesitated on the third step and turned around. "Do you think they'll bother us? I mean, we're just touristas, not movers or . . ."

"Or moosers? I'm afraid, *missy*, that I am."

"But you don't . . ." She hesitated again.

"I don't *look* like a Terran? I don't think it matters in the end. They detest all coffers and gulls, not just movers, not just Terrans. They even hate the remnants of the old Cuddle-Dong aristocracy, and how long have *they* lived here?"

"But, I'm a harper!"

"Perhaps they will pause and ask about that before they rough us up."

Méarana took a breath, let it out. "They may be only a gang of idle young men hanging out on the street corner."

"As harmless as that sounds . . . We could be judging them unfairly. But idle young men on a street corner in the small hours of the night do not inspire cozy feelings." He nudged her in the small of the back. "At the bottom of the stairs, turn right, then go down the next street to the left. The streets here are a tangle, but I've got good bearings and we can circle around them. Go. Before they notice us."

The harper and the scarred man hurried down the rest of the staircase and turned toward the next street, away from the phundaugh. Just before they reached it—Tchilbebber Lane, the sign announced—there was a shriek from the direction of the three-points, followed by the patter of rapid feet, followed by the drumming of many feet. Donovan looked back. There was a man in a billowing dust-coat sprinting up Beachfront Highway toward them. The Young 'Loons were pelting after him. He touched Méarana. "They're not after us," he said.

But they ducked around the corner anyway. Mobs, even small mobs, had a way of expanding their horizons on encountering targets of opportunity. <RUN!!!> cried Inner Child. "Brisk, now," the scarred man told the harper. "But no need to run."

"That poor man!" said Méarana.

"He'll go up Beachfront. We'll wait a little ways up this lane until they pass by, then we'll make our way to the hotel."

"Shouldn't we try to help him?"

"Two of us against twenty? Three if that poor fool turns and stands. More likely, he'd keep running while we divert the crowd. That's what I would do."

"No, call the policers!"

"Méarana, *this is Harpaloon*. The policers come out in the morning and count the bodies . . . Quiet, here they come . . . Well, damn the gods!"

The deities he cursed had neglected their duties—for the fleeing man turned and came pelting up Tchilbebber Lane with the 'Loonie mob on his heels.

"Let's get out of here," Donovan started to say, but the man reached him and threw himself upon him.

"Pliz, pliz, you-fella. You help poor Terry-man! Bud-mash fella-they chase him no reason! Aiee!" And he ducked and crouched trembling behind Donovan.

His pursuers staggered to a halt when they saw the harper and the scarred man and their quarry hiding behind them.

"Just like a mooser," one of them said. "Hide behind a shawner and a clean's skirts."

"Out of our way, coffers," said another. "Shoran, we maun teach this Terry trash his manners."

"You hear that, ye walad?" said a third. And he was chorused by the laughter of his companions.

Donovan spoke up. "This lady is a harper—an ollamh. *Air hwuig shé?* You will not touch her."

The first speaker, whom Donovan took for the leader, said, "Shoran, we don't care about coffer bints, shawnfir. Just you be stepping aside so we can teach this dog to step aside for us like a good little mooser."

Donovan turned to Méarana. "You had better take yourself to the hotel."

"Donovan . . . ?" She spoke with uncertainty, but in her heart there was none. She knew what he meant to do. "I'm sorry." She shrugged her shoulder and felt the knife drop into her hand, keeping it concealed from the mob. She emptied her mind of all but her mother's training. It seemed she would learn how well the instruction had taken. But, twenty?

"Step aside!"

"No, no, pliz," cried the Terran behind them. "Big dhik! You-man save me!"

Donovan turned and took him by the collar of his tunic, raising him to his feet. "I'll not save a man on his knees," he growled.

The leader of the gang grinned and stepped forward. "Hazza moontaz! We'll take it from here."

Donovan turned to him and bowed lightly over his

folded hands. "Ah, no sahb. This-man no let dacoit takee. Hutt, hutt, you changars! You chumars!"

The gang leader's face froze in surprise. Then it broke into an even broader grin than before as he did the arithmetic. "Hey, boyos, shoran we have us a twofer! And you, shawnfir, you're two brassers short of a whorehouse."

"I do not normally use a pick to play," said the harper, bending slightly forward and balancing on the balls of her feet. She held her knife underfisted, ready to slash or stab. "But I can pluck at your heart strings either way."

The scarred man's lips had been moving. Then Donovan sighed and pulled a teaser from his pocket. "Fudir, are we agreed?" "No other choice." "Take over, Brute."

Debate was not the Brute's forte. He struck without warning, teasing the leader so that he dropped twitching to the paving stones. Simultaneously, he drove the bunched fingers of his left hand into the brisket of the man's companion, doubling him over. Méarana, in a catlike crouch, swiped her knife at the man before her, causing him to leap backward for the sake of his intestines. The other Terran wimpered.

Two down, thought the Brute, **only eighteen to go.** Méarana might be able to knife two of them if she would not hold herself back. But they would not prevail, even if the other Terran, quaking beside him, helped. He saw bats hefted in the crowd and caught the glint of at least one pellet gun. **Well, it was fun for a while.** He teased a second youth, but the field only numbed the yngling's left side.

A shot rang out.

The Brute started, felt no pain, and turned in panic toward Méarana. **No! Not her!**

But the harper, too, was unhurt. The 'Loonie mob had frozen at the gunshot. Habituated the Preeshdad 'Loons might be to violence, but few there were who embraced it from the sharp end.

A voice boomed from the darkened alleyway on the left. "Throw down your weapons! You are surrounded!" And he was seconded by a voice from the right: "All men in place, Captain!"

The 'Loons looked to the blank rows of shuttered shops and tenements flanking them on either side of the lane. Did they see shadows moving into place? "The coffer riot cops?" "Damn mover regime . . ." "Where'd *they* come from?" Then someone in the middle of the mob hollered, "Let's get out of here!" And with that cry, they broke and scattered down Tchilbebber Lane to the Beachfront Highway.

The Terran fell to his knees and began to kiss Donovan's fingers and the hem of his tunic, calling him his savior and summoning blessings from the gods. The Brute nearly kicked him, but Donovan and the Fudir stopped him. **Yeah,** the Brute said bitterly, **it's "Brute, save us," when you have it to do; but it's "Brute, fall behind" when the drums stop rolling.** He surrendered control before either Donovan or the Fudir had taken it back and the scarred man staggered. Méarana and the other Terran kept him upright, grabbing an arm apiece.

"That was close," said Greystroke, dusting his hands and throwing down the bat he had taken from one of the gang members.

"They're gone, Cu," said O'Carroll, who stepped from the shadows on the right. "I followed them to the corner and they kept running. Are ye feelin' none too well, Fudir?"

Greystroke stepped close to Donovan. "That was a fool play, Donovan. You could have gotten Méarana hurt! What possessed you to face down a lynch mob?"

The other Terran handed Donovan back his teaser and began to brush at and straighten Donovan's clothing. The scarred man batted his hands away. "Call it a dislike of lynching," he told the Hound. "Especially of Terrans."

"This-man much aruḷ," the Terran said to Greystroke. "Save poor Billy Chins from ākāmiyam. From impiety and wickedness. He the shower of blessing, the gracious one. Me aṯangku him. Always his khitmugar."

Donovan groaned. "Aṯangku? Is that the way it's to be? Always a *mooser*, you?"

Greystroke had frowned in puzzlement before turning to Méarana. "It might be best if you take passage with us off planet."

"We'd be glad to have you," said Hugh.

"You're following Bridget ban's route," the Hound said. "From here she went to . . ." He flipped open his pocket brain. ". . . to Dancing Vrouw. You are in luck."

"I usually am," said Donovan, "but the question is whether it's good luck or bad."

Hugh chuckled, and Greystroke spread his hands. "We can take you there. Rinty and I have business on Yubeq, and Dancing Vrouw is along the way."

Donovan did not miss a beat. "Are you still looking to arrest me?"

Greystroke shook his head. "No."

"Then, I guess you're not the officious little prig you used to be."

Greystroke smiled. "And you aren't the wheedling, lying little scrambler you once were."

"Good. Then we can both drink to the men we've become." He and the Hound locked gazes.

Hugh sighed. "I don't know," he said, looking into the depths of the darkened lane. "I rather liked the lying little scrambler, myself."

AN AISTEAR

There is a Terran custom called aṭangku. *The term means something like "obey, be submissive," with overtones of "be contained in another." It means, in short, "to moose." The practical form it takes is that saving another's life is much like taking it, for the savior takes ownership of the life and the one saved devotes himself thereafter to paying rent. It is thus that Donovan has acquired, in the person of Billy Chins, his very own servant.*

The scarred man is not pleased with this turn of events. What need has he of the burdens of ownership? Yet, when he attempts to dismiss Billy, the man falls to his knees on the bricks of Tchilbebber Lane. If the Beloved of Heaven will not have him, his life is worthless and his only recourse is to destroy it!

This strikes Little Hugh as a bit excessive; but Donovan gauges the promise meant, and a part of his mind entertains dismissal for no better reason than to exercise such power. To hold another man's life in one's hand is an intoxicating thing; and the temptation is correspondingly strong to take a good stiff drink. Donovan studies the soft pendulous lips, the basset eyes. A man of little use in a fight; but perhaps other talents lie buried.

"Lady Harp be go offworld," he warns the man. "No kambak Harpaloon."

"No like kambak here." And Billy takes the sandals from his feet and claps the dust from their soles. "I go with thee, hutt, hutt. I serve the Child of Wonder. I cook. I wash your clothes. I unfasten your sandal straps. You never unplis of Billy Chins. You see."

Donovan glances at Little Hugh, who is smiling into his hand. He sighs, knowing defeat from long acquaintance.

"Okey-doke," he tells Billy. "You-fella come by early-early Plough-and-Stars, all bungim wantaim. No kambak you forget hankie. Cart luggage b'long us, too. We travel jildy, this man's ship." And he indicates Greystroke, who conceals his delight over the additional passenger.

Méarana also assures the wretch. "No more 'Loons where we are going, Billy," she says. "You'll be safe with us."

Outwardly, Greystroke's vessel is as forgettable as the man himself. Her lines, her name, her colors, even her registration number are unremarkable.

Inwardly, it is a different story. All the flamboyance squeezed from Greystroke's persona has been lavished there. Fluted and spiraled columns frame the doorways; murals swarm in the spandrels. Control knobs wear the heads of beasts. Colorful flowers blossom from clay pots and planters; and the odors of champa flower and kyara wood delight the nose.

After Méarana has seen her stateroom and admired the chatterchuff pillows—and the taffy and lace and the bathroom!—she shows all to Donovan as if she herself had decorated it. "Now, this," she says in mild rebuke, "is first class!"

And Donovan looks it over and plumps a pillow with his fingers. "I have never seen a more agreeable cell."

That they are aboard by something stronger than an invitation the harper cannot deny. Bars may be made of silk and chains of solid gold, as she had told Jimmy Barcelona. But if more than an invitation, it is less than an incarceration. They are not Greystroke's prisoners. Not exactly.

Certainly, the Hound wishes to sup at the banquet of their knowledge, meager feast though it be. And why not?

They fare on the same quest, and by all appearances she would get the better of the bargain. The Hound and his Pup cannot know less *than she at this point.*

Not for the first time, she wonders if the scarred man might not err in playing a lone hand. Some Hounds might weight self-interest above all; but surely not Greystroke and Little Hugh! Of the three that she had always suspected, they are the other two. But she had gone to Donovan because of who he was, or who she thought he might be, and what sort of fool consults a specialist only to ignore his advice?

Donovan would not have the Kennel find what her mother sought before he decides whether they can be entrusted with it. Fair enough. But it raises the finer point of whether Donovan can be entrusted with it.

And on that she has a single datum. When it had come to the test, when Donovan had once held absolute power in his hands, he had opened those hands and allowed it to float away.

Her own desires are more dangerous. While Donovan seeks what Bridget ban sought, she seeks Bridget ban. For that *finding, the harper might well sacrifice the whole of the Spiral Arm.*

Billy Chins insisted on waiting service on Donovan, hovering behind his master's chair, anticipating his every whim. If Donovan took but a single sip, his glass was replenished. If he but expressed a desire, the object of it appeared on his plate. And should those whims not be forthcoming, Billy would enquire anxiously after them. In consequence, Donovan's plates were, like the Dagda's cauldron, never empty.

Neither could Donovan carry a burden from one room to another save that Billy wrested it apologetically from his grasp and bore it for him. "Aggressively servile," is how the scarred man described him. It became a sort of game: Donovan trying to accomplish some small task un-aided, and Billy endeavoring to thwart those efforts. Little Hugh thought it all great fun.

To celebrate the breaking of orbit, Greystroke prepared a dinner of sable tiger fronted by a medley of vegetables. The tiger was graced with a sauce of sea-grapes and zere-shik barberries and was accompanied by a black wine pressed of slipskin girdiana.

During the postprandial drinks Donovan raised the ques-tion that had been in the back of his throat since the con-frontation in Tchilbebber Lane.

"'We have you surrounded'?" he said.

Greystroke swirled his wineglass before taking a sip. Hugh laughed aloud. "The 'Loons were between Greystroke and me."

"Still, two against twenty . . . ," Méarana suggested.

Hugh set his own glass on the table. "I noticed the two of you ready to take them on."

"The harper was supposed to run for help," the scarred man said. "But she didn't. And it wasn't even her fight."

"When it is twenty to one," says Méarana, "it is my fight."

"How noble." The scarred man sneered. "When it is twenty to one, I usually find a reason why it's not." He gath-ered the sardonic looks of the others, sighed, and glanced at his servant. "But blood calls to blood. I am a Terran. It was foolish of you, harper, to stand with me."

"You've called me a fool more than once," she replied. "Why carp at proof?"

The scarred man turned to Greystroke. "What I'd like to know is where you hid the amshifars. You were too much on the spot."

Greystroke waved his hand. "Oh, they were in the beer, of course. You pulled that clothing trick once before."

———————

That the ship was thoroughly bugged was a proposition that compelled assent through reason alone. Empirical proof was not required. When Billy Chins "kill big-big cockaroacha" in Donovan's stateroom, the smashed listening device was mere anticlimax. The harper and the scarred man communicated therefore using Méarana's code, but not so often as to pique Greystroke's curiosity. It was a conceptual code, not easily broken without "Rosie's Thesaurus." But it was imprudent to wave red flags at bulls.

175.10 and 854.12, he advised her. Slow and steady. The trail is two years cold. How could there be urgency? Privately, he hoped that the colder the trail, the less inclined Méarana would grow to pursue it.

And what of Bridget ban? asked the Silky Voice. *Will you abandon her?*

She is past abandonment.

You don't know that, the Sleuth pointed out. *There are no clues. There is no evidence.*

And so no reason to suppose her still among the quick. No word for almost two years.

The absence of evidence, the Sleuth insisted, *is not the evidence of absence.*

He was answered by the toll of a distant bell that echoed in the timeless dark within his head.

<Fear> shivered him, and Inner Child swept the room anxiously.

Stop that, Child, the Brute grumbled.

You know the real reason, the Fudir told them all. *The trail points into the Wild. To Ōram or Eḥku or some other, more nameless world. Worlds where the jungle has crept over all, where treachery and cruelty await the occasional "dude" from the Periphery. What hope is there of finding her out in the Wild?*

"None. But that's not the real reason at all," Donovan

answered. "The real reason is that you and I would die out there."

"Who will die?" Méarana asked, and Donovan realized that he had spoken aloud. Billy Chins, who was folding clothing, looked up in sudden alarm.

But Donovan only shook his head. "Mostly people that you've never met."

The ship's day following, Hugh came upon Méarana in the ward room, drinking of Greystroke's tea and reading from Greystroke's library. He poured a mug of his own from the samovar and sat across the table from her. The harper tracked him from the corner of her eye.

"We enter the Silk Road early tomorrow," the Pup said eventually.

Méarana laid the viewpanel on the table, screen side down. She picked up her tea and sipped. "Is everything . . . What do they say? 'In the groove?' "

"Oh, yes. Greystroke is a road scholar and certified superluminal pilot. We usually have a small ceremony when we enter the roads. A dinner, some toasts. Perhaps you would play for us."

Méarana dipped her head. "I would be honored."

"That's all right, then." He reached out and lifted the viewscreen. "What have you been reading?"

That Greystroke's dibby had not been tracking the files she and Donovan read was beyond credibility. Hugh had to know when he walked in exactly what file she had up; and that meant his question was intended for something other than information.

"An odd story," she said. "Some scholar has discovered that everyone on the Old Planets is descended from only twenty-seven different ancestresses."

"So you don't spend all your waking hours trying to trace your mother . . . ?"

Méarana looked away. "How could I? Until we reach the Vrouw I've no hope of learning anything new."

"It's a hopeless search. You know that, don't you?"

"All searches are hopeful, or there would be no search. That's why I'll find her and you won't."

Hugh shook his head slightly, perhaps in admiration. "I think you're wrong, but I rather hope you're not." He looked again at the view screen. "Only twenty-seven?" he said. "How can that be? Millions were transported during the Clearances."

"The author meant that everyone on the Old Planets has at least one of these women as an ancestor, not that they had no others."

"How can he know that? People were too busy surviving to track their ancestries."

"He claims to have discovered an old Commonwealth fact: certain genes he calls *sinlaptai* are passed on from mother to daughter. They change a little bit with every generation. By counting the number of changes he can tell us how long ago the clan-mother lived."

"Really . . . !"

"And by studying their distribution within the Old Planets he can learn where these clan-mothers lived."

"Sinlaptai."

"He says it's an ancient term meaning 'little thread shapes' or 'mighty Kondrians.'"

"Oh. Which are they, 'little' or 'mighty'?"

"Both, somehow. He doesn't say where Kondria is, either. Maybe the mighty Kondrians discovered the little thread shapes. I think he expected his readers to know the term."

"Which means . . . ," said Hugh, holding his tea cup in both hands and sipping from it. ". . . you aren't one of the readers he expected. What is his name?"

"Umm . . ." Méarana took the screen up again and back-scrolled to the title. "Sofwari. D. J. Sofwari, it says here. But if you're asking why *I'm* reading it, the idea of twenty-seven clan-mothers intrigued me. I've been thinking on a song cycle."

"Don't tell me. Let me guess. Twenty-seven stanzas."

"It's a technique called 'brute-think.' Pick something at random and play with it until an idea occurs to you. I found this a few years ago, in a random search. I go back to it now and then and see if my muse has come up with something."

I am become as duplicitous as the Fudir, Méarana chided herself. *If the Hounds backsearch the household gods on Dangchao, they'll find the record that it was accessed; but they'd not know if it was Mother or I who read it.*

"Fudir's engrossed in a story book called *Commonwealth Days.* Fairy tales. He's chasing a dream far longer lost than your own, Méarana."

"I haven't lost my dream, Hugh. I'm still holding it."

Hugh rose from his seat and gathered up his tea cup. "Lucy, be careful of relying too much on the Fudir. He's a man who uses people."

"Why, fash it, mon! 'Tis no small thing to be useful! Many men live their entire lives without achieving so much! He tricked you into leaving New Eireann during the Dancer affair; but that was best for everyone, yourself included."

"Do you suppose that makes it better?"

"I heard the story from his own lips . . . Perhaps you should hear it there as well."

"The problem with stories," said Little Hugh O'Carroll, "is that life never ties up so neatly. Some ends are always loose."

The Pup fell into a pensive mode, standing with cup in hand. Méarana studied him with a terrible intensity that eventually drew his attention back from the depths to which it had descended. "What?" he said.

"Nothing. I was looking for a man from a story."

When they slid onto the Silk Road, Greystroke held the promised ceremony, and after dinner, Méarana played a range of music: ancient tunes by Paxton of Terra; the gentle "Fanny Poer" by the legendary blind harper O'Carolan; the savagely sarcastic "On, Ye Heroes, On to Glory!"; the elegiac song cycle "Green, Oh, Green" by Galina Luis Kazan of Die Bold. But most of all, she played snatches of tunes from the Dancer cycle. She chose passages of camaraderie—among Greystroke and the Fudir and Little Hugh—hoping with her strains to ease their strains. If she could not mold them into what they once were, she could at least remind them of what that had been.

Greystroke was a master of indirection, and this was true no less of his interrogations than of his appearance. Hugh was a bit more direct, as only an assassin can be; but he had learned during the guerilla on New Eireann how to lie low and wait things out. The Fudir knew this, and knew something about lying low himself. He spent his time reading *Commonwealth Days*, then passing on to *Rimward Ho!* and then to *Customs of the 'Loon Tribes*, all of which Greystroke had in his ship's library.

"It appears that Donovan has given up the search for your mother," Greystroke told Méarana one day in the refectory.

"Oh, he was never looking for her," the harper allows. "He was only looking after me. It was an agreement he reached with Uncle Zorba."

Greystroke's lips quirked. He had some experience with agreements with Zorba de la Susa. "So Donovan is your chaperone? Your bodyguard? You know of his disability . . . ?"

"About two-sevenths of it."

If the precision puzzled Greystroke, he made no sign. From the samovar, he poured a cup of Gray Thoughts, a blend made especially for him by the tea masters of Peacock Junction. "I noticed you the other day with a medallion. I wonder if I could see it?" He carried the cup to the table and sat across from Méarana.

The harper hesitated only a moment. Donovan had been correct. Greystroke could sneak up on you in more ways than one. She pulled the medallion from under her blouse and handed it, dangling from its chain, to the Hound.

He studied it closely, tracing the abstract shapes on the obverse with his finger.

"Rude," the Hound said after a moment, "but not without craft. This is the souvenir your mother brought back from Thistlewaite, the one you showed Gwillgi?"

"Aye."

"But you and Donovan were making inquiries on Harpaloon, not Thistlewaite."

"Mother told me that she bought the piece on Thistlewaite, but it had come from Harpaloon." Méarana blushed. "I thought as long as we were there, I could find some matching pieces."

O Vanity, thy name is Woman! What sort of person, in search of her missing mother, would pause to shop for jewelry? Surely, one who would blush to admit to it! That the same individual might also blush to lie to a League marshal only equivocates the sense. Hounds are always sniffing around after scents, but what they flush is not always what they think it is.

"It isn't Harpy work, though . . . ," Greystroke ventured.

"No, none of the jawharries . . ."

". . . it comes out of the Wild."

"What?"

"Isn't that what Jawharry Boo Zed told Donovan? Enjrun or Ōram or Eḥku, he wasn't sure of the name." Greystroke shrugged. "Somewhere out in the Burnt-Over District."

One may also flush from anger. "Mother bought me that piece!" the harper said and reached for it as if it were Donovan's throat.

But Greystroke paused and ran his fingers over it. Had he felt the writing on the back? Donovan thought it derived from the old Taṉṭamiž script, though he had not yet identified the alphabet. But the Hound only grunted. "It's broken off. The red stone once projected below the rim of the disc. Was it always thus?"

"I hadn't noticed," Méarana said, blushing.

"It looks a bit like a tornado." He held it up to the light. Méarana could see the writing on the reverse when the light caught it. "The artisan brought out the grain of the gem to make it look like it's whirling." He handed it back to her and Méarana stuffed it quickly inside her blouse. "A red tornado in a black disc," Greystroke mused. "On my homeworld, Krinth, tornados sometimes blacken the sky. And I've heard of white tornados on Ogilvy's World— funnels of snow and ice that screech down from the arctic— and can flash-freeze a man in a moment's passage. Maybe a red tornado is a hot one, volcanic." He laughed, though not entirely with humor.

"I never thought it was representational," Méarana said. "I took it as symbolic."

Greystroke shrugged. "Every symbol represents something. Your mother's last gift to you . . . I can see why you'd want to learn all you could about it."

"No," said Méarana, "you're wrong. It's her latest gift, not her last."

Greystroke's lips parted, but he changed his mind. He

hadn't come to crush a young woman's illusions. Besides, Zorba would one day watch the recording of this session and judge how his protégé's daughter was treated. "The Friendly Ones decree," he told her. "But until we know Schoedinger has cut the thread, all possibilities remain."

The "cold comforts of Krinth" were proverbial across the Spiral Arm. But he had meant to console her, even to encourage her in his own fashion, and of the three, he had been the one most selflessly in love with Bridget ban, and that should count for something. "Thank you," she said.

Greystroke rose, but paused and turned back. "Oh," he said. "I nearly forgot. One of the jawharries was murdered. I thought, maybe, you would want to know."

A cold hand stroked Méarana's heart. "Who . . . ?"

Greystroke held a hand to his ear, consulting his dibby. "We picked it up on the newsfeed as we crawled upsystem . . . Ah. Here it is. A woman named—oh, by the Owl!—En . . . wel . . . um."

"Enwelumokwu Tottenheim," Méarana answered. The numbness spread. "Enwii."

"Yes, that's the one. At Côndefer Park. Another 'Loonie attack, apparently. Like what nearly happened to that poor Chins devil. They scrawled irredentist slogans on the shop walls. The Marshal of Preeshdad said there had been a string of incidents recently. I'm sorry." He offered her a small kerchief from his sleeve. "I didn't know you felt so about her."

"No, it's not that," Méarana cried. "We only spoke a few minutes; but the woman was so terribly cheerful and friendly." *Hound's business?* Enwii had said. *That's a magnet for trouble. I don't want to be involved.*

Violence was common in Preeshdad, and jewelry shops were tempting targets . . . Maybe it was inevitable that one of the places they had visited should be attacked. But Méarana shrank from Greystroke, suddenly wary of who he was and what he might do in pursuit of a prize for the Ardry. She did not believe in coincidence.

And neither did Donovan when she told him about it.

He went immediately to the 'face in Méarana's stateroom and found the Preeshdad marshal's report readily accessible. "The prick," he said. "He *wants* us to know about it."

"Why? Was it a warning? Did he and Little Hugh . . . ?"

"What? No. Greystroke can be guilty of a great many foul deeds. Terrifying you counts as one. But he'll never wear the Badge of Night."

Méarana sat and leaned over her folded hands. "None of you want me to find Mother. You keep throwing obstacles at me. You keep trying to discourage me. You, Greystroke, Little Hugh. They spread doubts about you. You spread doubts about them. You keep secrets from me."

"What secrets have I kept from you?"

"Ōram," the harper said distinctly. "Ehku. Enjrun."

Donovan closed his eyes. Greystroke really can sneak up on you. "That cāracan," he said. "That son of a whore."

"I guess I wasn't supposed to hear about those places."

Donovan looked around the room. "Should we invite Greystroke and Hugh to sit in personally, or is it enough that they can listen when the mood strikes them?"

"At least Greystroke . . ."

"If the Gray One were really interested in finding Bridget ban, he'd be out looking himself, not trying to find out what we know. By the gods, I hope he did hear that!" He struck the table hard with both fists. The 'face jumped and a Friesing's World death hoot fell off its hook on the wall and clattered to the floor.

Billy Chins came scurrying in from the common room, his face creased in anxiety. "Why such shout-shout? Is master want Billy?"

The scarred man rubbed his face and for a moment all

was silence. Then he pushed to his feet and walked over by the door, where he picked up the fallen instrument. He played a few notes in the horrid and unnatural intervals of the Qelq-Barr Mountains, then placed the hoot once more on its hooks, but it fell again to the floor. This time Billy Chins rushed to retrieve it and held it defensively in his hands.

The Fudir turned to Méarana. "Greystroke had a reason for trying to frighten you. No, stay, Billy. You deserve to hear this." He returned to his seat and tapped the screen.

"The Preeshdad Marshal said this Tottenheim woman was savagely beaten. But I saw the morgue photos on the upload, and there was nothing of the savage in it. It was a careful and methodological beating, designed to extract the maximum of information. Kǎowèn, it's called."

"Kǎowèn? Maximum information? Enwii didn't know anything! She had a—"

Donovan put a finger to her lips. "And now Those know she didn't know anything."

"Those?"

Donovan seemed to withdraw into himself. "Something is following us."

VI A SNAKE IN THE GRASS

The great 'Saken philospher Chester Demidov, known as "Akobundu," once described the United League as "raisins in a bowl of porridge." This struck many of his readers as just another of his obscurities; but people who put raisins in their porridge—and there were some— understood what he had meant. The best philosophy begins in sense experience, and a bowl of porridge is as sensible as it gets.

The raisins are the great clumps of civilized planets: the Old Planets, the Jen-Jen, Foreganger-Ramage-Valency, and elsewhere. Within these clumps, great and powerful worlds lie mere days apart, with war and commerce bustling between them, with cities large and impressive, and with those activities that make of life something more than being alive. It is here you find Akobundu's "grand continuum of culture": great literature, music, high art, travel, the enjoyment of nature, sports, fashion, social vanities, and the intoxication of the senses. The nature of a civilization could be gauged, he had said, by the point along this continuum where its people draw the line and say, "Below this lies the merely vulgar."

Everything else is the porridge. These comprise the more widely-scattered solitaries, like Peacock Junction or Ugly Man, the barbarous regions like the Cynthian Hadramoo. These may boast great accomplishments, but they are not where the action is.

The Greater Hanse is one of the raisins, and a juicy one at that. There, fortunes are made—and many a second sib arrives in the dewy-eyed hope of making one. The Hanse chews them up and spits them out. It grinds them like polishing grit, and the result is a gleaming money-making machine—once the grit is washed off.

On Akobundu's continuum, the Hansards set great store by the social vanities, pursuing their rivalries not only in board rooms and markets and entrepôts, but in balls and cotillions, in fashion, in clubs and organizations, at dinner parties, and in orders of nobility. But they draw the line at the intoxication of the senses. "Drink dissolves profit," they say; "and dreams go up in smoke." A man obsessed with pleasure seldom thinks clearly, and women are consequently a sort of weapon to intoxicate one's rivals. They do not launch missiles at one another, so much as mistresses. Befuddle a rival with perfumes and tender

*caresses and you can diddle him in every way that she
does not.*

Dancing Vrouw had been settled initially from Agadar and
Gladiola, and it is said that when the first ship had set down,
after a harrowing voyage through then-uncharted roads, the
landing party officer had stripped herself naked and, from
a sheer and undiluted joy, whirled through the thigh-high
spindle-grass of the landing field. Consequently, the blazon
of *tawny a nude danseuse all proper* appeared in the flags
of every state but one on the Vrouw, and was quartered in
the arms of most of the Merchant Houses.

There is an addendum to the legend that involves an
Ursini's viper and the inadvisability of stepping on one,
even while dancing, but it is a complication seldom mentioned by the tour guides and myth-mongers. The bite
proved nonfatal, though chastening, and both it and the
dance have provided fodder for local proverbs ever since
and a warning against excessive exuberance. The one contrary state that eschews the danseuse emblazons a snake
on its flag with the motto, "Don't Tread on Me."

A counter-legend holds that the landing officer had sim-
ply been a native of "Dancing," said to be a city on Old
Earth that had anciently been a member of the original
Hanse. But what sort of romance can you spin off that?
Naked women and serpents in the garden of a fresh new
world were by far more fascinating.

The Steelyard was more than a spaceport. It was also the
chief Counting House of the Vrouw. Thus, although located in the capital of the Eastern Cape Circle, it had extra-
territorial status, and merchant princes from every Circle,
and even from other Hansard planets, stationed factors
there.

Groundside customs was more thorough than on

Harpaloon. The Toll-Clerk, as he was called, studied their Kennel passes with great intensity, even employing a loupe to verify the watermarking of their papers, and required a retinal scan of each of them. Billy Chins proved a problem. A *chumar*, the lowest caste of Terran worker, he had little in the way of papers; and no one had ever thought his retinas worth scanning.

Rules meant much in the Greater Hanse, and their functionaries did not accept bribes to overlook them. However, everything was for sale, including entry visas, so the distinction was a fine one and not always apparent to out-worlders. There were regulations on how to bypass the regulations. These required three oath-helpers to swear to Billy Chins's good character, and a native of the Vrouw to purchase the contract. The Clerk summoned a Trader from the Floor, and shortly a wide-bodied man in a marten-rimmed, sleeveless coat and wearing a silver medal on a neck-chain stepped off the lift.

"What is then all this?" he asked the Clerk and, the situation being explained, he turned to Billy Chins. "You-fella Terry? Good-good. We process, jildy. Khitmutgar, you? Oho! Who thy master? This one?" A skeptical eye was cast over Donovan, but swift handshakes proved both members of the Brotherhood. The Trader switched to the Tongue. "This shalt proceed swiftly, my brother, and at a nominal fee. I hight Hendrik ten Muqtar, senior trader of the House of Coldperk. I will ask of thee no more than but a single marek, for honor's sake." He made a complex gesture with his hands. "But as for the Purse of the Steelyard, they will accept no-but less than one hundred mareks, however middling our contract."

"Pliss, pliss," said Billy Chins. "Me-fella blong this-man, Donovan. No blong you-fella." To Donovan, he added, "I go long you. No go long him. Plis no send Billy Chins away!"

Donovan fluttered his fingers and addressed ten Muqtar. "Forgive him his intemperance."

"It makes naught. Here. Behold the standard contract. Thou shalt enter names here, and here. Aye, the light pen, so that it may scan. Oho! A Kennel chit! Had I but known of him, thy fee would have soared. Deep pockets hath the Kennel."

When all was completed to the jot and tittle of Hansard Commercial Regulation §189.3, Part V, paragraph 6.2 (a), Billy Chins tugged on ten Muqtar's coat and said with something like awe, "Ally-all Terry here got plenty somtaing, laik you-fella?"

Ten Muqtar flashed them a quick sad smile and spoke to Donovan. "Tell your boy that the Hanse placeth no bars to those willing to work, and that many of the Original Folk have become here wealthy. But thou wilt have noticed that when the Clerk required a Trader to buy a Terran's contract, he sent for a Terran. We prosper here and enjoy great liberties, but the doors of society are closed to us."

"As oppressions go," said Donovan, "that doth pale beside a Harpaloon lynch mob."

"It is much of a such," ten Muqtar said with a shrug. "Here, much business is done at dinner parties and on the courses of golf. Where a man's expectations are greater, smaller slights grate the more."

The skywalks ran above the Trading Floor and Méarana and her party paused while crossing to gaze over the banisters at the activity below.

A mob of Harpaloon drunks did not shout and mill as wildly as did the press on the Floor. They cried out or sent messages over headsets, buttonholed and bargained, waved fingers in the air in an arcane code. A display board at the far end listed cargos and vessels arriving in orbit and the

Traders, who sat like lords around the periphery of the Floor, sent their Runners to ask and offer prices, the two hunting up and down the scale until they met and cleared the cargo. This was for the most part accomplished while the vessel was on the crawl, and a ship's contents might be sold and sold again before ever it reached High Dancing Orbit.

The throng of arrivals followed the walkway to a broad outdoor plaza at third-storey level. It was come on to winter in that quarter of Dancing Vrouw and the wind drove light flurries of snow across the paving stones and into the sleeves and shoes of inaptly-dressed out-worlders. Incomers scattered, hailing skycabs or huddling in the tramline station or scurrying across the plaza to the Roaming Qaysar Hotel.

This hotel, a stolid, seven-storey building of dark ironwood timbers and light masonry, was said to be the largest primarily wooden building in the Spiral Arm. Flanking it on either side were Factor Houses from around the Vrouw: from nautical Giniksper to tropical Dangerminda to Kalmshdad in the Northern Waste. Farther off, stood the more modest entrepôts of other Hanse worlds—Yubeq, Hanower, Rigger, and elsewhere; so that overall the prospect before them was of a solid wall of buildings, diverse in size and style and color. Parti-colored House arms flashed in light-signage, in holo-projections, or in cloth flags.

Greystroke had booked them rooms on the seventh floor of the Roaming Qaysar and, having stowed their belongings, they foregathered in the suite's common room before a wall-spanning window. Below, lay the city of Pròwensh-wai: a faery jumble set along crooked streets, bisected by broad, straight avenues, interrupted by white plazas and green parks. Stairways twisted up bluffs where streets dared not go. Here and there, clocktowers, minarets, and kokoshniki pierced the skyline.

It was a city that delighted in wood and its possibilities. On the buildings below, cornice, tympanum, spandrel, gable, jamb, and shutters had been set into parquet or carved into basilisks, wyverns, griffins, distlefinks, gargoyles; into flowers and leaves and lacework. Statues emerged from the walls of the greater buildings.

"Is look strange-strange," said Billy Chins. "Never off Harpaloon, me."

"'Tis broader spread than any city I've played," Méarana said. "Even Èlfiuji is more compact."

"You should see it when night falls," Greystroke added. "They call it the Carpet of Lights. And at midwinter, when the snow covers all, they put candles in every window, and in small bags lining every walkway. Over that way," he pointed, "is the Tower of the Snake. Remind me to tell you that story. You can recite it for drinks, Donovan, when you return to Jehovah."

Donovan did not rise to the jibe. "Where's the Toll Gate?" he said.

"Right behind the hotel. You can't see it from this angle. It's one of only two entries from the international enclave into Eastern Cape Circle itself."

Donovan cocked his head. "Where's the other?"

"You can scale the outside wall of the Hotel," said Little Hugh, leaning close to the window and pointing off to the left. "There are stretchers and dog's-teeth in the masonry. Then—see there?—you can jump from *that* ledge over onto the roof of *that* storage building and shinny down the rain pipe."

Méarana shot him a glance to see if he was joking, but with the Ghost of Ardow it was hard to tell. He could get into and out of the most unlikely places. "We'll take the easy way," she said.

Hugh exchanged a glance with Greystroke. "Sometimes that *is* the easy way."

"Enough said of that," the Hound cautioned him. He turned to the harper. "I don't know what you expect to find here that Gwillgi failed to find. According to the Hotel's records and the Toll-for-One, Bridget ban stayed here only two days. She never even entered East Cape."

Donovan grunted. "Makes you wonder why she came down at all."

Hugh glanced at him. "We've all worried at that. If we knew why she came down . . . Thank you, Billy." The khitmutgar had found the suite's bar and had assembled a tray of drinks. As any good servant might, he had, on the flight from Harpaloon, identified everyone's preference. They moved toward the center of the room. "If we knew why she paused here, we might know where she went afterward. But if this was just a stopover . . ."

"Why come planet-side for a mere rest stop," said Méarana.

Hugh pursed his lips. "Sometimes you just need to get outside of a ship."

"Maybe she was expecting to meet someone," Donovan suggested. He had remained at the window, where he gazed down at the roof of the storage shed.

"Gwillgi thought so," said Hugh, "but she met no one of whom the hotel staff was aware." Both Donovan and Greystroke snorted. "Right," Hugh added. "But Gwillgi checked into everyone staying in the hotel and . . ."

Donovan turned from the window. "Everyone?"

Hugh nodded. "Staff *and* guests. Gwillgi may not be as *persistent* as Grimpen, but he does dot all his t's."

"So, you may be right," said Greystroke, who had materialized by Donovan's side and nodded toward the perilous route into East Cape. "There's only one flaw: no trace of her anywhere in Pròwenshwai."

There's always a trace, murmured the Sleuth.

"Greystroke," Donovan said in a low voice, and moved the Hound a little apart from Hugh and Méarana, who were sampling a plate of hors d'oeuvres that Billy had prepared. "You and I both know that the jawharry at Côndefer Park . . ."

". . . was killed by a Confederate courier. Elementary. Who else combines stealth and cruelty in such exquisite balance? Has it convinced *her*?"

"To give up the search? Not yet."

"It might have been a coincidence, but . . ."

"It wasn't."

"Agreed. And you can't go forward assuming it was. The question is: What is the courier's mission? Is he hunting what Bridget ban was hunting? Or is he hunting you?"

"Me!" Donovan could not stop Inner Child from looking around in alarm. "No," he said, turning back in time to glimpse Greystroke's pity. "No," he said again. "If he was hunting me, why torture the jawharry?"

" 'Following the hare,' " Greystroke quoted, " 'the hunter starts a deer.' Sometimes one path crosses another. That's all chance is, you know. The Friendly Ones weave causal threads. Sometimes they cross, and we call that chance. Once you crossed the courier's line of vision, he may have wondered what you were up to."

"You suppose he recognized me."

Greystroke nodded. His eyes rose toward Donovan's scalp. "You bear certain distinguishing marks."

But Donovan shook his head. "No. I've haunted the Bar on Jehovah for a great many years. If They had wanted to find me . . ."

"They may have wanted only to find you *there*. As long as you stayed in place, swilling whiskey, what did They care? Donovan-the-sot is no threat to them. Donovan-on-the-roads may be a different matter."

The scarred man said nothing. He looked out over the whittled city.

"If you went back to Jehovah," Greystroke said, "they'd likely lose interest again."

Donovan felt turmoil within. <Safe!> said Inner Child. *But,* said the Silky Voice. *The odds* are *better there,* said the Sleuth.

"Méarana," whispered the Fudir.

"She'd be safer with us," said Greystroke.

Méarana, talking with Billy and Little Hugh on the other side of the room, laughed. Donovan and Greystroke both watched her silently for a while and, perhaps attracted by their gaze, she turned and smiled at them, waving to them to join the others. And so they did, and they chatted of inconsequential matters before proceeding to dinner in the hotel's restaurant. But Donovan could see worry behind the eyes of all of them—except Billy Chins, who, having delivered himself utterly into the hands of another, had not a worry in all the known worlds.

Sometimes, the drink worked, and sometimes it did not. There were shards in the ruin of his mind; and sometimes drink floated them to the surface, if not to the service, of his consciousness. The barroom of the Roaming Qaysar stood in the under-cellar of the building in a series of rooms made up to look like caves. It was called a Vine-stoop, and served a kind of wine called a hoyrigen, which referred to that morning's press. It was not yet aged; it was not yet fully mature. It had not the quick numbing of the uiscebaugh, which stunned like a ball-peen hammer. It was more like drowning.

After dinner, the scarred man took himself down to the stoop where he could sit in dim light and be as much alone as a man like him could ever be. Around him, inside and out, swirled whispers and comfortable laughter, and the

occasional clink of stolid Hansard toasts. They sought contentment, the Vrouwenfolk did. The beedermayer, they
called it; the gemoot'. But always there was the main chance
looked for, the edge sought; and so contentment was an
elusive thing, enjoyed only by the sliders and touristas who
just *adored* the quaint customs of the cutthroat merchants
of the Greater Hanse.

The tables were rough-polished ironwood, with no adorn-
ment save a short candle that floated in a red-glass bowl.
The flame took nothing from the darkness, but he blew it
out anyway; and when later the *gellrin*, the waitress, tried
to re-light it, he sent her scuttling with a well-aimed growl.

Watch the one in the corner, he heard the whispers. *He's
surly when drunk.*

How little they knew him here! He needed no drink for
that.

"She *will* be safer if she goes with Greystroke," he assured himself.

𝔗𝔥𝔢 𝔠𝔬𝔲𝔯𝔦𝔢𝔯 𝔡𝔦𝔡𝔫'𝔱 𝔨𝔦𝔩𝔩 𝔱𝔥𝔢 𝔧𝔞𝔴𝔥𝔞𝔯𝔯𝔶 𝔦𝔫 𝔱𝔥𝔢 𝔎𝔞𝔰𝔭𝔢𝔯, the
Pedant pointed out. 𝔑𝔬𝔯 𝔞𝔫𝔶 𝔬𝔣 𝔱𝔥𝔢 𝔬𝔱𝔥𝔢𝔯𝔰.

"No, Greystroke would have told us had there been
others."

Would he?

"Yes," said Donovan. "He means to scare us off. For
that, an abundance of bodies is more persuasive than one."

<One was enough. Oh, it was.>

𝔖𝔦𝔩𝔢𝔫𝔠𝔢, 𝔆𝔥𝔦𝔩𝔡.

You know what it means, said the Sleuth.

Nah, but you're gonna tell us, aren't ya, smart-ass?

It means that, even if it was *Donovan who crossed the
courier's path, it is Méarana that he's interested in.*

Inner Child trembled, and the scarred man spilled some
of his day-wine.

You don't know that.

So, she's not safe, even with Greystroke and Hugh.

"I said she'd be 'safer,'" Donovan pointed out. "I didn't say she'd be 'safe.'"

She'll be glad to know that.

𝔗𝔥𝔢 𝔎𝔢𝔫𝔫𝔢𝔩'𝔰 𝔰𝔲𝔠𝔠𝔢𝔰𝔰 𝔯𝔞𝔱𝔢 𝔞𝔱 𝔭𝔯𝔬𝔱𝔢𝔠𝔱𝔦𝔫𝔤 . . .

"You're an ass, Pedant," said the Fudir. "Probabilities don't matter. What difference to the corpse that it was one chance in a million that slew him?"

Resentment swelled within him like a rancid bubble. 𝔍 𝔰𝔢𝔫𝔰𝔢 𝔍 𝔞𝔪 𝔫𝔬𝔱 𝔴𝔢𝔩𝔠𝔬𝔪𝔢 𝔥𝔢𝔯𝔢.

"That's the first sense you've made all evening."

The Pedant broke off, and Donovan became acutely aware that there were things he had known that he had now forgotten. "Smart move, Fudir. Pedant's our data base."

"Ah, who needs him?"

There was something about Bridget ban, said the Sleuth. The late Bridget ban.

Donovan gestured to the gellrin, and wagged an empty carafe. "Red," he called.

Sleuth, said the Silky Voice, *why would this agent of theirs be interested in Méarana?*

A worm of hope stirred painfully in the Fudir's breast. "Because he hopes she will lead him to Bridget ban?"

She may be alive? After all this time? Or does he simply not know she's dead?

Their agents use the Circuit like everyone else, said the Sleuth. *If one of them had capped her, they'd all know by now.*

"Or he hopes Méarana will lead him to whatever it was Bridget ban was hunting. The weapon that would protect the League against Them. She would not have told them what it was when they caught her. She would have died silent."

The gellrin came by with a fresh carafe, and it was on this occasion that she sought to re-light the café-candle and Donovan snapped at her.

"Great," said the Fudir after she had stalked off. "It's one thing to piss the Pedant off; quite another to anger the waitress. What do we do when *this* carafe runs dry?"

Wave a Gladiola Bill 'stead o' the empty. She'll come running.

"Brute," said Donovan, "there is something charming in your simplicity."

Yeah. And sometimes ya need the charm.

"But what was it about Bridget ban, Sleuth?" said the Fudir.

I've forgotten. The Pedant knew. He never forgets anything.

"Well, kiss him on the lips. Maybe he'll tell us."

He had raised his voice. A couple at a nearby table who had been drowning in each other's gaze turned and looked at him. "Why don't you drink your own wine," the woman snapped.

Maybe it was the dim lighting, but he thought for an instant that the woman was Bridget ban herself, warning him off. Her hair was shorter and darker than the Red Hound's— but hair can be dyed, and cut. Her complexion was dark, like hers—and it might prove golden in a better light. But . . . No one lops eighteen thumbs off her height for the sake of mere disguise, and the woman was that much shy of the witch's height. The scarred man, who had begun to lean forward, slumped back in his chair.

After all these years, the witch's spells were still potent. A good thing he had left her when he had. He closed his eyes—and a dozen others in the stoop relaxed. Two put weapons away.

The Fudir remembered a bright spring afternoon atop a wooded hill overlooking the Dalhousie Estate on Old 'Saken. He and Bridget ban had been scouting the estate under the pretext of bird-watching. The breeze had been gentle and cool, flowing off the Northbound Hills, and the birds had trilled and piped; and Bridget ban had placed her hand upon his arm, perhaps forgetful for just a moment of their purpose, and said with pure delight . . . "Listen, that's a rubythroat! We have them at home on Dangchao."

Let the Pedant settle for factual memories, for bricks dry from the kiln. The memories of touch and smell, the sound of her voice, could immerse him like a living river lazy on the plains.

"There's an interesting bird," he heard the remembered Fudir say. "A double-bellied nap-snatcher." It had been the approaching ornithopter with two security guards in it. He and Bridget ban had been using aliases on that scramble. Méarana's mother had called herself . . .

The fact would not come. The kiln had grown cold.

A strange sensation crept over him, as if something loomed behind him, vast and implacable. And he was sitting with his back against the wall. Inner Child shivered and the Brute clenched his fists under the table.

I feel it, too, said the Silky Voice. *And it's not the first time.*

He waited, and he felt the others waiting, too.

A time went by and then another time, until slowly, the feeling abated, like a pool of spilt wine soaking into the thirsty dirt. Though no candles had been lit, the room grew sensibly lighter.

The release was a long-held breath expelled. Inner Child began to cry and tears stained the scarred man's cheeks.

Later that night, Méarana awoke and found herself unable to go back to sleep. She kept thinking of poor Enwii, killed brutally for what she did not know. Little Hugh had thought the murderer a Confederate agent who, while on another mission, had recognized Donovan. But he might have been watching Donovan on Jehovah and had followed him from there.

In either case, she was responsible for Enwii's death. The

scarred man would never have left Jehovah but for her importuning.

It was this thought that had unsettled her sleep, and which kept her now awake.

Restless, she arose and took her harp to the common room, where she played on muted strings a suantraí for Enwelumokwu Tottenheim. The chords wept, but she found her heart was not in it; or perhaps that her heart was too much in it. So she laid the *clairseach* aside and sat in silence in the darkened room.

Eventually, she grew aware that, opposite her sofa, the door to Donovan's room stood ajar, and curious at this anomaly, she crossed the room and peeked inside.

The room was empty.

The bedclothes were rumpled, thrown aside and Méarana remembered Little Hugh's bitterness when he told of the Fudir abandoning him twenty years ago. That must have been some knock on the head the Fudir had given him, to hurt so after so long.

There was a Terran Corner in Pròwenshwai and the Terrans of the Hanse ran to wealth and power—more perhaps than other Hansards found comfortable. With the Brotherhood's aid, Donovan could hide indefinitely. Stepping inside the room, she checked the fresher, half expecting for reasons she could not name, to find he had hanged himself.

But no body dangled from the "rain shower," no body lay blood-drained in the tub. She chided herself on the expectation, blaming the late hour and her own feelings of guilt.

Returning to the sleeping quarters, she threw open the closet and found his meager wardrobe still inside. His kit littered the vanity in wild confusion. If he had fled, he had fled without his clothing, without his personal items. But what did that prove? He had left such ephemera behind in Chel'veckistad, too, when he had walked out on Bridget ban.

She had picked up his brush. Now she laid it down and noticed, tucked to the frame of the vanity's mirror, a palm-sized hologram. She plucked it up and held it to the lamp-light that speckled through open window-blinds.

Four figures sat at an outdoor café table on the sunlit cobbles of the Place of the Chooser, the great public square in Èlfiuji, in the Kingdom on Die Bold. It was one of those images that strolling artists would take of touristas. Dono-van, Greystroke, her mother, and Hugh. The image was old, but only Hugh had noticeably aged. He had not then ac-quired the hardness in the corners of his mouth, and still retained something of his youthful insouciance, as if the world were a joke and only he knew the punch line. Bridget ban sat in the middle—difficult to accomplish in a group of four, save that Greystroke had managed to fade a little into the background and was nearly obscured by Donovan and her mother. Méarana smiled a little to note that detail. The Gray Hound was a dear little man, if a trifle too cold for her comfort.

Mother, dressed in the travel garb of a Lady of the Court, sat turned at three-quarters but with her head fully facing the imager. In the depth of view, she was the most forward. Her smile, broad; her eyes seducing the viewer; her red hair captured in midflight, as if she had just then tossed her head to look at the artist. Her left arm draped Little Hugh's shoulders; her right hand covered Donovan's on the table. Greystroke's hand rested on her shoulder. They were all smiling, playing at the time the role of chance-met strang-ers; but Méarana thought they were smiling, too, because they were happy.

Hugh's eyes and his smile were directly for Bridget ban, and no mistake, for he was turned in her direction. Dono-van and Greystroke smiled into the viewer, but in the drift of their eyes, they, too, looked on Bridget ban; Greystroke, because he had placed her in his line of sight to the imager; Donovan, because though he faced one way he glanced another.

He had been the Fudir back then, Méarana reminded herself. Donovan had not yet been awakened, and the others were then uncreated. She wondered what it meant that he had kept this hologram until now; and wondered if the other three had copies as well.

Of course, Hugh's bitterness notwithstanding, the Fudir had not run out. He had, more accurately, run off. He had reasoned that what had to be done he had to do alone. It had been no more an act of abandonment than throwing oneself on a hand grenade.

But that had been a different man. The wreckage that now called itself by Donovan's name was timid where the Fudir had been bold. He had fled into the Corner of Jehovah on the mere realization of Méarana's identity. She had tracked him down then—more accurately, she had lured him to her.

Returning to the common room, she replaced her harp in its case, slung it over her shoulder, and slipped out of the suite.

But in making her way to the rear exit—and to the Eastern Cape Toll Gate—she passed by the hotel's exercise rooms and, glancing therein, saw the scarred man running in the simulator. She watched him for a while, knowing a certain relief that she did not examine too closely. Then she slipped the door open and quietly entered.

The track was a multi-belt surrounded by a hologram of scenery. The scarred man ran through an urban landscape and the belt conformed itself to it, taking him uphill and down and around corners. He ran with ferocious concentration, oblivious to everything but the sim and his own body, and it seemed to Méarana that he bulked a bit larger than usual. His face was set harder. His arms and legs appeared muscled.

But it was only a seeming. Physically, he was unchanged. It was the same skin; the same skeleton. The muscles had always been there. Yet, what informed the body seemed more substantial, like a big man wearing a smaller man's clothes. She lowered herself onto a nearby floor mat and sat cross-legged. Without conscious thought on her part, the harp found its way to her hands.

He had programmed the running boards for random hazards, and so vehicles and other pedestrians appeared in his path, coming out of side streets or doorways or simply moving more slowly, causing him to dodge and weave and, in one case, pirouette gracefully around a matron with three dogs on leash. Méarana's fingers picked out a running beat on the strings, hunting for the melody that would capture this determined running machine.

He turned! And the sensors in the simulator shifted the direction of the treadle by ninety degrees as he ran up an alleyway to all appearances directly toward the harper.

Startled, Méarana rolled to the side; but of course the onrushing approach was only an illusion created by the rolling belt.

The scarred man skipped a beat, and slowed his pace. Then he pointed at her and a grin split his features and he laughed.

It was a horrid, flaccid laugh. It reminded Méarana of the voices of people she had heard talking in their sleep. She plucked a staccato chord. "You must be the Brute," she said.

The scarred man nodded in time to his running.

"Donovan and the Fudir have sometimes complained of

sore muscles in the morning," she said. "A sign of age, they thought. Now I know why."

The Brute smiled again and made a flip with his hand.

"Who cares about them, right? You're mute. You don't control the voice, they told me."

"Aaaasleeeeb," the Brute moaned.

"When Donovan and the Fudir are asleep you can speak, a little. You must have some access to the speech center of your brain or you'd not be able to communicate with them."

The shoulders rolled in a great shrug. **"Naaaad maa shaaaab."**

"You don't know about brains and paraperception, is that it? All you're good for is combat and physical exertion?"

Another smile and a thumbs-up.

"I understand. If it's all you're good for, at least you're good for it. You're . . . Don't take this the wrong way. You're the animal part of Donovan's soul, aren't you?"

The Brute scowled and there was something red behind his eyes. Then he tossed his head, a great deal as a horse or a dog might do it. "Easy, fellow," she said. "Each of us is an animal—sensation, perception, emotion, and action. There's an 'I' . . ." She plucked a chord. ". . . that simply touches the strings and hears . . . An 'I' that doesn't know *music*, but only *sound*. An 'I' that thinks, remembers, and imagines, but does not conceive. Am I making myself clear?"

The Brute shrugged and gave a half smile. He raised his right hand and pinched his thumb and forefinger about an inch apart.

"But the 'I' that only *hears* the sounds and the 'I' that *understands* the music . . . Those are the same 'I.' The animal and the person, we're one. I can't imagine what it must be like to have them split apart."

The Brute wiggled his hands. Then he held up all ten fingers and splayed them.

"Split ten ways? Donovan told me there were only seven."

The Brute scowled and seemed to count on his fingers. Then he shrugged, held up all ten fingers and wiggled them, following up with a "who knows?" look. His eyes retreated and worry crossed his features.

He slowed to a modest pace, cooling off. The simulation vanished from around him and a series of numbers appeared above the hologram platform, to which the Brute paid no mind. He counted again on his fingers; then, held up seven as firmly as a row of spears. But then three, followed by a shrug.

"I don't understand."

The belt stopped, and the Brute came and sat beside her. Méarana flinched and pulled back, and the Brute hung his head.

Méarana stroked the back of his neck. "I'm sorry. I didn't mean that. But you are a little scary."

The Brute grinned and shook his head. **"Uh *lod* sgairee. Sbozabee,"** he moaned. A lot scary. Supposed to be.

The harper returned his grin. "Sure, who would be afraid of a fluffy bunny?"

The Brute rocked with silent laughter. But when he subsided he reached out and took her chin in his hand and stared into her face.

The animal body, she knew, had been trained in every martial art that muscle memory could hold. She knew that, should anything alarm him, he could with a flick of his wrist snap her neck. There had been the Xiao family in Main Tooth, in the Out-in-back of Dangchao, that had kept a pair of hunting poodles. And one day their son of four, in all innocence, had poked them the wrong way, and the devoted pets had become killers. That the Brute could speak in a limited fashion made him somehow more frightening.

"**Bready,**" he said. "**Uh'd dye voryuh.**"

But the harper did not know what he meant.

When she led him back into the suite, she found the other three in the common room and in a state of consternation over their absence. They unleashed a cacophony of demand, worry, and rebuke.

"There you are!" "Where were you?" "Oh! Master no bandon Billy!"

Billy threw himself at the Brute's feet and grabbed hold of his ankles. That woke the scarred man and Méarana could see the Brute cast one last glance in her direction before he sank beneath the sand of Donovan's awareness. The scarred man looked around the room in anger. "What the devil is going on?"

"That would be my question," said Greystroke.

Hugh took both the harper's hands in his. "We were worried about you. In case . . . You know."

"So you didn't run out this time, Donovan?" Greystroke said to the scarred man.

"In case we were followed here from Harpaloon?" Méarana said to Hugh. "Not likely."

"Nor impossible. There are fossil images in the berms of the Roads. A clever man can follow a ship, and from the blue-shift know where she had exited. So . . ."

"So," said Greystroke to both the harper and the scarred man, "isn't it time you told us everything and handed the job back to the professionals?"

"Before the Confederate catches up with you?" added Hugh.

Donovan swatted Billy Chins on the side of the head. "Stop that now, or I really will set you free! A life spent groveling is not worth living."

Billy Chins released Donovan's ankles and scrambled to his feet. "So sorry, master. I no serve you good? I still serve you?"

"Serve me, if you must. But do it on your feet! What am I doing out here?"

"You were sleepwalking," Méarana told him.

"Well," said Greystroke, "what's your answer?"

Donovan nodded to Méarana. "It's her answer to give." To the harper, he added, "It's the smart move. I've told you that from the beginning."

"I know. But . . . The 'professionals' searched for two years and gave up the hunt."

Little Hugh stuck his chin out. "Greystroke and I have not. And we never will until we know where and how she . . ." He paused, and finished in a different voice. "Until we know."

"Then you ought to understand. I can't sit on Dangchao and simply wait."

"Remember the jawharry on Harpaloon," said Hugh.

"I do. And that's one of the reasons I can't quit. I owe her something more than quitting."

Hugh suppressed a smile. "Scared you on instead of off?"

Donovan shook his head. "We're all tired. It's the middle of the night—and nights on the Vrouw are uncommonly long. Let's sleep on it and in the morning . . ." He left unsaid what the morning would bring.

Everyone returned to their rooms. When Donovan turned to close his door, he found Greystroke in the room with him. He bobbed a finger. "Heel-and-toe, right?"

"I walk in your footsteps."

"You know it. So, get this over with."

The Hound walked to the work desk by the wall and sank into its chair. He waved Donovan to the reading chair in the corner.

"She doesn't understand," Greystroke said when they were both settled. "She doesn't know how dangerous it is."

" 'It is the young who catch the gliding snake.' "

Greystroke cocked his head. "Stop being the inscrutable Terran."

"A Terran proverb. The young do dangerous things in innocence."

"So, what's *our* excuse? Never mind. This is no longer just nosing around Lafrontera. It's not just taking ordinary chances on raw settlement worlds or staying in posh hotels like this one at Kennel expense. It's not a bleeding *lark*!"

"She knows that."

"Does she? There's an agent of Those of Name nosing around. That's not a mob of 'Loonie simpletons. That's . . . Fates take it! She's *her* daughter!"

"Then maybe you understand why she won't give up."

Greystroke opened his mouth to say something, thought better of it, and crossed his arms. "When I remember twenty years ago . . ." His eyes lit briefly on the hologram on the vanity mirror. "Ah, well . . ." He fell silent for a time. "You'll stay with her?"

"I promised Zorba."

"No, *he* promised *you*. I know how he operates. But I don't want you in this only because your personal skin is threatened. A man like that is too likely to disappear once he thinks he safely can. And where would that leave *her*?"

"There are other men," Donovan observed, "who cannot abandon her because they have not stepped forward in the first place."

Anger flashed briefly on the Hound's bland countenance. "She came to you," he pointed out. And Donovan wondered whether the anger was over his jibe or her choice.

"Don't worry it, Hound," Donovan said. "It all lies in how the gods decide."

"The gods," said Greystroke, "are merely despotic. But behind the gods sit the Fates, and they are deadly."

"How could she go to you or to the Ghost for help? She needed someone . . . unencumbered."

Greystroke snorted and looked inward for a time before he pulled a brain from a pocket and tossed it to Donovan.

The scarred man caught it on the fly, looked at it, looked at Donovan.

"It's one of my private codes," the Hound explained. "If you ever need me, encrypt it with that and send a message to the Kennel. They'll forward it over the Circuit to wherever I am. Rinty and I will come as quickly as we can."

Donovan said nothing, but looked at the Hound.

Greystroke colored and looked away. "We have to be on Yubeq shortly. On assignment."

"That wasn't a ruse?"

"No. We really were going your way."

Donovan studied the pocket brain, turning it over and over in his fingers. Then, abruptly, he clenched his hand around it. "Why?"

"Why do you think?" He nodded toward the hologram. "Twenty years ago, the four of us were partners. I don't like you; and you don't like me. (Please. Spare me the wheedling Terran excuses.) But among the four of us, you and Rinty had a bond; and now he and I have one. And we were all bound to *her*, of course. But between you and me is the missing link. Just answer me one thing. *Tell me you will not abandon her.*"

Now it was Donovan's turn to anger. "Do you think I would do that?"

Greystroke's silence was eloquent.

Finally, Donovan waved a hand, and the Fudir answered, "No, sahb. I do no such a thing."

"Because if you do . . ."

"Yes, I know. You'll defend Méarana to the last drop of my blood. My beard is on fire, and you come to warm your hands at the blaze."

Greystroke put his hands on his knees and pushed to his feet. He looked away. "I used to think that perhaps I . . . But no, I needed but one look at her." His glance was iron. "You and I agree on one thing, at least. We both wish it were someone else going with her."

Donovan temporized. "What more risk can there be than what we saw on Harpaloon? Bangtop, Siggy O'Hara, and the other places . . . I am as capable as the next man of booking passage on throughliners and rooms in hotels. And once we reach the Chit and the trail peters out, perhaps then she will give it up."

Greystroke seemed about to speak; but shrugged and turned away.

After the door had closed, Donovan continued to sit in the reading chair, looking nowhere in particular, and turning Greystroke's pocket brain over and over in his hand. He glanced at the hologram, noted that it was out of place and wondered if it had been Greystroke or Hugh who had fingered it. "I am become cane in the sugar-mill," he said, reciting a proverb of his people, "and a bit of straw in the waves of the sea."

In the morning, Greystroke and Little Hugh were gone, and their rooms as if no one had ever slept there. Méarana found herself oddly distraught by their absence. In their company, she had not felt so alone in her quest. Billy hardly counted at all, and Donovan had proven less than she had expected—although in another sense, he was more. Yet, a man can accomplish very little if he is of two minds about it, and Donovan was seven—or ten, if she had understood the Brute correctly. The Hound and his Pup had given her briefly the illusion that she had more allies in her quest, and indeed the greater illusion that they would lift the burden of her quest from her.

Did that desire make her a bad daughter? Or did it mean only that she was afraid she might fail? Sometimes she remembered that she had but twenty years metric in her *crios. Despair is the one unforgivable sin,* her mother used to tell her, *for it is the only one that never seeks forgiveness.* Yet Méarana could not but feel the beat of its wings nearby.

Mother had first told her that maxim when a very young Lucia had thrown her child's harp from her in frustration over its intransigent strings. There had been tears, and strong encouragement. She had persevered and gained eventually a small degree of fame in and around the Old Planets. She would persevere in this task, too.

She had no memory of ever having met Greystroke before—and what sadder fate than that could be told of any man? But she did remember Hugh from her childhood and remembered how Mother had brightened at his visits. She had formed certain conclusions from that, conclusions that she now saw were utterly fantastic, and now recalled that Hugh had always borne a sad and winsome countenance on his sojourns. After a time, he had no longer visited.

Now, inexplicably, he had abandoned her again. Duty had called, Donovan explained, but duty was a cold lover and false in the bargain.

"Is that so?" Donovan told her when she had said so. "Wherefore, dost thou seek thy mother?"

"That is love, not duty," she explained.

"Love," said Donovan, "*is* a duty, and a hard one."

They had gathered around the breakfast table in the common room and Billy Chins provided from the hotel's larder plates of egg and bangers, tomato juice, daal and beans—

and a concoction of his own which he called fool. He brewed qalwah, which tasted much like ordinary Vrouwish kaff, save that it was bitter and muddy. "Billy savvy duty," the khitmutgar said, taking the seat his master had ordained him. "Duty, me, to sahb Donovan."

"You may wish otherwise," Donovan said. "Let's talk plans. No, Billy, you stay here. You may as well hear what you're getting into. You may decide it's more efficient to kill yourself now."

"He doesn't mean that, Billy."

Donovan tore a piece of naan in two. "Don't I? There's a Confederate courier somewhere on our backtrail. That is not certain, but has more certainty than it ought to. We can't afford to assume he will stay back there. If he knows we left Harpaloon with Greystroke, he may learn through other contacts that the Hound was bound for Yubeq. So he'll follow down the Spiral Staircase to Dancing Vrouw. At that point, if he's tracking the fossil images in the berms, he'll see the blue shift and know that we stopped here. Tracking is slower going, so we have perhaps another day before we can expect him here. He may be in the coopers already and crawling down-system. So, let's finish up and—to use a Terran phrase—'haul ass.' If we leave here before he shows, he'll not know where we're going next, and we'll lose him."

Billy Chins nodded vigorously. "Hutt, hutt; go jildy! Bungim paus, me." He started to rise, but Donovan held him back.

"Some matters must be checked out before we go. To-morrow, we go."

"Oh, Fudir," said the harper. "We spent *weeks* investigating on Harpaloon."

"Then," said Donovan, tossing his napkin to the table, "there's not a moment to lose. Billy. This big-deal samting. We go, mistress harp and me, but come back no long time.

No ansa him the door, less *this* knock." He rapped his knuckles on the table in a tattoo. "You hear that, you answer back *this* . . ." Another, different tattoo. ". . . but only if alla pukka. If alla dhik, no knock-back. Savvy, you?" He ran Billy through the sign and countersign several times before he was satisfied. "No special knock, no ansa door. No 'room service,' no maid. No for nogat nothing."

"I with you, me," said Billy. "You see. I go with you wokabout. Out to Rim? I go. Out to Rift? I go. You wokabout place nogut, Billy Chins there. I good man, you see."

Unaccountably touched, Donovan extended his hand, equal to equal, and Billy, after a moment's hesitation, took it.

They took the easy way in.

"There were only two reasons why the Kennel never got a sniff of her," Donovan explained to the harper after the Toll had franked their visas and issued them their green cards against their deposit of funds. "Either she entered East Cape in secret—in which case, we've no hope of picking up any trail—or she used a name they never thought to check. Normally, on official business, she would have used her office name—Bridget ban—and on personal business, she would have used her base name."

"So Gwillgi only checked to see if 'Bridget ban' had entered East Cape, and she went in as Francine . . ."

Donovan steered her down a corridor of the Toll-for-One building. The walls were tiled in pale masonry with a frieze at head level relieved into wreaths and tendrils. "Gwillgi is not stupid. He checked both names. We know she was on Harpaloon as Francine Thompson."

"Then what . . . ?"

"Bridget ban was not name-lacking. Gwillgi checked all the Kennel knew of."

"Then . . ."

"The Kennel may not have known all of them. You told

me once that your mother believed in the Four Strengths. Courage . . ."

"Courage, prudence, justice, and moderation."

Donovan nodded. "If one is to believe in gods, those beat Greystroke's Friendly Ones."

"Yes, four to three."

Donovan shot her a surprised glance. "You seem more cheery than earlier."

"The sun is up. It's easier to be cheery in the sunlight."

"Even winter sunlight? Never mind. Prudence. The witch had the courage to take risks, no doubt of that. Otherwise, she'd have come home by now. But she would have been prudent enough to leave . . . breadcrumbs."

"Breadcrumbs?"

"Old Terran fable. A trail of clues. The Sleuth deduced that. And I had to get him drunk to get that out of him. That helps sometimes, if we all get cheery-drunk together. Then the Pedant quit and we all forgot . . . Aaah, you don't want to hear all that. Listen, and mallum bat. Your mother did not expect problems. She told you she'd be back soon. But she coppered her bets. She kept the Kennel updated on her whereabouts, if not on her whyabouts. She wasn't ready to tell them what she was looking for. If it was a wild goose, she'd look foolish, and—you had some taste of Kennel politics—no Hound wants that. And if it was the goose that laid the golden eggs, she wanted first dibs."

"Goose?" said Méarana. "Dibs?"

"Here we are."

They entered an office which, like most such offices throughout the Spiral Arm, bustled with earnest activity. Clerks filed, frowned at screens, read hardcopies, entered data by voice, key, and touch. "If only they had the artificial intelligences of Olde Earth," he told Méarana, who only laughed.

He flashed his Kennel chit and the Vrouw must have

been more accustomed to dealing with League agents than either Thistlewaite or Harpaloon because the reception clerk merely glanced at it, handed them a set of forms, and directed them to a nearby table to fill them out. "So much for the Kennel mystique," Donovan muttered.

"By the time we fill these out," Méarana said, "the Confederate will catch up."

The forms were "smart-forms" or "gloogardies" in the dialect of the Eastern Cape. They were laminas several hairs thick sandwiching a processor. The embedded logics were standard "spreadsheet" and it was only a matter of scribing the right data into the right entry fields, after which they propagated automatically. At the table, Donovan tried three light pens before finding one that worked; then hunted through the paperwork to find the forms he really needed. LEAGUE REQUEST FOR UNNATURAL ALIEN IDENTIFICATION and LEAGUE REQUEST FOR ALIEN IDENTIFICATION CARD USAGE LOG. There was even a space for entering the Kennel chit number.

"Unnatural?" said Méarana.

"Not naturalized." Donovan poised his pen, then hesitated.

"What's wrong? Did you forget the chit reference number?"

"It's in the back of my mind," Donovan complained. "But the Pedant is still in a snit, so he's not letting it out." He pulled the lanyard by which the chit hung under his blouse, and read the glowing number off the back side.

When he turned the forms in, the Clerk said, "You haven't entered an Alien Identification Card Number for the Usage Log Request."

"I can't enter the Card Number until you process the Identification Request."

The Clerk gave him a patient look and handed back the

second form. Then, taking the first form, he went to a form reader and inserted it in the scanner.

"What name did you ask after?" the harper asked him.

"Julienne Lady Melisonde. That was the name she used when she and I were scouting the Dalhousie Estates on Old 'Saken. It's a shot in the dark. If it works . . ."

It did. A Julienne Lady Melisonde "of the Banry's Court" had entered East Cape Circle with High Taran papers nearly three metric years before, exited later that same day. Alien Identification Card Number, thus and so. Donovan copied that onto the second form and handed that one again to the Clerk, who slid it through the reader.

"How did you know . . . ?" Méarana asked.

" 'The whisper of a beautiful woman can be heard farther than the roar of a lion.' But it was the only other name of hers I knew. *And* it was one that Gwillgi might not have known of. She used it for just that one scramble. Ah, here come the payoff . . ." He wagged his green card. "Unnatural Aliens have to deposit funds with a Hansard bank to prove they will not become a burden on the public purse during their stay. Then they use the cards for purchases, hotels, meals, entry swipes to public buildings . . . This list . . ." Which he took from the Clerk's hand. ". . . should tell us where she went, who she contacted . . . Here we go . . . Ah! She went to two places. The Gross Schmuggery— that's the jewelers' bourse—and the Planetary Tissue Bank."

Méarana took the sheet from him and read it. "The jewelers' bourse. So she was still trying to trace the medallion. But why the Tissue Bank?"

The Director of the Planetary Tissue Bank was a broad-chested man named Shmon van Rwegasira y Gasdro. He was coal-black in complexion, so that his eyes and teeth seemed to float in the air just before his face. He shook hands in the brusque and hearty Hansard fashion and ushered them into an oppressively comfortable sitting room paneled in dark woods and decorated with serious leafy plants on tall column pedestals. Bookcases alternated with pen drawings of vaguely anatomical aspect. He called for a pot of kaff and engaged them in chatty conversation until it arrived. The supreme virtue of the Hansard was comfort, which they called *gemoot*, and van Rwegasira was a past master of it.

When fellowship had been brought to a proper pitch, the Director asked them what had brought the Kennel to the Tissue Bank. Donovan said, "We are investigating the activities of Julienne Lady Melisonde of High Tara. She came to the Tissue Bank on 17 Herbsmonat, 1176, local. In metric time . . ."

But the Director waved off the conversion. His holo-screen already displayed the calendar. "Yeah-well . . . I remember her. It's unusual for outworlders here to come. To receive two such visitors in quick succession is unheard of."

"Two," said Donovan. He exchanged a glance with Méarana. "Who was the second?"

Van Rwegasira pursed his considerable lips and ran his finger down the screen that hovered before him. "That one was, umm. Yeah, here it stands. The other was named Sofwary of Kàuntusulfalúghy." He looked up and blinked owlishly. "They are not in trouble, are they? You are not hunting them down to, ah. . . ." His grin was at once appalled and fascinated. The Kennel had a reputation in popular culture.

"No. Just the opposite. They may be in danger, and we must warn them."

The Director looked troubled but nodded. "The Tissue Bank maintains the samples of nearly all residents in the Eastern Cape Circle, as well as of three other Circles with whom we have contracts. This provides to our government a resource-value, both for the health care—for cloning replacement tissues via retrogression to stemly status—and also for the law enforcement—for the matching with the crime scene traces. Our cross-tabulation keys are the finest of their kind and the archives have sometimes been used by *regswallers*—how do you say it? Rights-wallahs? Lawyers?—yeah-doke, by lawyers, to establish correctly the property-inheritance. Since only five years there stood the well-famous case of the False Hubert of Miggeltally, who claimed rights to the van Jatterjee commercial empire and we . . ."

Donovan interrupted the public relations speech. "But what of this Sofwari and Lady Melisonde? What was their purpose in coming here? Did they come together?"

Van Rwegasira blinked several times, shook his head. "No. Professor Doctor Doctor Sofwari came on the third of Leafallmonat and spent here six weeks with our dibby manager, making many visits. Genealogical research, by my notes. That is the searching for the ancestors." The Director shrugged, as if to ask what madness outworlders might be capable of.

"And what of Lady Melisonde?" said Méarana.

The Director worked his lips as he studied his logs. "She appears the same purpose to have had. Mina—she was then my dibby manager—has here that Lady Melisonde was after Sofwari asking. She provided to her a copy of his analysis." Van Rwegasira looked up from his reading. "That was improper, yeah? We have not the authorization one man's work to give another. Mina was reprimanded for the infraction, naturally."

"Then, you'll not show it to us?" asked Méarana.

"That is another pair of boots! Always, we cooperate with the authorities. I will have a brain immediately filled." He subvocalized and a light appeared on his holoscreen. "Now, stand there other matters in which we may the Kennel serve? No? Then I will say what a pleasure this has been? Perhaps . . ." And this he added with exaggerated diffidence. "Perhaps I may mention this service to my colleagues?"

To enhance his prestige among his friends. Donovan imagined him subtly scoring points. *As I explained to the agents of the Kennel when they consulted with me . . .* He removed his cap so that the Director could see his scars. "That would not be wise, sir."

The Director was too dark to go pale, but his eyes widened ever-so-slightly, and he nodded. "Yeah-doke," he said. He ran a finger across his lips. "No word to any over this."

"In fact, it would be a good idea to erase any record that this visit even occurred."

"Of course."

"It is for your own safety."

Rwegasira was now plainly sweating. "Yeah-well."

AN AISTEAR

Departing *Dancing Vrouw, the harper finally achieves her wish. She and the scarred man and their servant travel first class on the Hansard liner,* Gerthru van Ijębwode, *Hanower to Siggy O'Hara. A splendid ship, it sports that combination of fashion, comfort, and social vanity for which the Greater Hanse is justly famed: Never has cloth so flattered human form; never has palate been so sumptuously pleased; never have manners and status been flaunted with such deadly purpose.*

The appointments are luxurious, and even steerage would excite envy. Decor favors the ornate fashions of the Hanse. Serious portraits and scenes of nature and sport alternate with shelves full of knickknack and scrimshaw.

*Among the more bookish folk of Ramage or Hawthorne
Rose, the Hansards are accounted unspeakably vulgar;
but a Hansard merchant prince can buy or sell half of Ramage and take Hawthorne Rose as pocket change; so what
do they care?*

"The best disguise," the scarred man told the harper at
lunch the first day, "is the truth, so long as it be not the
whole truth." He had by nature an aversion to wholeness,
and was partial to partial truths. Being smaller, they fit
better in his mouth.

Donovan had acquired for the duration the guise of Āvalam of New Chennai. This caused Billy no end of amusement, for in the Terran patois Āvalam meant "a noise made
with the mouth in defiance." Ostensibly, he had an agreement with House van Abimbola to locate and deliver jewelry in the style of Méarana's medallion.

This was the partial truth. Donovan actually did have
such a contract. Inquiries at the Great Shmuggery had un-
covered no further clues on the medallion's origin, but they
had aroused the interests of several importers.

"I understand the precaution," said the harper, now
Ariel pen Drehon of New Cornwall.

"Billy no samjaw," said the khitmutgar as he poured the
wine for them. While the ship was well-staffed for the
comforts of her first-class passengers, these often traveled
with their personal servants. In the background a string
orchestra played pleasant incidental music; waiters circulated with dimsum carts bearing small portions on small
plates.

Méarana assaulted once more the ramparts of his ignorance. "You see, Billy, when the courier reaches Pròwenshwai and learns we've gone, he'll check all the departing
passenger manifests."

"He think we chel with Hound," the pudgy little man announced. "Old Terry kahāvata. 'Thou goest with the one who brought thee.'" His teeth showed.

Donovan had taken the measure of those ramparts, and knew them unscalable. "Thou art the very Bood of wisdom," he told him, sweeping his hand over the servant in the Sign of the Wheel.

"Don't mock," said the harper. "It's a reasonable guess. But, Billy, the man will *nolangtaim* learn that we were still in the hotel after Greystroke left the system. So we must have left on a commercial liner."

"But why we buy *two* tickets? We go twice as fast?"

"The other tickets were in our own names," she said. "When he finds them, the agent will think we left on *Lola Hadley* for Jemson's Moon."

Billy's eyes turned white and round. "We go Jemson's Moon? That much budmash place."

"No, Billy, we go Siggy O'Hara."

The servant's eyes welled up. "I am confused."

Méarana sighed, but she did not engage Donovan's I-told-you-so smirk. "Billy . . . Don't take this the wrong way, but . . . What did you *do* in the Corner of Preeshdad?"

For the first time since she had met him, Billy showed animation. His hands took life, defined with their trajectories the circumference of his answers. "Oh! I sell insurance, me. Explain risk analysis, premiums, benefits. Price cheap; but goods big-big."

"Billy," said Donovan, "if you try to sell me an insurance policy, I'll dismiss you, and you'll have to kill yourself."

By now Billy was certain Donovan would do no such thing; or almost certain. "Ha, ha," he said. "Master much funnyman. No sell policy you. Risk too great."

Now it was Donovan's turn to say, "Ha, ha."

"Policy very simple," the Terran continued. "I tell dukāndar merchants how much they pay for we not spoil him, the shop."

The harper found her voice. "Billy! You ran a protection scramble? That is terrible!"

"Oh, no, lady harp," he protested. "Terran Protection Service, Limited, good value. No let 'Loonie gangs burnim dukān, kill dukāndar. That big dhik!"

The scarred man laughed and slapped the table so that silverware complained. "A protection scramble that actually sells protection . . . You're well away from that, Billy. If you protect shopkeepers from 'Loon gangs, sooner or later the 'Loon gangs get you. As one almost did."

Billy Chins acknowledged the memory by grasping the scarred man's right hand and laying kisses on it. "Sahb Donovan most-blessed!"

Donovan yanked his hand back. "My name is Āvalam. Try to remember."

"I understand the false names and the decoy tickets," said the harper, "but why maintain the charade on board ship? The Confederate couldn't have reached Pròwenshwai in time to board 'Hurtling Gertie,' even if he guessed we were on her. And if he were on board, the pretense of the names would not survive the prospect of your scalp."

The scarred man did not answer right away. A plate of "invention" sat before him: the flesh of deer enhanced with a dark, mushroomy yeagersauce. After a while, he placed his fork on the plate with the morsel still impaled. "There are only two kinds of people: the careful and the dead."

"And you are not dead—at least in some respects."

Donovan's grin cut through the scarred man's lips. "The Purser knows us by our ticketed names. It will be less confusing to him, and draw less attention to us, if we continue using them. Otherwise, he may remark the matter in official reports; and these will run back to the Vrouw, and into the courier's ear."

The harper nodded slowly, glanced at Billy, who anxiously took that as a command to refill everyone's water glass.

On the dance floor, the luncheon entertainment had begun. Scantily clad women leapt about, swirled their silk veils to wild music, and rhythmically slapped their shoes and short leather pants. For a time, the harper and her companions watched, each immersed in thought. And while Billy's thoughts as he followed the dancers' undulations were easily read, Donovan's were farther away. Méarana asked to hear them.

"Your mother's breadcrumbs," he answered. "I understand the witch's prudence in leaving a trail, and even her caution in making it hard to find. But so far as I know, only three people know she ever called herself Lady Melisonde."

"Then she expected one of you eventually to follow her."

"So it would seem."

"So which bothers you more? That she might have left the trail for Greystroke or Little Hugh—or that she might have left it for Donovan?"

The scarred man went rigid and a conflict raged through his features. He began to mutter, both hands gripping the table's edge. Billy rose. "I fetch doctor, jildy," he said.

But the harper held him back and he sank slowly back into his seat. "It is only a way he has about him," she said.

"Sahb Donovan much sick."

"Yes." The harper turned reflective. "I should not have brought him out here."

"Why you do that to sick man, then?" Anger informed Billy's moon-face.

She sighed. "I don't know, Billy. I really don't. I thought . . . maybe I owed it to him." But what she meant by this was not for a stranger's ears.

On the second day out, their steward informed them of the
Second Officer's invitation to sit at his table. Proper attire
was required; but it was a big Spiral Arm and "proper"
covered a wide range of attire. Donovan decided to wear
the same outfit he had worn to the palace in Jenlùshy, since
it was still resident in the anycloth's memory.

But in rummaging through the valise in which he had
stuffed it he discovered two ceramic cassettes, each about
the size of his hand, tucked in a pocket in the valise. One
was white, the other white with red stripes. Inner Child
recoiled, thinking them bombs planted somehow by the
Confederate courier, and the scarred man ended in the
undignified position in which the harper, rushing in, found
him.

"What happened?" she cried. "Are you hurt?"

Only in his dignity; but he said nothing. Instead he pulled
the two packets from the valise and examined them more
closely. "What are those things?" the harper asked.

Donovan noted dataports of antique design. *Something
plugs in here,* the Sleuth noted. *And something else there.*
Faded writing ran across the shells. On the one, a script
much like the curlicues of the old Taṇṭamiž on the other,
madly jambled curls and hooks and dots unlike anything
he had seen before. Or had he?

𝕳𝖆𝖍, said the Pedant. 𝕾𝖔𝖒𝖊𝖙𝖎𝖒𝖊𝖘 𝖞𝖔𝖚 𝖓𝖊𝖊𝖉 𝖙𝖍𝖊 𝖔𝖑𝖉 𝖋𝖆𝖗𝖙,
𝖉𝖔𝖓'𝖙 𝖞𝖔𝖚? Achilles emerging from his tent could not have
edged his voice with greater triumph.

"Where have we seen script like this before?" Donovan
asked. He aimed the question at the Pedant, but received
an answer from the harper.

"Why, those are the border decorations on the signage
in Preeshdad!"

The scarred man's anger was two-dimensional. One di-
mension was the anger of the Pedant at being upstaged.

The other was the anger of Donovan at the ease with which a unified mind could process what to him came only through wrangles. Had the Fudir not insulted the Pedant, had the Pedant not sulked, he would have recognized the matter straight-off.

Méarana took one of the cassettes from him and tried to read the ancient Taṇṭamiž. "Vu-ra-gith," she said haltingly.

"Birakid," Donovan said in sudden recognition. He rocked back on his heels as he realized what he had found so cunningly inserted in his goods. "Birakid Shee'us Nakopthayiní. The Specklings-Down of the Headmen."

The harper started and dropped the cassette, but the Beast caught it on the fall.

"The Holy Books of Harpaloon!" she said. "How did they . . . ?"

The scarred man's smile was grim, but there was a touch of genuine happiness in it. "A parting gift from Little Hugh. He and Greystroke must have overheard my wish to read one."

Inner Child feared reprisals from the devotees, but the Fudir reassured him. "There are supposed to be hundreds of these books. Hugh is smart enough to leave a dummy behind. They may never realize that two are missing."

"But how," Méarana said, "may one read them?"

The scarred man studied the antique dataports, and the Sleuth shook his head. "Long-forgotten technologies," Donovan said. He sighed and tossed the cassettes to his bed. "Our remotest ancestors poked reeds into mud and baked the mud into brick. We can still read those ancient thoughts, millennia later. But it seems that the greater the technology, the more ephemeral it becomes. There is a lesson there, harper. But what, I do not know."

JOR (MADHYA)

The Spiral Staircase is unusual among the roads of Electric Avenue, for on its course it crosses the strata of the Spiral Arm. Most roads, for reasons past understanding, remain on particular "tiers" parallel to the galactic plane. The science-wallahs make brave sounds about rotating plasmas and angular momentums and delaminations, but the plain truth is that they do not know, and the brave sounds are to prevent the rest of us from learning that. In consequence, there are stars in the skies that are forever out of reach.

The Spiral Staircase is an exception that tests the rule. A great whorl of plasma, it starts at Ramage, high above the Galactic Plane, corkscrews around Alabaster and Siggy O'Hara down into the Greater Hanse roundabout, and passes below Thistlewaite before climbing again on an extension called the Grand Concourse, whence once more past Siggy O'Hara to Boldly Go, and all the way to Gatmander, where it becomes the Wilderness Road.

"Hurtling Gertie" is bound nonstop to Siggy O'Hara and the harper and the scarred man use the enforced idleness to study the scraps that they have gathered, arranging the pieces this way and that in the hope that they will form a picture.

"Why are we not stopping at Bangtop-Burgenland?" the harper asked when Donovan had announced this change of plan. She sat in a swing chair in the common room of their suite. Her harp nestled in her lap while she tuned it to the third mode.

First-class suites in a Hansard throughliner are broad and spacious and rival the Hadley liners in their luxury. The sofas and settees are low and comfortable and upholstered in fine, soft leather cured from the hides of Megranomic longerhorns. Colorful tapestries covered walls with stags and hunters and mountain streams. Satisfied burghers stared contentedly from engravings. Fine aromas wafted from well-stocked galleys. A team of servants had been assigned to look after their creature comforts, and Billy Chins had with delight taken these in hand. As sahb Āvalam's khānsāmmy, his majordomo, he speckled them with instructions, half of which the staff did not comprehend—or affected not to.

"Is easy, mistress harp," Billy told her as he aimlessly polished and straightened a room already tidied by the now-departed staff. "We stop—pursuit catch us."

"If there *is* pursuit. Fudir, are you simply being prudent, or do you have a reason?"

The scarred man curled on one of the settees across the room, with a reading screen in the crook of his arm. A sinuous man when not outright sinister, this twisted posture seemed his natural pose. He wore a saffron housecoat and beaded moccasin slippers provided by the room's eager stewards. Now and then he touched the corner of the screen so as to page through the text. "I have half a dozen reasons," he answered without looking up. "And if Donovan weren't reading this book, I'd have even more."

Méarana had been looking at Billy and saw understanding there before a mask of studied incomprehension took its place. *He has guessed his master's condition,* she thought. "Willeth thou share with us thine reasons," she asked in an execrable imitation of the Tongue, "or at least one of them?"

Donovan continued to read. Reading wanted eyes, not lips and ears and the scarred man had attentions to spare. The Fudir answered. "We know *what* your mother was looking for—the source of the medallion. We can be reasonably sure she learned it, and that she went there. What we don't know is *why* she thought the medallion important. Or *how* it was supposed to protect the League against the Confederation."

"No possible, sahb," said Billy with a sad shake of his head. "Names much-much addykara, aah . . . have much-great power. Hold Terra," he added more softly, and held his hand out as if cupping a ball.

"And this somehow means we don't stop on Bangtop?" Méarana persisted.

"It means we squirt Bangtop a Kennel inquiry as we pass through the coopers," the Fudir explained, "and they send a reply via the Circuit, care of High Kaddo Platform at Siggy O'Hara, so it will be awaiting us when we arrive there. Why crawl down and back for something like that? Here, Billy." He tossed the khitmutgar a packet and a brain. "Take the packet to the concierge and have her queue it for the Bangtop squirt. Two messages: one for the jewelers' bourse in New Dreading; the other for the tissue bank in Licking Stone."

"You'll ask about Sofwari-wallah, too," said Méarana.

The Fudir made a sound of exasperation. "I'm not old-hammered. Sofwari's name has come up twice—three times, if he's the one who left the package on Harpaloon. That's once or twice too often for my comfort level. Either she was following him or he was following her." He hesitated and looked up from the book, and Méarana knew that Donovan had joined them.

"How can a man read with all this racket!" He tossed the screen aside.

Méarana knew Donovan meant chatter among his components. Being as fragmented as they were, they tended to rattle when set in motion. Sometimes she wondered how the man could think at all.

"There is a third possibility, you know," Donovan told

them. "Neither was following the other, but both were following the same trail. Sofwari put her onto it. That seems clear. And she probably wanted to cross-check with him when he reached Harpaloon, but they missed connection. Sofwari must have arrived there *after* she left, thinking he had gotten there first. Otherwise, why leave the brain? But he did arrive first at Dancing Vrouw and departed before she arrived. Even a harper should see why."

Méarana tuned a few strings. "They went 'round the Staircase in opposite directions. After they parted on Thistlewaite, Mother came home to do her research. When she returned to Thistlewaite and learned that Sofwari had not waited for her, she went to Harpaloon to intercept him. But he had not gotten there yet. She lost patience and went down the Staircase to Dancing Vrouw."

Donovan grunted. "And likely, passed Sofwari, who was coming up at the same time. You *do* understand."

Méarana strummed a chord, frowned, twisted a key a quarter turn. "I don't understand any of it. Why did Mother come all the way back to Dangchao to do her research? She could have done most of it from Thistlewaite and left with Sofwari. Why did Sofwari not wait for her on Thistlewaite? Why did it take him longer to reach Harpaloon than Mother allowed for?"

The scarred man showed his teeth. "Oil and water, girl. A Hound is relentless on the scent; but science-wallahs move in fits and starts. How could Sofwari abide on Thistlewaite, while the tissue banks of the Hanse beckoned? But once there, he could linger weeks in study at each depository. There is an unworldliness about his sort that more efficient folk like your mother cannot grasp. It never occurred to her that he would *dawdle*." A grunt of laughter was pulled from him and he muttered softly, "Yes, Pedant. I was sure *you* would understand."

"But why did *Mother* 'dawdle?' Why did she spend two

weeks at home on research she could have done almost anywhere? Ourobouros Thistlewaite was back in-circuit. At worst, she need have gone up the Silk Road no farther than High Tara."

"Ah." The scarred man's smile was like a knife wound. "There was one thing she wanted to access that she could only do on Dangchao."

"And what was that?"

"You."

The harper struck a false note, and looked to the scarred man with a surprise that she quickly suppressed. She tucked her head to the harp. "I doubt that," she murmured, addressing the strings and pretending to tune them.

Donovan nodded to his servant. "What do you think of all this, Billy?"

The khitmutgar flipped his hands ulta-pulta. "No savvy alla runaround. Go here. Go there. Romance, I think."

"Romance!" said Méarana; and the scarred man cocked his head with interest.

"Why you say that, boy?"

"Sahb! Man chase woman; woman chase man. What other reason ever?"

Donovan barked laughter. "Oh, that would be a fine joke! What weight honor and duty when Kam'deev the Bodyless looses the arrows of love!"

Méarana played a discord. "I'm not certain I like that."

The scarred man shook himself and pointed at Billy. "Before I forget . . . That brain I gave you has the dibby that Sofwari left for Bridget ban. It's nothing but columns of numbers. Actuaries work with statistics and data bases. See if you can parse it."

Billy studied the brain in his hand, and a shy smile stole across his features. "Oh yes, sahb. Child of Wonder shows much faith in poor Billy Chins. I work this no long time, you see."

Donovan grunted. "See me when you get back and we'll discuss it."

Billy hurried off to do his duty and Méarana said, "Do you think he can do it?"

Donovan spread his hands. "He claims to be good with that sort of thing. Don't let his dialect fool you."

Reading and harping then claimed them, and for a time a soft melody floated in the suite's air. "The Hunt for Bridget ban." It was a variation on a melody of hers that her mother had especially liked and, playing it, she felt as if the music drew her mother toward her. But she plucked it from the *third* mode; and Méarana was quite aware of what that signified. Even in its gentler chords the third smacked of anger—more fire, and the yellow bile. She had chosen it without thinking. Yet, until she knew who had wrought her mother's fate, against whom might the anger be directed?

A few minutes later, Donovan rasped in his throat. Grateful for an excuse to break off a strain that had grown too labored, Méarana stilled her strings with the flat of her hand. "What is it?" she asked him.

Donovan struck the reading screen with his knuckles. "This is an *abridged* edition of *Commonwealth Days*— compiled on Ladelthorp eighty metric years ago. The publishing history cites an original edition three hundred and fifty years earlier on Friesing's World."

The harper nodded. "And?"

"And which edition did your mother read?"

"Ah."

Donovan tossed the reader screen aside. "Send another message to your pal, Tenbottles, and ask him to find out. And while he's at it, check the editions and revs for all the other books as well. Meanwhile, I have to write a summary report for Greystroke and Hugh and drop it on them when we pass through Yubeq."

Méarana raised her brows. "We're not holding things back anymore?"

"Of course, we're holding things back. Only not the same things."

Mèarana bent over her harp and plucked out a small, cheerful melody to hide her smile. "You ought to become friends again."

Donovan grunted. "Call it gratitude, for want of something better."

The harper laughed. "Fudir might be grateful for the Harpaloon sacred books. I doubt Donovan is."

"It wasn't that. Or not just that. Greystroke . . . Never mind what Greystroke did. Using the Hounds is the logical thing to do. The Kennel can better track Sofwari. He cannot have covered his tracks so well as a Hound."

"And if we find Sofwari, we find Mother!"

"Or we'll find where she's buried."

It wasn't a fair shot. Donovan had dug deep and pulled the dart from some dark quiver of his mind. She hadn't been expecting it, and the point sank deep into her. She turned and fled from the common room. Donovan looked away. "But more than likely," he told the now empty room, "he's gone missing, too."

Fifty metric minutes passed before Billy returned, and Donovan had begun to wonder at his absence. When he reappeared, he clutched a message packet in his hand.

"This come for sahb!" he said in a voice as shaky as the hand.

Donovan took the packet and saw that it was addressed only to "the man with the scars upon his head." And who in the Spiral Arm knew that such a man was aboard *Gerthru van Ijębwode*? He grabbed Billy by the blouse. "Where did you get this?" Inner Child gibbered: <The courier! On board!>

"Please, sahb! Message, he find me at concierge. Signal-man not savvy 'the man with scars'; but he knew you wear him, the skullcap. I say, too, Where you get this? Sahb! He come in upsquirt from Nee Stoggome during the fly-by. How this man send him know you here?"

Donovan studied the packet seal more closely. An external receipt stamp from the signal room. Place of origin, Dancing Vrouw, forwarded via the Circuit. CONFIDENTIAL. That meant that the message had been decrypted automatically from a standard "blindside" commercial code. Anxiety drained suddenly from him. He clapped Billy on the shoulder. "Simple, boy! He sent the same message to every ship that left Dancing Vrouw. Place a bet on every number and you win every time!" The scarred man broke the seal and extracted the slip.

DONOVAN, the slip read. TWO HUNDRED THOUSAND IN GLADIOLA BILLS OF EXCHANGE TO YOUR ACCOUNT AT JEHOVAH'S TRUST WHEN YOU ABANDON YOUR USELESS SEARCH.

It was not signed, of course. Its mere existence was signature enough.

"What message say, sahb?"

Donovan shook his head. "It says, 'Don't throw me in the briar patch, Bre'er Fox.'" He smiled at Billy and crumpled the message in his fist. "Someone wants to pay me to do something I've been aching to do."

"What was that?" asked Méarana, who had emerged from her room, eyes raw and face red and puffy. She held the harp against her chest like a shield.

Donovan tossed the crumpled message and it arced gracefully into the flash hole, where it flared into ash. "An offer to buy a double-gross of your medallions."

The harper cocked her head and plucked a few random notes. She said, "A generous offer?"

Donovan nodded. "Very."

"Then, I suppose, we had better find some."

Donovan sighed, and closed his eyes, and . . .

. . . *and the table is dark wood, longer than it is wide, and no less well-wrought for being imaginary. The room it centers is vague and shades off into shadows in which flare dim lamps that cast no pools of illumination and whose muted reflections glimmer in the table's polished surface. Ten padded, high-backed chairs ring the table and before each lies a pad of smart paper and a light-pen.*

Seven of the seats are occupied, each by a version of himself.

Donovan looks around the circle. "Whose idea was this?"

Pedant's, *says the Sleuth. The Sleuth is a whippet of a man, so lean that he seems taller than his companions. Sharp eyes flank a thin, hawk-like nose and confer an aspect of alertness, as his prominent, squarish chin bestows determination.*

"I've always wondered what you looked like," *says Donovan.*

Irony becomes you, *the Sleuth responds.* Would you like me to describe your self?

"What need? We are identical septuplets, are we not? Only the seemings differ."

𝕿𝖍𝖊𝖓, 𝖙𝖍𝖊 𝖘𝖊𝖊𝖒𝖎𝖓𝖌 𝖎𝖘 𝖜𝖍𝖆𝖙 𝖒𝖆𝖙𝖙𝖊𝖗𝖘. 𝕽𝖊𝖈𝖆𝖑𝖑 𝖙𝖍𝖆𝖙 𝖆 𝖒𝖆𝖓 𝖘𝖍𝖆𝖗𝖊𝖘 𝖆𝖑𝖑 𝖇𝖚𝖙 𝖆 𝖋𝖗𝖆𝖈𝖙𝖎𝖔𝖓 𝖔𝖋 𝖍𝖎𝖘 𝖌𝖊𝖓𝖊𝖘 𝖜𝖎𝖙𝖍 𝖙𝖍𝖊 𝖈𝖍𝖎𝖒𝖕𝖆𝖓𝖟𝖊𝖊. 𝕭𝖚𝖙 𝖙𝖍𝖎𝖘 𝖉𝖔𝖊𝖘 𝖓𝖔𝖙 𝖘𝖍𝖔𝖜 𝖍𝖔𝖜 𝖆𝖑𝖎𝖐𝖊 𝖆𝖗𝖊 𝖒𝖆𝖓 𝖆𝖓𝖉 𝖈𝖍𝖎𝖒𝖕, 𝖇𝖚𝖙 𝖍𝖔𝖜 𝖑𝖎𝖙𝖙𝖑𝖊 𝖌𝖊𝖓𝖊𝖘 𝖒𝖆𝖙𝖙𝖊𝖗 𝖎𝖓 𝖙𝖍𝖎𝖓𝖌𝖘 𝖙𝖍𝖆𝖙 𝖒𝖆𝖙𝖙𝖊𝖗.

Donovan thinks he would have recognized Pedant even without his ponderous pronouncements. His body appears somehow corpulent; his face massive, like a man who has lately enjoyed a very large dinner. His gray, watery eyes give him a dreamy, introspective countenance. He rumbles with laughter. Aristotle compared the act of knowing to the act of eating. In either case, you take something in, and you make it a part of yourself.

It is the sort of irritating "factlet" that Pedant emits like particles from a lump of radium—allieviated only by his periodic sulks, as if he withdrew into a private club where the members never speak to one another.

Donovan's inner eye flickers from one persona to another. "So, what's the agenda, and why the elaborate visualization?" He looks to the Fudir, who usually has control of the visual cortex, but the scrambler sits at the far end of the table, his expression masked by distance.

"Will you take the bribe?" the Fudir asks.

"Two hundred kilobills?" Donovan laughs. "Why not?"

To his right, farther down the table, the Brute rumbles. That version of Donovan seems as large as the Pedant, but harder, more solid, yet at the same time lithe and athletic. The hardness extends even to the eyes. *We shouldn't run out on her,* he says. *Can we be bought for so little?*

"It's not that little. It's enough to keep Fudir drunk for as long as he likes."

The Fudir shakes his head. "You're the one who needs to numb the fear with spirits."

"Or is it," says Donovan, "to numb the spirits."

"A nice play. But, which spirits?"

"The spirits of the past who haunt your present."

"Bastard."

"And it's less that we abandon her, Brute, but that she abandons her."

Méarana will never abandon her mother. Beside the Brute sits a veiled figure who speaks with a silky and seductive voice.

"Do you think so? She's on the edge of retribution even now. The smallest push . . ."

Retribution? For what?

"How often has Bridget ban abandoned the harper? Why not return the favor just this once?"

Is morality transitive, then? Does her abandonment justify ours?

Bridget ban was sent on assignments, *says the Sleuth.* That's not abandonment.

"A touching faith in logic, Sleuth. But it's not what something is that matters, it's what that something seems. I never said she *intended* to abandon the quest. I said she felt *entitled* to do so."

The Fudir speaks from the far end of the table. "How would you know how she feels, Donovan? You'd need feelings of your own to recognize them in others."

Donovan cocks his head. "Perhaps you ought to ask Pedant to purge those memories. The ghosts seem to bother you."

"Not his memories to purge. What of *your* ghosts? You're the one Those tortured. I slept through the whole thing. Small wonder you run in fear."

A smaller version of Donovan, one with large, wide eyes and prominent ears, slips from his chair and scampers about the perimeter of the room. From the ill-defined darkness come the sound of door latches jiggling, of bolts shutting home. <The courier hasn't caught up yet; but we should bar the doors.>

"Those aren't real doors, Child," *Donovan chides him.*

<And Zorba . . . Zorba will hunt us down if we abandon her!>

"If we bring her back safe, Zorba has no complaint coming."

"And what of Bridget ban," *says the Fudir,* "and her discovery? Does Zorba not want those as well?"

"His threat covered only the harper," *Donovan answers.*

"If he wanted a broader contract, he should have laid out the terms more clearly. Let it go, Fudir. Bridget ban is gone. Zorba knew that. Eventually, even Méarana will know it. And whatever she discovered—or thought she had discovered—is best left lost. Weapons that save the world have the power to wreck it."

Don't be so sure.

"Sure of what, Sleuth? That she's dead? Or that dreadful weapons should be left alone?"

That the courier has been left behind.

"Ahh. Don't let that message spook you. You're reading too much between the lines."

𝕿𝖍𝖆𝖙'𝖘 𝖜𝖍𝖆𝖙 𝖎𝖓𝖙𝖊𝖑𝖑𝖎𝖌𝖊𝖓𝖈𝖊 𝖒𝖊𝖆𝖓𝖘. Inter legere, 𝖎𝖓 𝖙𝖍𝖊 𝖔𝖑𝖉, 𝖉𝖊𝖆𝖉 𝕽𝖔̄𝖒𝖆𝖛𝖆̄𝖘𝖎̄ 𝖙𝖔𝖓𝖌𝖚𝖊. "𝕿𝖔 𝖗𝖊𝖆𝖉 𝖇𝖊𝖙𝖜𝖊𝖊𝖓."

Surely, a man smart enough to send messages to every ship is intelligent enough to learn on which ship it found its mark.

"You don't expect they'll really pay up, do you?" says Fudir. "Two hundred thousand Bills, just to go home and drink? We used to do that for free. The likelier payment is knives between our ribs, not bills between our fingers."

<If Those of Name know that Bridget ban was tracking down some sort of weapon against them, why would They give up the quest even if we do, even if Méarana does, even if Bridget ban failed?>

"What matter? We'd be out of it—back on Jehovah, the harper back on Dangchao. Off the bull's-eye."

No. If Bridget ban found the weapon before They killed her, They would already have it. But if They killed her before she found it—or if the finding of it killed her—They don't yet know where it is, either.

Donovan says, "That the finding is what killed her is not the best argument you could have mustered for pressing the search."

Think it through, Donovan. If the harper is the best handle for tracking Bridget ban, and hence for finding the weapon, how long before Those come for her? And who will be there to protect her?

Silence descends upon the group, into the midst of which the Fudir eventually drops the comment, "Zorba would not like that."

"What! Are we to look after her for the rest of her life?"

That would seem the logical deduction.

And are we not duty-bound to do so?

"No proof of that. If the harper stirred a pot, that's her look-out, not ours. She's no child, to escape the consequences of her own decisions."

"Oh, that we could escape the consequences of ours!"

"It's a tough Spiral Arm. No one ever promised safety or success."

You can't mean that!

"Can't I? All in favor of taking the money, raise your hand."

Ghostly images raise hands: Donovan, Inner Child, Sleuth.

"Sleuth!" says the Fudir.

It's the rational course.

"Damn reason! But that leaves four opposed."

He, the Brute, and the Silky Voice raise their hands—in consequence of which all eyes turn to the Pedant.

But the ponderous body shakes the massive head. I am facts, and to take the bribe or not cannot be answered with facts. "Is" does not equal "Should." Neither logic nor fear nor sentiment nor brute strength nor any other fragment of who we once were can provide an answer. Rather, the contrary.

Three to three with one abstention.

The Fudir raps knuckles on the table. "The point is moot. We can do nothing until Siggy O'Hara. I say we accompany her within the Circuit. Anything we learn, we can turn over to Greystroke and Hugh."

Donovan sighs. *"I remember when we were only to escort her to High Tara."*

The Brute rumbles. **Just a question here, but anyone else wondering about the empty seats at this table? Pedant, you set this up. Why ten chairs?**

The massive face appears startled. 𝔍 𝖉𝖎𝖉 𝖓𝖔𝖙 𝖗𝖊𝖆𝖑𝖎𝖟𝖊 . . .

I did. *Like the Brute, the Sleuth had access to the sensory inputs.*

"Why do ten imaginary chairs matter more than seven?" *says Donovan.*

Child, you have the imagination. Did you . . . ?

<Not me, Silky. I'm the Guardian. I imagine threats.>

Yeah? Too many of 'em, you ask me . . .

Impatient with the chattering, Donovan opens his eyes and . . .

. . . and he was back in the common room, to find that he had staggered slightly and that the harper had grabbed a hold of his arm to keep him from falling. "Are you all right?" Méarana asked, and Donovan saw his opening and ducked into it.

"How . . . long was I out?" he asked, with more confusion than he ought.

"A few moments. You muttered."

Donovan imitated a chuckle. "Good old Fudir. He does run on. I . . . don't feel well." He allowed her to lead him back to the settee and lower him gently into it.

"Billy," she said, "fetch sahb Donovan an orange juice." While the khitmutgar rushed to do her bidding, Méarana arranged pillows around the scarred man. "Better?"

Donovan tried to speak, only to find the Fudir holding his tongue. His voice slurred like that of a man following a seizure. The Fudir realized that this only abetted Donovan's plans, and let go. "Yes," Donovan choked out. "Better. Thank you, boy." He drank the proffered juice, handed back the empty glass. "Méarana . . . I think this journey is taking too much from me. I'm tired and confused. We should lay over for a time, recover my strength." He wheezed for effect, trying not to overdo it.

The harper sat across from him and leaned her arms on her knees. "Do we dare? What of the Confederate courier?"

"Oh, mistress," Billy sang from the sink, where he was cleaning the glass. "He follow long *Lola Hadley* to Jemson's Moon. Sahb Donovan tell so."

"No," Donovan replied. "He'll query *Lola* over the Circuit, and by now they know we're not aboard . . . It will take a while. *Lola* can communicate only while passing through encircuited systems. So we have a lead on him, but he'll untangle the skein eventually and . . ." He enclosed both her hands in his. "I don't know what I can do when he catches up."

"Maybe we should have . . ."

"What?"

Méarana disengaged. She looked away. "Maybe we should have accepted Greystroke's offer and turned everything over to him." She would not look at him and her hands worked a harp she did not hold.

Donovan spoke as if in reluctant admission. "Greystroke and Hugh have better resources . . . Why mind the stove, if they will cook the meal?" Donovan had never believed that the harper was chasing after Bridget ban "because a daughter knows her mother." What daughter has ever known that? She was chasing Bridget ban because she was chasing Bridget ban; and had been chasing her all her life. "Let it go."

The challenge struck hard. Donovan could almost see the fracture lines streak across the quartz of her resolve.

He could almost see her crack; and he knew that the next words she spoke would be to abandon the quest.

"When we reach Siggy O'Hara," she said. And Donovan waited for her to finish, but she only shook her head and turned away before she could weep, and retired to her own quarters.

VII THE FREEDOM OF CHOICE

A *certain freedom comes from the abandonment of obligation; a sense of boundlessness from the lack of bonds. So the remainder of the transit to Siggy O'Hara ran more carelessly than had the initial part. A kind of melancholy settled over Méarana's playing, not only in what she played privately in their suite, but even in what she performed in the first-class lounge at Captain-Professor van Lyang's request. A sweet sadness informed her choice of mode and tempo. Méarana, it seemed, had begun to accept the facts.*

Except that Bridget ban's death was not yet a fact, as the Pedant periodically reminded everyone. It was merely a reasonable abstraction from the facts that the Sleuth had drawn. Yet no one loved a puzzle better than the Sleuth and from time to time the scarred man found himself unwillingly wondering how that death might have come about.

Inner Child was just as happy not to know, because to learn it they would have to track the Hound to the end of her trail; and the closer they approached that end, the closer they would approach their own.

No, the best of all possible worlds was that Méarana resign herself to reality and abandon the quest. That would satisfy Zorba—and those who had offered the bribe.

There lingered, too, the possibilities that the Confederates had learned of Bridget ban's objective, that they would not pay the bribe, that they would not leave Méarana unmolested. Donovan told himself not to worry over the future, although as the Fudir reminded him, the future was all that one *could* worry over. You may forget your cares, he told Donovan, not without a little satisfaction, but do not be so sure that those cares will forget you.

Meanwhile, he resigned himself to too much keening of the goltraí from the harper's *clairseach* and to wondering from time to time why there had been three empty chairs at an imaginary table. He could see but three possibilities: That he had lost parts of his mind and had forgotten even which they were; that there were emergent fragments yet unrealized; or that the Pedant had been careless in imagining the boardroom. He settled on the third possibility as being the most comforting; but the Fudir reminded him, too, that while the truth set you free, it seldom did so in comfort.

And so they came to Siggy O'Hara, a world named after an ancient battle on Olde Earth, in which a Duke O'Gawa had defeated "Toy" O'Tommy. The very reasons, let alone the passions, of that battle had been long forgotten, but every local autumn, O'Haran nations staged mock combats in which fantastically armored reenactors fired off cannon and muskets and swung long, two-handed swords. It was all great fun and hardly anyone was ever killed. Scholars fretted over authenticity and thought the armor used was an anachronous mixture of ancient Yùrpan and Nìpný fashion. They doubted that the two original armies had painted their armor blue and gray, or even that they had worn turbans. But authenticity had never been a concern of the reenactors. It was an autumn celebration, a last carouse of color before dead winter.

The harper, the scarred man, and their servant Billy Chins left the "Hurtling Gertie" at High Kaddo Platform in the O'Haran coopers, and checked into the Hotel of the Summer Moon under their own names, there to await passage to Ramage on the upper curl of the Spiral Staircase, whence to Jehovah, and home. Far below them, the Siggy sun was a pinpoint, brighter than most and with a faintly crimson cast.

Harping was less iconic among the O'Harans than in most of the Periphery. In olden days, the system had been isolated from the mainstream and had developed its own peculiar traditions and musics. Only with the Opening of Lafrontera had history caught up with her. Traffic had coursed through from Alabaster and the older inward worlds, like the wave front of an explosion. The settling of Wiedermeier's Chit, Sumday, and other worlds had been an unsettling period for the O'Harans. Long-standing customs had teetered and very nearly toppled. Though never as wild as Harpaloon on even a quiet day, Siggy O'Hara had afterward, tortoise-like, pulled in her head, and vowed that such times would never come again. Commerce with the rest of the League was tightly controlled by the "Back Office" of the McAdoo.

Days passed while they awaited a ship to take them to Alabaster and Ramage. None with open berths were scheduled, but Donovan visited the shipping office each morning in case new vessels had been logged on the Big Board. Most of Lafrontera was outside the Circuit—Siggy O'Hara was its outermost station—and inbound ships oft gave no notification other than swift boats dispatched down the roads ahead of them. Ships might arrive only hours behind their beacons. Not long ago, all traffic had operated that way.

While they tarried, a message caught up with them from

Little Hugh, confirming that "Lady Melisonde" had contacted the tissue banks at Licking Stone, Bangtop, and there, too, she had obtained a duplicate of the files copied by Debly Jean Sofwari and "thank you for telling us about the science-wallah." If that last had been intended sarcastically, it did not come across in the machine-printed code groups in which the message had been couched.

"You guessed right," he told Méarana at lunch that day in the hotel's restaurant. "Sofwari was on Bangtop while your mother was at home prepping. He went the long way 'round and she tried to head him off."

"Was he trying to evade her, or had they planned to meet?" the harper asked. "Thank you, Billy." The khitmutgar had interposed himself between the station's staff and his masters, taking the serving dishes from the waiters and spooning portions onto their plates.

"It's Greystroke's problem now," Donovan said.

Méarana pursed her lips and dropped her eyes. "I suppose so."

"That nogut, lady harp," Billy said. "Pickny-meri always belong mama. No one-time never have em." He screwed his brow a moment in thought, then said, enunciating very carefully, "Daugh-ter, she belong always to mother. Never give up."

"Billy!" Donovan said sharply. "It has already been decided."

The khitmutgar cringed. "No beat him, poor Billy. Not Billy's place, talk him so."

Méarana looked sharply at Donovan, but said nothing. She turned to Billy. "It's not final," she told him, "until we board a ship. Donovan, what else did Hugh have to say?"

The scarred man's eyes dropped to the decoded text. Gwillgi had been alerted and was asking questions on Kàuntusulfalúghy, in case they knew where Sofwari was.

I could have done that, the Sleuth told him, *if I had realized his importance earlier. Pedant stuffs his facts away like a magpie. I can't reason from what I don't know.*

A poor workman blames his tools.

The scarred man's fist clenched. **Quiet! The both o' youse!**

And so before Donovan could answer Méarana—*nothing of consequence*—she had plucked the message slip from his hand and read it. "Maybe Gwillgi can learn something," she said.

"He'll learn that Sofwari never reconnected with Bridget ban. A blind alley."

"But we may learn," she said with some of the earlier excitement in her voice, "what Sofwari was searching for, which had *something* to do with what *she* was searching for."

"Let the Kennel roll over the rocks. Something may crawl out."

She looked at Hugh's message again. "What does he mean in the postscript: 'Fudir, what is the Treasure Fleet?'"

Donovan snorted. "It means he is playing the game, too. He learned something on Bangtop and isn't telling us what it is."

"Then there *is* something to learn! What *is* the Treasure Fleet?"

Donovan snatched the message back. "How should I know?" But he felt a stir in the back of his mind and thought that the Pedant had some bright ribbon of fact tucked away back in his nest.

Later, Méarana, concerned that the scarred man was sinking back into the glum haze in which she had initially found him, pried him from the comfortable chair in which he preferred to await, drinking soggy, the arrival of a ship inward bound for Alabaster. "Let's go for a walk, old man," she insisted. "Let Billy have some time to himself."

"*He* doesn't have a self," the scarred man retorted. "I have it. Right here." And he clenched his left hand into a ball, as if crushing some small and inconsequential object.

But she persevered, and eventually Donovan threw on a cloak and placed a skullcap on his head and followed her out of the room. Billy, who sat at the dining table with a portable 'face, looked up from the screen with a question in his eyes.

"*The Fudir* and I are going to the Starwalk, Billy." This was a cue to the scarred man that Donovan would not be welcome. "We'll be back for dinner. We'll eat in the restaurant, so you don't need to cook anything." In truth—though she would never say such a thing to his face—Billy favored Terran foods, which she found peculiar in flavor.

"It lacks the True Coriander," the Fudir explained when she mentioned this on the esplanade and they had turned their steps toward the Grand Erebata.

"And what is the True Coriander? You told me once, but I've forgotten."

The Fudir's look became distant. "No man knows. We find it in some ancient recipes, but whether vegetable, meat, herb, or a mineral like salt, who knows? It grew only on Olde Earth and its secret has long been lost." He shrugged. "What we really mean when we say that, is 'all that we have lost since we lost Terra, and all that we hope once more to have.'"

The Grand Erebata was an oval atrium that ran end to end through the hotel, and from whose rim jutted diving platforms. Low-g gravity grids at one focus of the ellipse were on the roof; at the other focus on the mezzanine, so that one could leap out into the great open space and fall leaf-gentle in whichever direction one chose. When Méarana hesitated at the brink and looked toward the mezzanine twelve storeys below, the Fudir growled and reminded her that they were in free fall and "down" was an aesthetic choice. "Why do you think they only allow these things in free-falling habitats?"

And so she leapt. And fell upward. Whatever the Fudir had said, it *felt* like up, since the residential floors she passed all shared a common orientation. Gradually, she gathered speed. The god Newton is not mocked. But she had called out her destination when she leapt and the tracers directed counter-grids that slowed her so that she alighted like a dancer on the Starwalk level.

The Fudir was waiting. Méarana slipped her hand through the crook of his arm and they set off around the galleria that circled the "top" floor of the hotel. Faux-windows enclosed them on all sides but the inboard. These reproduced the vista beyond the hotel's shielding and served all the purposes of windows without the hazard of placing a thin pane of glass between hotel guests and hard vacuum. And so they walked, it seemed, through a great glass torus.

While nearby stars were individual points of yellow and white and red and blue, they were no more than free particles thrown off by a great slurry: the Spiral Arm. In that great Core-ward swath of light, individual stars were lost, no more than bricks in a great white wall.

"The Orion Arm," she said, pointing this out. "It's like there is no Rift between us."

"Oh, the Rift is real enough. From Ramage, you can see it clearly. But their 'Orion Arm' is only a part of our Perseus Arm split off by the Rift. Or so the Pedant tells me. This view . . . You get a sense of how small the League and the Confederation are. The vast majority of those stars out there have never shone on human folly."

" 'It's a big Spiral Arm.' That's what they always say. Oh, look! That bright star. The display says it's Siggy Sun. It looks so far away. Yet, we're in Siggy System."

"Those stars," he said, as if not hearing. "They are not

only leagues away; they're years ago. This is a vista of time, as well as space. Blind Rami, were he visible from this angle, would be Blind Rami two centuries ago. Jehovah, a millennium. They are not even contemporary. There are thriving worlds out there where, had we 'scope enough, we would see barren wastes, because *this* light, here, today, is from a time before they were even terraformed."

They had begun their perambulation, slowly clockwise around the torus, as was the custom. Now and then, they stopped to activate a placard identifying this or that distant sight. The Crab Nebula, looking not much like a crab from this direction, hung off in the galactic west, just within the borders of the ULP.

Several large telescopes, called "Hummels," were mounted to High Kaddo Station, and these fed special images to the faux-windows. By touching a spot, that portion of the skyscape would swell in magnification as the Hummels obediently redirected themselves. The Fudir summoned a close-up of the Crab.

"It's as if we zoom out into the cosmos," said the delighted harper. Then, "It's quite beautiful."

"It's much larger than the Crab they once saw on Olde Earth. That was a much younger nebula. In fact, they actually saw it born, though they didn't know it at the time. You see, there was once a star there—a massive, giant star, 'so it is said.' Then, about the dawn of human civilization, the star exploded and collapsed into something the science-wallahs call a pulsing star. It's deep in the heart of the nebula to this day, spinning like a madman and strewing his dusty remnants all over that sector—the Badlands, it's called. It tangles up the roads; so no one goes there, except to mine helium. But light takes six millennia to make the Newtonian crawl from the Crab to the Earth so it did not light the sky there until Old Year 1054. Zhōgwó sages made note of it. Later still, when they could measure such things, the Murkan wallahs found it already eleven light-years wide. That's Earth-years. Today, from Earth, it would appear to be forty light-years wide. But if you actually went over there, you would see that it's more like seventy light-years wide, and still dispersing. That was one hell of a firecracker."

Closer by, he picked out the sun of Alabaster for her. "He's the next star up the Spiral Staircase," he explained. "Other stars are closer to Siggy across the Newtonian flats, but a ship would take centuries to reach them, so in a paradoxical way they are actually farther away. Some say there are undiscovered turnoffs and byways on Electric Avenue that we will one day find. Others say that there are multiple road networks, mutually interpenetrating, but unconnected, so you cannot slide from one network to another. Those inaccessible stars may harbor scores of leagues and confederacies and commonwealths."

"But not human. If there's no connection between their roads and ours, men could never have reached them. 'All Men are One.' "

He shrugged. "Only a fancy of mine. The roads we know may be the only network, and all those other stars as empty as were once the ones we filled. Yet all the human stars, after all the years of settlement, I can cover with my left thumb." He held that thumb out so that it blotted a portion of the sky. "Well," he grudged, "maybe not all of them." He held up his other thumb. "There, that does it." Méarana laughed and the Fudir tapped the window with his knuckles. "All that immensity . . . It makes you feel how small you and I and the whole of humanity really are."

"In all that immensity," the harper answered, "even superclusters of galaxies are small, so I don't see what importance smallness has. I look at it and marvel that all that immensity has produced you and me."

The Fudir chuckled. "Seems a bit overkill. 'The mountain labored and brought forth a mouse!' " A comment that would have been a sneer from the lips of Donovan, was gentle amusement from the Fudir.

"Why not?" said Méarana. "How many acorns lie scattered to make an oak? How many sperm are expended to make a man? Why shouldn't it take a universe to make a world?"

The Fudir paused and stared at her. "By the gods!" He turned to face the Spiral Arm. "By the gods . . . I will never again look upon the night sky without seeing it as . . . as a mass of sperm." Then he could contain himself no more and threw back his head and laughed.

Méarana colored and walked on ahead of him. He hurried after. "Don't be offended."

"You don't take me seriously."

"That's not true. I . . ."

They had come to the portion of the perimeter opposite their entry point and the stars beyond the viewing windows had thinned. There were still more of them than she could count, but she could see that they grew sparser. And beyond that sparsity, nothing. "The Rim," she said.

The Fudir broke off his fumbled apology and simply nodded. "Aye. Technically, the tail end of the Cygnus Arm is out there somewhere; but yes . . . It's a big Spiral Arm, but it reaches an edge at last." He gazed across the thinning carpet of light. "The closer stars are Lafrontera. They shade off into the Wild. There are human worlds out there that have never been Reconnected. When the prehumans broke up the old Commonwealth of Suns, they scattered us far and wide. But most of the worlds out there are empty, barren, never terraformed. Here . . ." He touched an information placard, scanned it quickly, then led her a few paces farther along, where he activated the magnification.

"Skelly Mike," an androgynous voice announced while

a highlighter circled a particular star. "A so-called 'trailer' at the far end of the Cygnus Arm. His orbit around the galactic core takes him beyond the Rim, almost as if he were straining to loose himself from the electromagnetic bonds that hold the galaxy together. His distance from Siggy Sun . . ."

Méarana stopped listening and stared at the vista in silence. "You think she went out there, don't you? Not to Skelly Mike, I mean. Into the Wild."

The Fudir shifted uncomfortably. "If you follow her path, when she left here, she looped through Boldly Go, Sumday, and Wiedermeier's Chit and circled back to here. If you extrapolate that trajectory, it continues through to Alabaster and then, who knows? Ramage, Valency, or one of the other stars in the SoHi district . . ."

Méarana shook her head. "She's not an inanimate object. She doesn't have a 'trajectory.' You think she went out there."

The Fudir sighed. "Yes, I think she went out there. The apparent back-tracking was to throw others off the scent. She could have done that by planting time-delayed drones."

Méarana would not look at him. "We'll never find her, will we? All those stars . . . We'll never, ever know what happened to her."

The Fudir did not answer for a while. What a god-awful haystack, he thought, in which to lose a single needle. Ah, Bridget ban. *Francine.*

She must have been beautiful, said the Silky Voice, not unkindly.

No, not beautiful; not in any conventional sense. But she had an inner light.

"And you were a moth to her flame," whispered Donovan. What happened to the "witch" whose spell you "barely escaped"?

The Fudir made no answer. Turning to Méarana, he said, "No. I don't think we ever will. I never did."

Hot tears flowed down the harper's face. She struck the Fudir repeatedly on the chest with both fists. "Then why, why, why did you come on this useless expedition?"

He took her by the wrists and stilled her punches; and she pressed herself against him and wept. "Maybe," he said, "I was looking for something else."

That night, Méarana sat at the desk in her bedroom reading *Customs of the 'Loon Tribes of Cliff na Mac Rebbe* hoping to find in its turgid pages some hint of why her mother had read it. But so far its only effect was to induce periodic slumber. The author's primary conclusion seemed to be that 'Loon customs were unlike any elsewhere in the Periphery; but surely that could be said of the customs of most any people. She sighed, pinched the bridge of her nose, and closed the screen.

The room darkned with the screen. What did it matter, anyway? She had broken poor Donovan's health, and all for what? What sort of Hell was it when love was alive and hope was dead? Maybe that was what Hell was: the graveyard of hope.

But the quest had not been entirely in vain! They had discovered some things that the Kennel had overlooked: That Mother had met Sofwari on Thistlewaite; that Sofwari had told her something that sent her back to Dangchao to spend most of two weeks behind the doors of her study. They had learned that she was searching for the source of the medallion, and that she had traveled as Lady Melisonde. All told, that was not much; but it was not nothing.

Greystroke and Hugh knew of these things now, and perhaps now the Kennel would resume the search—and have better luck in it than she could hope to have.

Perhaps it was time to think of herself. That was all Mother ever thought of.

It is the nature of man to be selfish, Mother had said. (And Méarana remembered a much younger self, sitting by Bridget ban's knee before a great fierce fire in Clanthompson Hall, while certain wounds of her mother healed.) It is a weakness passed down from our uttermost ancestors, the original sin from which all others arise. It emanates from the ancient brain stem and spreads by electrical synapses to the cortex, establishing by repetition its debilitating pattern.

The more these patterns of self-indulgence dominate, her mother had cautioned her, the less your capacity for reason. The brain stem is not in the final analysis a thoughtful companion.

But her mother rejected predestination. Whether the curse is carried in the genes, as the Calvinist prophet Dawkins had claimed, or whether it involves apples and serpents, as still older allegories run, a man can school his soul to a "second nature" and so overcome the curse. By diligent exercise, he can establish habits of thought that temper or block these signals with neural patterns of their own. With prudence, justice, moderation. And courage.

And Bridget ban had displayed to her awestuck daughter images from the emorái *machine of her very soul: the sparking footprints of thought running through her mind.*

There were too few such moments in her memory, though each one burned there with a certain intensity, as if like diamonds they compensated with their brilliance for their rarity. She had found herself when young wishing that her mother would be hurt again, forced thereby to convalesce at home. A minor wound—a child is none too clear on such matters—one that did not truly hurt. Had that not been a kind of selfishness?

Mother?

Yes, Lucy?

Who was my father?

Oh, he was a brave man, a clever man. We had a great adventure one time, he and I and some others.

Perhaps she had shown courage enough in pushing the quest this far. Perhaps it was time to show prudence, and give the whole thing up.

But what, then, of justice?

She grew aware of a soft tapping at her door and thought it might have been ongoing for some time. Rising abruptly from the desk, she went to the door and threw it open.

It was Billy Chins. He held a message packet in his hand and had his data 'face tucked under one arm.

"It's late, Billy," she said and started to close the door.

"Please, missy," he said, thrusting his hand out. "This come when you and sahb on Starwalk. This tok address him you, from home. I forget till now, but now I think, maybe mama come home and this tell you so?"

Méarana did not believe that, but stranger things have happened and she snatched the message from his hand in a spasm of hope and broke the seal. Billy watched with half an eye while he set his reader screen on her desk and woke it.

The message was from Hang Tenbottles and it contained only the unabridged edition of *Commonwealth Days* that her mother had read. It had been peeled off the master copy at the Archives at Sannaklar on Friesing's World. Weirdly disappointed—she had had no right to expect anything more—she tossed it to her desk. "And what are you doing, boy?" she snapped. Billy had had no cause to raise her hopes even so unwittingly as he had.

He was setting up his 'face as a holo stage. "Oh, please, Mistress Harp. Sahb Donovan, he larim—I mean, he 'give up.' Āmmasmarpaña kranā. He is kaput! No more help you find mama-meri. So he no laikim tru for see this. I show you, even if he beat me for such."

He had activated the stage and a holo image now hovered above it. Méarana crossed over and studied it.

"What is it, Billy?"

"Is dibby from Sofwari left by Harpaloon. Make no meaning, alla code numbers. But Billy smart. He have *second* dibby, come from Dancing Vrouw, and I think, Billy, I say, why not run matchim up? So I find him the Vrouw data in the Harpaloon dibby." He beamed.

Méarana sighed with exasperation. 'I'm sure the dibby Sofwari left on Harpaloon included the data he had already harvested on Bangtop and Dancing Vrouw."

Billy's head bounced enthusiastically. "And Thistlewaite. Even earlier files from other places. But, missy, tissue bank on Vrouw, *she no use code numbers*, so I translate some of dibby. Find code numbers mean for birth-worlds, for people-groups, and so. Then put those into data columns for Bangtop and Thistlewaite and find more by the crossing of references. Then I do same with Bangtop data from Rinty. Is Sofwari find thirty-two people-groups!"

"I'm sure that is very interesting, but . . ."

"So I make map by birth-worlds of different groups. Also other maps, time plots, frequency plots, correlation plots, and so cetera. Billy hard worker. But they tell no nothing. See here."

Méarana saw that the holo was a map of the Periphery. One corner of the map bore a legend:

- Group 1:
- Clanmother: Anandi
- Origin: ca. 2000 years bp
- Central Locus: Megranome

In the holomap, Megranome glowed bright red. Abyalon, Old 'Saken, and several worlds in the Cynthia Cluster were orange; Die Bold and Friesing's World, yellowish; and Venishànghai and scattered other worlds were blue.

"What means it, Lady Harp?" Billy implored. "Billy, he make sense of data, but not make sense of sense."

Méarana laughed at his syntax, but then reflected that the tangle had gotten it straight. The dibby meant the map; but what did the map mean? She flicked through some of the other groups: Kadrina, Khyaddy, Geeda . . . All female names, alphabetically ordered not according to Gaelactic but according to customary usages on some of the Old Planets. Most showed a "central locus" within the Old Planets shading off to other worlds. A few bore the note "Origin Before Cleansing."

She recalled that Sofwari had been doing genealogy. She studied the map now showing. "This map means that 7200 years ago, some woman named Taruna—Now, how could he know her name? Right. Someone he *code-named* Taruna lived somewhere across the Rift, and her descendants wound up on Old 'Saken and a few other worlds, probably during the Cleansing, and from there later descendants emigrated and settled on still other worlds. The color codes seem to indicate where Taruna's mighty chondrians appeared most frequently."

Billy's expression showed bewilderment. "But . . . who cares?"

Méarana thought about the way a drop of dye spread through a glass of water. "I think it shows patterns of migration and settlement."

"We know him yet. Old Planets, numma one settle; then people walkabout other pless."

"Billy, when they did 'walkabout,' they sometimes found people on the new worlds. Where did *those* people come from?"

The khitmutgar stammered a bit and Méarana said,

"Look . . . See Lummila here? Her—what was the other term? 'Little thread shapes.' Her little thread shapes are 8100 years old, which means she lived Before Cleansing. But where are most of her descendants? On Venishànghai, other worlds in the Jen-jen, and on New Chennai, Hawthorne Rose, and Agadar. So the prehumans planted us on more worlds than the Old Planets. But the Old Planets rediscovered star-sliding first and started the Reconnection."

"Okay, mistress. But was Dao Chetty cleansed Old Earth and settled poor Terries across the Rift."

"That's what everyone still believes, but . . . Well, never mind." She copied the files to her own machine. She wasn't sure why Mother had found this interesting. She wondered which of the "clanmothers" she herself descended from.

Billy hesitated, and shifted from foot to foot.

"Yes, Billy, was there something else?"

"I tingting me . . . What is you say, I *think* . . . maybe is got clue that dibby. Billy don't know what, but maybe you see him the clue? Maybe say where mama-meri go?"

Méarana sighed, folded the projector fibers, and handed Billy his deactivated screen. "Maybe Greystroke can figure it out."

Billy still did not move. "Billy says no wrong, you. But what mean him your mama when Greystroke find her, not her pickny-meri. What mean him you?"

Méarana's lips thinned and she stood bolt upright. "Are you scolding me? How dare you lecture me on duty!"

The khitmutgar bowed his head. "Mistress Harp. Who know duty more than Billy Chins?"

"Sahb Donovan is waiting for a flight to Alabaster, and you have to go with him. Do you expect me to roam Lafrontera, to go into the Wild—alone?"

Billy gathered himself and stood to attention, touching his forehead with the back of his hand. "No, memsahb! Billy Chins go with! You better go-with man than Donovan."

The announcement so surprised the harper that she sank slowly to her desk chair, strangely touched by the little man's offer. "I thought Donovan possessed your life, and if you left him you would have to kill yourself."

Billy shrugged. "Aţangku much complex custom. You think mama-meri you go into the Wild, yes?"

"Yes, I think she went into the Wild."

"And we go follow, we die that place?"

"Very likely."

Billy spread his hands. "Then custom satisfied."

Méarana laughed, but it was a sad laugh, a goltraí. She placed a hand on the man's shoulder. "Does Donovan really beat you?"

Billy hung his head once more. "Should no speak budmash of master. Billy try the patience no few time."

"There's no excuse. I will speak to him for you."

"No, no, lady harp. Big dhik. Such-much trouble. Silence better." He bowed himself out of the room with his screen tucked once more under his arm. "Donovan," he said at the door, "he take him the money from Those to give up hunt for mistress mother. I no serve man like that. Where you go, I go." And then he closed the door softly behind him.

Méarana sat speechless at her desk for a time. That could not be! Surely, Billy was mistaken! That Donovan might give up the quest because it was hopeless, or because he could contribute nothing to it—those motives she could comprehend. But that he would do so for money seemed beyond even Donovan's calculating nature.

Did it mean that he was not the man she thought he was?

No, it must only mean that Billy had misunderstood some comment of his. Perhaps he had vocalized one of those internal arguments of his, for she had no doubt that among the splinters of his mind were some mighty sharp slivers.

She began shutting down her screen and it reminded her that a file was open. The edition of *Commonwealth Days* that Hang had sent. She would have to remember to copy Donovan in the morning, although she wasn't feeling particularly friendly toward Donovan just now. From curiosity, she entered the table of contents and saw that it was nearly three times longer than the edition she had already read. The Friesing Worlders had evidently intended a reference encyclopedia. Small wonder the Ladelthorpis had brought out an abridged popular edition! She had toyed earlier with the notion of a song cycle based on the tales, but this volume would make it a grand opera!

She saw it two-thirds of the way down the table of contents: "The Treasure Fleet."

After that, she got no sleep at all.

VIII MONSTROUS REGIMENTS

They broke fast in their suite, a sparely furnished room, in keeping with O'Haran aesthetic norms. The walls were bare, save for a single print: an orange circle on white. On the counter, a trickle of water burbled across a bowl of small pebbles and into the recirculator. A tree the size of Donovan's palm grew there. Everything was shining chrome, black lacquer, muted colors. Compared to the dense, dark décor of Dancing Vrouw, the riotous intricacies of High Tara, or the haphazard eclecticism of Harpaloon, the room exuded serenity and peace.

Which was just as well, for the scarred man furnished none. Seldom chipper at breakfast, he grew nettlesome when he found his plans inexplicably awry. He expected plans to go awry. It was in their nature. But he at least expected the glitches to be explicable.

"What do you mean, you plan to keep going?" he asked.

The harper was drinking her usual breakfast of black coff, known locally as *kohii*. "Boldly Go isn't that far down the Concourse," she said over the cup. "It was her next stop, and you can't go planetside there anyway. Why should it bother you?"

"It doesn't bother me. Only, it's foolish; and I hadn't thought you a foolish woman. Beside, it's outside the Ourobouros Circuit. What if you get in trouble? What will I tell Zorba?"

"Tell him I released you from your promise."

Donovan grunted. "I don't think it works that way."

Billy Chins placed a plate of freshly baked biscuits on the table between them and backed away. "Biscuits pliis sahb?" he said, cringing slightly.

"Did you look at the files I sent you last night?" Méarana asked.

The scarred man scowled, wiped his chin with the back of his hand, and looked at the clock. He raised his eyebrows.

The harper relented. "All right, you need your beauty sleep more than most. Look at them, and then we'll talk."

"Do biscuits pliis sahb?" Billy asked again.

Donovan turned to him and said, "Will you sit down and be quiet, boy?"

Billy ducked. "Yes, sahb. Billy sit him down jildy." He took a seat at the table and picked a biscuit from the platter, though he nibbled it with no great sign of appetite. Méarana opened her mouth to say something, but Billy turned beseeching eyes in her direction and so she said nothing.

"I need to get out," she said abruptly, pushing herself from the table. "I need air and trees and brooks; or I need cities and bustle. Something beside hotel apartments and liner staterooms and recycled air and water *and artificial miniature streams in a damned porcelain bowl*!" She strode across the room to where her harp rested on one of the chairs.

The other two stared at her openmouthed. Donovan shuddered as the Fudir took control. "Alabaster," he said, "is plenty outdoors. Ever see the Cliffside Montage? It's out in the Prehensile Desert past Luriname. The prehumans carved the side of an entire butte into the most intricate shapes and figures. It's the farthest of all their artifacts from the Rift." He fell silent as it became clear Méarana was not listening.

He tried another tack. "Boldly Go isn't safe. The matriarchs are always looking for fresh blood, and have been known to kidnap women touristas and 'adopt' them. Without a Circuit Station, you couldn't call for help."

"I can take care of myself," she said, picking up the harp. She began to prowl the room, playing.

> *"Away, away on the Rigel Run* [she sang]
> *And off through California."*

"What's that you're singing?" said Donovan.

"A song I'm working on about people who heaped together all their most precious treasures . . .

> *All we are and all we hope to be*
> *Are outward bound, for hope can never die . . .*

"and they set off to find a refuge from their oppressors in far-off California.

> *Our green, familiar world is fading into time . . .*

"You said something like that yesterday. Time is distance; or distance, time. It's just fragments of song for now.

I can't decide whether it is a goltraí, a sad song of exile and farewell . . .

> *So farewell to ye, all of ye, grand treasure fleet,*
> *You carry our hopes far awa'.*
> *We'll hold ourselves true to ye, never submit . . ."*

"Treasure fleet," said the Fudir. "You're building a song on Hugh's teasing question?"

"California," whispered Billy Chins.

Donovan turned to him. "Do you know what that means? California?"

But the khitmutgar shook his head. "No, is sounding nice. Cali-forn-ya." He rolled out the syllables. "What means it, the word?"

Méarana shrugged. "A place of hope, perhaps; which would make it a geantraí. It could be both, maybe. The sadness of exile followed by the triumph of hope."

Donovan threw his napkin down on the table. "You live in a fool's world, harper. I know what your hope is, what your 'California' is. But, hope dies! It must. Because it hurts too much while it lives." And he strode out of the room and slammed the door to his sleeping quarters.

Billy ate another biscuit, stuffing the thing whole into his mouth, and chewing as he began to clear the table. On his way to the kitchenette, he paused and swallowed. "All bungim waintim?" he said open-faced to Méarana. "You pack him, the luggage?"

She nodded. "Last night."

"Me, too. I come with. You Billy's new memsahb."

"Oh, Billy, you can't help me on Boldly Go. They allow no men on the planet."

"Maybe no help there. But maybe help . . . find 'California.' Is tramp freighter *Reginão Luck* pass through this week for Matriarchy. Big Board, him say so. They take him, the passengers, so Billy make book two berths."

She looked toward the closed door. "I can't . . . just walk out on him."

"Why not?" Billy answered. "He would."

Méarana put her harp in its case, strode quickly to her room, and fetched her bags. She returned to find Billy in the suite's foyer with his own meager belongings. "I should buy you new clothes," she told him. "The Kennel can't object to that, can they?"

But the little man shook his head gravely. "Billy most objectionable man."

They left quietly; but that night, on board the *Reginão Luck*, the harper sang no songs.

Traveling in the limited appointments of a tramp freighter throws one among a class of rough men and women, unaccustomed to the pampering of passengers. The harper's presence meant an addition to their profit but they did not otherwise know what to do with her. There were no stewards.

Into the lack of service stepped Billy Chins. The Corner of Harpaloon had toughened him far more than his obsequiousness had made apparent. Out from under Donovan's thumb, he came out of himself more. He could talk the talk that freighter crews understood, and a certain swagger began to inform his steps. He was still "mistress harp's khānsāmmy," and while he never quite spoke with her as an equal, neither did he bow and scrape as he used to. He collected their meals in the freighter's galley and served them to Méarana in her quarters, always ensuring that she had eaten before he did.

Throughout the brief transit to Boldly Go, Méarana could not shake the guilt for having abandoned the Fudir. Playing for the freighter crew lightened the melancholy and dark; but she could not quite find the joy, and she wondered if she had left a portion of her art behind her in the Hotel of the Summer Moon.

"It wasn't right," she told Billy the day they rendezvoused with the Freight Center in the high coopers of Boldly Go. "I spent years in the finding of him, and minutes in the leaving."

But her servant only said, "Sometimes the search please better than the find."

Bumboats did not drop down-system from the Freight Center, so Méarana and Billy had to wait two days for the regular shuttle run to Stranger Station, the passenger terminal. Arriving at the complex, they found the usual transient hotel, shopping arcades, and other facilities. Boldly Go was an important nexus on Electric Avenue, with connections to Sumday, Gatmander, and Alabaster as well as Siggy O'Hara; and over the next few days, while they waited for the bumboat to drop, several liners and smaller ships entered Boldly Roads for rest stop, maintenance, or terminal activities, and several more passed through "on the fly," dropping and picking up passengers and freight and squirting and receiving comm traffic. Although not as large as Jehovah or Old 'Saken, the interchange at Boldly Go was a prize worth plucking. There had been a war with Foreganger twenty years since and no more than five had passed since Yves Whitefield's mercenaries had briefly seized the transit points. Without an Ourobouros station, the Cooperating Matriarchs of Boldly Go relied on their own Amazon Joint Navy—which had fended off both attempts.

Boldly Go was not a popular destination, and the bumboat carried mostly locals on leave from jobs on Stranger Station. These kept to themselves, chatting in high-pitched, excited voices. The outlanders were a mixed bag: two news agency crews, a dame from Angletar in a blue, head-to-toe *borke,* an Alabastrine businessman in a flowing green-yellow-red striped dashki, a High Taran in fringed cloak and kilt.

The pilot, a thickset woman with close-cropped hair, viewed her outland passengers with obvious disdain. Méarana's long, red hair came under her disapproving eye, as did the head-to-toe *borke.* But the pilot reserved her greatest disdain for Billy Chins and other men onboard.

"Once we reach Charming Moon," she said, "you *bikes* are off my boat! We got a nice holding facility there for males. Got urinals and everything. Whatever your business with down below, you can telepresent. And no complaining about the time lag. Be happy we don't make you do it up here, where you'd have to wait five hours just to trade hellos."

"Well," said the woman in the *borke,* "so would your people on the ground. The inconvenience works both ways." This earned her a scowl from the pilot.

The Alabastrine spoke up. "Boot I'm to meet with high ooficials of Bannerhook Indoostrials, oover the impoortation oof . . ."

"Sure you are, hooter. If you're important enough, someone will come up to Charming. Maybe take your fee personally." Some of the locals tittered at this sally, though Méarana did not understand the humor.

The express boat was equipped with Ramage-built Judson 253 alfven engines, rated for in-system use. So even though Stranger Station was almost thirty-two units up, the crawl was only eight days. By grabbing the strings of space and pulling herself along, the boat could "borrow" some of the local speed of space and maintain a constant acceleration of two standard gees down to Hera Orbit, where she would flip and decelerate at the same rate, "paying back" into the fabric of space. Within the vessel, counter-grids kept the apparent gravity to just over a single gee.

Once the boat was underway, the passengers unstrapped and moved about the cabin. A few headed toward the café, others remained seated and donned virtch hats so they could immerse in games or plays. In the café, the news crew from Sumday set up a game of five-handed rombaute at one of the tables. Méarana sat at a table with Billy, ignoring the scandalized glances from the Bolders. Mixing the sexes at table!

The woman in the *borke* joined them, introducing herself as Dame Teffna bint Howard. Méarana sent Billy to the service bar to buy three winterberry blues. Shortly, a woman from the other news crew—Great Rock News on Alabaster—joined them as well. She had a White Carthusian with a twist and a small deck salad of chaffered lettuce and wet walnuts. "Do you mind if I sit here?" she asked, without awaiting an answer. She belonged to that class of people, Méarana surmised, who never imagined unwelcome.

She introduced herself as Jwana Novski. Typical of Westland Alabastrines, she was tall and lean, with coal-black skin, long thin nose, and blond hair—but she spoke without the characteristic "hoot." When asked, she explained that news faces on her world strove for a general Gaelactic accent. "We're quite aware that people in the older sectors don't take us seriously because of our accent."

The Angletar dame asked what had brought two off-world news teams to Boldly Go, and Jwana said that they were to cover the trial of a celebrated wildman named Teodorq Nagarajan. Succumbing to the wanderlust that his kind often suffered, he had worked his way into the Periphery on a trade ship and had made a name for himself on a number of frontier worlds with his antics. He had, apparently on a dare, gone down to Boldly Go, where he had been caught. "He is what we call a 'hunk,'" said Jwana, making a fist with her right hand.

"But how could a man get down from Stranger Station?" asked Méarana. "Aren't we screened before embarkation?"

Jwana bobbed her head toward Dame Teffna, as if to say *How do we know what's under the wool?* But Méarana thought customs inspectors were not so dim that they would not look underneath!

"Oh," said Jwana, "they can be bribed as easily as anywhere else. And if a man is hunk enough, they might even 'solicit the bribe,' if you know what I mean."

The face for the other news team heard her and laughed. "If he took a bath first!"

Méarana glanced at the Angletar dame, but the woman's eyes were hardly visible through the white grill across the eye-slot. "Mo' to the point," said the dame in a silky contralto, "I heah that his, ah, vigah, might result in an extended sentence."

Billy had returned by then with the drinks and sandwiches. "What strapim for man he go down?"

The Alabastrine pushed her chair a little away from the Terran. "I don't understand your, um, accent."

Méarana said, "*Fou-Chang's Gazetteer* mentions that men are not allowed on the surface, but doesn't say what happens if they go."

"Oh, well," said Dame Teffna, "there's not much immigration to Boldly Go. So poor Teodorq will have to, ah, 'contribute' to their gene pool, as much as he can for as long as he can hold up."

Billy Chins laughed. "Then why not plenty men more go down there jildy?" Jwana and the news face at the other table, who was playing dummy that hand, laughed as she rolled the dice.

"Saving only one thing," said Dame Teffna from behind her screen. "When they finish with him, they cut his head off."

The news faces and Billy stopped laughing.

"Surely, y'all knew that, dears," said the dame. "It does take some of the edge off the humor."

"Here," said the news face from Sumday. "This is a flat of the man. He was in Pish-Toy City on the Southern Scarp—that's on Sumday—and he tried to rescue what he thought was a princess being abducted, and . . . Well, he got himself in the news back home, like everywhere else he's been. Be a shame to shorten him." She handed the flat to Jwana, who passed it on to Dame Teffna. "I've seen him. He was on Alabaster, too." When the Angletaran sighed over the picture, Jwana leered. "I told you he was a hunk."

Billy Chins blinked, and looked at Méarana before he handed the flat to her. "Billy Chins no like piksa men. Like piksa women." But his eyes, the harper saw, were bright.

Méarana took the "piksa" from him and saw that it was a normal flat holo. It showed a very large man with raven, shoulder-length hair pulled back in a tail. He wore a sleeveless vest made of blue canvas. Both shoulders were intricately tattooed. He stood grinning on the top step of what Méarana thought an official building while police freed him of his bonds.

And around his neck hung a medallion in the same style as Méarana's own.

"Billy," Méarana told her servant. "Change of plans. This is a man I want to see."

The news faces exchanged knowing looks and Jwana again made a fist with her right hand. "I like a woman," she said, "who knows what she wants."

Boldly Go's single continent, known simply as The Mainland, rose from the One Great Sea just north of the equator. Elsewhere, scattered strings of volcanic islands marked the submarine rifts of her oceanic plates. The official history was that she had been settled exclusively by women to begin with; but other accounts claimed a later Revolution; and still others a plague affecting only males. The survivors, they said, had made a virtue of their necessity.

Whatever the beginning, the end had been the same. Across the quadrant, men told themselves that the matriarchs did not really mean what they said, and the whole planet was just waiting for the right man to come along. They were invariably surprised to learn that, yes, the matriarchs really did mean it; and whether they had been waiting for the right man or no, he was not it.

For their part, the matriarchs maintained a corps of Amazons to keep the "bad ones" of the desert from troubling the settlements, and to caution their sister matriarchs. Alliances among "Nests" were quick, heartfelt, and abandoned on a moment's bad faith. Still, the Sisters of the Corps, though they fought one another lustily when one matriarch offended another, maintained the Amazon Joint Navy, second to none in Lafrontera. K. P. Charakorthy, the famed "Pirate of the Blue Sun," had learned this when his fleet had come for booty and honor and had departed with neither. It had cost Boldly Go one city—J'lala on the Purcell River—and Charakorthy his entire fleet.

Charming Moon was one of three moderate-sized bodies that stirred the One Great Sea into unusual and irregular tides. The old Commonwealth seed ships that had salted this region of the Spiral Arm had found the Sea already pregnant. Certain chemical reactions almost always tossed off amino acids and eukaryotes and sundry other bits of living matter, although they seldom elaborated further. So Boldly Go was already terraformed and waiting when the Ramage settlers made their way there.

Méarana left Billy Chins on Charming Moon with some

misgiving, but comforted herself with the thought that if he had survived among the 'Loons, he could last a week or so in the relatively benign Men's Room. He would have to pay the genetic tariff, but the harper suspected he would enjoy it.

She dropped to Boditown, capital of the Nest of Boditsya, where the Wildman was in custody. Being a curiosity as well as a prisoner, access was relatively easy to obtain, even for touristas. Méarana learned he was housed in Josang Prison, called the prison and, using her Kennel chit to get past an underling, spoke with the Warder herself. During the visiphone conversation, she noted a display of crystal animals on the shelf behind the Warder's desk, and so before visiting the prison in person, she purchased in an import shop a lovely crystal horse made by Wofford and Beale on New Eireann. Officially, it was not a bribe, but it did smooth the way to the Visitors' Room.

The Visitors' Room was entered through the main offices on Josang Avenue, a bustling thoroughfare with self-directed ground traffic. Méarana had not seen the insides of many prisons, and those only on sims and immersions, but she had not expected a brightly lit and tastefully decorated waiting room done in earth tones and furnished wth planters and chairs and tables. Bowls of patchouli and fragrant pit-roses from the Thatch Mountains gave the room a less-than-incarcerating air. The chairs were comfortable and there were no barriers between visitors and prisoners.

Méarana turned to her escort. "Not exactly escape-proof."

The Amazon sergeant laughed. "Where on Boldly Go could he hide?"

They brought him in a few minutes later. Teodorq Nagarajan was every bit as impressive in person as he had been in the holoflat. The raven hair, the broad, white smile, the smoothly muscled chest and arms, the impression of sheer animal power very nearly overwhelmed. What she had not expected was that he would be so short. He stood at only five feet and five thumbs, a head shorter than Méarana.

Nagarajan was bare-chested and walked with a panther's grace. Each deltoid had been tattooed with a man's head whose beard flowed past the elbow. His pectorals were likewise adorned, though with a dragon and a tiger. When he turned—and Méarana suspected his turning was meant for display—he revealed a pair of oversized cat's eyes on his scapulas. Thus adorned, he would appear ferocious in attack, and vigilant to any who approached from the rear.

His jailors had not taken his medallion from him, for it dangled on its golden chain, flanked by flaming dragon and growling tiger. The disc seemed to rest cupped between dragon's claw upholding it and tiger's paw protecting it.

The barbarian paused in the doorway, assessed the tactical situation, and eyed Méarana and the Amazon in almost a tactile manner. Then he swaggered to one of the chairs and flung himself into it, throwing his right leg over the chair arm, and propping up his chin with his left arm. "Awright, babe," he said in passable Gaelactic. "Ain't no bed in this room, so yuh ain't here for that. Too bad. Dames here, they think looking purty is a crime, so yuh be the first looker I seen. Hey! We could do it in one of these here chairs, if yuh like."

Méarana smiled. "No, thank you."

"Hey, don't mention it. After all, if yuh don't ask . . ."

The Amazon chuckled. "You see what they're like. That's why we keep them off the planet."

Méarana did not want to argue with the escort. "I wonder if he even knows why he is here."

The Wildman grinned. "I stole the Queen's girdle."

"What!"

The Amazon growled. "And you set foot on the Holy Motherland."

Nagarajan twisted in the chair so that he could see the sergeant. "Well, I couldn't very well steal the girdle without coming planetside, now could I?"

Méarana shook her head. "Why?"

"The girdle? Oh, me and this alfven-tech on the *Gopher Broke*—that's a trade ship I hitched a ride on. He told me about some ancient hero name of Herglee what pulled off these ten stunts. Which I told him doing the scuppers below the engines to pay my passage qualified as cleaning out some old horse stable. Well, another stunt was stealing this queen's girdle. So I said, big deal; and he said, so's why'n't *you* do it; and one thing led to another, and . . ." He spread his arms wide. "Here I am." He grinned and added, "We was drinking at the time."

"You mean you took a bet with a stranger to steal the Queen's girdle?"

"Well, it's more like one of them belts wrasslin' champeens wear; but . . . Yeah."

He was so matter-of-fact about it that Méarana decided not to pursue the matter. "How are they treating you here?"

"Not too bad. Ol' Johnson's getting a workout, but after a while it's hard to keep up." Snicker. "Problem is, they's all so you-gee-ell-why."

Méarana thought she picked up about half his dialect. In some ways, it was worse than Billy's patois. "Who is Johnson?" she asked.

Nagarajan winked and fondled his crotch. The Amazon laughed and when Méarana looked her way, the sergeant explained, "He talks about his sperm-ejector in the third person."

And the sergeant distanced it with technical terms, but that wasn't her business. "I notice you wear a rather striking medallion," she said to the prisoner. "May I see it?"

The door opened behind her and the two news faces entered with their female assistants. They took seats to the side and studied their notescreens and discussed image angles and lighting while they waited for their turn. From their hesitant speech, Méarana deduced that they were 'facing with their male technical crews on Charming Moon, and had to wait four beats for the lightspeed lag. To the harper's surprise, the door opened again and Dame Teffna bint Howard also entered.

"Oh! You were so right, Jwana," the blue-garbed woman purred. "He *is* a hunk."

Nagarajan leaned toward Méarana and spoke as if they were old friends. "That must be one ugly babe."

"Why so, sahb Nagarajan?"

"Hey, call me Teddy. Only one reason for a gal to cover herself up like that."

"She might prefer to hide her beauty to avoid harassment."

The Wildman considered that possibility. "One buck gets yuh five yer wrong. Smart money's on ugly."

Considering what had happened the last time Nagarajan had made a bet, Méarana was not about to take him up on it. He was quite capable of leaping the chairs and disrobing the Angletar dame on the spot. She did not ask him what a "buck" was. "I was wondering where you had gotten that medallion."

Of all the questions the Wildman expected to be asked, that one seemed pretty far down the list. He lifted the medallion and studied it as if he had never seen it before. The disc was ruby red and yellow amethysts had been worked into it like the flames of a fire, reaching up around and through it. Minute diamond dust suggested sparks when the light caught it. "This? I taken it off a dead Nyaka warrior."

"Ah. And do you know where he got it?"

The massive shoulders shrugged. "Uh, no? He was dead?"

"You're sure."

"I killed him, didn't I? They stay dead when I do that."

"Where do these Nyakas live?"

"Some boonie planet out in the Burnt-Over District. Why you so interested?"

"Do you know the name of the planet, or how to get there?"

Nagarajan's hand shot out like lightning, and seized hold of the leather thong by which Méarana's own medallion hung.

But Méarana was not called Swiftfingers for no good cause, and her knife had leapt from its sleeve and hovered now underfisted a scant thumbwidth from the Wildman's left eye.

Dame Teffna and the two news crews fell silent. The Amazon sergeant stood away from the wall and her hand had dropped to her stunner. But she made no move to draw it.

A frozen moment passed. Then a smile blossomed on Nagarajan's face. "No harm, Sarge. The lady and me was just showing off our jewelry." He tucked the medallion back into Méarana's blouse. He had barely glanced at it, but the harper suspected he had examined it quite carefully in that instant. He was a man quick with his senses. He smiled again, catlike. "Yuh need to put the killer in your eye," he murmured so she alone could hear. "A man sees in your eye that yuh ain't gonna stick him first, he maybe feels too cocky. I ain't no enemy, so I tell yuh this. Never threaten your enemy and let him be. Better t' just let him be and forget the threats."

Méarana made the knife disappear. Nagarajan sat back in his chair. The leg once more swung over the chair arm. "So, you come in from the District, too?" he continued in a low voice. "An' now you can't find your way back? No worries. I got all the roads mem'rized." He tapped his temple with a finger like a tent peg. "Oh, wait. One problemo. The memory's inside my head, which is gonna get lopped off the next couple days. That's why those ghouls . . ." He meant the news faces. ". . . come to gawk. Heads roll around Lafrontera like bowling balls, but when is it a head so handsome as mine?"

"I'm surprised they haven't shortened you already," said Méarana. "Your modesty is hard to take."

Nagarajan guffawed and slapped the arm of the chair. "But they still wanna know what I done with the Queen's girdle, which I ain't telling. An' no, before you ask, they won't let me go if'n I do. But they're getting tired of asking, and are just about ready to cut things short, so to speak. Tell yuh what. You're a harper by your nails. I want yuh to sing my story, so I don't die forever. Come back tomorrow after these ghouls are done and I tell yuh chapter an' verse on the Exploit of the Girdle."

"And you'll tell me how to find the source of these medallions?"

The barbarian smiled. "Whaddaya think?"

When Méarana stood to leave, Dame Teffna did, too. She embraced each of the news faces, bidding each good fortune with their interviews. "Ta," she said, "I shan't stay about to have that beast sticking his paw between *my* breasts! My dear," she purred to the harper as she caught up, "that must have been simply awful."

On Josang Avenue, Méarana hailed a jitney, one of the open-sided electric cars that cruised the streets of Boditown. "Are you staying at the Hotel Clytemnestra?" Teffna asked. "May I share the taxi? Oh, thank you." She lowered herself onto the bench beside the harper and snapped open a fan hand-painted with chrysanthemums and waved it briskly before the grill in her hood. "Terribly arid here. Would you like some lotion? This heat can*not* be good for your skin."

"I imagine," said Méarana dryly, "that it is hotter in there than it is out here."

The taxi driver had just settled into her seat and, hearing this remark, barked a short laugh. "One gold quarter-piece," she said. "For the both of you together."

Méarana opened the scrip belted to her waist, but Dame Teffna laid a hand on her wrist. "Do pa'don me, dear." Then to the driver, "Twenty minims in Venishànghai ducats, or three-tenths of a Gladiola Bill."

The driver made a face. "I lose on the arbitrage, ladies. Not enough foreign currency to make it worthwhile. Half a ducat. I won't take Bills."

"Half a ducat! My dear, that is terribly steep. Perhaps thirty minims five."

The driver considered that. "You could walk," she suggested.

Teffna sighed. "Oh, very well. Forty. And done."

"Forty *each*," said the driver.

The Angletaran laughed. "Done."

The taxi jerked away from the curb and headed east on Josang. "So, you went in to see the foreign bike, did you?" the driver said conversationally. "He pretty as he looks on the news-bank? No wonder everyone wants to 'visit' with him. They say Wildmen have bigger sperm ejectors than most bikes. That true?"

"I wouldn't know," said Méarana. "I went there to interview him."

"Interview," said the driver. "That what they call it on your world? Where you from, if you don't mind my asking."

"Dangchao," said the harper.

"Angletar," said the borked woman.

"Never heard of them. How do you handle bikes there?"

"I'm sorry," said Méarana. "Do you mean 'men'?"

"Is that the Gaelactic word? I guess so."

"On Angletar, we keep them in clubhouses," said Dame Teffna.

"Ours are free-range," Méarana explained simply.

Dame Teffna turned to her. "Oh, you can't let them run loose, dear. You must understand the distinct duties of the two sexes. Men talk about God and politics, and kill each other now and then—usually because of the talk. Women keep everyone fed and laugh at the men. That's why we wear these *borkes*—so they can't see us laughing."

Boldly Go did not depend on tourism. Consequently, no swarm of functionaries greeted them at the hotel, and there was an interval when Méarana and Teffna stood alone in the hotel's drop-off area. Méarana turned to the other woman and spoke through clenched teeth.

"Donovan, have you lost what little of your mind you have left?"

The Angletaran managed somehow to convey an attitude of social offense without a single part of her body showing. It was all in the posture and in the tone of voice. "What on Earth are you talking about?"

"What 'on Earth'? Who talks like that? Why else hide under that, that body-tent? It's an obvious way to conceal yourself."

"A little too obvious, wouldn't you say?" the dame murmured. "Do you believe them so obtuse that they would not 'check under the hood'?" And so saying, the dame lifted the face-veil of her *borke*.

And the face was undeniably female: the cheeks were fuller and more rounded; the forehead vertical and lacking in brow bossing. The eyebrows were arched and sat above the brow ridge rather than on it. And though the mouth was

wider and the chin more square than was the female norm,
the diversity of humankind throughout the Spiral Arm
more than covered such variations. Almost, Méarana apologized.

Except that the face was also undeniably Donovan's. If
Donovan had a sister, she would look like this. Or, more
accurately, if he had a crazy old aunt in the attic. Teffna
waited with an expression very much like the Fudir's smirk
for the harper to comment.

Méarana closed her eyes and took in a long, slow breath.
"I saved myself five 'bucks,' anyway. What if they 'look in
the trunk'?"

"What do you usually find stashed away in the boot,"
said the dame, lowering her face-veil once more. "Rusted
old tools."

Dame Teffna had scoured her hotel room for intrusive de-
vices upon checking in and did so again. "No reason to
suppose the authorities have any interest in 'Teffna,'" she
said, "so the odds are against the room being bugged, but
I'd rather learn that precautions were unneeded than to learn
that they were."

It was a single room, tastefully done, but in that perfunctory manner that catered only to unmindful business
travelers. There was a bed, a desk with an interface and
holostage. A comfortable desk chair and a more comfortable reading chair with a gooseneck screen. A copy of the
local holy book. Méarana waited until the cleansing ritual was completed before blurting out, "How did you manage it?"

Teffna sat on the edge of the bed. "You left a trail, dear.
I checked with ticketing and . . ."

"No. I mean . . . this." She waved a hand at her face. "If
I hadn't already known Donovan, I'd never have seen the
resemblance."

"Oh. He and the Fudir handed over control. What else could they have done?"

"But . . . Who are you?"

"*They* call me the Silky Voice. You can call me Donna, if you like. It's a title women use on Angletar and would cover nicely if you slip up."

"So, how did you . . ." She waved her hand again.

"Oh . . ." She touched her forehead in the center. "I live straight back, in an apartment the size of an almond—the hypothalamus. I have control of the glandular system, and that regulates basic drives and emotions, promotes growth and sexual identity, controls body temperature, assists in the repair of broken tissue, and helps generate energy. I'm the nurse."

" 'Promotes sexual identity,' " Méarana suggested.

Donna spread her arms in a familiar gesture. "Those who chopped up Donovan's brain thought there might be call for an agent's seductive side. Honey, they got *me*."

"You do sound more seductive than Donovan," Méarana allowed.

"The fourth Tyrant of Valency sounded more seductive than Donovan. I don't mean sexual seduction. For various reasons, I couldn't pull that off. I mean the sort of thing that your mother was so good at. Persuading people, getting them to go along with her plans."

"I would have said your features were 'strong' or 'handsome.' "

"My dear, you tell a woman that when you have no finer adjectives on hand. There's an enzyme that converts testosterone to estradiol. Certain fatty tissues swell or shrink, but the bones don't change. So a bit of water retention obscures the brow ridge and moves the eyebrows north. The laryngeal prominence softens because the angle of the cartilage shifts. The testicles, ah . . . I believe 'recede' is the proper term; but they're still there. Look, do you really want to know all this? It took several days of stretching and swelling and contraction; and it hurt, a lot."

"And here you are. I take it you read the story of the Treasure Fleet."

"'. . . And so the Fleet departed,'" Teffna recited, "'stuffed with all the wonders of the Commonwealth, her berths filled with the sleeping settlers, carrying the hopes of all true sons of Terra. They set their course on the Rigel Run and far-off California. But though the loyal folk of the Commonwealth waited and waited, nothing was ever heard from them again; and in the end the Commonwealth submitted.' But the Commonwealth was long dead when that was written down on Friesing's World. Why do you think it is any more than a fable?"

"Because you were ready to give up, and now you're here."

Donna rose and crossed the room, where she fiddled with her sundries on the vanity. "Is that the only reason I would have followed?"

"Isn't it?"

"Do you suppose there ever was a Treasure Fleet?"

"It doesn't matter."

Donna turned around in surprise. "Why not?"

"It only matters if Mother thought there was, and went looking for it. Remember the message Sofwari left on Harpaloon? We'll find her down that path, whether a treasure lies at the end of it or not."

"If you find *her* at the other end, would that not be treasure enough?"

The remark astonished the harper. But perhaps the Silky Voice had a gentler perspective on such things than Donovan. "I think . . . I think they had found a secret road somewhere in a place called California and they hoped to create a safe haven—colonies far to Rimward of the prehuman zone, from which they could strike the prehuman heartland from the rear."

"And this secret road led them to the Wild? By the gods, girl! No wonder they call it the Wild! What could be wilder than such speculations?"

"But if there is . . . No wonder Mother went in search of it. What if there is a remnant out there of old Commonwealth technology? Something that would 'ward us from the Confederation for aye.' "

The older woman grunted. "Like it warded the old Commonwealth? A great deal of hope to place in a couple of maybes and a fable."

But Méarana was adamant. "Could a fable keep my mother from returning home? She is no fool. She must have known something else. There is something still out there. A Lost Colony—decayed, or devolved, or defunct—and this . . ." She brandished the medallion. "This is connected somehow."

"Enter the Wildman, Teodorq Nagarajan."

"Yes. He knows where these medallions come from and tomorrow he'll tell me."

Donna laughed—and Méarana thought she heard an echo of Donovan in the laugh. "He will tell you nothing. Your mother was no fool? Neither is he. What is your quest to him?"

"But, he told me . . ."

"He told you to come back tomorrow. His reasons are teleological. They are formed to an end—his end. He considers how he might delay that. So, he has not told the Boldlys where he hid the girdle. They delay the execution, hoping to learn. He tells you he knows where your medallion comes from. Maybe you have influence and can free him, or delay the execution. He doesn't know that you do, but he doesn't know that you don't, either, and so the bet is worth the flyer. I don't doubt he'll play some similar game with those news people from Alabaster and Sumday. He'll put off his day of doom as long as he can with things like that. He'll try to give everyone he comes in contact with some reason to stay the axe. He's a clever sod. Don't let that barbarian simplicity fool you."

"Then, we have to rescue him."

"Do we? Why?"

"Because he does seem to know something we need. Because being a man is not a crime."

"It's a crime here."

Méarana looked the faux-woman in the eye and cocked her head.

Donna shrugged. "I never said I wasn't a criminal."

Méarana leaned her elbows on the writing table and rested her chin in her hands. "Now, how do we break him out? Security seemed rather loose. He could overpower the sergeant and walk out the front door."

The old woman gazed toward the ceiling. "And how do you plan to take him off-planet? Buy tickets on the sky ferry to Charming Moon, maybe?"

"That's Donovan speaking. There's no need for sarcasm. Billy can rent a ship, bring it down to some agreed rendezvous, and haul us off. And then . . ."

"And then eight days' crawl at least up to Stranger Station—where the the station police for the Joint Matriarchal Council will simply ignore our fugitive asses . . . ? I don't think so."

"But actually, I was thinking of taking him legally," Méarana said. "Maybe I can use my Kennel chit to commandeer him. That was how Greystroke pulled you off New Eireann."

"You have a fairly broad definition of 'legally.' And while

I admire the flexibility, remember your are not a Pup. I don't know that the matriarch's courts would hand him over to an 'authorized representative' with an expense chit."

"You have a chit, too. Maybe if both of us . . ."

"*Dame Teffna* doesn't have a chit, especially one that identifies her as Donovan buigh of Jehovah."

"Oh."

"Yes, dear. Oh. What you need is a 'get out of jail free' card."

"A what?"

"A notarized League warrant, chopped by a Hound."

Méarana slumped. "Where would we get one? Even if Greystroke is still on Yubeq . . ."

"He is."

". . . a swift-boat would need weeks to reach Siggy O'Hara and queue a message on the Circuit, and weeks for the O'Harans to swift-boat the answer back here . . ."

"Let me think."

"And that's assuming Greystroke gets the message and responds right away."

"I said let me think!" Donna strode across the modest room and sat once more on the bed, where she fell into closed-eye silence. Méarana heard the other woman mutter under her breath in a tone that she recognized as Donovan's. She rose and padded silently to the other side of the room, where she drew the curtain aside.

The sun was setting behind the hotel, throwing long shadows forward into Boditown, as if night were advancing on it in columns, like an army. It was a small town. Smaller than Jenlùshy, *much* smaller than Pròwenshwai, likely no larger than Preeshdad. But it was less ramshackle than either Preeshdad or Jenlùshy, the buildings solid, wider than they were tall, embracing central courtyards. Trees were plentiful, at least along the winding streets and in several parks visible from her vantage point, though sparser toward the red-lit horizon, where housing gave way to rolling grasslands and security bastions against the *bad ones*.

She heard Donovan say, "But we dare not draw attention to ourselves. We've only got the one." And she turned from the window to see Dame Teffna rise from the bed and go to the 'face on the writing desk.

"Do you have something?" she asked.

Teffna pulled from her scrip a standard brain, which she inserted into the receptor. "While I was changing into my dainty self back on Siggy O'Hara," she said, "I sent a Circuit message to Greystroke. He heard back from Kàuntu-sulfalúghy, by the way. Sofwari last contacted the College of Scholars about eight weeks after Bridget ban dropped from sight. He was on Ampāyam, heading out the Gansu Corridor to collect samples in the Wild. As far as they know, he never came back."

"Then we should heigh for Ampāyam as fast as e'er we can!"

"Don't slip the leashes yet. First things first. There's more than one world out the Gansu Corridor. Greystroke can't leave Yubeq just yet, but he did send Little Hugh to Ampāyam to suss things out. He also sent me a warrant."

"A warrant! Then we *can* get Teodorq out of prison!"

"We could . . . except the warrant doesn't say 'Teodorq Nagarajan' in the right places. I'll have to make some changes the Gray One might not approve of. But if it works, we'll be well away from here before the paperwork clears the Kennel. No Circuit station here."

"Can we have it ready by tomorrow? I already set up an appointment."

Dame Teffna shook her head. "I don't know. It's many years since I've practiced the skills. A League warrant is not the easiest thing to alter, and this is one world where I cannot call on the Brotherhood. There are any number of sisters in the Brotherhood, but I'd rather not lean on divided loyalties."

Méarana had never seen Donovan so conflicted before. "I understand. If you're caught . . ."

"If *you* are caught. I can't present the warrant. My chit identifies me as Donovan, remember? That's why I'm worried. If you present it and it doesn't pass muster, then you're for the women's prison. It wasn't supposed to be this way. *Vagōsanā!* It wasn't supposed to be this way."

The harper suddenly understood. "Donna . . . Who was the warrant for?"

Without a word, Dame Teffna turned the screen of the face so that Méarana could see it. She leaned closer.

The warrant was "to secure the person of Donovan buigh of Jehovah and deliver him to the custody of Greystroke Hound or his Pup."

Méarana turned to look into Donovan's eyes. For once, they were steady. For once, all of Donovan was looking back. "This is . . ."

"I promised Zorba I would take care of you," Teffna muttered. "I had to catch up and drop to Boldly Go with you. I had to visit the prison with you. I had to be close enough in case the *bad ones* came looking for fresh blood for their cloning tanks. Rama-rama!" She struck the desk. "What if one these tarka devis harm you? What I tell then Uncle Zorba, hey?"

Méarana reached out but Donna flinched, so she touched the screen gently instead. "This was your 'get out of jail free card.' In case you were exposed . . ."

"I would find some way of telling you where to find it and you'd throw some serious Kennel weight around and spring me."

"So if you alter it to spring Teodorq . . ."

"Greystroke wouldn't like writing a second one. He

stretched a point to write this one. The Kennel doesn't give them out as party favors."

The harper shook her head. "You can't take the chance. We can pick up clues to the medallion elsewhere."

"Of course. But where? We could wander Lafrontera for years before we stumble on them. Besides," and he entered a command even as he was speaking, for the Fudir's skills at forgery did not require the Silky Voice's silence, "Nagarajan deserves to be rescued for his own sake."

Méarana cocked her head. "He does? Why?"

"He staged a panty raid on an entire planet on a drunken bet. A man like that belongs on a hopeless quest."

They sat in a drab outdoor café whose striped canvas awning fended off the blistering midday sun. Lazy fans stirred the tepid air. The white strap-chairs and tables, the "spressaba," and other tattered and faded equipment seemed to have come from their packing crates already sun-worn and in need of repair. Dame Teffna wore a white *borke*; Méarana, a more dignified cut. She had programmed the anycloth to a trim powder-blue coverall with tabbed pockets and epaulets. It was not a uniform, certainly not a Pup's uniform, but it suggested that it might almost be one. She wore no insignia or patches. That would have been pushing matters too far. The Kennel would, in the Fudir's words, "throw the book at her" if she crossed the line from "special representative" to "impersonating a Hound."

"But," said Dame Teffna, "the Boldlys may not be too clear on what a 'special representative of the Kennel' can do. So act as if it means more than it does. Act like the true quill. Show confidence, but try not to lie more than is necessary. The Kennel really does want to learn where Bridget ban was going when she . . . Where she was going. So it's not a lie to say that the Kennel wants Nagarajan as a material witness."

"Donna," said Méarana, "I know how to act like my mother."

The Fudir wagged his head. "I wish it were me going in. If they detect the forgery . . ."

"All the more reason why you can't. Donna, I appreciate the risk you've taken for me."

Dame Teffna lifted her coffee and the tasse vanished behind her face-veil. "What risk?" she said as she put it down. "You're the one they'll seize if my handiwork fails. That's the hard part, you know. It's not hard to risk yourself. It's risking others that gnaws at you." She toyed a moment with the empty tasse. "What time is your appointment?"

Méarana glanced at the Salon of Justice across the street. A heavy, three-storey building, it consisted of a central cupola and two wings. One wing housed the prosecuting magistrates, the other wing housed the police and their laboratories.

"It wouldn't do to be late."

"I know that."

"Does Judge Trayza know why you made the appointment?"

"I told her clark it was Kennel business and let it go at that."

"Good. Good. That helps create an air of importance. 'Need to know,' and all that."

"I'm no fool." With a brisk, snapping motion she opened a tunic pocket and pulled out a timepiece of the Die Bold style. "It's time for me to go."

"Is that set to metric time?" Die Bold and the other Old Planets famously preserved their ancient dodeka time scales in the face of not uncommon confusions with other League worlds.

"All three," she said. "Doo-dah time, Taran Green Time, and it picks local time off the planetary tock." She meant the satellite system that transmitted the standard times around Boldly Go. "Stop fretting. I'll be fine."

Judge Trayza Dorrajenfer was a tall, graceful woman, elegantly dressed in a flowing dark-blue robe and a gold filigreed circlet binding her hair. Her office was an airy room on the first floor of the north wing, adjacent to her courtyard. Everything was done in plaster or plastic or metal, except the desk and chair, which were wood imported from Kwinnfer in the forested northeast. In the corner stood a rack of spools that Méarana took to be law books. A small fountain emitted a fine spray that kept the room cooler than it otherwise would have been.

The judge came from behind her desk and took Méarana's proffered hand between both of hers. "Welcome to my chambers, Méarana Harper," she said, guiding her to a pair of shapeless bags which, to the harper's surprise, turned out to be chairs. When she sank into the one indicated, it conformed itself to her contours.

"My, these are comfortable, your worship."

"Please. Call me Trayza. You've never seen smarticle chairs?"

"I've heard of them, but I've never seen them. I'm surprised to find them here—"

"There may not be another set on all of Boldly Go. These are imported from Valency, where they are all the fashion. The smarticles are micron-sized particles, I am told, that use the same sort of techne as anycloth. That *is* an anycloth outfit you are wearing, isn't it?"

Méarana had the judge pegged now. She had been born to money, and while she had the graciousness of her class, she also had more than her share of its conceits. In her first few sentences, she had alluded to her wealth in that indirect manner the wealthy had—*There may not be another set on all of Boldly Go*—and put Méarana in her place.

Bolt-for-bolt, anycloth was expensive, but a full, dedicated wardrobe was the mark of class.

"Why, yes," she told the judge, fingering a sleeve. "Where I go, it can be important to travel light. On my estate on Dangchao . . ."

"Dangchao belongs to Die Bold, does it not?" the judge asked. "I've always wondered if there were some ancient connection between your world and ours."

Méarana doubted that, but she would not secure Nagarajan by debating demographics with the judge. "I really don't know much about the migration era. There is a science-wallah drifting about the Periphery collecting facts that may answer that question. I think he may have stopped on Charming Moon to swab cheek samples."

"Him? Everyone thought he was mad. There was a woman, about ten or twelve weeks earlier, asking about him. She was a League marshall, so when this wallah bike showed up, we thought she had meant to take him into cutody for his own safety."

"The League marshall—the Hound—did you meet her?"

"Me?" Trayza laughed. "I am only a simple servant of the courts. We don't see many Hounds here, so *everyone* was chattering about her. There was talk of a reception. But she landed in Nest Admantine on the western plateau, and the *bad ones* had cut the monorail line out of the mountains. So . . . What may I do for you, mistress harp?"

Méarana handed over the brain and a print copy of the warrant. "I have been requested by Greystroke Hound to secure a prisoner in your custody."

The judge did not glance at the print copy. "Let me guess. The Wildman, Nagarajan. You visited him two days ago." Méarana was not surprised. Boditsya did not run a surveillance state, but that did not mean they lacked the means to discover where she had gone since landing.

"Yes," said Méarana. "We—that is, the Kennel needs him as a material witness in a case."

The judge grunted and held the print copy of the warrant. "What is the case, if I may ask."

"Ah, this is embarrassing . . ."

The other woman made a face. "No need to rub my nose in it."

"They don't tell me everything, either," Méarana said to take out some of the sting. "The warrant came to Siggy O'Hara because I was coming this way." Donovan often said that the truth was the best sort of lie, and she understood now what he had meant.

"The Kennel is using harpers now?"

Méarana shrugged. "You know how thin the Kennel is spread. They often use auxiliaries for minor tasks. I happened to be in the right place, and I had a special advantage."

"Really. What advantage does a harper have for the Kennel?"

"My mother is a Hound. You almost met her when she was here."

The judge retreated a little in her bag chair. "The case involves her?"

"Yes, but you will understand that I can tell you no more than that." Leave the matter vague, the harper told herself. Bridget ban had come to Boldly Go asking after Sofwari. Later, Sofwari appears. Then the Wildman comes, apparently on a feckless adventure. Shortly after, the daughter of Bridget ban comes with a warrant chopped by Greystroke demanding the person of that very Wildman. Greystroke could not have known of Nagarajan's imprisonment when he wrote the warrant. And that meant the Kennel really had intended to pick him up before he had even landed on Boldly Go. Perhaps the Wildman had deliberately gotten himself imprisoned to escape the Hounds—only to find he had jumped from the kettle to the fire.

Méarana let these thoughts circulate unspoken. It was a tissue of misdirection, and a tissue will bear not too much weight. Such things are more persuasive the less they are stressed, and when they hold just enough truth to give them substance.

Judge Trayza rose from her chair. "This is not something we like to do. It sets a bad example to other bikes, that they can come down here and get away with it."

Méarana also rose. The judge would not contest the warrant. No one begins a refusal with such protestations. She would have to justify her compliance first. The harper followed the judge to the desk, where she took a chair designed to subordinate those who sat in it.

"I will release Nagarajan to you on a single condition; namely, that when the Kennel is finished with him, he will be returned to us to complete his original sentence."

Meaning that the Nest of Boditsya fully intended to execute the man for the crime of being a man. Méarana unhesitatingly agreed. The important thing at the moment was to secure his person. She would decide what to do with it once she had it.

Trayza considered the harper. "Will you be able to retain control of him? It does neither the Kennel nor the Nest any good if turning him over means turning him loose."

Méarana emptied herself the way her mother had taught her and sat very still, allowing her eyes alone to speak. *Let them see the killer in your eyes,* Nagarajan had advised her. "My mother is a Hound," she said when the right amount of time had passed. "She taught me certain things, and that I know these things may certain you. I have people awaiting above on Charming Moon, and between here and Stranger Station, to where might a man escape?" All this in sweetly reasoned tones. Not sarcastic; certainly not threatening.

But with just enough condescension to carry the conviction.

The judge dropped her eyes and muttered that she hadn't meant to suggest that the Kennel would assign a task to one unqualified to bear it. She plugged the brain into her desktop 'face. "You'll need this requisition for the chief Warder at the . . ." She hesitated, unplugged the brain and reinserted it. ". . . at the prison, and you'll have to sign a re . . ." She re-plugged the brain a second time. ". . . a receipt."

"Of course." Méarana refused to look at the balky insert. Donovan had warned her that his alterations might not pass the quality control checks.

The third time, the insert loaded up and the harper, with some effort, did not show relief. The judge checked certain fields on the screen against the corresponding fields on the paper copy, pursed her lips; then with a small sigh of annoyance added her own proviso about returning the prisoner once he was no longer needed. She did the same thing by hand to the paper copy, and Méarana initialed and dated the amendment.

Give her anything she wants, Donovan had advised, *so long as we leave with the Wildman.*

"I wish I knew what this was in aid of," Judge Trayza said as she handed over the franked warrant and the release form.

Méarana took the paperwork and the brain and shook the judge by the hand. "No. You don't," she assured the woman. "There is one dead and one missing already in this affair. The less any of us know, the better." Make it sound mysterious; make it sound deadly. Make it sound like Judge Trayza Dorrajenfer of the Nest of Boditsya did not want to inquire further.

On the shuttle to Charming Moon, Teodorq Nagarajan sat between Méarana the Harper and Dame Teffna bint

Howard. He wore a pair of manacles, courtesy of Josang Prison, and grinned at the stares he received from the other passengers. A great many Boldlys resented his temporary escape from the death sentence. So, too, had the news faces from Alabaster and Sumday. "We came all this distance," Jwana had complained at the hotel, "and now there's no story."

But Nagarajan was content with that. He would rather Novski gripe at his good luck than exult in his bad. He nudged Méarana with an elbow after the shuttle had entered free fall. "I knew you'd come back for me, babe. Just couldn't let me go to waste."

"Please," said Méarana, "don't make me change my mind."

AN AISTEAR

Billy regarded the new member of the troupe with some disfavor and, on the crawl to Stranger Station, explained to the Wildman his position in the scheme of things. But Nagarajan took the Terran by the folds of his kurta and lifted him off his feet. "Hey," he explained, "Teddy don't take orders from no flunky. Lady Méarana is the boss. Wasn't no mention of you in the bargain."

"Dame Teffna" traveled with them on the same bumboat, but Méarana knew that Donovan and the Fudir were already reasserting control, for the Silky Voice grew huskier with each passing day, and from time to time she gasped a little in pain. "I control the androgens and estrogens," she explained privately at one point, "so I could force them to live as a woman. But they could shut me up in the hypothalamus, and I'd rather not make my body a battleground."

Teodorq told Méarana that the medallions had come from a world out the Wilderness Road. This surprised her, because Sofwari had last been heard from on Ampāyam; but he had been searching for clan-mothers, not medallions, so she told Billy to make reservations for the next ship to Gatmander. Donovan, eavesdropping, did likewise.

The *Furious Joy* had once been a liner working the Ramage-Valency region; but she had grown old and worn and less attractive to the sort of passengers her owners desired. So a consortium had bought her up and hired a down-at-luck captain to bring her out to Sumday, and the *Joy* now made the circuit from Gatmander to Sumday to Boldly Go carrying an eclectic mix of passengers and cargo.

Captain Lu-wi dan Fodio made a point of hosting his passengers to "the captain's dinner" and seating them with his officers on a rotating basis. The fare was plain; the entertainment, recorded. But dan Fodio was sincere and friendly and his officers polite, if a bit distracted by their duties. Yet Méarana thought the meals were in many ways more genuine than the more formal affairs on *Gerthru van Ijębwode*. Captain-Professor van Lyang had maintained an aura of dignity. Captain dan Fodio did not. He would roar with laughter whether he was hearing an anecdote for the first time or telling it for the fortieth.

Billy Chins made one attempt to wait table and Méarana ordered him to sit down and act like a passenger. There were seven of them at the table: Second Officer bPadbourne ("the P is silent," he explained), a shipwright named Weems from Gladiola seeking opportunity on the frontier, a wealthy bummerl named Konzaquince, and a rather more furtive woman who gave the name Patel and said nothing about her purposes. To have Billy Chins stand behind her chair and spoon potatoes and brusselballs onto her plate as if she were some High Taran aristo while Teodorq and the others contested for the serving bowls struck Méarana as ludicrous.

The eighth seat at their table, bPadbourne told them, belonged to a passenger who was ill at present, and remaining in his cabin.

It was Donovan, of course. He appeared on the third day out, his features now restored to their normal appearance. He came up silently behind Billy Chins and clapped a sudden hand on the man's shoulder. "Well, well," he said, and Méarana noted how Billy froze in fright on hearing that voice. "I see we've picked up a new playmate."

Nagarajan had pulled his hair back into a tail and wore the sleeveless jerkin that showed off his shoulder tattoos. Without moving his head, his eyes danced from Donovan to Billy, assessing their relationship.

Billy had turned in his chair and, after a moment of demonstrative surprise, embraced Donovan by the waist. "O sahb! Sahb! Such-much joy lukim you!"

Donovan pulled out the empty chair and sat beside him. "Billy," he said, "my old faithful khitmutgar, how I've missed you since you ran out on me."

"No, sahb. Billy no-never run! But Mistress Harp, she go willy-nilly wanpela tasol . . . I mean, she go on alone. Billy can no let such happen! Sahb Donovan be angry-angry supposem lady be hurt. So I go with help her. I do your will always, sahb; even you no ask."

After dinner, the four of them remained at the table and discussed the venture on which their mutual fates had placed them. For Nagarajan's benefit, Donovan reviewed the mystery of Bridget ban's disappearance, the evident importance of the medallion that Bridget ban had given her daughter, and the hints contained in the ancient Terran legend of the Treasure Fleet. Something that would "ward the League for aye." As far as the Wildman was concerned, League and Confederation meant nothing; but the chance to be immortalized in song was decisive.

"One last item, and maybe the most important," Donovan concluded, "is the fact-collector Sofwari. Somehow, his work convinced Bridget ban there was more in the old legend than a tall tale. But Sofwari went up the Gansu Corridor and has not come back."

"It's not some geegaw we seek," Méarana reminded him. "'Tis my mother."

The scarred man shrugged. "Find one, find the other. There is a bare chance the one is still functional."

"You told me once," Méarana said, "that all quests fail, and it is only how they fail that matters."

Donovan's smile was full of teeth. "I still expect we will fail."

Billy blinked. "We no find old machine?"

But Donovan shook his head. "It's the finding of it that might be our failure. Bridget ban sought it, and never returned."

"All right," the Wildman said, "I can see yuh need a fighting man, which that's me. But I like to know who I'm throwing in with. I ain't no dummy. I got looks, charm, bravery, fighting skill with all sorts of weapons . . ."

"Humility," suggested Billy Chins.

"Yeah, that, too, 'cause I only listed half my sterling qualities. But a man can't have everything and I don't claim to be no big brain. Every gang needs a leader, and my inner sense tells me it ain't Billy here. He strikes me as a sneaky, whiny little bastard. In a fight, yuh can depend on him for the rabbit punch—and I ain't putting yuh down, yuh Terry wart. Some fights are better won from the back than from the front. Not my style, but we gotta be what we call 'multitasking' here. So are yuh the brains here, Donovan?"

"Me?" said Donovan. "I have more brains than you might think; but I'm only a broken vessel."

Teodorq shrugged his massive shoulders. "Broken stuff is generally pretty sharp. And that leaves you, Lady Harp. I'm real sorry, me, about yer mother. That's tough breaks, and I feel for yuh. But what a fellowship we have here! I want the glory. Lady Méarana wants to find her mother. Dovovan wants to find a wonder-weapon. And Billy Chins wants to kiss Donovan's ass so bad he'll do a prostate exam with his tongue."

The little Terran cried out in fury and lunged from his seat, his left hand having pulled a stiletto from inside his blouse.

But Teodorq's massive hands moved like twin snakes and seized Billy's wrist in a certain grip, causing him to go white and drop the dagger. The Wildman looked first at the scarred man, then at the harper, then he grinned and pointed to each in turn. "Hideout gun in the back of your waist—a teaser, right? And that dagger yuh showed me once before. Sweet. Smart enough to draw. Smart enough to hold back and see what played out. Here, boy." He handed the dagger back to Billy Chins, who took it with smoldering eyes.

"Yuh got guts, boy," the Wildman said. "Pulling on me is usually a one-way trip to the boneyard; but I wanted to see what yuh was made of. Yuh may be a weasel; but a weasel got sharp teeth and ain't bad to have on your side when yer on the sharp end."

Méarana spoke up. "Are ye done playing games, Teodorq? Would ye hae me sing a satire on ye? Billy, sit down! Where we gang is gae dangerous, an' we all maun work together or we'll nae ayn of us come back."

"As your mother 'nae' came back," said Donovan.

Méarana turned on him. "What I said about everyone working together applies to ye in spades, Donovan buigh!"

The scarred man's face twisted as he tried to sneer, smile, and smirk at the same time. But the harper spun to face the Wildman. "And now, we'll hae no more dancing. Where did your medallion come from?"

Teodorq pursed his lips and looked toward the ceiling. "An export shop on Gatmander."

Méarana could scarce believe it. "Ye've nae took it off a Nyacki warrior? For such mickle return I sprang ye from Josang Prison?"

"Yuh had yer goal, babe; and I had mine."

Donovan said, "The release form says she gives you back when she's done. There's a Pup on Ampāyam who'd be glad to escort you there."

The Wildman shrugged. "What can he do? Put me under a *second* death sentence? Yuh can only kill me once, old man."

"Billy Chins knows things," said the khitmutgar. "Not death, but wish-for-death."

"Oh, don't get your shorts in a knot," the Wildman told them. "I said I was with yuh—to death and glory. The export-guy on Gatmander gotta know where it come from. An' I seen other pieces like it here and there out in the Free Worlds." He stood from the table. "I'll need to buy arms when we hit Gatmander," he said. "Yuh don't wanna roam the Free Worlds without yuh be armed—and with more than a teaser." With that, he left, whistling.

Billy rose to follow. Donovan held him back a moment.

"Don't kill him. We need him."

Billy nodded. "I make nice-nice, me. Billy patient man."

Méarana watched the khitmutgar go. "There will be trouble between those two, sooner or later."

"Later, rather than sooner," the scarred man said. "Billy is no fool. Having Teodorq along shortens the odds against coming back."

"You don't think we're coming back, do you?"

"No."

"Then why are you going?"

"That's what worries me. I'm not half so afraid of Those of Name as I am of what might be left over up here." He rapped his skull with his knuckles. "It's what might awaken in the closets of our minds."

Méarana reached for the harp case that sat at her feet; but the scarred man shook his head.

"Don't try your harper's tricks on me. Why do you play that thing anyway?"

She took the harp out and played a glissando, listening to the jangle of the chords. She began to tighten the ones that had grown slack. "To bring faith, and joy, and love."

Donovan grunted. "It's a big Spiral Arm. You have your work cut out for you."

"I'll be happy," the harper answered, "if I can bring them to just one person."

The scarred man shifted uncomfortably in his seat. "That's a more modest goal, and—if it makes *you* happy—a self-fulfilling one."

"No," said the harper in an almost distracted manner. "Just you, Donovan. Just you. I want you to believe in something, to find joy in something, to love something."

The mocking smile reclaimed Donovan's lips. "Why, then you are in luck," he said. "I believe I'll have another whiskey. Because I love it. And . . . I expect I'll enjoy it, too."

"Ah, such a joy is fleeting. It doesn't last."

"That's why you have to drink more than one."

IX ON THE VERY EDGE OF SKIES

Gatmander's sun lies more distant than most and he gleams in her sky as a blue-white diamond. Young Gat women are known to hold their splayed fingers to the sky and imagine the sunset in an engagement ring. Daylight on Gatmander would be called dusk most anywhere else.

She should be a colder world than she is. But her sun is hotter and compensates somewhat for his distance by his temperament. Partly, too, being a large world, Gatmander squeezes her core like a woman hugging herself for warmth. In consequence, her heart seethes from the pressing love of gravity, and some of this grills her surface. And partly, too, the water vapor in her air seizes and hoards what heat her star and core grant from above and below. This vapor falls as snow for almost half the year and melts grudgingly in a summer more like spring. The species planted by the ancient terraforming arks had made the best of a bad deal and have adapted with admirable dispatch. Behaviors changed, features were bent to new uses, and new features appeared in the blink of a biological eye as the god Lamarck awoke sleeping "junk genes" to tackle new environmental conditions.

Taken all for all, she is a bleak world. Tundra in the high latitudes, taiga over the temperate zones, oak and maple in the tropics. A bare million souls live in no more than a few score cities, with maybe another two million scattered in towns and villages across the Canda landmass. The other continent, Zobiir, splays half her bulk across the north pole and supports nothing but massive glaciers and a precarious research base on her Southern Bay. The people are friendly enough, but embrace a kind *of enthusiastic fatalism. Their literature runs heavily to huddled, lonely women yearning for hot but distant lovers.*

The harper and the scarred man landed with servant and bodyguard in train at the groundside spaceport near Gudsga, which was what passed for the planetary capital. Gatmander supported a single planetary government, mainly because no one saw reason to support more than one. That was theory. In practice, each city governed its own hinterland of towns and villages and sent a couple of *boys* to Gudsga to sit in a council they called the *loyal shirka*.

Passengers unboarded the shuttle by means of mobile stairs and walked across the field to the terminal. It was morning and the sun was behind them, casting bluish shadows across the field. The sky itself was lightening from black to gunmetal gray.

The terminal was little more than a large shed, and there were no formalities to their entry. Gats saw no reason to bar either those mad enough to come or sane enough to leave. The sign across the entry read: WELCOME TO GATMANDER: THE END OF THE ROAD. Méarana wondered if the Gats had meant that the way it sounded, or if they had intended only a bald, factual description. For it was here that that Yellow Brick Road and the Gorky Prospect, having combined into the Grand Concourse, came to an end, and ships had to circle halfway around Black Diamond Star to reach the Wilderness Trail into the Wild.

In theory, this should have made her a lively debarkation port, with companies of settlers moving through, drinking the local *vawga*, buying last-minute trinkets, seeking last-minute joys. The planet could have called herself "Last Chance" with some justice. But she had become a cul de sac on Electric Avenue. The worlds out the Wilderness Road were more advanced than those along the Gansu Corridor. Many had large populations and, though their technology was primitive, colonizing them would be problematical.

Billy found something akin to a hotel, called a "bed-and-breakfast." Hotels were not a major industry on Gatmander. She held few attractions for off-planet visitors, and native Gats were homebodies. Consequently, some families earned a little hard currency by renting out rooms and serving meals to strangers.

The next morning the family served them breakfast; or, as they put it in the peculiar back-handed syntax of the Gat born and bred: "Unto us there is an occasion for breakfast." Méarana immediately understood why the room and board was so inexpensive. There was barely enough board to count as a splinter. A bowl of some coarse-ground cereal called "fortitude" liberally greased with dollops of butter and syrup and washed down with a fatty milk called *chā-cha*. Méarana supposed the cereal was called "fortitude" or "grit" because one needed that virtue to consume it.

She was alone in her fastidiousness. Billy usually resigned himself to whatever food he was given; and the Fudir was, as always, indifferent. Teodorq seemed actually to enjoy the meal and asked for seconds, and Méarana made note to avoid the Wildman's native cuisine.

Their hosts, sahb and memsahb Dukover, were neither friendly nor unfriendly. They smiled at the right times and spoke the pleasant formalities, but their attitude was summed up in the Gatmander hospitality motto: "Guests Happen."

"These Gat-fellas," said Billy Chins later that morning as they walked toward the mercantile district, "they talk such-much funny-style."

Teodorq laughed, but before Billy could frown, he pointed down a side street and said, "The shop's down that way."

The wind was chill and blustery, channeled by the dark,

narrow lanes between the warehouses. It carried a touch of sleet. Gatmander's long winter had ended, and its long spring was underway. Flower buds peered suspiciously from plots and pots; *krunsaus* watched for shadows. The world had a long orbit and would be some while making up its mind. When they turned up Chandler's Lane the wind blasted them so that, even wrapped in the "snow-cloak" she had been loaned, Méarana shivered.

Or did she shiver from hope? Teodorq had promised no more than the name of the world from which the medallion had come; and the shop-owner might not know even that; but despite all past disappointments, she had come to expect some great breakthrough. But what of it? Were the outcome a sure thing, hope would be superfluous.

Teodorq paused before a weapons shop and studied the window holo display with longing. "Remember what I told yuh, babe," he said. "I can't be no bodyguard without I got weapons to guard yuh with."

"Later, Teddy," said the harper. "*After* you've led us to the shop."

She moved on and the Wildman followed. The Fudir hesitated. The Pedant wanted to study the weapons and the Brute concurred. Thus did hunger for knowledge and lust for combat find common ground. Between them, the two influenced the memory and the animal body, and so the scarred man forgot for a moment where he was going and his body turned to the display.

A variety of weapons were mounted on stands and pedestals: automatic pellet guns, revolving cylinder pellet guns, electric teasers, induction nerve dazers, brass knuckles, daggers and knives in an alarming range of shapes and sizes. A two-handed broadsword with an elaborately jeweled pommel leaned against the side of the display. Hand-lettered cards announced the provenance of the weapons. Zhenghou Shuai. Ākramaṇapīchē. Kaṇṭu. Enjrun. Worlds he had never heard of. Worlds of the Wild. Peoples to whom the crafting of a weapon was a work of art. Gloriously filigreed, garishly pastelled, engraved, burnished, some, indeed, could be intended only for ceremonial use. That saber, for example. That automatic. But for the others, their form followed their function.

Beautiful, the Brute sighed—delighted by the craftsmanship or by the functionality, who could say?

𝔄𝔩𝔩 𝔬𝔣 𝔱𝔥𝔢 𝔭𝔢𝔩𝔩𝔢𝔱 𝔴𝔢𝔞𝔭𝔬𝔫𝔰 𝔞𝔯𝔢 𝔣𝔯𝔬𝔪 Ākramayapīchē 𝔞𝔫𝔡 𝔎𝔞𝔶𝔱𝔲, said the Pedant. 𝔗𝔥𝔢 𝔪𝔬𝔯𝔢 𝔲𝔱𝔦𝔩𝔦𝔱𝔞𝔯𝔦𝔞𝔫 𝔢𝔡𝔤𝔢𝔡 𝔴𝔢𝔞𝔭𝔬𝔫𝔰 𝔞𝔯𝔢 𝔣𝔯𝔬𝔪 𝔈𝔫𝔧𝔯𝔲𝔫, 𝔞𝔰 𝔴𝔢𝔩𝔩 𝔞𝔰 𝔰𝔬𝔪𝔢 𝔪𝔲𝔷𝔷𝔩𝔢-𝔩𝔬𝔞𝔡𝔢𝔯𝔰 𝔞𝔫𝔡 𝔣𝔩𝔦𝔫𝔱-𝔩𝔬𝔠𝔨𝔰. 𝔈𝔩𝔢𝔠𝔱𝔯𝔬𝔫𝔦𝔠 𝔴𝔢𝔞𝔭𝔬𝔫𝔰 𝔞𝔯𝔢 𝔬𝔫𝔩𝔶 𝔣𝔯𝔬𝔪 𝔝𝔥𝔢𝔫𝔤𝔥𝔬𝔲 𝔖𝔥𝔲𝔞𝔦.

And you know what that means, the Sleuth whispered. *It's an elementary deduction.*

But since he would not draw it, the scarred man remained bemused. Pedant said, 𝔐𝔲𝔰𝔱 𝔶𝔬𝔲 𝔞𝔩𝔴𝔞𝔶𝔰 𝔰𝔥𝔬𝔴 𝔬𝔣𝔣?

Oh, look who's talking. Are you sure you're the memory and not the ego?

𝔒𝔥, 𝔱𝔥𝔞𝔱'𝔰 𝔶𝔬𝔲𝔯 𝔧𝔬𝔟.

The Sleuth sniffed and dropped out, and the scarred man found himselves staring at a catalog of weaponry. Then the Pedant dropped out, and he forgot what the catalog had been.

"I hate it when those two assholes quarrel," muttered the Fudir.

You could try being nicer to them.

They started to turn away, but Inner Child kept their eyes glued to the display. <Those could hurt us, if we ever found ourselves on the wrong side of them.>

"You're supposed to be cautious and wary," Donovan growled, "not paralyzed with fear. You're useless."

This time he did turn away—to find that Billy Chins had lingered.

"Sahb let Wildman have such-much weapons? Who guard us against our guard?"

"Billy," said the scarred man, "we are truly awed by the depth of your trust."

"Trust be better found hiding neath caution," the khitmutgar replied. "How much sambai long—I mean, what protection are broke old-fella you and liklik meri if the muscle turns on us?"

"I'm more concerned that he'll try to run out on us. He's not aṭangku, only a contract worker. To some of these Wildmen, 'honor' means everything. To others, it means nothing." He clapped a hand to Billy's shoulder. "They practice *taqila*. If you're not of their tribe, they'll pretend to be your friend, look you straight in the eye, and lie like hell."

"Master sahb lucky, then," said Billy with a wide grin. "Eyes belong-you never straight enough look into!"

Donovan directed a playful swat to Billy's head just as Méarana turned about and pointed from up the lane. "Teddy's found the place!"

CHENG-BOB SMERDROV'S IMPORT-EXPORT, SPECIALISTS IN WILDWORK, was a large, barnlike structure formed of "grown wood." Its bins and shelves held the most chaotic concatenation of gimcrack and miscellany this side of Jehovah's Starport Sarai. Cheng-bob himself was a bear of a man, bushy of beard and ruddy of cheek. His eyelids were folded at the corners and his nose was long and straight. He smiled to excess.

The importer sat on a high stool behind a wooden counting board, leaning his beefy arms upon its well-worn surface. "As it pertains to me," he was saying to Méarana as Donovan and Billy entered, "there is no occasion of memory. Many diverse goods from many diverse worlds pass through this building. Importer-exporter is a trade unto me, but art-critic is not."

Teodorq waved his medallion. "Yuh sold me this bauble no more'n six moons ago. Yuh can't remember that?"

Cheng-bob spread his hands helplessly. "Many Wild-men pass before my gaze. What makes one more memorable than another? It is for the buyers of Valency and High Tara that these goods are assembled. Wildwork is much in vogue in that quarter of the Arm. For me only rarely is there an occasion of retail."

Méarana showed the man her own medallion. "Here is a second piece. You can see they came from the same tradition. This may also have passed through your hands."

The wholesaler took both medallions and compared them. "Many are the pieces that pass through here. They are bundled into lots for auction when the buyers appear, and such lots want both diversity *and* similarity. But once they are gone and Gladiola Bills of Exchange have taken their places, of what use is the memory of them?"

"Please, sahb," said Billy. "If we say what world, can you show us lots belong from there?"

The harper sighed. "Oh, Billy, it's the name of the world we're trying to find out."

Billy ducked his head and tugged his forelock. "Oh, mistress harp. Billy see him sword up street belong-him such-much colors."

"Pastels?"

"Card, he say sword belong world Enjrun."

Donovan scowled, angry at the Pedant for having forgotten that information, and at the Sleuth for not sharing his deduction. He cursed himself for a broken old man.

"Do you have any lots of Enjrun merchandise in your warehouse?" Méarana asked Cheng-bob.

The proprietor shrugged. "This is an occasion of looking." He slid off the stool and led the way into the back, where the shelves and bins were filled with shipping cartons. Some bore the names of art houses on Valency and elsewhere, others bore only lot numbers. Their entry into this portion of the building triggered an occasion of activity on the part of the warehousemen. A forklift floated down an aisle with a pallet, a supervisor at the other end of the aisle scanned lot numbers into her dibby and attached amshifars to the containers; but Méarana had the sense that moments before, none of these things were happening.

Cheng-bob called out, "Kola! Where are the lots from Enjrun that *Vettery's Cat* brought in last month?"

The supervisor spoke into her throat-mike, listened with a hand cupped to her ear, and called back, "Ngī!"

Cheng-bob hollered thanks and led them down the front aisle. The rows, Méarana saw, were labeled in traditional consonantal order: k, ng, c, ñ, and so forth, and made a bet with herself that the bins in the cross direction were labeled in vowel order: a, ā, i, ī, and so on. The syllable ngī thus represented the second row, fourth bin.

Which was where the importer took them. "This lot was brought by the trade ship *Vettery's Cat*," he explained as they strode briskly between the striped lines of the walkways.

"Your memory is now working quite well," Méarana said.

Cheng-bob turned his head. "What art the lot holds is unknown to me. The billings, accounts, and shipments are not."

"Is *Vettery's Cat* in port now?" Donovan asked. "We'd like to speak to her captain."

Cheng-bob did not break stride. He spoke briefly into his throat-mike, then said, "No, there was an occasion for departure to Ōram and Zhenghou Shuai sixday last. Here is the lot, unconsigned, to be auctioned when the buyers appear from Valency and High Tara."

The container was standard intermodal, slightly taller than a man, and possessed a double door on the side facing the aisle. It was festooned with stickers identifying the trade ship and the exporter, a notary's seal testifying to its provenance, a tentative valuation, a large amshifar to track it.

"Is that a regular thing?" Donovan asked. "I mean the art dealers coming here." Méarana began unfastening the clasps that held the doors closed.

"Oh, yes. The arrival of the buyers is unto us the occasion of a festival. The Gatmander Festival of the Wild Arts. Although, this is an occasion of honesty to me . . ." He lowered his voice. ". . . some of the artists are Gats. As you know, poor Gatmander is at the tail end of nowhere. 'On the very edge of skies,' as our anthem puts it. And . . ."

Méarana turned suddenly from the container. "What was that?"

Cheng-bob blinked puzzlement. "Our . . . anthem?"

"Yes. How does it go?"

"It is sung thusly . . ." And then in a voice innocent of key and scale, he sang:

> *'On Gatmander, far Gatmander*
> *On the very edge of skies,*
> *There is occasion for—'* "

"Out to the edge!" the harper cried. "Out to the edge! *That is what Mother meant.* This is where she came!" Then, more quietly, she whispered, "This is where she came."

Donovan felt a glow of satisfaction for which he could not account, but the Fudir seized control of his tongue. "Sleuth! You *knew*! And you said nothing?"

His outburst frightened the exporter and he took a hasty step back. Teodorq, too, appeared startled and uncertain; but Billy placed a hand on the scarred man's arm and said, "Sahb rest. No time now bicker-bicker," and he led him to a low crate in another storage bay and caused him to sit there. The scarred man seethed with rage and humiliation.

𝔜𝔬𝔲 𝔠𝔞𝔫'𝔱 𝔱𝔞𝔨𝔢 *all* 𝔱𝔥𝔢 𝔠𝔯𝔢𝔡𝔦𝔱, the Pedant told the Sleuth.

"Oh, shut your food-hole," said the Fudir. "Both of you."

Sleuth, you think you're clever, the Silky Voice purred, *but cleverness without communication is sterile.*

Not every puzzle can be solved by smooth talking and seduction, Silky.

"And not every problem is a puzzle," said Donovan.

"Never mind all that," said the Fudir. "Did you see the way *she* looked at us?"

Over by the cargo container, Teodorq Nagarajan scratched his head. "What's wrong with the boss?"

The harper turned once more to the latches and swung the doors open. "Never mind him. He'll be all right after he gets some rest." She stepped inside the container, then stepped out again. "And *I'm* the boss," she told the bodyguard.

Teodorq turned to Billy, who had rejoined them. "She's the boss?"

The khitmutgar shrugged. "She always was."

The shipping container held cases equipped with stacks of flat sliding trays. These, Méarana and the others slid out and in. There were earrings and pendants, medallions and brooches, bracelets and wristclocks, buckles and bangles, frets of interlaced wires. About half were done in the style of Méarana's medallion—brightly colored stones set into gold or silver or aluminum—which Cheng-bob told them was called "parking stones" by the natives of Enjrun. No finer "parkingers" could be found, he assured them, in all the Spiral Arm.

Méarana did not know what she expected to find. In deeper drawers nestled cups and mugs, vases and breakstones. The art was beautiful, barbaric, compelling. But none of it brought her any closer to her mother. What had Mother seen in the art of Enjrun that sent her into the Wild after the source?

"What Enjrun lots belong here maybe two metric years ago?"

Méarana had to look twice to assure herself that it was Billy Chins who had asked. His Gaelactic had been improving over the months they had traveled together, and he could now frame whole sentences without falling into the Terran patois. The khitmutgar spared her a shy smile. "Maybe art your mother see, now long-time passé."

Cheng-bob tapped his front teeth with his thumbnail while he thought. Then he activated his voice link. "Kola! Did that old wood carving leave with Donozay Mpehle last Art Festival? No? It was paid for, wasn't it? Canceled? Ay!" He signed off. "A high relief wood carving sits in the outsize bins. As it pertains to one and all, it is an occasion for admiration; but as an occasion for purchase, not at all. Perhaps it is an occasion for firewood."

The carving was in kşau, the very last bin in the rack used for outsized items, and when the shroud had been pulled aside Méarana saw immediately why it had neither been sold nor consigned to the mulcher. It was much too beautiful to destroy, and far too ugly to display.

A high-relief carving made from a light red-orange wood which Cheng-bob called "blood maple," it seemed intended as an altar piece for some Wild cult. It was too large and garish for most private dwellings. It would disturb the tranquility of Peacock Junction or overthrow the domestic order of Dancing Vrouw. It was not playful enough for High Tara or serious enough for Die Bold. Any art dealer would, on first impression, desire it and, on second thought, know it to be unsaleable.

The figures in the carving were relieved from the wood, as if like dryads they had always dwelt within. They were running away from a spot in the center of the perspective. The varied sizes gave the crowded scene the illusion of perspective. The smaller figures were fleeing into the wood, the larger fleeing out. Several of the latter were attached to the base block only by a single foot, and so seemed to be leaving the wood panel entirely.

Not all the figures were fleeing. Some danced around the focal point with raised arms. The running and dancing men were cacophonies of bright reds and blues and yellows—war paint, or ceremonial body paint. The backdrop was a night sky in black lacquer, in which a single white star gleamed. Red lightning ran from the star to the focal point, where it engulfed the figure of a young girl standing with arms outstretched to the sides and head thrown backward as if to glimpse the star above her. Head, arms, feet, breasts emerged from the red flame in bold yellow. The remainder of the body was suggested only in the shape of the flaming torrent. There were dabs of red—at the mouth, at the tips of the breasts, even—by God!—at the tips of the toes and curled fingers.

That was craftsmanship!

Only a connoisseur would ever buy such a piece. Only a philistine would dare display it. Graceful curling letters ran along the base of the work.

Méarana pulled out her medallion, and held it at arm's length before the carving.

The medallion was an abstraction of the same scene. The black ceramic was the night sky, the diamond was the star, the ruby sliver was the lightning. It was broken off, she remembered. Perhaps there had once been a brown-and-green segment representing the ground; or perhaps the parkinger had wanted to suggest emergence by breaking the circumference. She turned the medallion around and compared the writing on the back side to that underneath the carving.

The letters on the medallion were plainer, lacking the ligatures and diacriticals that the woodcarver had rendered. It was a simplified font of the same script. And as near Méarana could tell, it was the same inscription. She turned to Cheng-bob.

"Do you have any idea what this means?"

The exporter pursed his lips and went to the pouch on the side of the rack. "According to Captain Barnes's testament of provenance, this work was the occasion of craftsmanship for one Henery Satéep na Fibulsongaram, a citizen of the Qaysarlik of Riverbridge on Enjrun and depicts a biannual festival in the City On The Hill called 'The Well of the Sun.' The title—and the inscription may be the title—is 'Fire from the Sky.'"

Méarana sighed and closed her eyes. "Thank you," she whispered. "Oh, thank you."

Teodorq scratched his head. "Yuh think yer mom went looking for these dancing savages?"

Méarana laughed, because as far as savagery went, Teddy ran rather closer to the dancers than to his present companions. But all things are a matter of degree and everyone drew the line somewhere. "Of course not," she said. "She went looking for whatever *that* is." And her pointing finger rested on the bright star from which lightning bathed the earth.

But Méarana could not take her eyes from the figure of the young girl engulfed in the flames, and a cold, deadly certainty engulfed her heart.

At dinner that evening Méarana was silent and uncommunicative. The Dukovers did not notice. Donovan, who talked to himself, did not notice. Teodorq, who talked to anyone, did not notice. But Billy Chins, their servant, who insistently helped their hosts in presenting the meal, took note and whispered encouragement to her.

"Maybe so, we find her, your mama-meri. Fella no look, fella no find."

Méarana gave him a wan, but grateful smile and attacked her "red porch," a cold vegetable stew dominated by beets, with all the enthusiasm it warranted. It added to the chill within her. In the whole time of her search—when time had gone by and gone by, when no word had come, when the Kennel had given up, when Donovan announced his pessimism, while she had wended the Roads out to Lafrontera—in all that time a small flame of belief had burned within that she would find Bridget ban at the end of it all. But the sight of that Wild carving had extinguished it at last.

Teodorq chattered on to no one's interest about the arms he had procured. "They still had my old nine that I pawned for eating money when I come in on the old *Gopher Broke*." His "nine" was an automatic pistol that fired off a magazine of bullets, but why it was called a nine neither the Wildman nor anyone else knew. "It's just what it's *called*," he had protested. He had also picked up a long sword called a "claymore," much to Billy's amusement.

"Why any-fella need him, pistol *and* sword? Suppose other-fella got him pistol. What good sword? And suppose other fella got him sword, the pistol is enough."

"Sure," Teodorq replied expansively, "until yuh run outta bullets." Then in a labored imitation of Billy's accent, "Sword, no run him outta stabs."

Méarana tossed her spoon to the table and stood up. "I'm going out to take the air." She turned and passed out through the sliding glass doors into the broad shrub-littered lawn behind the house. The grass had the same ragged quality of everything else on Gatmander. The bushes seemed to grow wherever chance had driven the seeds, and were trimmed in what could be only described as the "natural look."

She grew aware that someone had come out behind her, and she did not look to see who it was. "I don't think I want to know you anymore, Donovan."

The scarred man was silent for a time. "I may not disagree," he said finally. "It's too much work. What is your reason?"

"I saw you hit Billy, back on Chandlers Lane."

"What are you talking about?"

"When you and he lingered at the arms shop."

"That? He teased me about my eyes. I gave him a swat. It was good-natured."

Méarana shook her head. "That isn't the only thing. You treat him badly."

"What about me?" asked the Fudir. "Do you want to know me?"

She turned and struck him on the chest with both fists. "Stop! Don't play identity games with me. I'm going into the Wild and I'm scared." There. She had said it.

"You should be. It's a rough and dangerous region. There are old settled planets out there that haven't made Reconnection. Human worlds where starflight is unknown, where men fight with gunpowder or swords. Travel is chancy—there are no scheduled liners—and the people are treacherous. They don't like Leaguesmen. They want what we have, and they know they can't have it because they can't build the tools to build the tools. You wouldn't last. Some tramp captain could drop you off on some primitive internal combustion world and never return to pick you up. He could sell you as a sex slave to some machraj or king."

"I don't think I—"

"I think you can trust Teddy. And even Billy might not run in a pinch. But there are limits to what the three of us can do. Do you want to risk it all just to find your mother's grave?"

"I know that now. She's gone. But I have to keep looking."

"Why? Do you think she would thank you? Do you think she would even know?"

Méarana shrugged. "She may. *You* plan to go on, though."

"There's something out there. It's just not your mother. Something that created an entire district of burnt-out worlds. The Burnt-Over District. It's what your mother set out to find."

"Then I'll find it for her."

The Fudir shook his head. "No. That's not your quest. Go back to Dangchao. Put all this in your songs. Keep Bridget ban in your heart. That's where I keep her."

"Do you? I hadn't noticed. But she was never an easy one to keep anywhere. She had a way of slipping off. You can't go out there, Donovan. No matter how despicable you are, I can't let you go." She took him by his shirt and shook him until he rattled. "You're coming apart, old man! You've grown unfocused, indecisive. Those six pieces of you are flying in all directions. And when any of them gets in a snit, you lose a part of yourself. You were more single-minded behind a bowl of uiscebeatha in the Bar of Jehovah!"

"It was the one thing on which we could all agree."

"Listen to yourself. Is there some part of you that *wants* to die? What good would you be to me if you were half-drunk all the time? Whose skills would you blunt? The Pedant's memory? The Sleuth's deductive abilities? The Brute's physical prowess? Keep them docile and you keep them useless."

"They're useless anyway," Donovan said. "The Sleuth thinks the rest of us are stupid. Inner Child is afraid of his own shadow. The Brute . . . What's the use? I could give you six reasons."

"Six. That would include Donovan."

He shrugged. "There's such a thing as too cold-blooded."

"Which means you can give me six good reasons why you should stay here on Gatmander and wait for us to return."

"I would wait forever. I can't do it. Zorba . . ."

"Don't use Uncle Zorba as an excuse! That's the very worst thing you could have said." She turned and swept her arm across the Dukovers' backyard. "What do you think of their landscaping?"

"Eh?" The scarred man took on an unfocused look while he tried to decide which of him was best suited to answer. But she did not wait for him to decide.

"Gats don't think of themselves as actors," she said. "It's in their very grammar. They are always acted upon. Stuff happens. They're just spectators. So, don't you tell me, Donovan buigh, that you are tagging along because circumstances forced you!" She looked up, saw a drape flutter in the sliding door, and Billy Chins appeared briefly to nod at her. She indicated that she had seen him and took Donovan by the arm.

"Let's go back and finish our *porch*."

The scarred man snorted. "What's the rush? It was cold when they served it." But he followed her meekly back into the Dukover house.

He had not swallowed more than three more spoonfuls when he realized what had been done to him. He turned a gaze already growing uncertain on the harper, and his mouth tried to open and form words. "You . . ."

"Sleep," she said. "I've paid the Dukovers to watch over you until we return. Rest. Find peace. We are commanded to love others as we love ourselves. Start with that."

When the scarred man was snoring, Méarana turned to Billy. "Are we ready?"

Billy spared hardly a glance for his former master.

"*Blankets and Beads,* she lose him High Gat Orbit tomorrow. Bumboat go jildy, two horae; then cargo boat early morning."

The harper nodded and turned to Sefr Dukover, the husband. "You'll see that our luggage gets on the cargo boat?"

"As it pertains to me, there is an occasion of compliance."

Méarana sought the intercession of heaven. "Just once, could you say, 'I'll do it'?"

The Gat twisted his face into a look of disgust. "As it pertains to off-worlders, there is an occasion of tolerance; but there is no occasion for offensive speech."

Teodorq returned to the dining room, still buckling a holster around his waist. "Cab's here, babe." He spared a glance for the scarred man. "I still don't like this."

"Who will sing Nagarajan glories, my good *pahari*?" asked Billy. "Lady Harp or old man? Old-fella, he be no-good sick. He for burning ghats. Not long time die in Wild."

Nagarajan wore his sword over his shoulder and he reached back to test its draw. "Didn't say yuh was wrong, I said I didn't like it. It's a bad omen to start a journey. Shoulda sacrificed a goat."

When they went to the cab hovering on the parking apron, Teodorq held Méarana back for a moment after Billy had gotten in.

"What'd he mean 'pahari'?"

The harper glanced at the khitmutgar, then at the Wildman. "Hillman, I think."

Teodorq snorted. "Shows how smart he is. I was a prairieman, born and bred." And he reached over his shoulder and refastened the thong on his scabbard to keep the sword in place.

The Silky Voice falls through an infinite space, though in defiance of the god Newton her rate of fall remains constant, so that she seems almost to float. From her throne high in the hypothalamus, she notes respiration, heartbeat, the rush of endorphins through the glands and ducts and bloodstream. And still she falls. There is no bottom. There is no such thing as a bottom. She may as well be falling up, or sidewise, or in upon herself.

Weariness envelops the Brute, his contant alertness grows lax, muscles loosen. He lies down on a yielding and undefined surface to rest himself.

We've been drugged, the Sleuth concludes.

"Brilliant," the Fudir answers. "I never cease to marvel at the quickness of our mind."

A child's voice echoes through the white fog that now fills the Dukover dining room, that swallows up all the edges and all the colors: <Who did this to us! Who did this!>

Méarana swims into his view.

"You . . . ," croaks Inner Child, but with Donovan's voice. No other word can express the immensity of the betrayal.

"Sleep," the harper says, not without kindness. "I've paid the Dukovers to watch over you until we return. Rest. Find peace. We are commanded to love others *as we love ourselves*. Start with that."

Then the eyelids drift together and the darkness takes him. Distantly, he hears another voice. "*Blankets and Beads,* she lose him High Gat Orbit tomorrow. Bumboat go jildy, two horae; cargo boat early morning." After that, whatever the world has to say, it does not speak in his world.

There is fog, but not fog, for even the smoky tendrils of fog have an amorphous shape and this darkness is without shape. It is not even, strictly speaking, "darkness." But for all that, it possesses substance. Paradox! Can there be matter without form? Can there be a geometrical figure without a geometry? Can there be a story without the words in which it is told? Every thing must be *some* thing before it can be understood.

And so form emerges from chaos. Substance undefined takes on the seeming of quarks. Quarks embrace and became baryons, and these join hands and became nuclei. Photons dance joyously around them and, subtly, somehow, become electrons. Atoms share electrons; molecule bonds to molecule; and so upward down the slippery slope to order. The whole beckons the parts and, by bringing them to closure, perfects them.

And so function follows form.

It is the *form* of Donovan that has been broken, and deliberately so. His matter remains the same. Those of Name had labored under the ancient error that the whole is grasped as the sum of its parts, and that by perfecting the parts the whole would be uplifted. But while a brick may be broken into molecules, what molecule is red and rectangular?

How much more true for a piece of work like man! When Those had with their cold deliberation cut the form of Donovan into parts, they thereby lost Donovan, much as a water molecule, split into its constituent atoms, ceases to be water.

Darkness becomes light. The shapeless fog becomes shape. But the pieces of Donovan do not become Donovan.

Instead, they find themselves arranged as once before around the the same long, dark-wood table in the same ill-defined room, with the same ten padded chairs arranged around it. The Fudir studies the six faces, so alike in their differences. "Being unconscious," he wisecracks, "is not like it used to be."

Donovan scowls from the other end of the table. "Are we to endure another tiresome committee meeting? Pedant, why have you brought us here?"

The more corpulent Donovan turns its massive face toward him. The gray, watery eyes appear troubled. 𝔗𝔥𝔦𝔰 𝔦𝔰 𝔫𝔬𝔱 𝔪𝔶 𝔡𝔬𝔦𝔫𝔤.

Perhaps, the narrow-faced Sleuth suggests, *it is simply memory induced by the drug.*

The Fudir wonders if it might not be imagination instead of memory. That would point to Inner Child.

<Not me!> the boy protests as he skips about the room, checking for entrances, checking for concealments. <Not me!>

Hush, Child. We're here to discuss Méarana's treachery.

It wasn't her. It was Billy.

But it was clearly she who instigated it. Billy was only her instrument.

Maybe, the Brute rumbles, **it was her purpose all along to lure us to the edge of the world and abandon us.**

If so, can you say she had no reason?

"Leaving us here," says Donovan, "may have saved our lives. That is reason enough."

If a life is no longer worth living, can you call it "saved"? What if she never comes back?

"This getting us nowhere," gripes the Fudir.

"Nowhere?" Donovan laughs. "We are lying unconscious in some gods-forsaken hovel on a desolate planet, awaiting the return of people who may never return. Surely, nowhere is precisely where we've gotten."

It was bound to end badly, the Sleuth comments. *I always said so.*

Had he? The Sleuth's hunger for puzzles had lured him from the Bar of Jehovah against his better judgment; and now, on the edge of the Wild, his better judgment had finally won.

Something like that, drunkard.

We cannot abandon her.

Wake up, Silky. It's her what's abandoned us.

Inner Child yelps suddenly and runs to the Silky Voice instead. <Help me! Help me!>

From what?

The room shakes, and the Fudir grabs the edges of the table to steady himself. An earthquake on Gatmander affecting his dreams? But a shiver runs through him, too, as if he were a tree and an autumn wind were shuddering the dead leaves from him. The impression grows that he is being watched.

Something is wrong with the table's geometry. Donovan still faces him down the long axis of the table, but the perspectives have all gone awry, for the empty seat is also at the far end facing him and it is not so empty a seat as before. Something inhabits it now; something remnant of the chaos. Perhaps it is man-shaped, perhaps not. There is too much shadow in it to say for sure. In a better light, it might have a face, and the Fudir is suddenly, irrationally glad that the light is not better.

"Donovan, in the seat on your right . . ."

But Donovan shakes his head. "No, on *your* right."

"Pedant? This is no time for jokes."

𝔚𝔥𝔞𝔱 𝔍 𝔰𝔢𝔢 𝔰𝔦𝔱𝔰 𝔱𝔬 𝔱𝔥𝔢 𝔖𝔩𝔢𝔲𝔱𝔥'𝔰 𝔯𝔦𝔤𝔥𝔱, 𝔞𝔱 𝔱𝔥𝔢 𝔣𝔞𝔯 𝔢𝔫𝔡 𝔬𝔣 𝔱𝔥𝔢 𝔱𝔞𝔟𝔩𝔢. 𝔓𝔢𝔯𝔥𝔞𝔭𝔰 𝔦𝔱 𝔦𝔰 𝔰𝔬𝔪𝔢 𝔭𝔬𝔬𝔯 𝔡𝔢𝔡𝔲𝔠𝔱𝔦𝔬𝔫 𝔥𝔢 𝔥𝔞𝔰 𝔪𝔞𝔡𝔢.

Or a bad memory that sits beside you, the Sleuth shoots back. But Silky sees it beside the Brute; and the Brute sees it beside Silky. All of them, likewise, at opposite ends of the table's long axis. Inner Child, of course, sees it everywhere.

If time ceases, you live forever.

Nervous laughter. *By definition, I would think.*

"Quiet, Sleuth! Who spoke? Who are you?"

Namaste. Greet the God within.

"Oh, no, you don't," the Fudir says. "No, you don't. Not that old trick."

Death is the life that never ends.

That's nonsense. Death is the end of life.

<Make it go away!> The child-Donovan hops onto the Silky Voice's lap and hugs her tight.

Death *is* non-sense, for in death the senses are not. Change brings pain, and life is change. In death there is no change, and so, no pain.

𝔚𝔥𝔞𝔱 𝔞𝔯𝔢 𝔶𝔬𝔲 𝔱𝔯𝔶𝔦𝔫𝔤 𝔱𝔬 𝔱𝔢𝔩𝔩 𝔲𝔰?

"He can't tell us anything, you hair-splitting fool." The Fudir's voice is just short of breaking. "He's only some leftover part of us, no less foolish than any of us."

𝔚𝔥𝔦𝔠𝔥 𝔭𝔞𝔱𝔥 𝔰𝔥𝔬𝔲𝔩𝔡 𝔴𝔢 𝔣𝔬𝔩𝔩𝔬𝔴? 𝔇𝔬 𝔴𝔢 𝔞𝔟𝔞𝔫𝔡𝔬𝔫 𝔐é𝔞𝔯𝔞𝔫𝔞? 𝔒𝔯 𝔡𝔬 𝔴𝔢 𝔭𝔢𝔯𝔰𝔲𝔞𝔡𝔢 𝔥𝔢𝔯 𝔱𝔬 𝔞𝔟𝔞𝔫𝔡𝔬𝔫 𝔥𝔢𝔯 𝔰𝔢𝔞𝔯𝔠𝔥? 𝔇𝔬 𝔴𝔢 𝔣𝔩𝔶 𝔱𝔬 𝔱𝔥𝔢 𝔥𝔬𝔲𝔫𝔡𝔰, 𝔬𝔯 𝔣𝔩𝔢𝔢 𝔣𝔯𝔬𝔪 𝔱𝔥𝔢𝔪?

"It's no Oracle, Pedant! Donovan, do something!"

Take any path. You cannot avoid what lies at the end.

<But which path is the longest to reach it? We can dawdle, if we must.>

Dawdle all you like. In the vastness of time, the longest life is no more than a speck. It is no more significant than a single man in the vastness of the universe. Your youth is dead already. There is rest at the end, a surcease from striving, relief from the Wheel.

"Donovan! The table!"

The seats are receding like galaxies from one another as the table seems to swell. Donovan, Brute, Sleuth, and the rest are red-shifting. The Fudir knows what this must symbolize. His mind is flying apart. He hears laughter like the crackling of dried autumn leaves. Brute to his left, Sleuth to his right are already out of reach, but he lunges forward and stretches his arms and . . .

. . . and his hand encounters a pile of jackstraws in the middle of a light game table. He is the only one sitting at it. The jackstraws, multicolored on their tips, are all a-jumble. The Fudir hesitates and reaches out as delicately as if he were picking a pocket and lifts a bright red straw from the top of the pile. He holds it a moment aloft and waits to see if the pile shifts.

It does not and he smiles and pulls a second straw out. This one is green at the tips and it must be slipped from under two other straws lying atop it. His hands do not tremble; the straws do not shift; and he lays the straw aside with a sense of quiet satisfaction.

A half-dozen jackstraws he has removed without rustling the pile when the tabletop suddenly grows reflective, doubling the number of apparent straws. It is difficult, from his angle, to distinguish the real straws from their reflections.

"That isn't quite fair," he says to no one in particular. He stretches out his hand and . . .

. . . and the Sleuth picks up one more piece of the jigsaw puzzle from the pile on the table. For a moment, he feels concern that he has disturbed the pile and the pieces have slipped and slid. But that is of no concern in assembling a puzzle, and so he dismisses the fancy. The border is well-nigh complete and he searches for the place where this latest piece will fit. He wonders what the picture will be once it is complete, and tries to anticipate the whole from the hints emerging on the edges. Trees, perhaps. A brook or river. A pastoral scene? He works without a picture. What joy if the solution be known beforehand?

The colors on the pieces fade until all are a uniform

gray. *That isn't quite fair,* he mutters. Though it does increase the challenge. He reaches out his hand and . . .

. . . and Donovan adjusts the position of a councilor. "Dzha-doob," he announces, then sits back to examine his position. Red to mate in twenty-five moves. Somehow, he knows that, but he does not wonder how he knows it.

It is a shaHmat board of the classic design. No modernist innovations, only a plain walnut battlefield, nine squares by nine in alternating black and red. The pieces are arranged in midgame. His emperor stands unmoved on the center square of his home row while his minions have been pushed forward in a complex arrangement of mutual support. The flanking councilors and leaping Hounds are in play on the princess side, although the fortresses still anchor the ends of his battle line. But the enemy princess dominates the midfield with a good chance to marry his prince and she has brought both her Hounds forward. A picture emerges. The arrangement is unstable. The least wrong move will send it all crashing into chaos. (Much like a pile of jack-straws, the fancy strikes him.)

He decides upon a move, but the councilor will not budge when he tries to lift it. Instead, one of his own minions changes color from Red to Black and shapeshifts into a Hound. The fog of war settles over the board, obscuring the opposing princess, shrouding his enemy's moves. "That isn't quite fair," he says to his unnamed and unseen opponent. He reaches out to take a different piece, and . . .

. . . and it isn't quite the right word. A three-letter word. "As ——— as a Thistlewaite skyscraper." The Pedant scratches his head, but his nails scrape a tender spot and he winces, bringing away fingers bright and bloody. The table bears a holocube an arm's length long on each side. He sits on a bright outdoor patio facing an ornamental garden heavy on green shrubbery and white concrete furnishings. 𝕿𝖍𝖊 𝕳𝖔𝖙 𝕲𝖆𝖗𝖉𝖊𝖓𝖘 𝖆𝖙 𝖙𝖍𝖊 𝕺𝖑𝖉 𝖁𝖆𝖑𝖊𝖓𝖈𝖎𝖆𝖓 𝕻𝖆𝖑𝖆𝖈𝖊. He recognizes the vista immediately. 𝕭𝖊𝖋𝖔𝖗𝖊 𝖙𝖍𝖊 𝖗𝖆𝖓𝖘𝖆𝖈𝖐𝖎𝖓𝖌 𝖇𝖞 𝖙𝖍𝖊 "𝕻𝖔𝖔𝖗 𝕻𝖊𝖙𝖊𝖘." It was a pleasant place, a pleasant sight. One could grow accustomed to the life of a Valencian tyrant, save that they tended toward the short.

As ——— as a Thistlewaite skyscraper. The Pedant thinks he ought to know this word. But *rickety* is more than three letters. He recalls that an old Zhōgwó dialect still informs the Thistle version of Gaelactic, and on formal occasions they employ special symbols. *Ngap ngap gung?* Three symbols, and the middle *ngap* would do for the last four letters of Ginnungap on Friesing's World: 230 Down. "Where the heat meets the ice." 𝕺𝖍, 𝖛𝖊𝖗𝖞 𝖈𝖑𝖊𝖛𝖊𝖗!

But when he consults the list, all the clues are written in the old Taṇtamiž script. He sighs because on a good day the script possesses two hundred and forty six letters. And it is unclear how some of them, like கோ, should be counted. Strictly speaking, ே ா are not letters in themselves, but only modifiers to க. Should கோ go into one space or three?

𝕿𝖍𝖎𝖘 𝖎𝖘𝖓'𝖙 𝖗𝖊𝖆𝖑𝖑𝖞 𝖖𝖚𝖎𝖙𝖊 𝖋𝖆𝖎𝖗, he complains. But as he does so, he hears the Poor Pete mob approaching the palace and wonders if an imaginary death at the hands of an imaginary mob in the imaginary sacking of an imaginary palace would be real enough for an imaginary person.

He stretches out his arms in appeal to being or beings unseen and . . .

. . . and she finds herself standing beside a burning ghat with her arms outstretched and entertains the fancy that the mourners gathered here are pieces in a game of shaH-mat. Her words here today may move them in the right direction or bring the enemy crashing down upon them all. The mourners, mutually suspicious of one another, are united, if barely, in the garland-wreathed body that lies on the traditional handcart beside the ghat. At least one, she knows, is a traitor. Complexity upon complexity, and the least wrong move would send it all crashing into chaos, like a pile of jackstraws.

The old man on the cart beside her bears a withered look: wispy white hair like a bleached field of wheat, broken here and there by puckered scar tissue. The mourners have done with their firecrackers and trumpets and now wait in silence for her words.

She stretches out her arms as if to embrace them.

Splendid and holy causes, she declares, *are served by men who are themselves splendid and holy. And that splendour and pride and strength was, in him*— a nod to the body —*compatible with a humility and a simplicity of devotion to Terra—to all that was old and beautiful in Terra.*

This is a place of peace, sacred to the dead, where men should speak with charity and restraint. We should speak of peace and of the good. But I hold it a good thing to hate evil, to hate untruth, to hate oppression; and, hating them, to strive to overthrow them. Those of Name are strong and wary; but, life springs from death: and from the graves of patriots spring living nations. Those of Name have worked well in secret and in the open. They think that they have purchased half of us and frightened the rest. They think that they have foreseen everything, think that they have provided against everything; but the fools, the fools, the fools!—they have left us our patriot dead, and, while Terra holds these graves, Terra unfree shall never be at peace.

She waits for the reaction, but when she looks, the burning yard is empty. The wind blows strong and rustles her short-clipped white hair, tickles the bald, scarred spots. Eloquence wasted; words sown to the wind. *That isn't quite fair,* she says.

For a moment there is no answer. Then the body on the cart speaks through motionless lips. *I heard.*

The Silky Voice does not wait to hear more. She turns from the dead man and flees and . . .

. . . and he is running, legs pumping, breath bellowing, falling into the rhythm that eats miles. The hurdle is directly ahead of him and he gathers himself and *leaps!* and hits the ground running on the other side. He hears the clatter of a hurdle and laughs to himself. Another runner spilled like a pile of jackstraws. He wastes no breath on speech. A culvert looms before him and he bounds across, noticing only in passing that the culvert is a chasm so deep its base is shrouded in shadow.

He passes near the face of a cliff, and rocks roll down it. He dances through them, a *grand ballabile*, with boulders. A dog—a tan-and-black "sayshen"—has joined him and keeps pace, leaping with him through the hurdles, dodging the sudden obstacles. A monstrous water buffalo bars the way snorting and the dog barks and snarls and frightens the larger beast off. A black-clad warrior confronts him and the Brute spars while the dog nips at his heels.

Far ahead, he spies the princess in flight, and he hastens to catch up, but a wall is suddenly in his path. Ropes dangle from it to facilitate his passage. But dogs cannot climb, and the Brute bends over to carry the sayshen in his arms.

And the dog is a wolf and it snaps for his hand. The Brute pulls back in time and the teeth clack on air. **That ain't hardly fair!** he thinks. He turns and runs toward the forest, but when he looks behind, the wolf has run after the princess, and . . .

. . . and he finds a hiding place in a bower deep within a tangled greenwood, where he huddles. There is rustling all about him, the sound of scampering feet as other hiders seek other harbors. A distant voice pipes out, Ready or not, here I come! and Inner Child hugs himself with anticipation. Adorned with greasepaint and camos, he knows that in this place he cannot be seen.

He waits because he is very good at waiting, and he listens for the sounds of pursuit. Far off, he hears occasional yelps as other hiders are discovered. The sounds come closer, but Inner Child does not move. Motion is the killer. It draws attention. But as they near his position, the cries of discovered players become more like shrieks of terror, cut horribly short. The footsteps become heavier. Trees part to allow the passage of . . . something. <It's not fair!> he thinks, though he dares not speak.

A voice like the sliding of continental plates speaks out from the forest.

Ally, ally, oxen free.

The massive footsteps come nearer. Inner Child waits.

"It" is coming.

They remember a fragment of ancient poetry. "Things fly apart. The center cannot hold." And "What rough beast, its time come round at last, slouches toward Bethlehem to be born."

Donovan peers above the parapet of the ruined building and his hands choke his spot-rifle. Bullets sing off the plasteel and he ducks back down. The assault has failed. The Protector's flag still flies over Coronation House. Bolt tanks have moved into postion at each of the streets visible from this position. The redoubt is surrounded, no question.

He rolls to another position, estimates where the closest tank must be, then pops up and "paints" the tank with his spot-rifle and ducks back down before the chatterguns walk in on him. He waits, but nothing happens.

"The protectors must have sanded the satellite," he says. "Our submunitions didn't lock onto the painter!"

He looks around. The parapet is empty save for the dead.

Where have his squadmates gone? They can't have abandoned him!

The sky turns white and the building shudders. He feels a tingling even through his insulation. The bolt-tank has fired. It will be several minutes while it recharges. But of course there are four of them, one at each intersection, and they will take turns. The Chancellery across the plaza— O'Farrell's post—suddenly flashes and the walls fall in on themselves as the building comes down. How much longer can he hold the Education Ministry?

A young woman touches him on the shoulder and he blinks in surprise. She is young, hardly more than a girl, unarmored, uninsulated, barefoot amid the broken glass and masonry that litter the rooftop. She wears a Doric chiton and seems too delicate even to live on this world, let alone in the hell it has become.

(But where is this world? Donovan wonders. What is this city? The buildings sport lions' heads with gaping mouths at their cornices, but is that an emblem of the regime, a whim of the architect, or nothing in particular? In the plaza below he had glimpsed a statue of a triton holding a three-pronged fish-spear.)

"There is a way out of this," she tells him, and her voice is like a melody.

He remembers that there is an old, unused system of subterranean steam tunnels connecting the buildings in the Old Quarter of the city. They had been bricked over and abandoned in place following the shift to beamed microwave power during the Long Recovery, but the tunnels are still there. Bullets spray the parapet once again and he rolls away from the edge, staying down below the merlons until he reaches the center of the roof. The others in his cell lie slumped and dazed at their positions, except those who, unmoving, will never move again. Some follow him with their eyes, but even that is too much for most. Defeat stares back at him. 𝔗𝔥𝔢𝔯𝔢 𝔦𝔰 𝔞 𝔴𝔞𝔶 𝔬𝔲𝔱 𝔬𝔣 𝔥𝔢𝔯𝔢, he tells them.

But that is not enough. The girl in the chiton stands a-tiptoe and whispers in his ear. "They need encouragement."

As if such things could be ordered up a ducat the dozen! *Listen to me, men.* And a few do, not many. *We have lost this day. But there will be other days! We knew this would be 'a mere gesture' when we first hoarded weapons against it. But there will be other gestures! We here will not be forgotten. The Protector has not fallen, but he has teetered just a bit. He has rocked on his executive chair, and like a man tipping too far back, he had flailed in panic for fear of falling.* A few grin at the imagery. Two pick up their weapons and crawl to him. *The next tip will topple him; or the tip after that. Our children, or our children's children will finish where we have started. One day they will say, "The lamp that was lit has been lit again."*

No one cheers. They are past cheering. But a grim determination takes hold of them. Which way is out, Section Leader? Which way?

We must go down, all the way down to the dark and the fog, before we can come up again.

Some understand. The old tunnels? They are still open?

Others say, We cannot move. We will stay and man the parapets, and maintain the illusion that all remain.

The gesture touches, though the wounded have little choice but to make it. He goes from one to another and exchanges grips with them. *The Rearguard dies, but never surrenders. Your names will always be known.*

Known or forgotten, our fate is the same.

If go down you shall, why not go down shooting?

The girl in the chiton seems to float above the ceramic tiles of the rooftop. "Words are bullets, too; and they wound long after the last bullet has been fired."

He leads them down the darkened stairwell. <Quiet!> he cautions them. <They may have infiltrated the building.> They pass dim and empty offices, long looted for anything of use, littered with casings and sabots and exhausted battery packs, and here and there, too, the corpses of those who came to seize the offices and those who would not leave them. It had surprised him how many believed in the Protector. It was possible that even the Protector believed.

They pass the broadcast studio and pause long enough to beckon to Issa Dzhwanson, the silver-throated actress, idol of millions, who has been for these past few days the clarion voice of their futility. But she shakes her head and like the men and women on the rooftop will not leave her post. *I will maintain the illusion. I will tell the world that reinforcements have come, not that the remnants have left. I will sow doubts in the mind of the Protector.*

<I cannot tell you where we go. Any lips can be brought to speak.>

If you do not escape, it will not matter that we fought, she says.

In the second subbasement he finds the wall that should have led to the old steam tunnels; but there is no door. He sinks to his heels and covers his face.

"But it is only a wall," says the girl in the chiton. "And walls have other sides."

The Fudir sends them to scrounge the maintenance shops for anything that can hack and dig and chop. He flips his goggles up and sees how dark the room is. "Set your zoots to black," he tells them. "Ramp your temperature down. If we can't be invisible, let's be hard to see."

They pick and chip at the wall he judges most likely to have bricked over the old tunnel entrance. The blocks are ceramic and hard to break, but once through the surface facing, progress is easier. He wonders. Are we digging in the right place? How thick is the wall? Is time running out? Will the Protector's men enter the building to seize it or simply stand back and bring it down, as they brought down the Chancellery? Seventeen stories tower above them.

Later, there is a clatter above of boots on stairs. The Fudir gestures and men pause, improvised picks half raised, and they listen.

"They will go up, not down," the girl tells him, and he wonders why no one else sees her. "Time has not yet run out."

Once in the tunnel they are faced with a choice. Left or right? The stone staircase behind them has been hidden by old furniture pulled in front of the opening. It will not long fool a diligent search.

"But they will likely not search," the girl says.

She is right. No roll was taken of those who seized the building. How could the Protected Ones know that some have left? But neither will it do to turn the wrong way and flee into a building already occupied by the Protector's men. To the river, then. The tunnels once extended that far. But which way is riverward?

Steam lines. Failure modes analysis. Possible ruptures. Condensing steam. Water, a lot of it. Mitigation plan. Run out into the river. Energy needed to remove water. Gravity assist. Conclusion: there will be a perceptible slope down toward the river.

He pulls an I-ball from his pouch and places it on the floor of the tunnel. It does not move. He kicks it right and it rolls a little way and then stops. He nudges it to the left with his boot, and it rolls, and then rolls a little faster, and then picks up speed, until it curves into the wall and comes to a rest.

This way, he says.

He leads his squad at the trot through the tunnel, their

handlights opening pools of yellow-green light for their goggles. The lamps will make them visible, should anyone else be in the tunnels, but speed matters more than caution now. They must reach the river while the Protected Ones are focused on the Education Ministry, the Chancellery ruins, and the other buildings the patriots have occupied in the Centrum.

The men stagger. It has been four days without rest, and the river is a league away. Twice more, he must play the trick with the I-ball, and each time they turn trustingly downhill.

We are running in circles, a heavy voice says. And a fetid, stale breeze chokes them for a moment with ancient dust. *Would it be so terrible to surrender? You will be Conditioned, but at least you will live. There is a limit to what the human body can endure.*

"But perhaps not to what the human spirit can," says the girl.

They pause for rest and he looks at each of his squad. Ten of them have made it out of the building. The others, left behind, must be dead by now, or on their way to reconditioning camps. Is this all that is left of the conflagration they had hoped to ignite? A boy, a woman, six men, and the girl in the diaphanous gown.

"So long as there is a spark, there may become a flame," she says.

It's useless, one of the men declares. His voice is heavy, though oddly not with defeat.

"One day," says a young man. He is dressed in a chlamys, fastened at the right shoulder, under which he is otherwise nude. His right flank is exposed. "One day, people will look back and remember the names of each one here."

But are you *here?* Donovan wonders. *Am I?* For all he

knows he may be lying unconscious on the floor somewhere on a world as yet unknown.

"You will never have better friends than you have this day," the young man continues. "Each of you owes your life to the others. You have acted with one will, one mind."

Donovan notes how the grime of battle has likened them. The same war paint, the same camouflage zoots. Hands, eyes, faces made anonymous by concealing goggles and gloves. He goes to each one in turn and embraces them, and they do the like. One is especially fervent, and bestows a kiss on his cheek.

"It will be dark," the girl says, "when we reach the river."

There comes a time when the body finds its limits, and then it finds whether there is anything beyond those limits. The river is wide at this point, but its banks are undeveloped and so there are none to see him. He wants nothing more than to lie there and sleep undisturbed until morning. After which, in the pitiless light of day, he will be considerably disturbed. **Very funny,** he thinks. But there are miles to go before he sleeps. There is a safe house in the O'erfluss District, if he can reach it. If it is still safe.

"Why assume it is not until we need to know?"

He looks around to see who has spoken, but he is alone on the river's bank. **Who was that?** he asks the night; but receives no answer save the murmur of the river's current, the creaking of insects, and the distant crackle of bolt-tanks and thud of buildings behind him in the Centrum. He uses the I-ball for its intended purpose, tossing it up and letting the stabilized images from its miniature cameras flash his surroundings on his goggles. No one is near.

Not much left of the Revolution . . .

"Whatever you rescue from a burning house is a gain."

He summons reserves of strength, rises to his feet, walks slowly to the edge of the river. **Sooner begun, sooner done.** He will probably drown halfway across; and it is a measure of where he has come to that this seems a happy end.

He wades in until the water is waist deep, then he stretches out and begins to swim. The zoot helps, since it has buoyancy pockets. The current carries him downstream, away from the firefight in the city's center and toward the great bridge, black-shadowed against the night sky.

It is tempting to give up and simply drift with the river. In the buoyant zoot, he could sleep all the way to the sea. But to reach the safe house he must make shore some place before the water-ferry docks, and so he strokes more briskly, now fighting the current.

And after a lifetime, he staggers up on the western bank of the river, and throws himself to the ground. It is marshy here. An old sugar processing plant gone to seed. Improbably, sugar cane has taken root and stands out of the water as bewildered as he.

"It's not too much farther," says the girl in the chiton. She sits atop a piling that once outlined the sugar loading dock.

He hears feet brushing through the riverside growth. Pulling back into the shadows, he slips a knife from his belt. The searcher whispers his name.

His true name.

It has been years, a lifetime, since he has heard it. And he recognizes the voice.

Rising from the shadows, he whispers urgently, **Over here.** He waits to see if he has made one last mistake, but recognition comes. **You made it out of the Chancellery, then.**

The other rebel steps forward and embraces him. "Glad to see you got free, Chief. Are there any more with you?"

"No. I . . . I thought for a while there were, but . . ."

"I understand." He kisses him on the cheeks, once on each. "I hope you do, too."

And with that the Protector's Special Security forces close in and pin his arms to his side and take the knife from his hands. They are not gentle. The goggles are yanked from his head. One of the Protected Ones punches him in the belly and he doubles over. Looking up, he catches the eye of the man who had been his friend. "Why?"

And the man shrugs and will not look at him. "'Close fits my shirt,'" he quotes the proverb, "'but closer my skin.'"

Donovan gathers all his strength—though there is little left to gather—and he reaches out with both hands and . . .

. . . and dimensions twist and their hands impossibly meet.

The Fudir holds tight; sees that Donovan has done the same at his end of the table, grabbing Silky Voice and Pedant. Sleuth gropes for Pedant; Brute for Silk. Inner Child clutches the Silky Voice like an infant his Madonna. <Go away!> he tells the shadowy apparition. <You're bad! Go away!>

. . . and then they are a ring, and the unshaped thing is excluded, and the table is normal in size and shape, and there are only the nine of them around it.

Each looks at the other, and looks at where the shadows had sat, and it is all gone. Donovan wrenches his hand from the Brute's grasp. Sleuth lets go. Pedant crosses his arms and leans back in his chair.

"Well," says the Fudir. "That was different."

"Laugh all you want to, you fool; but that is what comes of your fissiparous activities."

"Mine!"

"Yes, yours. And all the rest of you. What are you, after all, but shards and pieces of me! By your very existence you fragment me."

The Sleuth turns to the Pedant. *What is the point of your gathering the grapes of experience if you fail to press them for the wine of wisdom?*

The naked young man in the chlamys says harshly, "Have you learned nothing? You have defeated Nothing itself. But you have defeated nothing yourself. You have preserved yourself intact, and which of you did that?"

"Who are you?" asks the Fudir. "And you?" The last is aimed at the young girl in the chiton.

"Parts of you," she says, "that you thought you had lost, but who were always there, close by, waiting."

"Was all that . . . ," says Donovan. "Was all that something that once happened to us? Was it memory, or imagination?" Had he really fomented a rebellion against some tyrant somewhere? Had they conditioned him out of the very memory of it?

The girl shrugs. "I know no more than you; but I would like to think that we will one day remember who we were."

The first part, says the Sleuth. *That was clearly symbolic.*

Symbolizing what?

"The facets of a diamond," the young man suggests.

Donovan stares at him and recognizes what he once was, a long time ago. And he knows that he cannot be that ever again. He has lost his youth.

"And is that not a gain," asks the girl, "as well as a loss?"

"I think," says Donovan, "that I will call you Pollyanna."

"Call me what you will, so long as you call upon me when the box has been emptied out. Every man loses his youth one day. You need not lose your happiness."

Méarana!

"If that is your happiness."

The Pedant smacks the table. 𝕽𝖊𝖒𝖊𝖒𝖇𝖊𝖗 𝖙𝖍𝖊 𝖒𝖎𝖓𝖎𝖔𝖓 𝖙𝖍𝖆𝖙 𝖈𝖍𝖆𝖓𝖌𝖊𝖉.

And the dog that turned.

"And the man who kissed us on the riverbank," says the Fudir.

He leans back in his chairs and considers. He can see it so clearly now and wonders why he has not seen it much earlier. Too busy mocking himself. Too busy fighting himself.

"We can't stay here. It would be a betrayal. She is our daughter, after all."

Finally, you admit it?

"Yes," says the Fudir. "Her chin. Her age. Half of what she is. Though it frightens me."

"It ought to," Donovan comments. "We can't let her go into the Wild, knowing what we know."

Have you forgotten? We've been drugged. We lie helpless on some Gatmander cot.

𝔖𝔦𝔩𝔨𝔶? 𝔍𝔰𝔫'𝔱 𝔱𝔥𝔞𝔱 𝔶𝔬𝔲𝔯 𝔧𝔬𝔟? 𝔜𝔬𝔲'𝔩𝔩 𝔫𝔢𝔢𝔡 *𝔱𝔥𝔦𝔰* 𝔢𝔫𝔷𝔶𝔪𝔢, 𝔞𝔫𝔡 *𝔱𝔥𝔦𝔰* 𝔬𝔫𝔢, 𝔱𝔬 𝔠𝔬𝔲𝔫𝔱𝔢𝔯𝔞𝔠𝔱 𝔦𝔱.

The Silky Voice summons glands into service. Enzymes race from their enclosures. Antibodies hunt down drug molecules, latch on, seize them and choke them tight, shove them out through sweat pores.

"As it pertains to him," he hears a voice say, "there is a fever."

And Donovan knows by this sign that he is near the farther bank of the river.

"There is still time," says the young girl in the chiton.

XI INTO THE WILD

Méarana had second thoughts about leaving Donovan behind, but her two companions assured her it was all for the best. "A man that sick can't help us," Teodorq told her as they rode the bumboat up to *Blankets and Beads*.

"We just go Wild look-look," Billy added. "You see. Back no-long time. Sahb get good care meanwhile."

But it was not whether Donovan received good care or bad that bothered Méarana, it was whether he received that care from strangers. And a friend was not measured by the good he could do you. "Maybe we could have waited a little longer."

"Ah, no, memsahb! Port Captain say long time no more trade-ship."

"What the little weasel means, babe," the barbarian told her, "is this was his best chance to run out on his master."

"You no say such, lack-wit! Mistress Harp need me now, not sick-man Donovan."

"Quiet, the both of you." She fell into a morose silence as the boat hurtled upward on Port Gatmander's laser lift. Teodorq tried to pretend he was an old hand at this sort of thing, but every time the vessel shuddered, the Wildman grabbed for the edges of his seat. Billy saw this and snickered, though by his own admission he had himself ridden a laser lift only twice.

Méarana sighed once more. "I hope our luggage makes it."

"No worry, memsahb. Dukovers handle luggage alla time. Cargo boat lift, yawn-yawn-time."

Méarana once more tried to relax, but almost immediately the boat began docking maneuvers and the gyros spun the great, gray world of Gatmander into her viewport. *Ah, Donovan. Sure, and it's all for the best.*

Blankets and Beads resembled more a small town in orbit than anything once called "ship." Domes, spheres, apses, barrels, and tubes joined in a complexity of angles, connections, and fusions, like a mass of soap bubbles. The resemblance to a town was heightened by the whimsical outer structures by which the pressure vessels were decorated to resemble buildings of different eras in the long history of

UP JIM RIVER 311

human habitation. The skin-style had been popular among shipbuilders a generation before, but had grown passé among the inner worlds. It survived now only among the thrice-used ships at the edge of civilized space.

She carried survey-class alfvens, for in the Wild she could expect no assistance from ground-based propulsion, and must pull herself along by the very strings of space. She also contained ffffg-imagers to analyze the berms of uncharted roads and probe for unmarked exits. It was a dangerous business, as the slightest miscalculation could take the ship into the subluminal mud to dissipate in a Ĉerenkov blink. Consequently, while her owners were tight enough with the ducat to outfit her with secondhand gear, they were wise enough to scrounge only the very best of secondhand gear.

The other reason for the trade ship's size was that such vessels often embarked on voyages years in duration, and when they did so took along families and friends. She resembled a small town because on many occasions she was one. This left plenty of room for passengers on those shorter jaunts on better-established routes when only the crew was aboard.

Méarana, Theodorq, and Billy Chins were welcomed aboard by the cargo-master, if welcome it be called—a subtle if unwitting indicator of their status in the ship's economy. The master's name was Mart Pepper, who projected by his attitude a preference for less animate cargo. He checked each of them against a list, and gave them a chit directing them to their quarters. The chit would brighten or dim depending on whether they were on the proper path or not. It would also open and lock their cabins, debit their meals from their deposits, and so on.

As he handed each of them their chit, Pepper muttered in a wonderful economy of syllables, "Cap'n'll bead-lighted tavya-come t'dinner-atse'n-point-five horae, metric," although he did not communicate a very heartfelt delight nor even that the sentence was composed of more than a single, very long word.

Méarana said, "We'll try to keep out of your way." But even that, Pepper indicated by his grimace would not be far enough.

Their cabins were in Dome Three, encircling what appeared to be a village green. It featured bushes, a fountain, children's playsets, and several dwarf maples. It was cleverly landscaped to appear larger than it was, and Méarana inferred the long-ago hand of a High Taran greensman.

There were a few other passengers already about on the green. One was a veiled woman with the grand title of Princess of the Farther Spaces from a small world on the farther side of the Burnt-Over District. She had negotiated a trade treaty with the League, had been suitably awed by what she had seen, and was returning with her eunuch and maidservant with a page full of promises.

"You pipple of the Farther Space," she later complained to Méarana in a heavily-accented Gaelactic, "you tink because we pipple got no ray guns, we stupider than you pipple. But we know it when we getting poked up the butt."

The fourth passenger was a thin, well-shaped man a little older than Méarana, dark-haired, long-nosed, with a dusky complexion, and garbed in a practical traveler's coverall. He sat by himself on a bench by the fountains and, so intent was he on a reading screen, that he had created a bubble of privacy that Méarana was loathe to break.

Lastly, there was a Wildman from Teodorq's own home world; though their bodyguard was not pleased to find a compatriot on board. "Paulie's o' the Hawk clan out in Overmount," he said. "Yuh can tell by his tats. They futter sheep out there, 'cause they can't get no women."

"Stay away from him, then," the harper told him.

When the dinner chimes called the passengers to follow their glowing chits toward the barrel vault leading into Dome Two, Méarana noticed the dusky man still engrossed in his screen; so she went to him and touched him on the shoulder. "Dinner bell sounded," she said. "They won't wait."

The man did not look up. "You are casting a shadow on my screen."

Surprised to be so admonished, Méarana stepped aside and glanced curiously at the man's screen—and recognized the gene map he was studying.

"Professor Doctor Doctor Sofwari! I have been wanting to meet you for a very long time."

At that, he did look up, his eyes showing surprise, puzzle, and pleasure in rapid succession. He rose and took Méarana's hand in his and kissed the back of it in a greeting gesture that the harper had not encountered before, but found unusually pleasant. "And I have been waiting even longer for a beautiful stranger to say that to me."

Méarana laughed and offered her arm and they walked together to the dining hall. "You and I," she said, "have much to discuss."

Teodorq Nagarajan knew he was destined for greatness. He was not certain what form this greatness would take, only that his village did not contain it. And so, not long after killing his first man, he had taken up the trade of the wandering champion. Partly, this was a necessity. Dead men have kinsmen. But partly, too, it was sheer wanderlust. On some worlds, he would have been called a mercenary though he often worked pro bono.

He followed rumors to the coast, where he found "the Big Encampment" to be wood-and-brick buildings, stacked cheek-by-jowl, some soaring to three storeys, and built by the strange green-faced men from over the Boundless Main. They had come, the coastalmen told him, in large canoes with blankets tied to sticks. But Teodorq set himself the task of "learning the ropes," in the sailormen's talk, signing on as a "landsman" and making several voyages with them.

He mastered the new by never allowing his sense of wonder to become a sense of awe. He learned to study a thing with narrow-eyed concentration rather than to stare at it in gape-jawed astonishment. Too many coastalmen had fallen into drunkenness and squalor from awe of the green-faced men.

In the Oversealand he saw wonders beyond wonders and learned that the "Big Encampment" was a poor imitation of the sprawling, brawling cities of Old Cuffy and Yavel-prawns and the other Great States. There had been employment there, too, and he had learned the art of the musket and the cannon. Although he regarded the latter as unmanly and the former as too slow to reload, he did not allow his sense of honor to outweigh his sense of practicality. He learned, too, a grave respect for captains who used men well, and contempt for those who used them badly.

Still, it was the "stunt" which lured him, and he sensed that in the massed armies of the Great States there was little scope for a man not "born with a cockade in his cap." He heard tales that far to the southeast, in the land of the swartsmen, were fabulous cities where men had caged fire in steel. And so he set out to find them.

His journey, had any of the skalds of his homeland known of it, would have earned him immortality seven times seven. He crossed inland seas and deserts, he passed the broken monuments of forgotten empires, he gazed on the ruins of a city that would have put to shame even the grand capital of Yavelprawns had it not been the hovel now of howling savages. He endured a winter beyond imagination in the high ice-mountains of Bellophor, where lived a degraded and cannibalistic folk who dressed in the furs of the White Grizz. And in the end he had come to the finest city on World, where an appalling stench of soot and fire blackened the very air, but in whose stamping mills wondrous weapons and other goods were forged. The smiths of the plains had fashioned swords upon anvils with mighty strokes of thick-hewed arms. Those of Old Cuffy and the other Great States had done so with trip-hammers and water-driven wheels. But in the cities of Varucciyam in the far southeast they had tamed the Fire itself! Ai, Tengri! Awe very nearly overcame wonder in his heart.

But he had schooled himself well, and he saw in the whirling "gears" and "driveshafts" but finer versions of the cams and blocks and tackle of the northwest, and in the power delivered by steam a more refined version of the power delivered by water unboiled. He hired himself out as usual, starting with the most menial deeds; found dishonor and treachery to be fine arts among the Varucciyamen; and taught them a bit of what honor meant on plains so distant that word of them had not yet reached their ears.

And then, one day a ship that sailed no ocean drifted down from the skies. That something so massive could float like a leaf was a wonder in itself, and Teodorq found himself asking, "How do they do that?" It shamed him that the proud men of Varucciyam abased themselves before these overskymen. Had not he, Teodorq sunna Nagarajan the Iron-Arm, stood before the squalid wonders of the "encampment" of New Cuffy, knowing that he stood before that which his own people could not build? And yet he had *stood* before it. He had not knelt or bowed or banged his forehead on the ground. That a man commands steel or fire made a man more dangerous, but it did not make him more of a man. Greed and pride and, yes, love and honor were to be found among all: among the plainsmen and the Varucciyamen, among the Great States and even among the feral tribes of the Ice Mountains.

And so it was with an eye practiced on a score of cultures that he had identified among the strange-garbed men of the sky-ship the "chief of the boat." This man understood the speech of the Varucciyamen, for this was not the first such visit, and Teodorq approached him and became once again a "landsman" on a new sort of "sailing ship."

And there he found his understanding blunted at last. The gulf that separated the overskymen from even the Varucciyamen was wider than the gulf of the Grand Crevasse that split the Wondering Mountains of Eastern Bellophor. Yet there were certain tasks that wanted less the How than the simple What. *What* this button did could be learned. *How* it did so was better left to the shamans.

Afterward he thought, in a moment of self-awareness, that he had moved so easily with the overskymen because he had not come to them with the same conceit as the Varucciyamen. He had seen, time and again in his wanderings, that none could count themselves the greatest of all. Conceit he had; but it was conceit in himself as a man, and not in his mastery of this tool or that weapon. The proud cities of the southeast, looking far and wide, had found no rival to their greatness. To learn their true place in "the Spiral Arm" had been a crushing blow and made of a once-proud people a race of lackeys.

And so Theodorq listened to the science-wallah aboard the *Blankets and Beads* with a practiced and a practical ear, if not with an ear tuned to full understanding. He heard the Whats and dismissed the Hows. He suspected there was more of the latter in the explanation than was strictly needed. Sofwari was one of those who enjoyed the mystification of others. It was common among the physically weak to seek their victories on other fields. For any man must feel that he excels at some one thing, and the more he fails in other endeavors, the more he elevates the one in which he does not.

Yet Teodorq detected no malice in the man, and wondered if he chattered on not to show off his kennings but simply because he took such joy in them that he could not conceive that others did not.

Teodorq understood maps, and the holographic projections that Sofwari showed them were only another sort. That the color gradients indicated the spread of certain clans from their points of origin he accepted on faith. In his own land, the migrations of the clans were recorded in the Great Lays and sometimes one came across a mountain or a river or a rock formation remembered from a Lay and would feel one's heart swell at the thought of ancestors who had once roamed there.

"But what was it that my mother found so interesting in these maps?" Lady Harp asked the wallah.

Sofwari turned the holostage toward her. Everyone could see, except Lady Harp, that the wallah was much taken with her. "It was the anomaly," he said. "The clan-mother I call 'Zhaamileey.' You see, the little thread shapes change over time for reasons that are not entirely clear. The rate differs from world to world, but for my purposes it only mattered that that between-world variation was small and randomly distributed. Then it could be treated as a constant for all practical purposes."

Teodorq made "get on with it" motions and was none too subtle about it.

"As you see," he told them in case they could not see, "this is a very old clade. Its most recent common mother—or DCM in Gaelactic—lived seventy-eight hundreds of years before present."

Lady Harp raised her eyebrows. "Which places her *before* the Cleansing . . ."

"Yes, but that is not the anomaly. Zhaamileey is in the wrong part of the sky. Her descendants are mostly on Harpaloon, not in the Old Planets or the Jen-jen. The marker was first seen among scattered creole descendants on Cuddalore and New Shangdong, those with ancestors among the aboriginal 'Loons. That was one reason to visit Harpaloon. The other was that the flow of colonists from all over the Arm makes her a wonderful sampling point."

"How do you explain the anomaly?" asked the harper.

Sofwari flipped a hand. "Two possibilities. Harpaloon is where Zhaamileey's descendants first appeared; or it is where they last appear. As for the first, Those of Name scattered our ancestors far and wide. Harpaloon may have been scattered a little bit farther. But the second is the more likely explanation. The clan of Zhaamileey was once more widespread, but died out across most of the Periphery, so that the 'Loons are a remnant, not an origin."

"Interesting . . . But there is a third possibility."

"So your mother said." Sofwari smiled in a kindly-meant manner and placed his hand over hers. Teodorq noted how the harper allowed it for a moment before slipping out. "One means no offense, of course, but your mother was not a science-wallah. Like many women, she was prone to romantic notions. She thought the anomalous pattern had to do with an old Commonwealth fable."

"The Treasure Fleet," said Lady Harp.

Sofwari bobbed his head side to side. "Yes. I had never heard of it; but she told me it was a well-known children's tale when she had been 'in barracks.' But archeology must be based on facts, not romances. One may as well believe in Babylonia or California or the Snowdrift Ride of Christopher Chu."

"California . . . ," Méarana suggested.

"A fabled land of eternal youth, of gods and goddesses, where the streets were paved with stars." Sofwari chuckled and leaned toward the harper, as if to impart a confidence. "But the truth of it is that it is only a nebula off on the edge of Old Commonwealth space."

"Is there a bright, hot, blue star nearby?" the harper asked. "Like the one at Sapphire Point?"

Sofwari wagged his hands ulta-pulta. "I don't know. Other science-wallahs specialize in cataloging stars. Besides, it's over in the Confederation."

The harper sang softly a capella,

*"Away, away on the Rigel Run,
And off through California."*

Sofwari sighed. "A science-wallah does not leap ahead of the facts, let alone for the sake of a song."

Teodorq chuckled and the other three turned to him. "Well enough, Sofwari," he said. "If our Bridget ban leaped ahead of the facts, yet here we are, tiptoeing after."

JHALA (DRUT)

In all her years knocking about the Periphery, Captain Maggie Barnes of the trade ship *Blankets and Beads* had encountered a great many irritations and not a few outrages. Experience had taught her that most could be dealt with by patience. To invest much worry was pointless, because the return on that investment was usually more worries. Other problems were like fungus. If you didn't sanitize right away, they just grew worse. Or "wusser 'n' wusser," as they used to say when she had been growing up on Megranome.

But what to make of this which Pepper had dumped into her now, alas, more ample lap?

She had been in her dayroom reviewing manifests with her First Officer when Mart Pepper brought in a bit of supercargo who claimed the authority to commandeer her ship. She studied the passenger's bona fides, and turned to First Officer ad-Din. "It seems to be a legitimate Kennel chit, D.Z."

The First Officer's full name was Dalapathi Zitharthan ad-Din, but to the joy of his shipmates, he would answer to his initials. He tugged at his beard. "Bumboat drops back to the Gat in a half-hora," he said thoughtfully. "Plenty of empty space on it for unwanted passengers. Otherwise . . . Our first stop is Ākramaṇapīchē. Folks marooned there don't usually find their way back to the League."

Barnes studied the chit more thoroughly. Its glow had died, of course, when she had taken it in hand; but it *had* been glowing. She had never heard of a Kennel chit being successfully counterfeited, but that did not mean it could not be done.

"This only means yuh have an unlimited expense account," she told her guest. "It means yuh can *afford* my ship. Don't mean yuh can *have* it." She handed the chit back and noted how it resumed its glow. Tag-alongs glowed when you were in the corridors that activated them. There was no way for them to recognize who held them. That bit of Kennel craft was closely guarded indeed.

Reluctantly, she concluded that this Donovan was exactly what he pretended to be: a "special agent" of the Kennel. The next question was what real authority a "special agent" might possess. "We'll gladly afford yuh passage to Enjrun. We was plannin' to stop there, anyways."

"We know," Donovan replied. "We checked with your owners at Chandler House before the bumboat rose."

We?

"The owners would have been asleep at that hour," D.Z. pointed out.

"We woke them."

"That why the bumboat was late?" Barnes was impressed with the throw-weight this indicated, but she did not let it show in her face. It might only show that people wakened in the middle of the night could be buffaloed more easily.

Donovan handed over a hard document and a brain. "It is also why we have a charter."

The paper declared "to all and sundry" that Gospender and Recket Trading Company of Gaznogav-Gatmander, had accepted charter of their trade ship, *Blankets and Beads*, to the Kennel of the High King, to be used as directed by Donovan buigh, their agent, or by Lucia Thompson, d.b.a., Méarana of Dangchao.

Barnes handed the brain to D.Z., who ran it through the sanitizer before inserting it in the reader. She held the hard up to the light. That was the G&R watermark, all right, and she recognized Kimmy Gospender's chop. She doubted that the brain would prove a forgery, either because it was not a forgery, or because it was a very good one. She handed the hard over to her First. "Verify this with Kimmy—voice-and-vision—before we hit the roads."

"Damn it, Barnsey, I've got a bundle tied up in trade goods for Ākramaṇapīchē and for Zhenghou Shuai, too! All on hire-purchase."

"Argue with the owners, D.Z. Seems they done sold us out." She folded her hands into a ball on her desktop. "And yuh ought to be aware, *Donovan*, that all my officers got money at risk on this here voyage. Legally, yuh can do what yuh want; but I thought yuh'd like to know."

Meaning that, illegally, who knew what could happen? Donovan smiled engagingly, and Barnes thought for a moment that there was something very familiar about that smile. "We appreciate that, Captain; and were this not of the greatest importance to the League, we would have delayed the charter until we found a ship free. But we can sweeten the pot two ways. The first is that after you drop us on Enjrun you can finish your deals at Ōram and Zhenghou Shuai, and then come back and pick us up. Our business should be done by then. If not, we'll dicker a little more. The Kennel can afford bonuses. Then you can do the rest of your trades—Kaṇṭu, Ākramaṇapīchē, and the rest—on the trip back. So all you lose is a little time backtracking to Enjrun."

"How d'ye know we won't maroon you on Enjrun?" asked D.Z. "She isn't the most pleasant world to be stuck on." Barnes shot him an irritated look. She did not want to aggravate the situation.

"Oh, that's simple enough," Donovan said. "I took out an insurance policy. Copies of the charter went to Greystroke-Hound and his Pup, and to Zorba de la Susa on High Tara. All three of them have a very deep *personal* interest in this assignment."

Barnes had started to say that she had never heard of this Greystroke, but stopped herself. De la Susa, she *had* heard of. "I thought Old Hound was retired."

"He'll come out of retirement just for this. It involves his goddaughter. We guarantee that Greystroke and Rinty will be waiting on Gatmander when *Blankets and Beads* returns and while they might not weep if we're not aboard, they will very much want to know where Méarana of Dangchao is. Captain Barnes, we are not your enemy. A Confederate agent is on the same trail, and no one will be happy if he reaches the end of it before we do."

"What's the second sweetener?" Barnes asked. "I hope it's sweeter than the threats."

Donovan spread his hands. "We can hook you up with a

consortium on Dancing Vrouw that's interested in some of the goods you buy on Enjrun."

Barnes cocked an eyebrow. A handshake with a Hansard Trading House was worth a great deal indeed. "What's the arrangement?"

"We have one end of a 60:40 for all the parking stone jewelry you can get. You help us, we give you half of our end."

Barnes pursed her lips and locked eyes with her Number One, who tipped his head ever so slightly to the right. "Half of the forty?" she asked.

"Half of the sixty."

Both she and D.Z. relaxed. Assuming Donovan spoke sooth, anyone who could wangle the long side of a Hanseatic deal was a man of considerable wangle indeed, and one worth dealing with.

But she could not shake the notion that she had once known this man, and that the knowing had not been a happy occasion.

Billy Chins was quite satisfied with how matters had fallen out. The mind-crippled Donovan had been discarded, leaving only the dimwitted Wildman. Now he need only follow the harper, and glory and renown would be his—and perhaps power, as well, if he understood properly the hints thrown his way. It was not quite clear what the harper and the scarred man thought they had found, perhaps not even to them. Whatever it was, it had killed a Hound and that was something very puissant indeed. *Fire from the sky* could mean a great many things, and none of them sounded harmless.

But for now he remained a servant and "Spud" deViis, the ship's steward, wanted to see him. It was not so bad to wait upon the harper, whom he had grown rather to like, but aṭangku could be an irritation. He followed his tag-along down corridors and through apses and bubbles and along a tube into Dome Five until he found the door plac-arded VICTUALLING and pressed the hoígh plate. The door slid open and . . .

. . . he stepped inside to find a bare room. He hesitated just the barest fraction. Had he come to the wrong place somehow? And in that fraction the door slid shut behind him.

Trapped! By whom? It was too subtle for the oaf Te-odorq; too treacherous for the harper. He backed into a corner, drew his stiletto and waited, ready.

A door opened on the far side of the room, and through it stepped Donovan.

Billy flung his knife, but Donovan stepped aside and snatched it handle-first out of the air. He looked at it and smiled at Billy, and Billy did not like the smile. "You ought to be more careful, boy," he said.

Billy fell to his knees. "Oh, sahb! Sahb! Billy fear such-much! Door close, and I think budmash trap for Billy. I think: does agent who follow behind us—catch up now long time? But master only make surprise poor Billy. Such joy to see sahb! O such-much sorrow, if knife find heart of master!"

Donovan shook his head. "I didn't mean careful with the knife. I meant careful with your syntax."

"Syn-tax, sahb?"

"In the hotel on Dancing Vrouw. You said 'out to the Rift,' and no Leaguesman would ever say that. We say 'into the Rift.' Only a Confederate thinks 'out' when he thinks of the Rift. For a long time, we couldn't put the pieces to-gether; but . . . Was drugging us your idea? We have you to thank, then."

Billy began to sweat. This was a Donovan he had never

seen before. "No, sahb! You wrong him, Billy. Billy Chins your khitmutgar!"

"Yes, that was slick, the way you arranged that. We don't know if we would have seen through it even if we had been whole at the time."

"No see-through! You protect Billy from 'Loonies! *You* ask *me* come with!"

"Clever, like I said. But I think that mob was bought and the whole thing staged. Art thou evenso a Terry?"

The last he had asked in the Tongue. Billy sighed and gave it up. "As thou sayest."

Donovan grunted. "So. Many of the Folk wear the collar of our oppressor. The next question is: what are we to do with you? Did you kill that woman on Harpaloon?" He turned the knife casually in his hand.

"No. That was my shadow."

"Ah."

"Thou knowest the shadows. The Names send us out in pairs, with the second to act if the first fails. The second agent hath always the higher loyalty quotient."

"Trust is not among Their many qualities," Donovan said. "Yes, we know the system. We once had dealings with a second."

"Ravn Olafsdottr."

"Yes. Knowest thou her?"

"By reputation only. May I rise, O best one?"

Donovan gestured with the knife, and Billy struggled to his feet, in the course of which Donovan produced a dazer in place of the knife. "Now, explain thyself, worthless one. Much dependeth upon thine answers."

Billy bowed slightly. "I was sent to question the woman at the park. She was what we call a *myan zhan shibang*—a sleep-agent . . ."

"We know Confederal Manjrin," Donovan interrupted

in that language before reverting to the Tongue. "Speak more quickly, that thy life be thereby prolonged."

Billy bowed again. "I found her much alarmed over the harper's visit. She desired instruction. I allayed her fears, and set out to learn what the visit portended. Easily did I find the Hound's daughter and, Lo! She led me unto thee. I thought that thou hadst . . . overcome thine infirmity. But my shadow took offense that the jawharry had held a Hound's package without reporting."

"Fool! She knew it not."

Billy shrugged. "Now my shadow hunts me, also, for I did nothing to punish her. For this reason did I attach myself to you, and in your protection flee my station on Harpaloon. Listen, and I will tell thee something. There is a struggle in the Lion's Mouth. 'The lamp that was lit has flared again.' Agent hunts agent. 'The names that were not forgotten have been remembered.'"

"What is that to us, but an occasion to cheer each side in turn?"

"The woman at the park had sympathy for that remembrance. So hath I. My shadow does not. Should *he* find thee, he will kill thee."

"He will try." Donovan held the knife in throwing position. "As you damn near did."

Billy closed his eyes and let out his breath. He sensed that he would live the day. "I feared a trap, and threw without thought. Who else knows of me?"

Donovan laughed. "Am I a fool? They all know. Captain Barnes. The whole crew. I told them before I arranged this meeting."

"What then is to be our resolution?"

"Doest thou truly reject Those of Name?"

"I do."

"And all Those works?"

"I do. I have trawled the League for others of like sympathy, dispatching them back to the Confederation, there to aide in Their overthrow. But my usefulness is now at an end, and I flee myself for my life."

Donovan nodded. "Give thanks to whichever gods please thee that thou livest this day for the morrow."

"Let me not question my fortune, good or ill, nor tempt the gods, but why extend my life for even one hour longer? Is there not a scripture that sayeth, 'Better safe than sorry'?"

Donovan grinned. "We are in the Wild, boy. And another scripture saith, 'The enemy of mine enemy is my friend.' Another good eye, another skilled pair of hands, would not be unwelcome—provided the eyes may be trusted and the hands not turn against us. And this trust will be proofed not by thy word, but by thy self-interest. For in the Wild 'We must all hang together lest we hang separately.'"

When Teodorq Nagarajan returned to his quarters in the "village," he sensed another presence waiting in the darkened room, and fell to a crouch without turning on the light. His eyes searched for that shadow within the shadows that did not belong.

"Just tell us one thing, Teddy," said a voice that had grown familiar to him.

Teodorq grinned and rose and turned on the lights. He tucked his nine back in its holster. "Yuh sure gave me a start, boss." The dazer in Donovan's hand worried him, but the scarred man held the weapon pointed to the ceiling, so he didn't worry too much.

"Just tell us one thing, Teddy," Donovan said again. "Did you provide the drug she used?"

"Sure. It's the potion we drink when we go on vision-quests to learn our true self."

Donovan grunted. "It works." He clicked the safety on and returned his weapon to its resting place. "You can put the thong back on the knife, too. Your answers were too guileless. You really thought you were doing us a favor."

Teodorq shrugged. "I couldn't let her go into the Free Worlds with only him to protect her."

"You're a loyal man, Teddy."

He shrugged. "She's paying me."

"Teddy, we have one more call to make. Contact Sofwari and tell him the team will meet in half an hora, on the Green."

"You want me to tell Billy, too?"

"That won't be necessary."

An important quality of a harper's art is the ability not to miss a beat. But when Méarana of Dangchao finished freshening up and returned from the vanity to the sitting room of her quarters to find Donovan buigh sitting in the big blue padded chair that she had taken as her favorite, it required all of her mastery to maintain her rhythm.

"You keep turning up," she said, "like a bad ducat."

"And you keep leaving us behind; so it evens up."

"After a while, one tires of dragging and pushing and prodding. Had ye not dragged your heels . . ."

"Are you going to offer us a drink? I thought you might have a bottle of uiscebeatha in your room."

"Harp, clothing, weapons, and uisce. The four essentials."

"I get by without the harp. In a pinch, I can get by without the clothing."

There was a cold-well in the suite's galley and Méarana produced from it a bottle of Gatmander *vawga*, called Shining Moon. "Will this do? It's been aging since at least last week."

Donovan said, "You better watch that stuff. Someone could dope it with gods-know-what and you'd never taste it."

Méarana had been pouring two drinks and at that she spilled on the counter. "That wasn't a fair shot."

"Because it hit the target?"

"No." She attacked the spill with a cloth. "Because it wasn't necessary." She carried the two glasses in either hand and gave one to Donovan.

The scarred man lifted his glass as if for a toast, but Méarana simply twisted hers in her hands, staring down into it. "To the quest," he said.

"There's no need to mock."

"Who's mocking? It may be hopeless, but aren't those the sort of things that needs cheering on? Isn't that what you always say? Anyone can cheer a winner." He tossed back half his drink in a single swallow.

Méarana took a sip and drank no more. "It seemed like a good idea at the time."

"Leaving me on Gatmander? We're sure it did. And as it turned out, it was."

The harper cocked her head. "There's something different about you." She found the second chair and sank into it. "I don't know why that should surprise me. You have more differences than any man I know. You came up in the luggage boat, of course."

"Of course. The pilot was greatly surprised. Most of his luggage has little to say."

Méarana would not look at him. "Almost, I wish you hadn't made it on board." When Donovan made no response, she turned to face him. "Because if you hadn't, I might have been able to forget. Now every time I see you, I'll remember what I did."

"We all have our sins," said the scarred man. "Sometimes, it's good to remember them." He paused, and added, "I remember some rather good ones."

She could not prevent the laugh from breaking forth.

But it was a trick and it made her angry. "Why did you come? This journey is hard enough without your constant pessimism."

"You can't sip this stuff," Donovan said to his *vawda*. "There's no point in lingering over the taste. It hasn't any. Just toss it back and let it hit like a hammer."

"You have odd ideas of fun." She studied her glass and then took the hard swallow he had recommended.

"You stocked this stuff. If we had to guess, you did it for its analgesic effect."

"You didn't have to guess," she reminded him. She set her glass aside and crossed her legs. "You haven't told me why you scrambled aboard the *Blankets and Beads.*"

"There are . . . all sorts of reasons."

"Try a few."

"Well, to find out what happened to your mother, for one."

"We had that reason from the beginning, and you were eager to quit back then. And don't bring up the weapon she was trying to find. Same objection."

"We promised Zorba we would take care of you."

"So you are here under duress?"

Donovan closed his eyes and exhaled slowly. Silence gathered, and Méarana could hear the faint whisper of the air recirculator and, outside her cabin, the murmur of distant voices on the green. Then he took a deep breath and said, "Because . . . I am your father."

The harper's expression did not change. "Is this the part where I go all warm and gooey?"

"We didn't think you would take the news so well."

"It's not even news. Why do you think I came looking on Jehovah? Mother had told me everything about my father but his name. He was strong, she told me, and wise, and deep down, a good man. Can you imagine the shock it was to find *you*?"

"Did she mention that we were handsome?"

She leaned half out of her chair. "Don't make a mockery of this, Donovan! I won't have it!"

"What did you expect after twenty years? We never knew you existed. She cut us off."

"And what did *you* expect? You ran out on her and took the Dancer for yourself. How do you think *she* felt?"

"You know why I did what I did."

"But *she* did not. She never knew. She went on her last mission thinking that the man she once loved had betrayed her without a backward glance. You never called at Dangchao."

"You saw what Those did to us. Would you have welcomed that wreck?"

"I saw what you made of yourself. If Those broke you, they had your willing help."

Donovan struck the arm of the chair with his fist. His empty glass wobbled from the impact and fell to the floor. *"Then why did you come to Jehovah? Why did you drag us onto this mad venture?"*

All the anger drained out of her, and Méarana sank back into her chair. "Because I wanted a father and a mother. I wanted both, but I would have settled for either one. Not to raise me. God, it's far too late for that. But to find the man that my mother once loved . . . ? That might have been worth the effort."

Donovan reached down and picked up his empty glass from the floor. He set it this time on the side table. "Did you find him?"

"I caught a glimpse of him once in the Corner of Jehovah, on the rim of a rusted-out fountain. I bought him a cheap meal."

The scarred man all but smiled at the memory. "You'll never find what never was."

"I'm not such a fool as that. I've always looked for what

might yet still be." Then she cocked her head. "Your eyes," she said. "They're stilled."

"Yes."

She said nothing for a while, but folded her hands under her chin and studied him. For a long time, she had hesitated to call him "father," at first from uncertainty, later from a more profound uncertainty. Now she was content to wait. It was a title that must be earned.

The rapping on the door interrupted the silence before it could fall, and when Méarana told the door to open Teodorq Nagarajan stuck his head in. "They're waiting for us, boss."

Donovan pointed to Méarana with a tilt of his head. "She's the boss."

Teodorq shifted his expectant gaze from Donovan to the harper with no change in his expression. Méarana rose.

"Let's not keep them waiting."

Teodorq nodded and left. Donovan rose and offered his arm to his daughter. "Come on," he said. "Let's go find your mother."

XII IN THE REMNANTS OF EMPIRE

Blankets and Beads entered stationary orbit above Enjrun and Méarana gathered her team in the conference room so Captain Barnes could brief them on conditions below. D.Z. unrolled a holomap on the table and they gathered around the topography that emerged. Miniature mountains loomed over green floodplains. Matchstick cities sat on earthen mounds. Captain Barnes handed out earwigs.

"The *noor jessers*," she explained, "once ruled this whole region." Her arms swept across the alluvial plain, the neighboring forestlands, and the northern foothills. "So most everybody south of the Kobberjobble Mountains will savvy the *loora noor jesser.* We've loaded the lingo into these earwigs, so yuh shouldn't have trouble being understood 'til yuh get to 'bout here." She pointed to the foothills. "Once yer in the high-up hills yuh'll need to hire local translators. Enjrunii don't take ducats or Gladiola Bills, but if yuh deposit some hard currency with the Resident, he'll fix yuh up with enough silver or gold for expenses."

"We'll put you down here," said D.Z., pointing with his light-pen, "at Nuxrjes'r, our regular trade stop. The name means something like 'the place where the river can be crossed.' You can call it 'Riverbridge'—or 'Noor Jesser' if you're disinclined to cough up the necessary phlegm. It's the southernmost point where native technology can bridge the river. The east-west pack caravans connect with the north-south river traffic.

"Nuxrjes'r got rich from the tolls, and eventually got an Empire from the riches. Then, depending on who tells the tale, she grew either too greedy or too tempting, or both, and the barbarians moved south from Kobberjobbles and east from the Blistering Badya. By the time the *Bonregarde* found its way into the Burnt-Over District, the old Nuxrjes'r Empire had fragmented into a dozen successor states and a rump imperium, ruled variously by barbarian warlords or *soi disant* counts, depending on which day of the week it was.

"*Bonregarde*'s lander put all their postimperial squabbles into perspective. The warlords and counts patched up a truce and agreed that Riverbridge would be a neutral city governed by a Board of Dūqs and everyone would smile for the off-worlders."

"That was about three generations ago," Captain Barnes said. "So far, the truce seems to be holding, though the

makeup of the Board can change sudden-like. Y'might say
they moved the fightin' from outdoors to indoors. But the
trade consortium made it real clear that if trouble gets out
of hand we stop a-comin'. So the Resident is like an impar-
tial referee. He enforces commercial regs, negotiates deals,
and judges disputes among the Dūqs."

Teodorq spoke up. "If this was World, there'd be a lot of
resentment boiling underneath. I don't know if these noor
jessers got honor or not, but judging what I saw back in
Varucciyam, they'll wanna either kiss your ass or cut your
throat—or maybe both. Not much in between."

The First Officer wagged his light-pen at Teddy. "Hear
him," he told the others. "His folk are more advanced than
the Enjrunii, but he's closer to their way of thinking. Everyone down there will be kissy-kissy on the surface, but
everything depends on what they think they can get away
with. And the farther north and west you go, the less kissy-
kissy they'll be."

Captain Barnes said, "Yuh'll meet with the Resident
first. His name is Oodalo Bentsen. He'll see yuh git outfit-
ted proper." Her pen swiped through the northern mountains. "The noor jessers tell us the parking stone jewelry
comes from 'upriver,' which means these here mountains.
The Kobberjobbles."

The holographic projection displayed a broad corduroy
of high-peaked crags and deep valleys through which the
upper reaches of the Arfidnux'r wound like a hungry boa
constrictor. "The noor jessers call that stretch of river the
Multawee, which they tell me means 'twisted.'"

Méarana spoke up. "Why not put us down where the
jewelry comes from?"

D.Z. pointed into the map. "Because we don't know
where that is. We deal only with the Dūqs in Riverbridge.
Where they get the jewelry from, they don't say."

The pilot, Wild Bill, snorted. "As if we had time to flit around the planet."

D.Z. said, "Men accustomed to treachery will see it everywhere."

Inevitably, eyes turned toward Billy Chins, who flushed and protested. "When Billy ever do such? One time, name him! Ask Donovan. I come to you be safe from shadow."

"Scared of his own shadow," murmured Teddy.

Billy turned to him and wagged a finger. "You be scare, too, if you know 'em, the shadows. Maybe now she no catch up; but who can say? Billy good fella, good man in fight. Stick by you. You see him!"

Sofwari raised a hand. "What about pickup? If you don't know where we've gone . . ."

"Yuh'll have yer beacons," Barnes told them. "They handshake with our satellites and keep yuh located. After we finish our business here, we heigh off to Ōram and Zhenghou Shuai. We'll pick you up when we backtrack. Don't lose yer beacons, or we'll never find yuh."

They discussed a few more items regarding equipment, local mores, and terrain. Then D.Z. turned off his lightpen and tucked it in his blouse pocket. "Anything to add, Captain?"

Barnes pushed her lips out and shook her head slowly. "No, but Donovan, would yuh be good enough to stay for a few minutes?"

The others filed out. Méarana gathered her notes, capped her pocket brain, but remained seated. Barnes looked from her to Donovan, who said, "Whatever you have to say to me, you can say in front of her."

The captain shrugged. "Have it your way. There's a bottle of Megranomic *kurutakki* in the cabinet, aged fifteen years in oak casks. I been saving it for a special occasion."

Donovan, who had risen at the implied request to fetch

the drink, paused half out of his chair. "And this is a special occasion? Because you don't expect to see us again?"

"I won't lie and say I'm optimistic. Best o' luck and everything; but . . . Like we told yuh, them hill tribes can be a might peckish. Pour us three, 'Kalim,' and be generous."

Donovan had poised the bottle over the first glass. Now he straightened and grinned at her. "I wondered if you recognized me."

"Didn't at first; but it come to me, bye and bye. Or should I call you 'Fudir'?"

Méarana suddenly understood. "Maggie Barnes! Of course! You were January's astrogator."

"He told yuh about that? That was in a different life. I didn't have these silver streaks back then, I tell yuh, let alone the cap'n's rings. But as I recollect, this man here, he come aboard *New Angeles* with phony papers. We coulda lost our license, so this ain't exactly old comrades well-met! Smuggling that O'Carroll fellow back to New Eireann to restart the civil war, that didn't sit right with me, either."

"That's not exactly how it was," Donovan suggested.

"Wasn't it? Well, that was near twenty year since, and it don't matter no more; so let's drink to it. I won't ask what phony pretense yer up to now. I'd say yuh was lying about being on Kennel business, except that Méarana here says yuh are, and her, I trust."

Donovan handed out three glasses. He lifted his and said, "To Amos January!"

"Gods rot his liver," agreed Maggie Barnes.

They threw back their drinks and Donovan sighed as he set his glass down. "Oh, that was smooth. *Kurutakki* . . . 'Eye of blood-red color?' "

"Close enough." Barnes held her glass a moment longer at eye level. "There's this fellow owns a distillery out near Thillainathan Flats, and he has his own grove of oak clones that grow as barrels. Can yuh imagine! Aged in living trees." She put the empty shot glass on the table in front of her. "Yuh know we was ten years gettin' back to known space? Yessir, that there is a fact. After January left New Eireann, an engine blew and we taken the Gessler Sun cut-off. Damn spanking new engine, rebuilt in the Gladiola Yards, and—" A snap of the fingers. "Well, the cutoff is one-way, and we found ourselves down in the Lower Tier. Not as bad as the Wild—or maybe it is. Ah, yuh don't want to hear old troubles; but . . . Ten years! And Micmac Anne a-waiting every one o' them back on Jehovah."

Méarana said, "I wouldn't mind hearing the story." Her fingers curled instinctively on imaginary harp strings.

"We saw a sight of strange things, and that's a fact. Maybe on the way back. There'll be time for it then. But I didn't want yuh to go down there, Donovan, if that's what yer name is, and maybe git yourself killed, without I tell you what a platinum-plated son of a bitch yuh were."

Donovan nodded. "Thanks. I hope we haven't lost the touch."

"Now git, before I lock yuh up."

Méarana paused on the way out and studied their pro-jected route on the holographic map. "Up Jim River," she said.

Donovan heard her. "What's that mean?"

"Jim River. It's a wild river on my home world. It's a nice lazy one in its lower reaches, but the farther upstream you go, the wilder the country gets. Swamps, deserts, moun-tains, rapids, wild animals—I'm talking Nolan's Beasts that have gone feral. Not everyone comes back down-stream." She paused in reflection for a moment. "So Dan-gchaoers say, 'I'm going up Jim River' or 'he's up Jim River,' to mean in big trouble." She gestured to the Arfidnux'r and the mountains beyond. "Looks like we're heading up Jim River."

Donovan laughed. "Méarana, we've been heading up that river since we left High Tara."

The night of their arrival from orbit, the G&R Resident hosted a banquet in honor of Méarana and her people, to which he invited several of the Dūqs in town for the "Star Market." The Resident occupied a palace built of white marble joined and set entirely without concrete. The flooring and trim was of an aromatic wood akin to cedar, and the roofing consisted of ruddy, semicircular terra cotta tiles known as "oyster shells."

The climate around Riverbridge was warm at that time of year, and Oodalo Bentsen wore only a plain white Enjrunii "jellybean," a skirt similar to a Terran dhoti that left his torso bare. This made manifest the extent of both his hairiness and his indulgence of his appetites. He liked to think he was bluff rather than crude, and hearty rather than overbearing.

One of the guests was Chuq Lafeev, who was the Rice of Jebelsanmèesh and held the Dūq for the jewelry trade. The locals dined sitting cross-legged on the floor around a great carpet, on which were set basins and plates of hammered copper containing the food. Oodalo had alternated his local guests with the visitors from *Blankets and Beads* and had placed Lafeev between Méarana and Donovan. Méarana found the local quite witty and not at all unsophisticated about his celestial visitors. He listened sympathetically to the harper's tale of her search for her mother.

"But of course," he said, "it remembers me, your mother. It was seven moon-crossings ago . . . Wait. Good Oodalo, how are crossings tabulated in your 'years'? So! Sugar and jazz." Méarana's earwig translated "sugar and jazz" as "thank you very much." A servant standing behind Lafeev scribbled hastily on a slip of reed-paper and handed it to the Rice, who glanced at the computations. "Ah, more than a year of your time. Only once, and briefly, did we meet, yet the impression she left is everlasting." He touched his forehead with his fingertips in a gesture of respect. "She, too, sought the source of the parking stone jewelry, and set off up-country in her flying cart. It fears me that she came to grief up there. Ay! A woman alone, and in the land of the Emrikii!"

"Do you know that for a fact?" Méarana said.

"Alas, never came she back. But perhaps," he added more brightly, "it was that your mother rode her flying cart all the way back to her ship in *feyityis*." He necessarily used the Gaelactic word for orbit, although he introduced a surplus vowel or two. Méarana supposed that the *loora noor jesser* did not have slender vowels and palatilization.

"That is most likely so," she said. One thing for certain, Bridget ban's ship was no longer in orbit. No one but the Resident's people had the ability to reach orbit; and even they could not have entered a Hound's vessel without the proper authorization codes. If Bridget ban had died in the high country, her field office would still be circling Enjrun.

"Unless the orbit decayed," said Donovan when she had given voice to this hope. "Even a Hound's ship would not survive uncontrolled re-entry into a thick atmosphere."

"Cheerful, as always. If the noor jesser—"

Lafeev chuckled. "Nuxr," he said.

"Noor."

"No, no!" Playfully, he enunciated. " 'Nu—' "

"Noo."

"X—" He breathed roughly.

"Huh."

"No, cough a little. 'Nu-x-r.' "

"Noo-huh-r."

Lafeev threw his head back and violated protocol with a belly laugh. The other Dūqs questioned him and he answered in a dialect that the earwig could not entirely translate. Méarana picked out the phrase "lazy throats," which evidently referred to the Gaelactic inability to hack and cough their way through the local *lingua franca*.

She caught his eye and said, distinctly, "Fitir," properly palatalizing the F, aspirating the T, and trilling the R. Her tongue, struck like a snake on the T. Then, before he could do more than begin to frown, she smiled. "Sure, and the Gaelactic plays as much with the lips and the teeth as your *loora* does with the throat and the tongue."

There was no mockery in it, and so he took the correction in good humor. "A man one day older is a man one day wiser," he pronounced. "By Owl, I swear it, I know not why he gave men such a myriad of tongues. But Owl knows all, and Owl knows best."

The courses that were brought out also alternated Gaelactic and Enjrun dishes. There was a bean salad called pully that Donovan said was much like the *fool* he used to get in the Terran Corner. Sofwari commented that pully and fool might both be forms of an earlier word. "My colleague, Gwenna Tong Thalasonam, believes that basic sound units may change and pass on like the little thread shapes. What is an *F*, after all, but an aspirated *P*?"

"Did my mother tell you," Méarana asked the Dūqs, "what she hoped to find up in the hills?"

Lafeev only shook his head. "Whatever it was, may Owl grant that she found it."

The way things had turned out, Méarana very much feared that Owl had done just that.

XIII UP JIM RIVER

$\mathcal{T}$he endarooa *Efranizi* set forth from the main docks of Nuxrjes'r two days later and rowed upstream until the southerlies freshened and the sail could be let down. She comprised two galleys linked by a platform on which sat fore and aft cabins and a mast from which hung a square mainsail and a triangular "lantern" sail.

"Remarkably stable," said Sofwari, "but not much for maneuvering."

The boat's captain, Pyar Allweed, laughed. "Don't need much maneuver on Big River. We sail-up straight during the 'soons; then let the current carry us back. We just reverse the sail-rigging and the rowers' benches. 'Course, working the Delta is almighty different."

"What," said Méarana, "is the 'soons?"

"Told you," said Captain Pyar, nodding his head toward the south. "When the southerlies blow, it brings the rain."

Behind them, dark and lowering, thunderheads boiled over the distant Mut'shabiq Delta.

"Well," Sofwari shouted above the howling wind, "at least we know why they build these little houses on top of the decking."

Méarana and her people huddled in a close wooden hut, whose canvas door periodically pulled loose of its stays and flapped like a sail with three sheets flying in the wind. Rain sprayed in through gaps in the planking, in the roofing, and through the front door itself.

"Cain't fer th' life o' me see why they bothered," said Paulie o' the Hawks.

Zhawn Sloofy, a guide and translator hired in Riverbridge, shook his head. "Alla time, Gaelactics complain.

Too wet, too dry, too hot, too cold. Why not stay home where everything more better?"

Paulie o' the Hawks had come down from *Blankets and Beads* to gawk at the women and had decided at the last minute to throw in with the expedition. "Youse're goin' inta hill country, aina?" he asked the harper. "What farkin good is a cow-kissing *plainsman* up there?" This, with a nod toward Teodorq. Méarana and Donovan had agreed that another pair of strong arms would not be amiss, and hired Paulie as a second bodyguard.

By morning, the rain had passed on, but a second front moved in right behind it and so by afternoon the downpour had resumed. After a time, Teodorq and Paulie said to hell with it, stripped to loincloths and moccasins, and went out on deck with the boathands, where they helped at odd jobs or squared off in sparring matches. Méarana made them swear not to hurt each other. The sailors watched the matches with interest and bet on the outcomes.

After several days of this, Donovan, in the persona of the Sleuth, announced that the patterns of wins and losses relative to the odds suggested that both Paulie and Teddy were fixing the fights to clean up on the side-bets.

"Which proves there is something those two can agree on," Méarana said.

The 'soons moved north in wave after wave. This had a certain predictable consequence. The river began to rise.

"What goes up, must come down," Captain Pyar told them cheerfully. "Ye'd best brace yourselves for some rough times."

Teddy and Paulie tied everything down, and laid out straps and lifelines as they had seen the crew do. "One hand for yourself; one hand for the ship," the captain reminded everyone.

By the fifth day, the river was over its banks and still the 'soons did not let up. On the shore, the farmers scuttled for high ground and the fields were underwater. The sailors and rowers made signs to the grain-goddess. Sloofy told Méarana that the entire valley depended on the annual rains to refertilize the alluvial plain.

That afternoon, a sailor perched high on the mast hollered, "She's a-coming!" and slid down the rigging to the deck, where he and his mates struck the sails and joined the rowers at the oars. The helmsman strapped himself to the tiller. Captain Pyar, the boat's carpenter, and the mate stood at the ready, clipped to the lifelines that ran the length of the deck.

"What's 'a-coming'?" Billy Chins asked.

Sofwari frowned. "A flash flood if I don't miss my guess."

Donovan grunted. "If the ship's company think it worthwhile to hang on for dear life, I for one will not call them fools." And he, too, grabbed hold of the ropes they had run in the aft cabin.

Méarana pulled the cloth flap aside and peered ahead into the steel-gray curtain of rain. The south wind sang through the ropes and stays. The water hissed against the twin hulls. The oars groaned in their locks as the rowers, assisted now by the sailors, bucked the surging current.

And then she saw it. The rain turned black and a wall of water bore down upon them. The rain that had fallen in the northlands was not only returning but, to all appearances, returning all at once.

The boat heeled as the water humped up underneath. Then the wave broke over the deck, and swept Méarana from the doorway and toward the stern. She heard Sofwari's cry of alarm as she scrambled for the lifeline; but Billy reached out and grasped her arm, hanging on against the force of the water, hauling her to safety.

The wave filled the cabin, lifting them and choking them

with turgid water. The cabin walls creaked and Méarana thought they must either burst or the cabin would fill up and drown them all. But the wisdom of the chinks in the wood-work now revealed itself: They acted as scuppers to drain the water out over the stern.

The rowers shouted as they fought to maintain position while a second surge, not as great as the first, lifted them and again drenched everyone on board. The ship heaved and Teddy heaved with it. Billy was dashed against a cross-beam and won a ragged cut. Donovan gripped the lifeline, looking grim. Sloofy asked the goddess why he had ever left the riverbank.

A third wave followed but, after the first two, it seemed almost a gentle caress.

By the time the surges had settled down, a break had come in the clouds and the sun beamed, however briefly, on the countryside. The damage to the boat could have been worse. The fore cabin had been stove in. A plank on the left-side galley had been sprung and was leaking into the hull. A rower had been brained by an oar that had pulled loose from its handlers. And a sailor had a bad cut down the length of his forearm that, under local medical standards, would likely fester and kill him.

The rower was wrapped in a sheet sweetened with herbs, and tied to the prow as a guardian against river hazards until they could raise a burning ghat. The carpenter went to work, first on the hull, then on the forecabin. Méarana used some of their medical supplies to treat the sailor.

"Captain Pyar says the worst is over," Méarana told them when she had returned to the cabin and hung the medical bag on a peg in the wall and taken a seat. "The watercourses up in the mountains bake hard as ceramic during the dry season, and the first rains sluice right off it. He expects the water to rise some more, but not such in a tearing hurry; and the rain will slack off to a constant drizzle. The current has pushed us back about a day's rowing, but now he can raise sail again and make it up." She rubbed her face with both hands. There was mud all over, courtesy of the first surge, and it streaked her cheeks and brow. "Ah, well. I was getting tired of the insides of ships and habitats anyway."

When they went out on deck, they could hardly see the edges of the river, so widely had the flood overspread its banks. Farmsteads and villas poked above the water atop earthen mounds. Catboats were putting out from some of them. Here and there the flood had undermined the embankments and toppled the houses into the waters.

At Rajiloor, the endarooa reached the end of its range. Above this point, the river emerged from the Roaring Gorge, a passage not only too narrow for the vessel to navigate, but one at the head of which was the first of the great waterfalls that marked the upper river. The town was mildly prosperous as a transshipment point because of this. Freight and trade goods were transferred here between endarooas from the lower Arfidnux'r and the durms that plied the upper river, or Multawee.

Like the farmsteads on the alluvial plain, the town of Rajiloor was built atop a rammed-earth platform. The mound had survived decades of floods through the judicious use of marble facings and terraces, culverts and cisterns to divert the water, and frantic repairs between 'soons. She also benefited from being on the lee bank where the river curved, so the floods coming out of Roaring Gorge sought the east bank.

Rajiloor had been a border town of the old Imperium; but a generation earlier the garrison had declared its general the True Qaysar. Before he could sail his troops downstream to debate the issue, a light-complexioned people of long dark hair called the Tooth of the Wolf had come out of the mountains and made themselves masters of the hinterlands, encircled the the city walls, and waited. When the food ran out, the imperial troops had hailed the paramount chief of the Wolves as the new Qaysar. More realistic than his late predecessor, the Wolf had kept the title "Qaysar" and possession of the Rajiloor Sak, but refrained from bothering downstream lords with other opinions. The key to success being ofttimes a judicious lowering of one's goals, the Qaysar of Rajiloor pretended that the Qaysar of Nuxrjes'r was his overlord, and the Qaysar of Nuxrjes'r pretended he meant it.

The sailors and rowers took their payout from the captain and vanished into a town in which every other building seemed a tavern or a brothel. The population was a mixture of Rajilooris, Nuxrjes'ri, Wolves, Harps, Emrikii, and others.

Méarana set up a headquarters in a wharfside tavern called The River Dog. The main room was low-ceilinged and was constructed of heavy cross-beamed timbers. The wooden tables were long and narrow, with polished surfaces, and names carved into them. The air was redolent of stale beer.

She sent Donovan and Sloofy to hire the durms they would need for the next leg of their journey. Sofwari went into town, with Teodorq to watch over him, to take more of his cheek samples. That left Méarana in the tavern with Billy and the other Wildman.

She had been wary of the little man ever since Donovan's revelations. But Billy, seeing how she sat away from him, only sighed. "Ah, missy. Was not Billy Chins *good* khitmutgar? When he not take care for you?"

"You could have told us you were recruiting for the CCW rebels," she said. Perhaps it was the deceit that grieved her most; although she could not say Donovan had been much less deceitful.

"Would Greystroke have permitted me aboard his ship if I had? At best, he would have left me to face my pursuer. At worst, he would have done my pursuer's work for her."

"You do him an injustice."

"Do I? For such stakes, would you have announced yourself?"

Méarana had to admit she would not. She spread the holomap across the table. The map was impregnated on a flexible substrate, so it would fold up and fit snugly in a carry-bag. Once unfolded, it shook hands with their amshifars and with the traders' satellite network, and displayed their locations within a half-league of actual.

The tavern-master spoke the imperial language after a fashion—a generation's occupancy by the Wolves had not obliterated all knowledge of the ancient *loora nuxrjes'r*— and Méarana desired to learn something of the conditions in the Roaring Gorge region.

"Ah sure, your honor, the Roaring Gorge is right peaceable the now," the taverner said. "Himself is after going through there no more'n two-three year back and taught 'em to bend the knee. My wife's cousin's younger son was with that army. Now, they might be a bit pouty, but if you carry our Qaysar's safe conduct—may Owl protect him— they won't dare be touching you."

"Are there any Gorgeous folk in town? We could use a native guide through that country, and we can pay well."

The tavern-master fingered his ear and his eyes wandered to the holomap on the table. "So I've heard," he said. "So I've heard. There be none of 'em staying here at the Dog, but there's always some what come down afore the rains, seeking after their fortunes. I'll put the word around, if you'd like."

Méarana nodded. "That would be nice." She pointed to the second great falls, the one that danced off the Kobberjobble escarpment. "We'll need to find the way past that.

They told us in Riverbridge that we might find guides here in town."

The tavern-master shook his head in admiration. "Ah sure, and that is a fine map your honor has gotten yourself. Is it some charm that a *trood* has recited into the cloth that makes it grow so? The Qaysar's master-general has such a high-low map, but it is made of plaster. I saw it myself when I was young and pretty and marched with the Owls, and I thought it surely a wonder, painted up and all in green and blue and brown. But *this* is like flying above the land itself." At this point, Méarana's question seemed to catch up with his admiration, and he tossed his head. "I hear tell of a trail past Second Falls that passes through the Harp country. Good fortune finding a guide. The Harps be enemies of the Gorge-folk and the Wolves alike. 'But red gold conquers all.' "

"Are these Harps enemies to regarders?" The locals called all off-worlders after the *Bonregarde*.

The old man laughed. "They'd not likely know of you, at all. They think the *nuxru noorin*, the river of light, is the mountain path that Fjin Cuul trod long ago, high up the Mountain of Night."

"Nushrunorn? Is that what they call the galaxy?"

"No, mildy. That's what we civilized folk be calling it. The Harps call it the *gozán lonnrooda*, the shining path. They are simple mountainfolk and don't know that it's just a local thickening of the aether that makes the light seem like a continuous band."

Méarana said nothing to this, although she noticed that even Paulie was much amused, though he could not have believed anything more sophisticated himself before he went on the Roads. "Will we have trouble with them?"

"No, mildy, for they worship the instrument you play. It is their totem. But when you reach the third falls, where the river will be impossible to use, you will find the people of Dacitti. They are a surly folk, not welcoming of outsiders. But they can tell you of the Well of the Sun."

"The Well of the Sun?"

But the tavern-master shook his head. "That is a long and very dry telling."

Méarana took the hint and reached into her scrip for a gold Fredrik. These bore the image of a recent Qaysar in Riverbridge, one who claimed, through marriage to marriage, a tenuous connection to the old imperial house. The current Qaysar, who really did have the old blood, had not bothered with such pretensions. The coin rang on the tabletop. "My men are thirsty, too," she said.

The tavern-master grinned and the coin did not bounce a second time before he had it for his own. He ducked swiftly behind the counter and poured three drinks from the same barrel and a fourth, his own, from another. When he set the mugs down before them, Billy laid a hand on the man's arm to stay him. "What was in the second barrel, friend?"

The old man blinked, puzzled. Paulie loosed the sword in his scabbard. "But I follow Owl," the tavern-master said, "and surely you do not!"

"Old man," said Billy, "you obviously believe you have explained something, but you have not; and the time grows short in which you may."

"Billy . . . ," said Méarana.

"Fermented beverages are forbidden to the children of Owl! If you'd drink a wee drop of the fruit nectar with me, sure and I would be pleased to pour it. Are there those among you who shun the creature as we do?"

Paulie suppressed a snicker. "How could you receive a vision from the gods without mead?" Méarana also accepted the beer, which was flat and room temperature. Enjrun had not yet rediscovered either carbonation or refrigeration. Billy shrugged and said he would try a nectar of peaches.

When everyone was settled once more, the tavern-master said, "As it once was in the long ago . . ."

The door to the wharf swung open and Donovan strode in with Zhawn Sloofy close behind balancing on his head what looked like a metaloceramic panel. "Make it not so long ago, Djespa. Save the long version for those who don't pay in gold."

Paulie protested, "I like a good story."

"You and he can stay up late swapping yarns, then."

The tavern-master shrugged. "As you will. The Well of the Sun is at the Edge of the World, about . . . here." His finger entered the hologram a little way north of Dacitti, and he hastily withdrew it and wiped it on his *qamis*, the baggy shirt favored around Rajiloor. Since the map clearly showed more world beyond the Edge, the Gaelactics smiled. "The story is that there is a tribe high up in the western Kobberjobbles that eats only once a day. They have a very deep well, which they fill with water; and into this well they toss the meats and vegetables that they have spent the day hunting and preparing. When the sun goes down to his place of rest, he falls into this very well and, of course, boils the water . . ."

"Of course," said Billy. Méarana glared at him.

". . . and this cooks the food, for the sun is quite hot, as you may know. Then, once night is fallen and the sun has cooled, the tribe draws up the meat and vegetables into a kind of stew called *moogan*, on which they gorge themselves, for they will not eat again until next sunset."

"One question," said Billy with a tightly controlled countenance. "The sun fell into the well, right? So how does it get out and run around to the other side of the world in time to rise in the morning?"

Djespa the tavern-master showed surprise. "But your honor, all men know that the world is a ball and the sun goes *around* it, so that though it seems to touch the ground far off in the west, it is only passing beyond the horizon. Surely, you regarders are as knowledgeable in such matters as our own failingsoofs."

"Now, my good Djespa," said Donovan, "if you would serve a pot of that fine beer for my man Sloofy and myself?"

"Not the peach nectar?" asked Méarana.

"Of course not," Donovan told her. "All sorts of bacteria out here in the Wild that our specifics don't recognize. Ask Sofwari about it. But nothing that can hurt a man can live in a pot of beer. It's the alcohol, you see. What's the matter with Billy?"

"Nothing. Did you hire the boats we need?"

"I did. And an interpreter who savvies the lingo in the Roaring Gorge. His name's Djamos Tul. He's a Gorgeous pack peddler, and will be joining us once he finishes selling his pigeons. They say the river will be more settled by then." Donovan took his pot and went to stand over the holomap. "We wish this thing had better resolution." He waved the mug. "We're not blaming Maggie B. The spysats are just to check for wars or tribal migrations, not to look for footpaths up the sides of cliffs out where they're never going to go. Sofwari back yet?"

"No. I don't expect him until dinnertime. You know how involved he gets in his work."

"He has a funny idea about work. We brought back a bit of trash he might find interesting." Donovan hooked a thumb over his shoulder at the panel that Sloofy had propped up against the wall. "There's an ancient city not far from here and the Rajilooris salvage materials from the ruins to shore up the terraces during the 'soons."

The scarred man held a huge amusement behind his belt and needed to loosen it and let it out. So the harper sighed and, taking her beer with her, walked over to the wall where the panel stood. Billy and Paulie joined her. Sloofy only shook his head at the insanity of regarders and applied himself to his beer.

It *was* metaloceramic. And who in the Wild knew how to make such stuff? She said, "Why, this must date from . . ."

"From the First Ships?" said Donovan. "From that era, certainly. The ruins these people are scrounging from may be the remnants of the oldest settlement on this world."

"Infamous!"

"Don't see why," said Djespa. "We need to keep the mound shored up, else it'd wash away in the next flood. What good does this stuff do, buried out there under the mud and sand?"

Paulie o' the Hawks agreed with him; Billy shrugged. "A culture has the sciences it can afford. If they didn't salvage this material, their own town would soon join it under the mud. Do you really want to ask that of them?"

But Méarana did not answer him, because she had already seen what Donovan had wanted her to see. Across one end of the panel ran the squiggly script used by the 'Loons of Harpaloon. "I think I know," she said slowly, "what friend Sofwari will find in his little thread shapes."

Donovan nodded. "That the 'Loons came from here . . ."

Djespa said, "'Loons, you say? Why, that be the name of the junk-quarry. Madéen o' Loons, as what the riverfolk call it. *Madéen* is a town; *loon* is a sickle blade."

"It was also," Donovan said with sudden thoughtfulness, "the name of Terra's moon. Luna."

Djespa turned and spat into a bucket. "Terrans!" he said. "Faithless djinni that lure people to their doom!"

The company set out two days later in three durms. These were massive, flat-bottomed boats, built of thumb-thick oak planks coated with tar from the seepages near Black Springs. Each was twelve double-paces in length and nearly three arm-reaches wide at the midpoint, and required a crew of five to handle.

Méarana and Sofwari rode in the lead boat, the *Mada-reenaroo*, with Djamos Tul, their new guide. They sat on cross-benches that ran athwart the boat. Donovan and Billy Chins rode in the *Green Swan* together. The two body-guards rode in the *Gadlin* with Sloofy. The space between the benches was packed with their luggage, supplies, and trade goods.

The boatmen themselves were a stolid lot and said little beyond the perfunctory greetings and instructions. "We take you to Candletown near the Roaring Falls," the head sweeper said. "Twelve Freddies for each boat. Six up, and six we gotta go back after we drop you off." Then he took a position in the rear of the boat and the others unshipped great sweeps and placed them in the locks. "Jennelmen," the steersman called out. "Dockside two, push off light! Push!"

One of the oarsmen shoved against the pier with his sweep. "Bow pair, maintain the gain." The two forward oarsmen stroked against the current while they waited for the other two boats to assume position. When the steers-man had assured himself that all was ready, he called out, "All four, normal pull, full stroke." He waited until the two bowsmen completed a stroke, then called, "Stroke!" and the two sternmen dipped into the water in synch with their brethren, pulling hard with the full length of their bodies. "Eki dumah!" the sweeper announced and then sang out a rhythm:

"*Kay,* kay-kay, kay."

To which the rowers responded:

"*Eki* dumah!"

On *Eki*, all four oars pulled together.

"*Kay,* kay-kay, kay."

"Eki dumah!"

Under this steady rhythm, the boat began to make way against the current. Behind them, Méarana could hear the other boats calling similar rhythms. After a while, she pulled her *clairseach* from its case and began to play along. One of the bowsman looked up in surprise and his oar caught a crab and smacked into the sternman's oar. The steersman hollered at them in the riverman argot and quickly had them back in synch, but by then the *Green Swan* had passed them, jeering and shouting "lu-lu-lu!" The Swan's sweeper showed his ass.

"Our steersman does not seem happy with you," Sofwari said. "He glowers. Perhaps your music can charm him as it charms me." He shifted to the bench ahead and sat facing the harper. "You play so beautifully."

"I can play ugly if you wish. My range is wide, and music has many purposes."

"None higher than beauty, and no purpose greater than simply to be."

Méarana strummed a bit of goltraí, but softly, so as not to distract the boatmen. "I think you have confused art with entertainment."

Sofwari opened his mouth to speak, but second-thought stopped him. "I'll consider that. I've only ever been on one side of the music."

She shifted to the "War Song of Clanthompson," a tune handed down in her family from the dark age after the diaspora. Fierce, angry, dissonant, and full of wild vengeance, it caused Sofwari to shiver. She stilled the strings with the flat of her hand. "Was that 'pretty'?" she challenged him.

"I never said 'pretty.' I said 'beautiful,' and there is more than one kind of beauty. There is beauty in the golden skin and flaming hair of a fierce young woman; but there is wild beauty even in tragedy and death. There is nothing delicate or fragile about it."

The harper regarded him for a moment in silence. "Now it is you who gives me pause."

"Almost," he said. "I am glad your mother is lost. Otherwise, I might never have met you."

Méarana smiled. "Your second thought saved you from the penalty incurred by the first. But don't try to be too clever. I'm not one to be gulled by clever words."

Sofwari bobbed his head. "I'll speak no parables if you will simply play."

The boatmen ate lunch on the river, taking turns, but they drew their boats up on the west bank when it was time for evenmeal. Because of the long curve in the rivercourse, the west bank caught the lee of the flood and so the silt was less deep. Stepping out of the boat, the right bowman pressed a copper coin into Méarana's hand. "Yez honor th'boat," he said in a thickly accented imperial.

The rivermen had with them a flask of what they called disl oil, which they used to ignite the still-damp wood they gathered for their fires. This oil was distilled from the rotted remains of the ulmo tree in the far south. A fungus that grew within the tree consumed its woody part and altered it to the oil. Donovan wondered if this were a natural thing, or one that had been created by the fabled engineers of old Commonwealth days.

On the second eve, they reached the ruins of Madéen o' Loons. Broken columns and walls and statues emerging from the mud revealed where portions of the city lay buried. The boatmen ignored the place, save to pull a panel from the ground to use as a makeshift table; but the Gaelactics explored the ruins. Even Teodorq was impressed.

He had found a statue whose face had been exposed by the recent flood. "This here is one stubborn fella," the Wildman said. "Look at the eyes and the chin. Do you suppose these people were black, or is that just the stone they used for the statue?"

Donovan found what he supposed the base of the statue, which bore an inscription in the old Taṇṭamiž script. "Hold fast forever," he read, slowly puzzling it out.

Teodorq looked about the ruins. "What happened to them?"

"Forever came and went."

Sofwari and Méarana wandered to the higher ground that marked the center of the site. From it, the science-wallah surveyed the vast, treeless, mud-covered plain east of the river and shook his head. "It is as if man and all his works have been wiped from the face of Enjrun," he told the harper. Three fires burned on the sandy shelf by the river bank, and the smell of wood and flame and meat were carried to them on the now-gentle southern breeze. "We might almost be the last survivors, in a few lonely boats, of a vast world-scraping tsunami."

Méarana was deaf to his poetry. She faced west and could spy in the far-off distance the glow of the Kobberjobbles that still caught the daylight on their peaks. "Up there somewhere," she said. "That's where she went."

Sofwari caught her hand. "You won't find her there. Her ship would still be in orbit, otherwise."

She pulled her hand from his. "I know that. But I may learn why she went there, and given that, where she was bound."

"I didn't believe her, you know, when she and I spoke on Thistlewaite. I thought the tale of the Treasure Fleet was pure fable; but she made the leap right off from my anomalies to the old legend. A leap of faith, for she had no data to prove her theory."

"Mother never let a few facts get in the way of a good theory."

"That's why we science-wallahs only tabulate facts. We

describe *what* happens and *how* it happens. But *why* it happens . . . ?" He shrugged. "Is gravity a form of love, as many say? All we can know is that it is the nature of matter to attract matter, as Shree Einstein decreed. To answer *why* it is natural exceeds our writ."

"Does that not make you feel limited?"

"Oh, no, Lucy! I have the whole of the universe to play with—from the little thread shapes all the way to galaxies, and everything in between. That there is more, who can deny? There is love and justice and beauty—and hate and bias and ugliness."

"No, Debly, those last three don't exist. They are only the names we use when the good is absent. And the opposite of justice is not bias, but fate; and the opposite of love is not hate, but indifference. And there is no thing that exists that lacks for beauty. You told me that yourself."

"So I did," Sofwari said in mild wonder. The breeze quickened and he shivered. "The damp air has given the sunset a chill." He put an arm around her shoulder. "You may share my cloak, if you wish."

"For a while, Debly. For a while. There. At the eastern horizon. That's the Spiral Arm peeking up. What did they call it?"

"The *nuxru noorin*. The river of light."

"Dangchao seems so far away. As if it were in a different universe."

Sofwari hesitated. "Did you . . . know that Donovan is your father?"

Méarana turned to him in surprise. "Did he tell you that?"

"No. He never speaks of his past. A man might suppose he didn't have one. I tested his little thread shapes, and yours . . ."

"I thought your *sinlaptai* passed only from mother to daughter!"

"Those of the mighty chondrians do. But there are other thread shapes. If you think there is a vast universe out there in the sky, it is nothing to the vast universe inside each one of us."

"If the universe is infinite, I suppose it is only fitting that we be, too. Why did you think I did not know?"

"The two of you do not act as father and daughter. Only, sometimes, when you look at each other."

"There is a history between us. Or rather, an absence of history."

"Oh?"

"The rest, you need not know."

They walked a little farther through the mud.

"I look at these ruins here . . ." Sofwari kicked at a shard poking up through the mud. "I am a bone-picker. I will never discover anything. I will only rediscover it. Whatever I may learn, someone unknown learned it ages ago."

Méarana said, "It might have been better if we had forgotten all this entirely—all the legends, all the wonders—for we live forever in its shadow." She leaned against him.

"No. As much pain as it causes me, ignorance is never better. It was not all wonder. There was decay and war and collapse. If all we can hope for is to repeat the glories of the past, then we can hope not to repeat the mistakes."

They heard Roaring Gorge before they saw it. It was a narrow cleft in the foothills of the Kobberjobbles—like a slit in a wall—and it howled and moaned at their approach, as if some great beast crouched within. Sloofy trembled in fear and even Sofwari seemed alarmed for a moment. Then he laughed and said, "The gorge acts like a megaphone for the waterfall at the farther end."

The steersman heard them and he said, "Sure, but the roar of the waterfall might also cover the roar of a genuine dragon." He laughed without waiting to see if he had

alarmed them. The other boatmen laughed, too, but Méarana noted how they looked at their passengers sidewise,
licked their lips, rubbed their hands.

Anticipation; but not a little fear beside. Surely, they had
been through the gorge often enough to know there was no
dragon.

The river narrowed and the current grew swift. The
oarsmen pulled the cotter pins and lowered the walking
planks that ran the length of the boat on each side. Then,
two at a time, they shipped their oars and took up "setting
poles" battened to the inside hull. These poles were almost
as long as the boat itself. The two sternmen stepped out
onto the walking boards and went to the bow of the boat,
where they lowered the poles into the water. "Bottom!"
one of them called, and the sweeper acknowledged. Then
they put their shoulders to the leather-padded butts on the
poles and began walking toward the stern, punting the boat
ahead. Then the two bowmen stowed their oars and did the
same, so that the four men were now walking stem to stern,
pushing against the current. One of the sternmen said
something low and angry to the steersman when he reached
the back end of the boat, and the steersman pointed em-
phatically to the shoreline. Méarana looked where he
pointed, but saw nothing out of the ordinary.

She took up her harp and began to play at random—a
jig, a taarab, a halay. She adjusted the tempos to match that
of the men walking the setting poles, and the steersman
grinned and beat the tempo against the handle of his steer-
ing oar. The right bowman, when he reached the head of
the plank, glanced across to his counterpart and, ever so
slightly, shook his head, a gesture his companion repeated
before they put shoulder to pole and pushed.

They made night-camp on a sandy shelf on the east side of
the river where the cliffside had broken away into rubble.

Upstream the river vanished into a mist created by the waterfall at the far end of the gorge. The roar was, oddly, more muted inside the canyon than at the approach, but they still had to speak up to be heard.

Donovan was the last out of the boats and when he set foot on the ground, he said in a distinct, though conversational tone, "Is that a sand viper?" And then, almost immediately, "But no, it is only a branch buried in the mud."

It struck Méarana as a curious performance—and she did not doubt for a moment that it was a performance, for Donovan did little without intent. She and the two Wildmen erected the tent. The boatmen had grown used to the tent-that-pitched-itself, and no longer gathered around to gawk openmouthed when Méarana activated the equipment.

Billy Chins and Donovan approached, talking in Confederal Manjrin. Donovan bent and looked inside the tent.

"Where are Teddy and Paulie?" he asked.

"They went back the boats for our supplies."

"Sofwari," said Billy, "go fetch-them."

The science-wallah looked to Donovan, who nodded.

"What's going on?" Méarana asked when Sofwari was gone.

"Trouble," said Billy.

"Nothing, we hope," said Donovan.

"I'm glad for the warning, whichever it is." Méarana retrieved her harp. She was still tuning it when the others returned.

Once they were gathered round, Donovan told them that Billy thought the boatmen were planning something.

"I thought so before we cast off," the Confederate said. "The old taverner was too concerned that we expect peaceful passage through Roaring Gorge, and a little too unconcerned with our gold and silver."

"I believe him," said Donovan. "When I claimed to see

a sand viper, I spoke Gaelactic. But several of our 'friends' turned around in alarm. I pretended to take no notice, and I don't think they gave it second thoughts."

"They have earwigs," said Méarana.

"Or they've had force-learning. But in either case, why conceal their understanding? They want to know what we are saying without letting us know they knew."

"I saw you test them," said Billy. "There were only four who reacted."

Donovan nodded. "Earwigs cannot be all that plentiful here. The sweeper on each boat has one." He looked at Theodorq. "Go find Sloofy and bring him here." The Wildman nodded and trotted off.

"Meaning no disrespect to Billy," Donovan continued, "I doubt a Rajiloor tavern-master has the wealth to subborn fifteen rivermen. Earlier today, we passed a boundary cairn on the riverbank. We passed from Rajiloor to Jebelsanmèesh."

Sloofy entered the tent, followed by Teodorq. The Wildman had loosened the thong on his scabbard.

The translator smiled. "What do my masters want with Sloofy?" But his smile slowly faded to match the faces he saw around him. "Have I done something to displease?"

Donovan spoke to him in clear Gaelactic. "When do they plan to strike?"

The translator went pale. He stammered ignorance, but Billy shook his head. "That will not do. We know everything. You need only tell us the rest."

It was a formula that had struck terror in many hearts; but it meant nothing to Sloofy.

"My companion," said Donovan, to make the matter plain, "practices an art by which others are brought to answer questions."

Now Sloofy began to tremble. "No, a'yaih. I am but a piece played on the shadranech board of great men."

"If you are so worthless," Billy suggested, "you will not be missed."

"I think," said Méarana kindly, "that you had better tell us everything."

Sloofy turned to her as if to his savior. "Yes, O sadie. I will withhold nothing!"

"It was the Rice of Jebelsanmèesh who hired you?" said Donovan.

"My master knows all things. Men of his gave me coins to purchase the boatmen, and promise of more when . . . the deed . . . was done."

Méarana turned to her father. "Lafeev seemed friendly when we spoke."

"But the Rice of Jebelsanmèesh," Donovan said, "is also the Dūq of the jewelry trade. And we are searching for the source of one of his best exports."

"But we're not interested in the jewelry," Méarana said. "We're looking for my mother."

"Lafeev could not imagine why anyone would go on such a mad quest. And I can't say I blame him. He decided it was a cover for our true purpose, which was to cut him out of the jewel trade."

Billy said, "A mind already wary will gaze on all with suspicion."

"When did they plan to strike?" Donovan asked the translator again.

Sloofy stammered. "They will kill me if I tell you."

Billy said, "And we will kill you if you don't." He spread his hands in helplessness.

"Hell of a dilemma," said Teodorq. "Ain't it?"

Billy continued. "But consider that at our hands, it might take far longer. You might live for many days before the jackals and kites find you."

Paulie said, "He don't look so happy about a longer life."

Donovan asked gently, "Are all the boatmen in the plot?"

The translator nodded. "No. There are three who have not been told, because they are not blood relatives. Neither has the abominable Djamos, whose mother was a slut from the gorge. When the hammer falls, these four will be given the choice to join the boatmen or to join you with the fishes."

"Tough choice," Paulie acknowledged.

Donovan looked across his shoulder. "Teodorq?"

"Aye, boss. I'll fetch 'im." And he ducked out the tent flap.

"When were they to carry out this deed?" Donovan continued to Sloofy.

"After we have crossed into Jebelsanmèesh, lest the deed offend the Qaysar of Rajiloor, and a little ways into the Roaring Gorge, so that blame may be laid upon the Gorgeous Folk." Sloofy swallowed hard. "Likely tonight, after you are asleep, and they have rested from their punting."

"Not farther up the gorge?"

"No, lord. They want to blame the Gorgeous, not actually encounter them."

Donovan nodded, looked at the others. "There you have it. Do you see any problems?"

Billy shook his head. "Yes. How are we to handle three durm boats if all the boatmen are dead?"

"We'll manage somehow," Donovan said. "Depends on the other three, I guess."

Teodorq re-entered with Djamos held by the scruff of his neck. "Found him, boss. Where do you want him?"

But Sloofy said, "The gods have maddened you. You face twelve men, at least. You have only two fighting men. And maybe this one—" He indicated Billy. "—is more than mere talk. But the soft one will be as nothing in a fight, and what use an old man and a *bint*?"

Donovan looked at Teodorq. "What do you think?"

Nagarajan scratched his head. "Three boats-full? I can handle one. Paulie can maybe handle most of the second. That leaves five for the rest of you. I don't think this thing-found-on-my-shoe-bottom understands what his friends are biting off."

The confidence of the "regarders" was beginning to undermine the translator's certainty. Méarana only wished it would bolster hers. But she knew not to show fear in front of the enemy. "I could play my harp," she suggested.

Billy began to laugh, but Donovan shushed him and both Sloofy and Djamos showed genuine alarm. Sloofy tried again. "Your occult arts will not help you."

Donovan turned to Djamos. "How much do you know about this?" he asked in the language of Riverbridge.

Djamos glanced at his colleague. "I knew these downstream dogs planned something ill, but I thought to stand aside and see how things played out."

"There's a brave soul," said Paulie.

Djamos shrugged. "Foolish is the man who dies in another's quarrel." But he saw the faces of Donovan and Billy, and he said, "But I see that the matter is settled, so let it be fighting the downriver dogs rather than aiding them."

They did not kill Sloofy. Billy wanted to, but Donovan said that would alert the boatmen. Instead, he would join them at their fire, which they built farther up the shelf, away from the others. In the dim light, it would not be evident that Sloofy was bound and gagged. Billy cautioned him to sit still because if he tried to raise an alarm he would die "the first death *and* the last." Sloofy understood. "What do I owe those upriver wharf rats?" he asked before they jammed the ball in his mouth. It was a rhetorical question. By his own admission, he owed them the second installment of Lafeev's payment.

"A man who is willing to kill another for his gold," Donovan told Méarana, "is seldom willing to die for it."

Méarana placed a camp chair outside the tent and perched her harp on her lap. She tuned it to the third mode, humming a bit to herself. The boatmen lay about on blankets a little ways off and watched with some curiosity. One man spread an ointment on another's shoulders. Yes, it could not have been an easy day for them, working the setting poles. Yet while it had been needful to reach the gorge before doing the deed, they did not want to linger too long in this place.

She remembered how they had rubbed their hands, licked their lips. Not anticipation, she realized. They were wharfside thugs, not professional assassins. They must nerve themselves up to the deed. They would probably start drinking soon.

She sang the "Tragedy of Hendryk Shang." A well-known poem on Die Bold, the translation into the *loor nuxtjes'r* was tricky. She rehearsed the words sotto vocce, letting the earwig suggest the proper phrasing, then doing it over because she wanted a poetic translation, not a literal one. She was not entirely happy, for the poetic standards for the two languages were very different; but great poetry was not her intent.

Hendryk Shang had famously sold his lord to his enemies for a bag of silver coins. But once Lord Venable was in his enemy's clutches, his captors refused to pay Shang, and so the man was left with no money, no lord, and no honor. Méarana sang the tale not as that of a good but desperate man who had succumbed to temptation. Such subtleties were for the concert halls of Èlfiuji not a sandy bench in the Roaring Gorge. She sang it as a satire. Shang as an object of ridicule and shame to his family, his friends, his profession.

*"For he had taken Lord Venable's money
And sold off Lord Venable's life."*

The boatmen were only half-listening, but Méarana noted how some shifted uncomfortably and two moved off a little way from the others and proceeded to get into an intense discussion with each other.

Afterward, she played ominously in the goltraí, disturbing their rest. When she was finished, she returned to the tent. Teodorq grinned at her. "I'd hate to have you mad at me, babe."

Djamos the translator was trembling and stared at the harp with bulging eyes. "You are not from here," he said again and again.

They sat huddled in the tent while different constellations appeared in the sky above the gorge. "Just before dawn?" said Donovan.

Teodorq nodded. "Makes sense, boss."

They took turns sleeping, but when it came her turn, Méarana could not sleep. She curled up in her bag and closed her eyes, but sleep was not there.

Or she thought it was not, for the next she knew, Donovan was shaking her shoulder. He held a finger to his lip. "They're coming."

"How many?"

"Three stayed behind. I don't think they like this, but don't see how they can stop it." He opened the back flap of the tent. "Teddy, Paulie, you'll go out the front. Billy and I will go out the back and flank them."

Debly Sofwari said, "What am I to do?"

"Do you have a weapon?"

He nodded.

"Do you know how to use it?"

He nodded again.

"Then use it."

"I've . . . But I've only ever shot vermin. In fieldwork."

Donovan nodded. "Good. Just bigger vermin here." He started out the back, then turned. "Try not to shoot your friends."

Teodorq pulled out his "nine" and chambered a round. Paulie looked at him. "You ain't gonna use your sword?"

"Why should I?"

Méarana was watching through the grill in the tent flap. "They've reached the fire. They found Sloofy. He's untied. Look lively. They know we know."

Realizing that surprise had been lost, the boatmen shouted and came at the tent in a rush. Teddy and Paulie burst out the front, the latter swinging his broadsword while Teddy went to one knee and braced his hand. He fired once, twice. A man fell. Paulie sliced the arm off a second. One bowled into Méarana and drove her to the ground. Her knife shot out and she stabbed him four times, rapidly, in the gut. He rolled off, groaning and clutching himself, and Sofwari stepped over and fried his brains with a dazer. The others scuttled back. This opened them to fire from Billy and Donovan, who had taken a position behind some rocks on the left. Another man dropped. Two more clutched parts of their bodies and staggered.

Then the boatmen retreated out of range and rummaged in their boats. Teodorq turned to Paulie. "That can't be good."

It wasn't. Boatmen going up the Twisted River sometimes had to hunt for their dinner, and a compound hunting bow had considerable range and penetration. They were arguing among themselves. Some were pointing to the boats. Méarana supposed these wanted simply to leave. The others, perhaps transported by rage, strung bows with grim concentration. They called out to the three men who had stood aside; but these replied by signs that they wanted nothing to do with the treachery.

"Come on," said Sofwari, taking her by the arm. "Behind the rocks with Donovan." As they retreated toward the shelf in the cliffside, Djamos paused at each man down and stilled his cries with a swipe of a curved knife blade across the throat.

"Not that one," called Billy. "I made a promise."

The Gorgeous pack trader looked down at the bleeding Sloofy. "You are a fool of a downriverman. You should have joined the starmen."

Sloofy replied between taut white lips, "Death was my destination. Does it matter who sees me off?"

Djamos withheld his blade and patted Sloofy on the cheek. "Enjoy the trip."

When the pack trader joined them behind the rocks, Méarana noticed that Paulie still stood beside the tent with his sword cocked at his right shoulder. Blood ran down the blade and out the pommel to drip on the sand by his feet.

Teodorq called to him. "You coming, hillbilly?"

"Just a sec. There's something I always wanted to try."

One of the boatman had gotten his bow strung and now fitted a quarrel to the string. He stepped cautiously along the riverside, sure of his own range, but uncertain of the starweapons. But there was something about the brawny man dressed in *serge de Nîmes* standing so calmly. He raised and loosed.

And Paulie whirled and swung . . . and the arrow spun off in two neatly-cleaved parts.

Paulie leaped for the rocks then and vaulted them ahead of a second arrow that glanced off the cliff face.

Teodorq nodded. "Not bad. Wanna try it again?" He nodded toward the boats, where all three archers were now armed.

Paulie stared at him. "Do I look crazy?"

Donovan said, "They'll try to work their way up on our right." The pocket had no natural barrier in that direction.

"They'll stay out of range of the beam weapons. Teodorq, you've got the best range here. How many bullets do you have left for your pellet gun?"

"In the magazine, or back in the tent?"

"Maybe they'll just leave us here," suggested Sofwari.

"They ain't fighting for no medals," agreed Theodorq.

Donovan powered down his dazer to save on the battery. He shook his head. "They want our gold and silver."

"That's in the chests on the boat," said Sofwari.

But Billy chuckled. "Tell him, Donovan."

"The money chest is in the tent. I switched it with your equipment chest. They'll figure that out once they look inside."

Teodorq braced his hand atop one of the rocks and tried a long shot at one of the archers. The bullet struck the man in the ankle and he howled, fell to the ground, rolled away. His mates went to him and carried him to the *Gadlin*, which was farthest from them. Then they fell to arguing with one another again.

Méarana sang out in the local tongue:

"O brave man, to seek your courage
In throats slit of sleeping men!
Your fame: the laughter of the taverns.
You could not slay the sleeping men!"

Billy snorted. "Sticks and stone can break their bones; but not words."

"Don't be too sure," said Méarana. "They take curses and satires very seriously in the north, and some of the boatmen are northern-bred."

"Think of it as psychological warfare," said Donovan. "What else can we throw at them?"

"Sahbs," said Theodorq. "Upstream."

From out of the mist slipped the silent shapes of four

large war canoes. The heads of beasts adorned their prows. The sound of their paddling was lost in the rumble of the falls. Djamos rose to his feet and cried, "The canyon! The canyon!" And ducked before the arrow he had tempted from the rivermen struck the rocks behind him.

Donovan looked at Billy. "My apologies," he said. "You were right."

The Confederate shrugged. "If Djespa could not buy so many rivermen, he could surely buy his own cousins."

Djamos said, "There is no price among brothers."

The men in the canoes laid their paddles aside and notched longbows while the canoes carried them silently forward. The command to loose must have been audible on the riverbank, for the boatmen spun suddenly about and their chests blossomed with feathered shafts. The two archers returned the favor, picking off two of the attacking party. Another man ran for the bow dropped by the third archer, but the attackers pinned him neatly to the sand. The three men who had stayed out of the fight ran for the cliffs, and two of them made it behind the rocks.

The *Madareenaroo* scraped off the sand and into the current with the surviving boatmen scrambling aboard. One fell off the gunnel with an arrow in his back. The durm spun slowly as the current carried it downstream. No one exposed himself at the sweep to keep her steady. A canoe caught up with her and pulled alongside. Men leaped from the canoe to pull themselves up the side. But now the advantage was with the boatmen, for the sides of the durm were high and they could fight back from a tactical height. Finally, the canoe's captain gave up and backed off. The Rajilooris jeered their attackers as they drifted away, as if they had won some sort of victory.

One of the boatmen who had made it to the rocks looked over to Méarana. "I wanted no part of it," he said. "You must believe me, Lady Harp." He made a motion like scratching his chest. She recognized him as the man who had given her the token payment.

"I believe you, Watershank," she told him. "You have acted with honor throughout."

Djamos moved swiftly, and his curled blade was out and at Méarana's throat before anyone knew that he had moved. "And now let us await my kinfolk," he said. "No. Make no move, or the harper's voice is stilled forever. And you, harper: If your lips part in a satire, your throat will sing before your lips."

Billy said quietly, "You are making a grave error."

The marauders in the canoes had beached themselves and now swarmed over the boats, tearing bundles open. Clothing and equipment were strewn on the sand. "My instruments!" groaned Sofawri. "My data!"

"It's not your head," growled Donovan, "at least not yet." He pressed the stud on his dazer and the green light began to blink. Billy noticed and carefully slipped his own gun into his crotch. Theodorq's nine had disappeared.

A contingent of warriors approached the tent. "All of you!" said Djamos. "Place your hands on your head! You, Paw-lee, put down the sword!" Then he stood, holding Méarana, and called out, "The canyon! The canyon!"

One of the warriors sent an arrow through Djamos's neck. The translator had no time even to register surprise, but opened his mouth in a gush of blood. Méarana spun away and Sofwari caught her. The warriors drew bows on the embattled group and one of them barked something incomprehensible, motioning with the arrowhead.

Watershank, the boatman, exclaimed and responded in the same tongue. The war chief rattled a command and Watershank opened his shirt to expose an intricate tattoo of a harp. This seemed to satisfy the chief, who motioned to Watershank to join them.

Watershank did not move. "Chief says, are any else here degenerate dog-farking gorge-dwellers?"

"Well," murmured Billy, "not if he asks *that* way."

"Watershank," Méarana said. "Tell him who we are."

"These people do not understand 'starmen,' Lady. I do not know if I can explain." He spoke again, making signs with his hands. The chief grunted and glanced at Méarana. He asked a question. "Chief says, where is your harp?"

"In my tent. Does he want me to fetch it?"

"Chief says, if you are harper, you can play—how do you say 'on the moment, without previous hearing it'?"

"Extempore."

"If you are harper, you can extempore a praise of his feat here in besting the mighty downriverfolk."

Méarana doubted such a lay would include the escape of one of the boats, or even a realistic assessment of the might of a band of wharfside thugs. "Does he expect me to use the tropes of the Harp—you are Harps—or may I use the tropes of my own world?"

Watershank grunted and said, "I will say your own country."

"Tell him my country lies far up the *gozán lonnrooda*, high up the side of the Mountain of Night."

Watershank looked frightened at this. "My Lady!" he wailed. "I did not know!" Then he turned to the chief and the two discoursed quickly and vehemently. Méarana did not know whether they were arguing or that was the normal timbre of their language. Then Watershank turned to her.

"Chief say, as riverfolk would have it, put the money in your mouth."

"I will go into the tent and fetch my harp. No one will stop me."

Donovan whispered in Gaelactic, "Méarana, are you sure you know what you're doing?"

She answered in the same tongue. "I told you. My mother trained me." She stepped through the warriors, more of whom had come curiously from looting the boats. Bows followed her, sweating bravos stepped back with uncertain looks. She heard the term *crootài* several times, and wondered if that were the local term for harper.

Inside the tent, she fell to her knees before her satchel and trembled. A body lay in the entrance to the tent and she remembered that a scant hour before she had killed that man. Mother had been right. When the time came, her training had held and no hesitation had stayed her hand.

Her fingers shook as she took the satchel and she paused a moment to gather herself. She remembered what Donovan had told her once. It is much harder to risk another's life than to risk your own.

Unsnapping the clasps, she removed the bolt of anycloth and inserted the datathread into her communicator. She searched through the memory until she found the image she wanted.

Then she slung her harp case over her shoulder, stepped across the body in the entrance, and walked uphill toward her companions. Passing Sloofy on the way, she saw that a Harp warrior had smashed his skull in. She wondered if the unfortunate Nuxrjes'ri had welcomed surcease by then and what it must be like to die so far from home amidst angry strangers.

Méarana wasted no tears on him. He had gone out looking for trouble, and ought have had no complaint at finding it. But she saw no good in using him cruelly, and gave thanks to her God that the Harp warrior had ended his pain.

She found a pole that one of the boatmen had been using as a quarterstaff in the attack. (How futile and pathetic their effort seemed now! But a man is as dead brained with a quarterstaff as he is when fried by a dazer.) She attached the anycloth to the staff and stabbed the pole into the ground.

The southern breeze caught the cloth and unfurled it. It was the green banner of Harpaloon: the harp embraced by the crescent moon.

Their captors jabbered excitedly among themselves. Then the chief stepped forward and embraced Méarana, kissing her lightly on each cheek.

"You have come at last," Watershank translated for him. "You have come at last."

XIV A CITY ON THE HILL

The canoes moved swiftly upstream. Behind them, one of the durms sent a dark plume of smoke into the sky. The other durm had been set adrift into the current with Watershank's friend aboard and a message that the Tooth of the Harp had made women of the Gorgeous, and Rajilooris were no longer welcome in the Roaring Gorge. With the sweep alone to keep the durm in the channel, the man had a desperate time ahead of him; but he had his life, and that was no small gift. The Harps had wanted to carve the message into the man's skin, but Watershank had asked his life as a favor of the chief. "Xudafah was a good friend to me on the boats," he said. "We exchanged the kiss of friendship. How could I take from him what is mine to freely give."

Méarana's party had been split up, and the only sounds she heard were the rush of the Multawee over the rocks and the rhythmic chanting of the warriors at the paddles. The sound of the waterfall grew steadily louder and the canyon closed up into narrow, sheer cliffs. Once, the canyon was broken by the mouth of a tributary stream that came bubbling and churning out of a split in the rocks and Méarana glimpsed up its length a series of tumbling cataracts.

They came around a bend in the Multawee and saw the blackened ruins of a stockade and scores of people penned behind wooden fences under the eyes of more Harp warriors. "Candletown," Donovan guessed. "Those poor bastards are Djamos's kinfolk. He was a pigeon merchant? What are the odds that at least one of his pigeons was a homing pigeon, and carried word back here?"

"No odds," said Méarana, "and it doesn't really matter anymore."

"I suppose the Harps found out about it somehow and hijacked the whole thing. That does matter, because they worship the harp. Who knows how it would have turned out if Djamos's kin attacked the boatmen?"

"Father, be quiet. I have to think." Donovan retreated into silence and, suddenly contrite, Méarana laid a hand on his knee. "I'm sorry. It's just that there's a thin line between honored guest and prisoner. Remember Jimmy Barcelona on Thistlewaite?"

"From what I've seen, they will deny you nothing."

"From what I've seen all of our lives belong to the chief, and he can do whatever he pleases. If he chooses to keep a harper in a wooden cage to entertain him on demand, who will deny him? If he chooses to keep the harper and kill all the harper's companions, can I do anything but threaten a satire?"

"I think that threat would mean something to him."

"I don't know how far I can extend the protection of my status."

"You can't ask Watershank."

"God, no. He's not our enemy; but he isn't our friend,

either. He may feel he owes us something because we gave him shelter behind the rocks. And he may have picked up more sophisticated mores in the old empire."

Donovan snorted. "I didn't notice many sophisticated mores in Lafeev or Sloofy or the boatmen." He studied the burnt stockade as they passed. "Look at that," he said, pointing. "Bunch-cords running down from the tops of the cliffs. That's how the Harps attacked the town. They tied the cords to their harnesses and jumped off. Closest thing to an aerial assault this world has ever seen."

"Billy can be my servant. He knows how to play the role. And Teddy and Paulie are my bodyguards. The Harps will understand a harper traveling with bodyguards and servant. But what am I to call Sofwari?"

"Or me," Donovan suggested.

"You are my *bongko*. You play the lap drum to give me the tempo."

"Méarana, I don't know an alap from a jhala."

"You don't have to. Your drums were destroyed by the boatmen and you must go through a purification ritual before you can make a new set. And you can't do that until your hand heals."

"My hand . . ." Donovan studied that extremity. "Oh. Yes." He curled his fingers and cocked his wrist. "Hurts like hell, too." He fell silent for a while. "Sofwari," he said after a time. "You like him."

"I didn't expect to; and he can be . . . exasperating. But he is both well-built and well-spoken, and that combination is not so common as to be dismissed out of hand."

"When Bokwahna tackled you, I thought I would die."

"Bokwahna?"

"The steersman on the *Green Swan*. A big man. When he overpowered you, I cursed myself for being on the flank instead of at your side."

"Was that his name? I never got to know him. Well,

we're best friends now. Who can be closer than the killer and the killed?"

"When Sofwari fried Bokwahna's brains, I loved him like a son."

She had dealt the death blow. Four times into the abdomen. Sofwari's shot had probably been redundant, but it was nice to remember that Sofwari had done that for her.

More silence passed and the canoes turned for shore. Donovan said, "He's not right for you; but we'll figure something out. He's one of us now."

Near the foot of Roaring Falls a path led up into the Foothills. It was a well-worn path and one easily ambushed in its narrower reaches; but those who had guarded it were dead and the Tooth of the Harp now owned it. The falls showered down in continual complaint from the ridgeline three hundred feet above and raised a mist within which shone a pale rainbow. Everything was damp and had a sheen of water over it. When Méarana closed her eyes, the falls sounded like a giant wooden door that was constantly rumbling open.

The Harps unloaded the canoes and strapped the bundles on the backs of himmers. These were a species of donkey native to the land: semiaquatic in the rainy season, and storing fat on their backs in the dry. Gorgeous boys, torn from their shrieking mothers, were pressed into service to drive the beasts up into the High Country.

"Look on the positive side," the Fudir said through the scarred man's lips. "At least they're taking us in the right direction." He nodded toward the towering massif of the distant Kobberjobbles, snowcaps shining in the afternoon light.

Days passed in endless walking. Each morning dawned chill and a hasty breakfast saw them on the way up. At the midmorning stop, the drivers adjusted and retightened straps on the himmers and everyone drank a bitter tea of cocoa leaves to ameliorate the altitude sickness that had begun to develop among the lowlanders. In the afternoons, the last waves of the 'soons spent their scattered remains on the highlands. Around the campfires at night there was singing of a high nasal sort that set Billy's teeth on edge, and some of the warriors played wild skirling music on whistles. Méarana filed it all away in that part of her mind that never stopped plucking the harp strings.

She would use it someday to play this journey to comfortable audiences on Die Bold and Jehovah, on Abyalon and High Tara, to audiences who thought themselves in their ignorance to be tough. It was a big Spiral Arm, but it was far away from here, and the whim of a border lord with a headdress of feathers meant more than the considered will of the Grand Sèannad in congress assembled.

They came finally onto a high plateau where the thin air blew unobstructed and the trees were strangely twisted. They met again the River Multawee in her upper courses. War canoes met them, drawn up on the riverbank. By then the boys pressed as donkey drivers had stopped crying and they faced the unloading with hot, stolid eyes.

The Harp canoes were more elaborately carved than the Gorgeous ones they had highjacked. Their prows arced into lions and gryphons and more fanciful beasts, each plucking with its claws a harp carved on the left-side bow. The sides were fretworked down their lengths: herringbones, weaves, floral patterns, all painted in bright gaudy colors. Watershank told her that each fret design and prow totem represented a different clan. He had never seen so many clans assembled.

"Harp country lies up there," Watershank said, pointing

beyond Second Falls to the Kobberjobble escarpment. "But chief says this plateau is now their—our homeland. Last year's harvest was poor and many died in Great Hunger Month, and so he has led us down to find glory here. The Gorgeous have been driven off the clifftops, and the Tooth of the Bear chased into Telarnak Valley. No other chief of the Harps has ever conquered so much· territory."

"He is a regular Alish Bo Wanameer," agreed Donovan; and Méarana remembered that the young Zorba de la Susa had assassinated the People's Hope.

When the war canoes had been packed, the Harp chief had the children of the Gorgeous lined up, and his men drew their swords. It took Méarana a moment to realize what the Harps meant to do.

"No!" she cried. "Ye cannae!" Donovan grabbed her arm, but she shook it off and stepped out between the boys and the men with swords.

The chief did not understand Gaelactic, but he understood a negative when he heard one. But because she was a harper, he explained.

"Chief says," Watershank told her, "that these children will grow to men, and these men will seek vengeance for their fathers, whom they saw slaughtered. When they do, they will fall beneath our swords as their fathers did, so why wait?"

"Because," Méarana said in the *loora nuxrjes'r*, "they cannot fight back."

The chief nodded. "Yes. That will make the work easier."

"Harper," said Billy Chins in Gaelactic, "this is not worth risking our lives. Their fathers were preparing to come downriver and slaughter us. We owe their spawn nothing."

Méarana did not look at him. She said, "I will sing of this."

A gasp ran through the Harps, as those who knew scraps of the imperial tongue told those who did not. The chief looked perplexed, unsure if he was to be honored.

"I will sing how the Harps so trembled before a band of children that they killed them, though they could not strike blows for their own honor. I will sing this in the City on the Hill toward which we journey. I will sing it in the wharfside taverns of Rajiloor; in the palaces of Nuxrjes'r. *I will sing it on the shining path!* On Harpaloon and Die Bold, from Ramage to the Dancing Vrouw. On worlds where they know nothing of you, they will know that you are killers of children."

Watershank trembled and fell to his knees. "She sang a satire on the rivermen," he told the chief, "and all but a remnant died."

The chief sneered. "Aye. Because we came and killed them for their gold."

"Can you deny that her singing brought you to her? The Weird twists like the river."

"So," said the chief, pale but determined. "If we must not kill them because they are unarmed, then we will arm them. Unless," he added as he turned to give the orders, "you will fight in their name?"

A voice behind her said, "I will be their champion."

Méarana turned and saw Teodorq Nagarajan grinning at her. "It's what I do, babe. Start thinking of the stanzas you'll sing about me." Then he faced the chief. "I will fight your champion alone; or I will face five others who are not champions, for I have not eaten since noon and I am weak with hunger."

The chief smiled as Watershank translated. *Here* was someone he understood! "I will fight you myself!" he declared.

But Teodorq declined. "I cannot deprive your people of

great leadership. Your people will need your strong hand to comfort the widows."

Chatter among the Harps rose and fell while the chief tried to decide if he had been praised or mocked. Méarana heard Donovan, sotto vocce: "I hope he is half as good with a sword as he is with a boast."

Eventually four men stepped forward; then, after his name was called, a fifth. They stood in a row, each with sword in hand. Teodorq looked upon those swords, and smiled.

"Them are what we called 'gladius' back on World," he said to Méarana. "They use them in sports matches." Then, to the men facing him, he said, "Are those your own blades, dedicated to the gods in your name and blood?"

They frowned, uncertain of the custom to which he referred, but Watershank explained and they began to nod. "Yea, mine own." "None other holds this!" Teodorq nodded.

"Then I claim the right to use my own blades, which for fear of them, they was taken from me and now lie in your canoes."

The chief smirked. "You seek to delay your fate, starman."

"Oh, no," Teodorq said, "but it may take me a moment." Then he cupped his hands around his mouth and shouted, "Goodhandlingblade! Gutripper! Your master calls you! There is work to slake your thirst!"

Everyone stood transfixed by this performance. Mouths spilled open and in the silence that formed, a high voice could be heard. "Here I am, boss! Come and get me!"

Debly Jean Sofwari closed his eyes and looked to heaven. "Holy Dear Wisdom! He put voice-activated amshifars in his sword hilts!"

Teodorq glanced sidewise. "'Course I did, wallah. I ain't fresh fallen off a bumboat. Done it on Gatmander. Those blades cost a pretty ducat, so I wasn't about to lose none."

He was already striding to the canoe from which the voices came. "I'll use both," he decided at top lung, but as if talking to himself. "I will slay three with Goodhandlingblade in the right hand; two with Gutripper in the left."

When he had extracated both swords from their bundles and turned again to face the group, there were only two swordsmen facing him. The other three had melted away, and most of the Harps were on their knees or hiding their faces from the talking swords.

Teodorq frowned. "It doesn't seem hardly fair, there being only two of you. But I tell you what. All Lady Harp wants is that these boys not be killed. Is that so unreasonable?" He waited for Watershank to translate this.

One of the warriors could not take his eye off the blade called Gutripper, the one which, if they fought, would be his to converse with. Teodorq saw this and offered to introduce them, but the man shook his head. "It seems honorable to me, now that it has been explained." And he, too, melted back into the throng.

"And that leaves you," Teodorq said to the remaining warrior, who stood trembling, sword-naked, but the point aimed at the ground.

The man sighed. "It is as fair a day as any to die."

When Watershank had rendered this, Teodorq nodded. "It is that. And you are right. Honor requires that one of you fight and that I defend. That is how the courts proceed in my homeland. It will be an honor to kill such a brave man as yourself."

"Well," said the other, hefting a round wooden shield to protect his left side, "one should not presume on honors. The Weird bestows honor, and winding are her ways."

"As you will." He held his two swords crossed before him. Watershank ran to the sidelines.

The Harp swung and Teodorq danced.

That was the only term that did him justice, Méarana

decided. He danced. He leapt and spun in a display that was as much art as mere battle. When he caught the Harp's sword in the V of his own two swords, he actually paused for effect before spinning and flinging the sword out of line and swooping low with Gutripper to slash at the man's calf.

But his opponent was no mean swordsman, either. His people made their living by cutting up other people, and it would be hard to show him a trick that he had not already seen. He avoided the cut, though with less grace than Teodorq.

His return cut was overhand and aimed at the spine Teodorq had exposed. Méarana sucked in her breath, but she heard Paulie mutter, "One-two-roll." And as if in time to the mutter, Teodorq spun against the man's knees and brought him to the ground.

Both scrambled to their feet and stood again facing each other, this time out of reach. Paulie said, "They got their measure now and can start fighting. The idea ain't to hit the other guy's sword. The idea is to hit the other guy. What you'll see are a few set moves and countermoves, then disengage."

And so it went. Sometimes the swords flashed so quickly Méarana could not see the strokes clearly. She also learned that the big round shield had an advantage beside the obvious one, and a disadvantage. The unexpected advantage was that it could be used as a weapon itself. The disadvantage was that it was heavy, and over time grew heavier.

As the shield dipped lower and lower, Teodorq's sword flicked up and over its rim more and more often. Slashes began to appear on the Harp's torso and arms. Once, on his thigh.

Paulie grunted. "So that's how he wants it. Better not ever try it on me." But Méarana did not understand what he meant.

And then Teodorq made a mistake.

Méarana had not seen a single slip or error in his performance. He spun his two swords, slashing and poking with left hand and right in an intricate ballet with no misstep.

Now he was open, and the Harp lunged with his point. Teodorq danced back, but it was not enough and the point pierced his arm. He did not drop Goodhandlingblade, though he backed away another two steps. He grinned at his opponent, and his opponent grinned back. Then, he stuck both his swords in the ground. And the Harp, after a moment longer, did the same.

"Boss!" Theodorq called to the chief of the Harps. "I cannot kill this man of yours, because that would deprive your people of a mighty champion! You must melt honey and butter on his head, and put mead in his mouth! He must have a new name from this day forward! I will call him Sword-friend and, should he ever come to my country, I will feast him and we will spar once more for our honor!"

When this speech was translated, the longest Méarana had ever heard the Wildman utter, the assembled warriors broke into an ululation. Dovovan whispered, "I told you Teodorq was more clever than you gave him credit for. Did you like how he handled that warrior?"

Méarana nodded. "I liked how he handled the other four."

Paulie, standing behind them, spoke up. "That poor savage never stood a chance. He ain't never seen men like Teddy or me. He knows how to use a sword, that one does; but he don't know how to use his tongue. So the one was sharp, but the other dull; and it was the weapon he did not look for that skewered him."

"But," Sofwari pointed out, "there are worlds where that trick with the locator unit would have gotten him burned as a witch. There are cultures where putting down his sword would have gotten him killed. I saw some, out along the Gansu."

The Wildman shrugged. "A man learns to sniff out the ways of other men."

"How?"

"Experience."

Sofwari thought about that. "That's a hard teacher."

"Yah," said Paulie. "You only get to see the graduates."

The captured boys were given food and drink and set on the path back to their own country. The oldest, a lean scar-faced lad who looked to be about fourteen standard years, turned about before they left. "We will come back to this place. And then we will kill you for the deaths of our fathers and the rapes of our mothers." But the Harps only jeered him, although some nodded and extended a welcome.

"It is only right," the war chief said, "to return the seeds to the ground in the hope of a future harvest." His henchmen drew their swords and waved them about, in case anyone was unclear on the scythes that would mow that harvest.

After that, Méarana and her people were led to New Town, where they were feted and praised, and where Méarana improvised a lay celebrating the sword fight between Teodorq and the Harp, whose name she learned was Crowfeeder. Those who had been there added color commentary for the benefit of friends and women. Méarana changed the ending a little bit. She had both men recognize at the same moment the heroism of the other, so that both plunged their swords in the ground at the same time. It made a better story that way, and flattered Crow-feeder. In her version, too, the other four warriors had not shrunk from fear of the talking swords, but because Crow-feeder dismissed them in order to fight alone. The war chief of the Harps recognized the alterations and gave an approving nod. In another year, when the song had been sung enough times, even the participants would believe it had happened that way.

A week later, a party of Harps escorted Méarana and her companions up past Second Falls onto the Kobberjobble Escarpment. The Harps called the peaks the "shining mountains" because the snowcapped peaks still caught the sun's rays even after he had set over the horizon. Having no notion of the geometry of spheres and rays, they believed the glow to be a property of the mountain peaks themselves.

Here, the party transferred to yet another set of canoes, lighter than the war canoes they had been using. This was the ancient homeland of the Harps and the villages and stockades were more substantial and showed evidence of long habitation. The walls were more than a fence of poles, but were plastered over with something like stucco, which gave them an ochre appearance especially striking in the setting sun.

The utility of the lighter canoes was demonstrated the first time they had to make a portage. The Multawee ran over numerous cataracts on its journey across the high meadows, and each time, the canoes had to be unloaded and carried around the obstacle.

Crow-feeder led the escort, which consisted of his personal following, now swollen because of his performance in the Fight at First Falls. Also with them was Watershank, because his knowledge of the *loora nuxrjes'r* was their sole channel of communication, and a young woman named Skins-rabbit. She had been captured from the Emrikii of Dacitti in an earlier war and was being returned to them now as a tactical offering of good will. She knew both the *tanga cru'tye* of the Harps and the *murgãglaiz* spoken by the Emrikii.

"What a tangled path when we find these Emrikii," Sofwari said. "We have to think in Gaelactic, our earwigs will render that in the *loora nuxrjes'r*, Watershank will translate that to the *tanga cru'tye*, and Skins will translate *that* to *murgãglaiz*. Any rabbit of thought that makes it through that bramble will surely be skinned by then."

Some of the villages they glided by were abandoned, and Méarana recalled that Harps were moving down into the Foothills, driving out the Bears and others who lived there. Méarana thought that a great injustice on the Bears, but Watershank told her that the Tooth of the Bear had earlier taken the land from the Tooth of the Raven, who now lived in a valley farther to the east. "It is the way of the world," he said. "One day, your people will come, and will drive out even the mighty Nuxrjes'r."

"That might be a very long time," Méarana said.

But Watershank shook his head. "In my time, or my childrens' childrens' time. But come, it will. Beside your might, we are as nothing. And those who have power, use it; unless stayed by fear or impotence."

Méarana would have argued further, but Donovan said, "Once the Ardry learns that a forgotten road runs from the Confederation into the Wild, can he afford to stay out? What if the Confederation rediscovers the road? In the end, the choice is not whether these folk remain free to slaughter each other's children and cut the throats of travelers, but whether they will be ruled by the Ardry or by Those of Name."

They had portaged around any number of cataracts and falls as they wended their way through the old Harplands, but when after a week, they came to the base of the Longfoot, they saw why none of those had possessed even so much as a number. Longfoot Falls was called Third Falls because there was nothing else on the river to match her, save her two downstream sisters. Unlike Roaring Falls and Second Falls, however, Longfoot did not tumble straight down. Here, the mountainside was steep but, save near the crest, not sheer. Instead, the Longfoot sluiced half a mile down the mountainside, jouncing and splashing and leaping from its bed like a child on an amusement park waterslide before plowing into the Gryperzee at its base. The rocky slopes were barren, save to the south of the slide, where twisted "crumb-wood" trees grew no more than chest high and slewed their limbs toward the east.

"It's a fairy wood," said Teodorq, uneasily. But Paulie only laughed and called him a "prairie dog."

Crow-feeder pointed toward the peak. "The Emrikii live up there, where none may molest them. They descend from their mountain only to take vengeance over what they call 'injustice.' But they never hold the lands of the people they defeat, being weaklings as well as cowards."

Méarana stared up the long slide of the mountain. It did not sound cowardly or weak, but merely prudent. *But there comes a time,* Bridget ban had once told her, *when there is no difference between them.*

It was a strange thing. She had not thought of her mother in many days, and now her remembered voice was so true, so real, that she almost turned, expecting to see her by her side. She took a deep breath. Let it out. The air would be even thinner atop the mountain. They must watch their supply of cocoa leaves. "How do we get up there?" he asked Crow-feeder.

"The canoes will be of no more use to you," said the Harp warrior.

Tell me something I did not know. But she smiled. "I did not ask how I might *not* reach the top, but how I might."

The man waved vaguely. "There is a trail. We will leave the yaams."

The yaams were a strange sort of hairy jamal, peculiar to the high mountains. They were ill-tempered and spat a lot; but they were sure-footed on mountain trails. A raft bearing two of them was being poled up the Multawee and would probably arrive in the morning.

It is no favor to abide by the terms of the agreement, she thought, but aloud she said, "Your openhanded generosity is widely known."

"And may the Weird be less strange on your journey."

"You're not coming with us." She did not make it a question.

"It is not our journey. Our journey is to the lower lands, where glory and pasture may be won. The Emrikii are savages and poor, and they do not know honor. There is no glory in entering their country. We will leave you one bag of the gold with which to bribe them, and the food of your own that you brought with you."

"Generous of him," Teodorq said sotto vocce.

He is afraid of the Emrikii, Méarana thought.

They built a campfire and spent a somber night in its flickering glare. It was nearing the time when Captain Barnes expected to return with *Blankets and Beads*. It would be good to return to the world of baths and books. Paulie and Teddy got into an argument over who had done the most work unloading the canoes and nearly came to blows, save that Donovan separated them. Sofwari, his equipment smashed in the Roaring Gorge, his notes reduced to what he had already loaded in his pocket brain, had fallen into a morose lassitude and hardly bothered swabbing cheeks anymore. Some gang of savages would destroy them, he told her, before they could be analyzed. There were no more honeyed words, no more clever insights. Billy said little, and watched everything with a glum fatalism.

Méarana sang a little, but she was tired and pleaded sleep. She went off to the side and sat just at the edge of the firelight, where she took her medallion out. She had had to make a new thong for it after it had been ripped from her neck by the Harps in the Roaring Gorge. *They are up there,* she thought. *The people that made this medallion.* She thought of how many hands it must have passed through to reach Lafeev's men in the city of Riverbridge on the banks of the broad Aríidnux.

Tomorrow, she thought, gazing up at the sky-rimmed mountain edge.

The raft arrived at midday and the yaams were loaded up for the climb to the City on the Hill. Crow-feeder took his leave. "May the Weird grant that you find your mother." Then he went to Skins-rabbit and said, "I grant you your freedom, Skins-rabbit, and bid you give them my kiss of friendship." And he took her in his arms and placed his lips on hers.

Then all was quiet once more. The wind soughed through the pine needles. The paddles of the departing canoes dipped and splashed. The Longfoot crashed and rumbled. High overhead, an eagle screeched. Suddenly Méarana felt as isolated as she had ever felt in her life. She shivered in the mountain breeze, and adjusted the anycloth in her jacket to pad up a bit against the chill.

She and Donovan went to Skins-rabbit, who stood on the riverbank looking after the departing Harps. When the last canoe had turned the bend and vanished behind a stand of hop-willow, she spat into the river.

Méarana had not expected that she had loved her captors. It was a hard world, but each man had his strengths and his flaws. There were none, as her mother had once told her, entitled to throw the first stone.

But that did not mean, she had always added, that there were none who deserved to be struck by it.

"Come with us, Skins-rabbit," said the harper. The girl would understand nothing but her name, which Méarana had learned to pronounce in the *tanga cru'tye*.

But the girl tossed her head and the twin black braids flew like whips. She said something in a vehement tone and reached to rip off the thigh-length flaxen shift she wore. Méarana stayed her hand and she and the girl locked eyes for a time. Then Skins-rabbits made a grim line of her mouth and dropped her hand.

"I think we get the message," Méarana said. "What is it, Donovan?"

"I think I know what she said. When you called her Skins-rabbits, I think she said, 'My name is Chain Gostiyya-Uaid.' "

"My earwig was silent."

"It wasn't my earwig. It was the Pedant. It was a language I learned . . . I don't know when."

"You never talk about your youth."

"If I ever learn I had one, you'll be the next to know." He said something to Chain in a tongue alternately liquid and guttural. Chain frowned, listened intently, and opened her mouth to reply. But then she shook her head and shrugged.

They walked back to the rest of the group, who had donned their backpacks and were waiting with the yaams. "It will come to me," Donovan said, though he did not sound certain. "Perhaps I once learned a language that was cousin to hers."

Chain led them to a trail that switchbacked up the massif. It was a pitiless trail, at times reduced to hand and toeholds carved into the face of the rock, and at other times to ledges that wound narrowly along the precipice. It was not a trail to be walked lightly. At one point, Billy slipped and would have fallen but that Donovan seized his arm and pulled him back up.

During the climb, Donovan mulled over the tantalizing half-familiarity of Chain's language. The Treasure Fleet had set out from Terra well before the Cleansing, and her people would have spoken the Taņțamiž *lingua franca* of that age. Yet, there had also been the Vraddies, the Zhõgwó, the Murkans, and the Yurpans with their Roomie under-class . . .

In the Age of Audio, languages changed more languidly than in the Age of Print. But while recordings preserved the classical pronunciation for longer periods, nonetheless consonants softened, vowels shifted, declensions dissolved. Among the descendants of the Cleansing, they had changed one way; among those of the Treasure Fleet, in other ways. In the Old Planets, different languages had been thrown together with the deliberate intention of hindering communication among the refugees, so the tongues of the Periphery were more thoroughly blended than those of the Wild. That was why he could understand occasional words, but not quite the whole sense.

The Sleuth was working on it.

Sometimes he missed the voices in his head. There had been a community in the cacophony, despite all their quarrels. Now and then, he heard a whisper of the Pedant's pompous ruminations, of the Sleuth's snide deductions, of the Inner Child's high-pitched worries. But now he had the sense that *he* was ruminating and deducing and worrying— that it was the same "I" even when done in parallel by separate portions of his mind. He even missed that sly old reprobate, the Fudir.

"Told you you would miss me when I was gone," his lips said.

And Donovan smiled as he climbed.

Then they were over the lip of the mountain and moving down through an alpine forest. High-crested light-blue birds cocked their heads at the parade and scolded them in shrill cries. Does with fawns bounded away through the dark beneath the canopy. The path was well-worn, but they saw no sign of the people who had worn it.

Then the forest opened out onto a broad, high meadow, and Donovan saw a checkerboard of regular, well-kept fields and small homesteads bordered by stone walls and rail fences. The houses crouched under low-slung turf roofs; and the smoke that curled from the chimneys drifted toward the ground. Men and women halted their plows with sharp commands to their himmers and stood to watch the passing strangers. Each had a long gun to hand, and some cradled theirs.

"They have firearms!" Méarana said. "Not even the Nuxrjes'rii have firearms."

Donovan called out to a farmer and waved. The man, after some hesitation, waved back. Because he had recognized the word? Or only because he recognized a greeting?

They came to a small bridge across a rushing mountain stream, one of the tributaries that would become first the Multawee, then the mighty Aríidnux. On the other side, on an island formed by a fork in the stream, houses stood cheek by jowl. But instead of crossing the bridge, Chain went to her knees on the stream's bank and splashed the water on herself, letting it run down her arms and dashing it on her face. "O Xhodzhā! O Xhodzhā!"

Sofwari had gone downstream a little way and now crouched there. "Strange," he said. "They have dug two tunnels *under* the stream. Why?" Slightly downstream was a statue of a goddess holding a lantern.

The people on the island studiously paid the newcomers no attention. The yaam Donovan held honked and yanked against his reins. Then he spit on Donovan. The scarred man made a pungent comment on the beast's ancestry in the Terran patois.

And one of the men across the bridge repeated the phrase, adding a gesture with his finger.

Some words, it seemed, changed very little over the centuries. In terms of communication, it was little enough, but it was a start. Donovan exchanged grins with the other man. *Yeah, life's a bitch.*

An elderly couple elbowed their way to the stream-bank. "Chain!" they cried. "Chain, gyuh xub pex dyŭshdū evda yodãí!" And then, although the stream was easily waded, Chain ran to the bridge and slapped across it on bare horny feet into their arms. The other Emrikii clasped their hands and cried, "Aw!" as a crow calls, but deeper and throatier.

Almost, Donovan could make out what they were saying. But the words eluded him like a tavern wench. He beckoned to the Harp translator, Watershanks.

"Lord Donovan," he said before the scarred man could speak, "these people don't like Harps. Much bad blood. Tell them I be riverman from Rajiloor. I am a riverman, really, for many years since I left Harp country."

Paulie's lip curled. "Seems the Harps breed for cowards as well as bugnuts."

Donovan was not certain whether the cold-blooded fighters of World were in any way preferable to the wild emotions of the Enjrunii. "Stick close by," he told Watershanks. "The more you talk the *loora nuxrjes'r* and the less you talk the *tanga cru'tye*, the more you may set their minds at ease. Sofwari, hold onto my yaam. Méarana, when you're ready."

Donovan, Méarana, and Watershanks moved to the foot

of the bridge. The Emrikii stirred uneasily, counting numbers, but clearly counting Teodorq and Paulie more than
once. They had recognized Teodorq's nine as a weapon,
and possibly the dazers that Donovan and Billy wore. The
people of this high valley did not have high tech, unless
one counted gunpowder and waterwheels, but they clearly
knew it when they saw it.

"Give them a friendly greeting," Donovan told his translator.

Watershanks said something to Chain in the *tanga*, and
the Emrikii murmured at the sounds and rhythms of their
enemies.

It was in Chain's hands to bring it all down on them, and
Donovan could see the knowledge of that power in her
eyes. All she need do is tell her people whatever vengeance
she wished. But she must know that the strangers, although
they had seemed on good terms with her captors, were
clearly not of them. Their strange clothing and accouter-
ments indicated great power. What could they wreak if
offended? Finally, she said something in the *tanga*; and,
after she had spoken the words, she knelt by the riverside
and cupped water in her mouth and spat it out.

Donovan said to Watershanks, "If you want to ease their
minds, every time you say something in the *tanga*, rinse
your mouth out and spit." The riverman stubborned up for
a moment. He did not want to be identified with his people,
not here and now; but that did not mean he wished to repu-
diate them. Yet, prudence won, and he did as Donovan
advised.

"We have come," Donovan announced, "seeking the
men who wrought this." And Méarana lifted the medallion
from around her neck and held it up for all to see. "For we
would know where the place is where this fire comes down
from the sky."

Not many could have made out the design on the

medallion, but excitement bubbled through the growing crowd. Donovan heard them say, over and over, "El bhweka ezgoyfrõ!" And "El zagwibhoyshiz!" And they broke into cheers that were quite different from the ululations of the Great Valley, and opened a path from the bridge into the village of Dacitti.

There was a great deal of handslapping and general cheer as they made their way up a broad path to the village green, and Donovan could see that his companions were heartened by the welcome. But a vague unease stirred within him. <Something is not quite right.> 𝕴'𝔪 𝔴𝔬𝔯𝔨𝔦𝔫𝔤 𝔬𝔫 𝔦𝔱. He looked about the village for escape routes. <Just in case,> his Inner Child told him. Meanwhile, he smiled at the people he encountered. They would not understand his words, but his friendly tone would come through.

Dacitti sat on a long, narrow island between the Xhodzhã and the Rjo-yezdy. Save for the farmers scattered about the valley, nearly all the Emrikii lived on this island. In consequence, the huts were crowded close and, in some cases were stacked three high atop one another, with access by ladders. There were well-trod paths between the huts and many of them had been laid with corduroy planks or paving stones. The paths were rectilinear, save at the lower end, where the two streams came together, where they were more tangled. Donovan supposed that this arrangement had originally been for defense—the two streams were not especially formidable, but did provide a moat of sorts to protect the village from attack.

Whatever threat had once motivated its construction, the valley of the Emrikii was now peaceful and secure. The other valley tribes had long ago joined their confederacy. The Oorah used to raid into Emrika to capture women, but now seldom tried. Harp bravos sometimes led war parties into the Kobberjobbles, but the path was too arduous, the sentries too vigilant, and the Emrikii warriors too disciplined. Now the Harps were leaving the Longfoot Valley—blaming a poor harvest rather than an Emrikii punitive expedition.

A large rectangular green occupied the center of Dacitti. It included a sheep meadow and a pond where fish were cultivated. Much of this cornucopia was laid out for the visitors that afternoon in a great feast. Damáire, who was village headman, bid them official welcome and when the platitudes and formalities had been completed, Méarana finally got an answer to her question.

"The sky-fire comes down up there," Watershanks told them as Damáire pointed to a flat peak at the far end of the valley.

"Every night," said Billy Chins, "to cook their food."

Damáire laughed at the humor of the starmen. "You are a funny man," he told the Confederate courier. "That is only a legend of superstitious Valley folk. No, it is the sperm of the sky. When the god grows horny, he comes to our world to impregnate her. The sky-fire is his thrust into her.

" 'Fire from sky meets womb in ground.
Thrusting deep within . . .' "

"Well," said Billy wooden-faced. "We wouldn't want to believe a superstitious legend."

"Sperm," said Donovan. He could not get out of his mind what Méarana had told him on the Starwalk at Siggy O'Hara. "Then why 'fire' from the sky?"

"Because the god has what we call 'the hots.' God loves the world, so he comes back, again and again. And it is a beautiful world, though I know no others."

Donovan could see between the three-stacked huts the newly plowed fields of Emrika valley rolling off toward forests and the mountains that rimmed them in. He could not tell Damáire he was wrong. He asked the headman how long it took the god to grow horny.

"Hard to say," was the answer. "Gods are not like us, but it must be exhausting, making a whole world pregnant. I will ask the *efrezde*-who-watches-the-sky. Her tallyboard may tell us when the world is to be screwed."

The *efrezde*-who-watches-the-sky spent several hours of prayer that night, using a sextant and jacobstaff to mark the positions of key sky-objects. But, as this was her station in life, she kept these observations updated daily, and it did not take long thereafter to complete her prophesy. "In one tenday and half a tenday," she announced at morning prayer, "will the fire come down and enter the Well at the End of the World." At breakfast later, she added, "So your arrival is timely. The other golden-skinned woman, who came in a sky-borne chariot, arrived last year. But it was not the proper time. So after a time among the Oorah she ascended into heaven."

The harper's knees nearly betrayed her. Donovan seized her by the arm and Sofwari took her by the other and between them they bore her up.

"Mother," she said, almost in a whisper.

Perhaps that was another word that the centuries barely touched, for Chain Gostiyya-Uaid turned to her and something like understanding was in her eyes.

XV   AND BEHOLD, A PILLAR OF FIRE

They set off the next day from Dacitti in a shower of red maiden and edelweiss and with wreaths of dragon's blood around their necks. Fifes and drums played them up the Broad Path to the ditch that connected the

Xhodzhã with the Rjo-yeszdy at the north end of the island. The Emrikii lined the Path and cheered and threw
confetti as they passed. A company of musketeers in
powder-blue jacks and cross-belts marched with them as
an honor guard. At the Xhorlm Ditch, the well-wishers remained behind and Méarana and her group continued
along the Xhodzhã High Road that ran the length of the
valley.

Méarana paused to thank Damáire, but he only waved
his hands and said, "V'gedda-boddi," which the translators
told her was how the Emrikii said, "you're welcome."

With them went a "long hunter" named Bavyo Zãzhaice,
who knew the way to the top of the Oorah butte, and Chain,
who spoke a bit of the Oorah language. Bavyo had the
broad stride and confident mien of one returning to his
natural home.

"He is a man-who-likes-aloneness," Chain explained
through Watershanks. "He lives in the forests and in the
Big Mountains, so he gets little practice in talking to other
people."

Indeed, their guide frequently went off by himself when
they stopped for night camp, to a lonely crag or an oak
grove, where he sat in silent contemplation. Méarana joined
him one evening on a great stone outcropping. There was a
gap in the forest through which a distant mountain pass
could be seen and the flat line of the plains beyond. The sky
had deepened to indigo save where the sun had lately gone
down, and there the clouds glowed a bright red. Bavyo said
nothing the whole time she watched the sunset.

The next day, as they crossed the lower slope and entered the Borigan Forest, Chain fell into step with her.
"Bavyo say," she stammered in halting *loor nuxrjes'r*, "yes,
he set beautiful." Then she scurried ahead to walk beside
him. He seemed to take no notice, and Chain looked everywhere but at their guide. Méarana smiled to herself.

Sofwari came to walk beside her. "What did she tell you?"

"Nothing. How goes your research?"

The science-wallah's face clouded over and he touched a pocket in his coveralls. "I have only the data from Rajiloor and Nuxrjes'r, but your intuition seems to have been correct, and this is the origin of the anomalous cluster on Harpaloon."

She took his hand and they walked companionably. "Debly, tell me something."

He hesitated. "What?"

"Why did these worlds crash so badly? The Dark Age was rough on the Old Planets. The prehumans deliberately mixed cultures and languages, and it took centuries to recover; but the Old Planets never forgot the past as badly as here. The Harps have a legend about ancestors who went out on the Shining Path, promising to return. But they never did. That would have been the expedition sent to Harpaloon. I've seen the landers in Côndefer Park, and even the 'Loons have forgotten what they were. No surprise, the Enjrunii never heard of the League or the Confederation. But I've mentioned the prehumans, Dao Chetty, even the Commonwealth. Nothing. It's like they never were."

They continued silently for a space while Sofwari gave it thought. A bird with a flare of red feathers at his crest called out from a branch they were passing and took wing to another tree. "This is outside my expertise," he said at last, "but my guess is that as rich as the Treasure Fleet was, it was not as rich as a world. What they took with them was nothing; next to the whole of Terra. In the end, there were not enough of them, or they lacked for something essential, or they spread themselves too thin. Perhaps if they had focused on fewer worlds . . ."

"I understand the world has to be receptive. Look at Gatmander or New Eireann. Had they seeded too few places, and the prehumans had stumbled across them out here . . .

No, their safest choice was to spread their seed as far and wide as they could. Who knows . . ."

"Who knows what?"

"Who knows what we would find in the Cygnus Arm, if we ever get there?"

She heard chimes, and looked around to see what the sound could be. The Harps placed "soul catchers" in trees and the wind rang the metal pieces woven into them. But this was far outside Harp country.

Donovan was answering his comm. unit. For a moment, the significance did not register. Then she realized. "*Blankets and Beads!* She's back!"

Their translators and guide did not understand the elation. Méarana tried to explain to Watershanks that their "endarooa-of-the-stars" had returned from a trade visit; and Watershanks tried to explain that to two people who had likely never seen an endarooa. A star canoe? What was that beside the wonders they had already seen? Ayiyi! The Scarred One spoke to a djinn invisible!

Donovan said, "They have a fix, but there are only four signals. They have another signal, very weak, from Roaring Gorge, and ad-Din wants to know what happened? Who's lost their beacon?"

Teodorq shrugged. "Mine went missing during the fight in Roaring Gorge. I ain't going back to get it."

Debly Sofwari ducked his head. "Same thing. When the Harps ransacked my equipment . . ."

Méarana grabbed him by the sleeve. "You were supposed to keep it on your person! Not stuff it away in your baggage! What were you thinking? If you'd gotten separated from us, we would never have found you!" She had begun pushing and shoving him; and he seized her hands at the wrist.

"Why berate me over what might have happened? If I had told you, what could you have possibly done about it?"

"D.Z. wants to know," said Donovan, wagging his comm., "if we want pickup."

Paulie said, "Easier than climbing up that mesa."

Méarana backed away from Sofwari. "Tell him no," she said. "We'll be on top tomorrow morning."

"The priestess back in Dacitti," Theodorq said, "said day after is when the god comes."

"Donovan, tell D.Z. that the ship should search for an approaching astronomical object. An asteroid or something."

Donovan did so, adding, "And D.Z.. it would *not* be a good idea to let *Blankets and Beads* come between that object and the mesa." He signed off and tucked the comm. back in his breast pocket.

Méarana, watching him, said, "How did you hide your comm. from the Harps?"

The Fudir grinned with Donovan's lips. "There's always one place you can stick things where most folks won't look."

The path to the top of the mesa was steep. Bavyo assured them that there were no turnoffs to lead them astray. He then wished them good fortune and turned to the main trail. Méarana cried with astonishment. "Wait!"

But Chain said through Watershanks, "He walks his own path. The Oorah trail is not his trail."

Billy Chins grunted. "Some guide."

"I will go with Bavyo," Chain announced. "He needs a woman to walk beside him, and how the barbarians used Skins-rabbits will not matter to him." She, too, turned her feet to the main trail, speaking a few words with Watershanks as she passed.

The others gathered round. Teodorq watched the two Emrikii depart. "That can't be good."

"Watershanks," said Méarana, "what did she tell you?"

"She assured me that the Oorah consider a guest as their most precious treasure."

"Fine," said Paulie, "but without we have an interpreter, what can they tell us?"

Donovan stood to the side with a thoughtful frown, running his fingers across his scars. "Oorah," Méarana heard him say. "The people of the village? Do you think it could be, or is it just a coincidence?"

The way was steep, though unlike the Longfoot trail, there was no point at which they had to resort to toe- and hand-holds. But the air was thin and cold, and there was trouble catching one's breath. Coming to a primordial lava flow, the trail passed through a slot cut through the rock and fashioned anciently into stairs. In the rock were carved the runes: கபார்தார்

Donovan stopped and ran his fingers over them, feeling out the shape of the figures. "Kapartār," he said, as if to himself. "Could that be 'guhbahdāw'?" He stood, staring and silent.

"I suppose it could be," said Teodorq. "But for my eyes it could be 'For a good time, summon Tsuzi Elkhorn.'" Paulie laughed with him.

Méarana said, "Donovan, what does *guhbahdāw* mean?"

"Hmm?" The scarred man turned from his contemplation of the carving. "Oh. It means 'beware.'"

Teodorq looke at Paulie. "That can't be good."

Paulie said, "Stop saying that." And the mountaineer made a sign with his left hand to avert the evil.

"Pedant talks about phoneme shifts. A 'bh'—or 'v'—tends to become a 'b,' for example; and a 'b' becomes a 'p.' But sometimes people pick up phonemes from neighboring folk and 'b' may become 'bh' again. This looks to me like the old Taṇṭamiž that we saw in Madéen o' Loons, or on the old captain's logs that Greystroke stole from the Harpaloon temple."

"I don't mean that," said Méarana. "I mean, what are we supposed to be wary of?"

"Life."

"We needed a sign to tell us that?"

Méarana started into the cut, but Teodorq suddenly grabbed her by the shoulders, lifted her up, and set her down behind him. "I think," he said, "that this is what yuh hired me for, babe. Paulie, you take rearguard. Donovan, Billy, in the middle with the scholar and the lady."

"I can handle myself," Méarana told him.

"Yeah? That's what the late Tsuzi Elkhorn said to me at Whisker Bluff. But she was only half-right, and it was a whole fight. So, shut up, babe. Without yuh, there'd be no-body to sing my story. I mean, yer the reason we're *here* an' not somewhere else. My head would be decorating a spike outside Josang prison, and yer old man would be a drunk in a Jehovah bar. And Debly, here, would be playing with himself and swabbing people's cheeks instead of being on this here quest where his name might be remembered for something that matters."

Sofwari began to protest, but Teodorq had already started up the cut. Donovan paused before following him. "I don't know," he said with a grin. "The Bar on Jehovah might have been the better choice."

Méarana pushed him along. "Move along, old man. Mount your head on a spike or mount it on a bottle of uis-cebaugh, you're embalmed either way."

The passage took them up onto the lip of a wind-whipped parapet. Emerging, they saw that the rim of the mesa was a ridge that encircled a great barren bowl of a valley. It was at least a thousand double-paces from lip to lip. The village of the Oorah was strung around this bowl like a wreath woven of greens and fir branches. Fields were set in terraces in the side of the bowl. Below them, huts nestled. Inward of the huts was barren rock: no vegetation grew, no trees, no bushes.

"Like the caldera of a volcano," said Sofwari as they made their way around the ledge.

"Except here," Méarana said, "the fire comes down from the sky, not up from the ground."

Thin lines of people filed into the caldera, each person carrying something which he laid in a great pile in the center of the bowl. Through the stiff wind they heard the faint murmur of singing and the people swayed to the rhythm of it.

"Offerings to the approaching god," Sofwari guessed.

One of the supplicants, turning back after dropping her offering, pointed and raised a cry, and heads began to turn their way.

"Perhaps we have interrupted something," said Watershanks.

Donovan stepped to the edge of the parapet and cupped his hands. "Halloo!" he called. "Nawn inki yergay mbetão!"

This caused a flurry of activity beneath them. People ran to and fro, sleeves were tugged, hats held out to shade eyes, more fingers were pointed. Finally, an old man was led out. Despite the cold, high-altitude air, he wore nothing beside a short skirt and what looked like a dusting of talcum powder over his chest, face, and arms. He bore a staff made of a thick, twisted tree limb and his hair was a rat's tangle. An acolyte held a megaphone to the man's lips.

"Ungloady pr'enna?"

Donovan thought about that, then shouted back, "Onkyawti por enya?"

Now the priest, if such he was, appeared puzzled. Then he made a sign on his body and said, "Ongalodai per enna?"

Donovan smiled. "He knows the ancient dialect!" he

told the others. Then he called, "Naan Donovan. Naan in-gey irke vendum!"

Tangled hair bobbed as the priest nodded vigorously. "Vanakkam! Ullay waruvangal." He pointed ahead of them. "Munney po! Munney po!"

Donovan turned to them. "He says welcome and come in, and we should go forward."

They found the path down through the terraces half a league farther on along the parapet. But once down to the next level they had to "pinnal po," go back the way they had come to find the stairs to the next terrace down.

"I had wondered about that," said Billy Chins. "Their village occupies the low ground, which disadvantages them. But they have created a maze through their crop terraces, so an invader cannot charge straight down. Though if the Emrikii learn to make rifled muskets, they could stand on the parapet and pick off people in the village."

"The Harps could take this place," said Watershanks. "They could rappel down the sides of the terraces like they did down the cliffs at Candletown." Whether that thought heartened him, he did not say. The Harps, in any case, were far away and getting farther.

The entire ring of habitations was called Ūr, or Oor; but different segments along the ring were called by different names. When Méarana and her company finally emerged onto the terrace where the houses were set, they found themselves in Mylap Oor, or "Peacock Town." There was a great stone statue of a peacock there under the shade of what they called a "funny tree." The peacock was said to be the goddess Fahbády worshipping the god Žiba. That one god might worship another struck Méarana as peculiar. Maxwell certainly did not worship Newton! And since the stone peacock gazed nowhere but into the empty bowl valley, how did anyone know what she worshipped?

A happy, laughing crowd met them and escorted them around the ring-village to the headman's house. Along the way, they passed bronze statues, mostly of young women, but including also some young men and a few older men dressed like the bonze who had first greeted them. Donovan told them, after asking their escorts, that these were the *nayanmars*, the sixty-three saints of Žiba. The statues were beautifully done and many of them were adorned with floral wreaths around their necks or with bouquets and jar-candles and joss sticks at their feet. It is the festival of "Rupa Đamupa," they were told by those who kissed them as they passed.

That evening, at a banquet in their honor, they learned that the festival celebrated the coming of the god in two of his aspects: Vrabha the Creator and Žiba the Destroyer. The headman, who was also the hierophant for the entire Oorah tribe, sat them on great embroidered pillows and placed cones of incense before them and decked them with leis. Then he brought in troupes of naked dancing girls, between performances of which he explained the traditions of the Village People.

Eons ago, Vrabha the Creator placed the Oorah on the mesa to bring life to the world by preparing a place where the god might come: the Vagina of the Earth, although the pagans in the Lower Lands called it the Well at the End of the World.

"But it is not the End, but the Beginning," he explained.

The speech had to run through Donovan's ears and out his tongue, which made at times for slow-going. The ancient Taṇṭamiž had changed in one way for these people and in another way for Donovan's, and so they spoke in the dead tongue that was their common ancestor. Donovan felt exalted. He was, however inexpertly, speaking as the Vraddies of the old Commonwealth of Suns had spoken in the glory days of Terra. He was, in some manner, at one with them.

"But the god is three in one," the old man explained. "He not only brings life, but he sustains it, and destroys it, and thus brings the wheel full circle; for the destruction *is* the conception. And so when the god comes, we hold this festival to honor his saints. We take our most precious treasures and place them in the Vagina of the World to be consumed by his love. Thus it has been. Thus it will be."

Paulie said, "This food tastes funny."

"It does have an odd flavor," Donovan agreed. He asked the headman what spices had been used to flavor the meat and the headman told him.

"Tānikam," he said. "What some folk call 'coriander.'"

Donovan paused with his spoon half-lifted. "Coriander?" he croaked. "*This* is coriander? But it grows nowhere else but Terra!"

The headman shrugged. "Perhaps it is but a different thing called by the same name."

Donovan finished swallowing. "It is not so much of a such," he said.

Méarana laid a gentle hand on his arm. "Sometimes a dream is more alluring than the fact."

But Donovan shrugged off the hand. "Then we should dream more realistically."

Méarana looked away. "She was here, wasn't she? Your headman confirmed it. They called her a reincarnation of Fahbády the Peacock. She came down from heaven in a chariot, walked among them, and then rose once more. You can't say my quest was unrealistic if we actually succeeded."

Donovan saw tears in the corner of her eyes, and did not

answer. Success was no proof at all. One man might succeed on the wildest of hunches; another fail after careful calculation. If the True Coriander had proven a disappointment, the same was not true of what it symbolized. He gazed at the bowl valley, which the verandah of the headman's palace faced. The Burnt-Over District, he thought. There must be places like this on a dozen worlds; places where the god returns at intervals and screws them over with fire from the sky.

That sort of repetition bespoke the mechanical, like the tock of a metronome. Whatever the original purpose had been, it was simply repeating itself now, like a scanner stuck on a bit.

"At least," said Méarana softly, "I know at last where she went."

"But you don't," Donovan told her. "She came here, yes; but she left to go elsewhere. And these people don't know where. This is the end of the trail."

"No it isn't," Méarana said, pointing to the stars that were appearing in the violet sky. "She went there."

And there was a blue star, brighter than all the others, rising above the eastern rim of the bowl, directly in line with the Vagina of the World.

"She's decelerating," Maggie Barnes told them over the comm. as they gathered for the night in the Longhouse of the Nayanmars. The building was decorated for the festival in banners and icons. And one of the bronze statues had been rolled into the building with them. The second-oldest, they had been told.

"No," the captain continued, "I don't know what kind of engines she's using, but they ain't what we use. She's a-coming our way at a fair clip. D.Z. says she has a two-year period relative to Enjrun's year and reaches conjunction at northern hemisphere spring."

"That fits. We think the harper's mother tracked down the object and rendezvoused with it—it's some sort of old Commonwealth tech—"

"We ain't stupid, Fudir. And I gotta say if it pans out, yer high-handed arrogance commandeering my ship may just damn-well pay for itself five times over."

"Short of what the Kennel will want kept confidential. Send the boat down for us in the morning, after the festival." He glanced at Méarana, who nodded. There was no urgency to the rendezvous, and it hurt nothing to be polite to their hosts.

The others were already bedded down, although Teodorq sat on his bedding against the wall with his nine in an open scabbard and Goodhandlingblade across his lap. "They seem friendly enough," Donovan told him.

The Wildman shrugged. "Then I lose a few hours' sleep before Paulie spells me. I'd rather be cautious and wrong than careless and wrong."

A bench ran along the inside walls of the longhouse and Donovan sat beside Teodorq. "You know, Teddy, I had my doubts at first; but you've been a good man to have. The way you handled those Harp warriors showed good judgment as well as bravery."

"Yeah. I'm good. It's what we call counting coup back home. The law of least effort. The real bitch is when yuh have to kill a friend. That's hard."

"Yes," the scarred man said after a moment, "I guess it is. But I know one thing harder."

"What's that?"

"Betraying a friend."

The Wildman thought about that for a while. "But sometimes yuh wind up on the other side. Like Arjuna or Cu Chulainn—the Original Hound from way back when. Then yuh got it to do. I'm gonna hate like hell to kill Paulie. He's been okay, and that was a good trick, cutting the arrow in midair."

"I don't understand. Is it that old blood feud between plainsmen and mountaineers?"

Teodorq shrugged. "Yuh best get yer sleep, boss. Big party tomorrow."

Méarana, too, was wakeful, and Donovan went to stand beside her in the doorway of the longhouse, where the blue star was already perceptibly brighter. "End in sight," he said.

The harper nodded, but said nothing.

"Afraid what you'll find?"

She crossed her arms and shivered; and Donovan laid his arm around her shoulders. "Maybe you and I, we'll complete what she started," he said.

"I don't care about old Commonwealth tech. Oh, I suppose it's important, but . . ."

"I wasn't talking about that."

"Oh." Méarana leaned against him. "Did you ever want something when you were a child, something you wanted so badly but never had, and you wanted it all the more for not having it?"

Donovan could not remember his childhood; but he said Yes because it sounded right.

"There was nothing special about her leaving, Father. Just a note. 'Back soon.' It should have been more. She should have said something more."

"You never know when it's the last time. No one ever knows. First times, though. That's different. You called me 'Father.'"

She leaned closer. "I was never sure before that I wanted to."

"You almost did, a couple of times. At first, I was afraid that you would. Later, I was afraid that you wouldn't."

"I guess this *is* the time when I go all warm and gooey."

Donovan laughed and, unlike the laugh of the scarred man, it was a pleasant one to hear. He kissed her on the forehead, and said, "I told you once that I'd always hoped something good had come out of the Dancer affair. I'm glad something did."

The Sleuth was shaking him awake. *Donovan! Fudir! Brute! We have trouble!*

Groggy, he opened his eyes a slit. Red dawn was stealing through the open windows. "What is it?"

𝕿𝖍𝖊 𝖔𝖑𝖉 𝖍𝖊𝖆𝖉𝖒𝖆𝖓 𝖘𝖆𝖎𝖉, "𝖂𝖊 𝖙𝖆𝖐𝖊 𝖔𝖚𝖗 𝖒𝖔𝖘𝖙 𝖕𝖗𝖊𝖈𝖎𝖔𝖚𝖘 𝖙𝖗𝖊𝖆-𝖘𝖚𝖗𝖊𝖘 𝖆𝖓𝖉 𝖕𝖑𝖆𝖈𝖊 𝖙𝖍𝖊𝖒 𝖎𝖓 𝖙𝖍𝖊 𝖁𝖆𝖌𝖎𝖓𝖆 𝖔𝖋 𝖙𝖍𝖊 𝖂𝖔𝖗𝖑𝖉 𝖙𝖔 𝖇𝖊 𝖈𝖔𝖓-𝖘𝖚𝖒𝖊𝖉 𝖇𝖞 𝖍𝖎𝖘 𝖑𝖔𝖛𝖊."

That means to be incinerated by the power beam.

"Yeah, yeah. And . . . ?"

𝕮𝖍𝖆𝖎𝖓 𝖆𝖘𝖘𝖚𝖗𝖊𝖉 𝖚𝖘 𝖙𝖍𝖆𝖙 𝖙𝖍𝖊 𝕺𝖔𝖗𝖆𝖍 𝖈𝖔𝖓𝖘𝖎𝖉𝖊𝖗 𝖆 𝖌𝖚𝖊𝖘𝖙 𝖆𝖘 𝖙𝖍𝖊𝖎𝖗 "𝖒𝖔𝖘𝖙 𝖕𝖗𝖊𝖈𝖎𝖔𝖚𝖘 𝖙𝖗𝖊𝖆𝖘𝖚𝖗𝖊."

That means . . .

"Oh, shit."

"And exceptionally deep, too," said the Fudir.

<The door is the only way out of the longhouse. The stairs up through the terraces are a maze. We are seven to several thousand.>

"Will they use force?"

𝕱𝖔𝖗 𝖆 𝖌𝖔𝖉 𝖔𝖋 𝖙𝖍𝖎𝖘 𝖘𝖔𝖗𝖙? 𝕺𝖋 𝖈𝖔𝖚𝖗𝖘𝖊.

"Armament?"

Billy and us got dazers, both fully charged. Teddy's nine. Méarana has a pellet gun, and Sofwari has the needler, if he ain't lost that, too. Knives, each of us. Méarana has three, two in the baggage. Paulie and Teddy have longswords. Watershanks has a knife, but nothing else.

"And all that against several thousand?"

A hefty fee for the ferryman; but otherwise, not a chance.

Donovan closed his eyes. . . . *and sees a young girl in a*

chiton. "There is a way out of this," she tells him, and her voice is like a melody.

The headman came shortly after the second morning hour. He was accompanied by flower girls strewing their path with spring petals, by a musician playing a morning rag, and by several very large acolytes.

Méarana told him, through Donovan, that she wished to dedicate her most precious treasure to the god: her harp. Teddy agreed and named his best sword. No one else admitted possessing a most precious treasure—Donovan had one, but he was not about to sacrifice her—but they agreed to accompany their friends down to the pile of offerings. And so, flanked by the flower girls—and the large acolytes—and followed by the musician, all of them singing in harmony, they set off in a procession to the path that led down from the longhouse.

Teddy and Paulie were also singing, in their own languages, a jarring dissonance. What words Donovan caught sounded bawdy, but given how the Oorah had conceptualized the power beam, somehow appropriate.

The musician had an instrument that Donovan knew as a steel guitar, but was known here as an ishtar. He played the rag in alap—slow and improvisational—adding each new note of the scale at the right time. The Pedant reminded him that an alap could meander for hours and the Sleuth wondered if that meant they had lots of time. "We don't know when he started playing," the Fudir reminded them.

When they reached the base of the path, the ishtarist upped his tempo to jor and a tabla man walking beside him added rhythm. Donovan told his companion in Gaelactic, "When he ups his tempo again to jhala, things will start to happen, fast."

Donovan could see the statues of all sixty-three saints.

The Sleuth told him that these must be the statues of earlier sacrifices. With each new pass of the god, the oldest-but-one of the statues was retired, melted down, and recast in the image of the latest sacrifice.

Their own children. Sometimes, an elder. No wonder they welcome guests.

"Thank the gods," said the Fudir, "that *she* came in the wrong season."

Bavyo must have known; and so had Chain, but Donovan wasted no breath cursing them. The Emrikii had likely interpreted their eagerness to find Oor as a willingness to be sacrificed. It may have saved an outlying farmstead from a bloody mesa-top raid.

The offering pile was large, but given the size of the ring-village, not terribly so. Donovan was reminded of the sacrifices to Newton he had witnessed, in which a bull was dropped from a leaning tower to smash on the flagstones below or—in more humane settings—was felled by a weight smashing his skull. (It was important only that gravity killed the beast.) The offal and tripe were burned to the god; but the tasty meat—the rump, the flank, the loins— were butchered and distributed to the poor in the temple's district. So a child of Oor might offer a beloved toy—but one that was worn out after much play.

A mongrel dog had been pegged into the ground by its leash. Seeing the harper's distress, Teddy turned and cried out for Donovan to translate, "I dedicate this sword, Good-handlingblade, to the god!" Under his breath, he added, "to the Chooser of the Slain." Then he tried to stab it into the earth. In doing so, he accidentally severed the dog's leash, and the animal, sensing its freedom, tore immediately from the bowl.

The crowd murmured, trying to understand whether this was a good omen or not. Teodroq tried to look sheepish.

Then the priest looked up at the sun and barked an order

and the well-wishing crowd turned to file out of the bowl. Watershanks cried out and ran after the dog. To catch him and bring him back? The priest knew better; and likely he had seen such last-minute changes of heart by previous volunteers. He signaled to one of his acolytes, who sped after Watershanks, caught him easily, and struck him on the side of his head with an obsidian-edged club. The riverman fell without uttering a sound. The acolyte checked him, then made an angry gesture, and left him lying there.

Donovan reached into his scrip and pressed a button on his comm. unit: 999 999 999. Méarana glanced at him, and he nodded. There was no mistake now. The Oorah intended them for kindling.

The lander from *Blankets and Beads* soared up and over the western rim of the mesa. It had come down quietly in the night and had been waiting in the wastelands for Donovan's signal. It circled the bowl once, to get bearings, and to scatter the flower girls and the musicians. They cried out at this apparition and one of them called to Holy Fahbády, who had come and gone in just this sort of chariot.

"Remember what we agreed," Donovan cautioned them. "One at a time up the ladder. Méarana first. Billy last."

The musician had recovered his ishtar and he and the tabla man resumed the rag they had been playing, although they missed notes and beats now from nervous glances at the chariot. They backed away at jor tempo.

The priest stood a moment longer. Perhaps the chariot was intended as the most precious offering of all?

The craft settled to the ground and the hatch popped open almost immediately. Kid O'Daevs stuck his head out. "Move yo' asses! Ten minutes to closest approach! Wild Bill takes off in five!"

They moved as one to the base of the ladder, and Sofwari helped Méarana onto the rungs even before it was fully extended.

The priest cried out and the burly acolytes rushed them. Teddy pulled his nine and shot the first. Paulie winged the second. Billy sprayed them with his dazer but, waving it back and forth as he did and not concentrating his fire, only numbed them.

It spread confusion, and that was enough. But the edge of the bowl was now lined with spearmen, who began to hurl their weapons. Paulie cleaved one spear as he had the arrow in the Roaring Gorge, and Teddy matched the feat. Billy actually seized one out of the air and threw it back, though being on the low ground, he did not quite reach the astonished spearman on the rim. Donovan called to Paulie, who faded toward the ladder.

Then an Oorah on the rim put a pipe to his mouth and huffed.

A dart embedded itself in Teddy's midriff. He looked down at it and said, "That can't be good."

It was not much of a dart, and by itself would have meant little damage. "Poison," he called to the others. Then, "Paralytic. Hurry!"

Sacrifices who tried to run were better handled by paralyzing them than braining them with obsidian clubs. The poison would leave them alive for the holocaust.

Teddy looked around, saw Donovan and Paulie on the ladder and Billy scrambling onto the lowest rung. He said nothing about waiting one's turn, but only gauged what time would be needed. The harper was helping Sofwari into the airlock. She looked up and their gazes met.

Teddy waved at her, then he bent and plucked Goodhandlingblade from the ground and sped after the retreating priest and his bodyguards. "Teodorq sunna Nagarajan of World!" he cried, waving the sword over his head and shooting left-handed at the spearmen on the rim. A second paralytic dart tagged him, but the adrenaline was flowing. "Teodorq Nagarajan of World! Remember me!"

The acolytes guarding the priests turned with their short-swords and bucklers, but Teddy dispatched them easily, for the battle-fury was on him. An upswipe to knock a buckler aside, then *thrust*, and one down; he converted his extraction into a backhand cut that severed the carotid artery of a second man. Two. Spin on the ball of the foot and hack the arm of the man trying to sneak around his left. Three. The others broke, and Teddy found his legs too heavy to chase them. The priest stood unmoving, facing him with no more than a hemlock sprig. Magic, he recognized, even powerful magic, though hemlock had no meaning on the plains of World. He sang his deathsong at the top of his lungs. Were three enough for an honor guard? He had not paused to count the men he had shot with his nine. Where was it now? Dropped when the clip ran out. His most precious treasure, left now as an offering for a god who was only some ancient broken machine, and not the true god at all.

A blowgun man toppled from the terrace. Teddy saw Billy in the mouth of the airlock, aiming with a two-handed grip on his dazer. Another shot, but the dazer did not have the range. "Run!" Billy called. "Run, you ignorant savage!"

But he could not make it back; nor could they reach him in the time remaining. Too many blowguns. Teddy saluted with his sword, converted smoothly into a swinging arc, and the priest's head leapt from his shoulders in a fountain of blood.

Then his body was a block of wood, devoid of all feeling. He fell face-first onto the obsidian ground.

But he gripped his sword the proper way around, a last defiance. Being utterly numb by then, he never felt it slide in.

Kid O'Daevs reversed the gravity grid and the mesa fell away behind them. The pilot threw in a sharp lateral vector to get off the bull's-eye, and none too soon, for the pile of offerings on the viewscreen burst into a great ball of flame. Superheated air wavered and grew purple, rose like a geyser, and the wind rushed in from the sides, buffeting the lander and calling up long-disused curses from her pilot.

Méarana did not watch. She sat buckled in her seat and wept.

Watershanks, she had hardly known; but Teddy had been with her for a long time and she had come to regard him as a shrewd and faithful retainer, with more bottom to him than she had at first perceived. And it was just possible that, had he not drawn all attention to himself with his wild charge, the paralytic darts would have dropped them off the ladder like so many senseless mannequins.

Her first impulse was to order the lander to go back and destroy the village. Teddy believed that a dying warrior required an escort of his slain to enter the mead hall, and why should the Oorah's religion be honored and not Teddy's?

But the lander was not a warship, and could do nothing but circle the village and scare everyone. Beside, how could she plead mercy for the hard and vengeance-minded children of the Roaring Gorge and not for the uncomprehending children of the Oorah Mesa?

And so she blamed Donovan. The lander had come down in the night. Could they not have made their way to it? So what if the night was unlit and the way out uncertain? So what if there were no place for the lander on the steep and forested slopes of the mesa? Or that Debly might have gotten separated from them while climbing down those slopes and, lacking a beacon, never-ever be found?

So in the end, she blamed herself. *She* had brought Teddy to this place, where he could die fighting savages. And it did not matter that he had taken a terrible pleasure in the dying.

As *Blankets and Beads* closed on the mysterious object, its size and scope unfolded. It was the largest vessel they had ever seen. Indeed, it was difficult to think of it as a vessel at all. It seemed more a work of nature. A dozen Gladiola arks could have nestled comfortably on its landing decks.

Yet it had been molded and shaped by human hands, carved and pithed and tunneled; shaven and smoothed and polished. Tubes flared; sensor rings glittered; pods that must have been alfven engines squatted symmetrically along a hull on which, scoured to ghostliness by long centuries of radiation, was blazoned the sunburst of the Commonwealth.

"That ain't a ship," Maggie B. commented. "That there is a world."

"What would it have carried?" her First Officer wondered.

"Anything," said Donovan, "and everything. Colonists in cold sleep, embryos or seeds of every species; fusion power; nanomachines to remake the chemistry of whole worlds; artificial intelligences and automatons to orchestrate and oversee the whole process. Libraries of libraries. *That*—is an old Commonwealth terraforming ark."

"Nanomachines," said Captain Barnes skeptically. "Artificial intelligences. Fairly tales."

"Giant ships," Donovan replied, indicating the ark.

"It's big and impressive," she agreed. "But I'll believe in a nanomachine when I see one."

"An ark explains the Oorah legend," Donovan said. "The god fertilizing a world made receptive. Méarana, remember Thistlewaite's Cautionary Books? The 'yin on ground' is . . ."

"The 'Vagina of the World.' "

"And 'yang from sky' is . . ."

"I get the picture. So the Oorahs are descended from the crew sent down to prepare the receptors."

"One of the crews. There must have been others. But something went wrong."

Ad-Din pointed to the viewscreen. "Maybe that." He tapped the screen twice and that section magnified.

The sensor ring was melted. Scopes and arrays had sagged, and bent. The hull itself was scorched and broken. Launch tubes and hatches were melted shut. A battle? A brush with the berm of a Krasnikov tube? Stringers of glassine metal ran aft as if in the wind. Whatever had happened had happened under acceleration.

"Looks like a wreck, all right," said Maggie B.

"Looks like *salvage*," her Number One said. "A Commonwealth ship? Even the wreckage is valuable beyond measure."

Maggie chuckled. "Do you want to put *that* under tow? We'll have to mine it in place."

"And don't forget," said Méarana, "parts of it are still working."

Burly Grimes, the chief engineer, modified a communications satellite; and Ripper Collins, the second pilot, flew it by remote so they could take a closer look. The ark had not reacted to their presence, but Barnes was taking no chances.

The telemetry was displayed on the holostage in the conference room for Méarana and the others to study. Ad-Din took copious notes and marked locations that might provide entry for salvage crews. "Most of it seems to be in vacuum," he commented, "but there are other sections still holding pressure and maintaining temperature. Here, for example . . ." His light-pen described a segement of the holo image above the table.

"After so long!" exclaimed Billy.

"Wait!" said "Pop" Haines, the Second Astrogator. "Back up the view there, D.Z. A little more. There!"

A ship, irregular in shape and bristling with sensor arrays, nestled against the ark's hull.

"It's an old Abyalon survey ship," said D.Z. in wonder. "I have a model in my collection."

"What's it doing all the way out here?"

"Dang if I know, Pop," said Maggie, "but I guess we ain't the first to come across this thing. All right, Mr. Collins, bring her back down the dark side."

Ripper maneuvered the probe up the ark's sunlit face and turned on its searchlights. "Be a few minutes," he said, "before we clear the north face. Newton! It's like surveying a planetoid."

As the probe cleared the "top" of the vessel, they could see that the other side of the ship was undamaged. There was a moment in which they glimpsed a second ship jammed into the vessel's side. Then something on the ark *rippled*; and everything went black.

They replayed the telemetry of the probe's last few moments. The second wreck lay half in and half out of the sharp-edged shadows cast by the probe's searchlights. Ripper magnified the image, cleaned it, enhanced it, threw it on the holostage.

"It's a Hound's field office," Donovan whispered.

A Kennel ship was nearly indestructible. Yet, *something* had cut it open and tossed it aside like an empty food packet. Méarana turned away from the suddenly blurred image.

Maggie Barnes spoke quietly to her First. "Did the scanners show any life-signs, D.Z.?"

The First Officer glanced at Méarana, then shook his head. "Hull breach. Sorry, m'lady."

Méarana turned on Donovan. "You told me from the start it would end this way. *Are you happy now?*"

The Fudir brushed his sleeve against his eyes and shook his head. "No. No, I—" The Sleuth told him it was the logical thing to expect. He listened for his other voices, but even the girl in the chiton was silent.

"Well," said Captain Barnes after a moment, "we know where *not* to land."

A handful of people could learn little about such a vast artifact from a brief visit. Even Bridget ban had intended no more than to confirm its existence and location. But the salvage laws required certain formalities, and one was to set a crew aboard the wreck. Second Officer "Fresh" Franq would take two power room technicians named DeRoche and Wrathrock to make a quick survey of what looked like the engines. Méarana would go because the least she could do was complete what her mother had started, so there was no help for it but that Donovan and the others would accompany her.

"A flying crow always catches something," Donovan told them. "We may as well watch for exotic materials, hard copy schematics, hand tools. Who knows? There might be something obvious—which is why you have to stay here, Billy. Méarana's mother was after the activation ray. 'Fire from the Sky.' Maybe we can locate the systems that power and control it."

"Be careful," Maggie B. warned them. "We know *that's* still working."

"It's a big ship," Donovan answered. "It's not as if we could break it."

Maggie shook her head. "The mucky-mucks can send fleets of experts to pick the ship clean. Before you set out to beat the odds, be sure you can survive the odds beating you."

Everyone in the Periphery romanticized the old Commonwealth. It had been an era when anything had been possible and so, in song and story, everything was. It had become an age of magic and wonder; of which little more than names had survived. Approaching the vessel, it was hard not to assume that the wildest legends were plain truth. Could such a ship have been constructed by a race any less than godlike? And this had been only one of a vast Treasure Fleet.

Yet: a Fleet now vanished, her descendants living as savages on half-civilized worlds. The hoped-for "end run" had never rescued Terra.

The 'Loons had pushed the closest—*they had almost made it*—but the Terrans had "moosed," and the desperate effort had proven in vain. No wonder the 'Loons despised Terrans, even if they had forgotten the details. If he could meet the men of the Commonwealth, Donovan wondered, would he find them as disappointing as he had the True Coriander?

Wild Bill Hallahan flew the shuttle to the ark's blasted side, well away from the active regions, and took them in through one of the open landing decks spaced down the length of the vessel. Approaching, they saw the shattered remains of boats, among which stood one in almost pristine shape. It was streamlined for atmospheric flight. "Dibs," said Wild Bill, pointing to it.

Hallahan settled the boat leaf-gentle on the landing deck, feeling for it with the skids. "No gravity," he announced. "Gotta lash her down. Wrathrock, DeRoche, come with me."

Skinsuit hoods stiffened into helmets when powered up. Donovan, Méarana, and Sofwari deployed theirs and disembarked. Second Officer Franq went to examine the flier, and the pilot and technicians joined him.

"Tao!" he heard Wild Bill exclaim. "The pilot's still in it!"

That brought Méarana and Sofwari on the double. But Donovan stayed by the boat and stepped behind the ladder and waited.

"No rush," he heard Franq say. "Just a skeleton wrapped in tin foil. That foil must be their space suit. I wonder if it generates a force field of some sort, because he's sure not dressed for a space walk."

"What was the gun for?" asked Méarana.

"Suicide," said Wild Bill. "He came back up after what happened happened and . . . lost hope. Don't know why he didn't rejoin the others on the ground. Maybe he was out'a fuel. Maybe his lover had been on board. We'll never know."

"There is a song in him, though," said the harper.

Donovan's patience was finally satisfied as first one pair of boots, then another, climbed down the ladder. He poked a gloved finger into the back of the first man. "I didn't think you could stay away, Billy."

The Confederate turned and smiled. "Of course not."

"Let me guess: you hid in the engine compartment? How did you evade your guard?"

Paulie was in the other suit. "I was the guard."

"This does raise some rather delicate questions."

"Donovan," said Billy Chins, "I have watched your back and you have watched mine for many weeks. I saved your life in the Roaring Gorge, and Méarana's during the storm surge on the Arfídnuxr. *What more can I do to prove myself?* I have been on this quest longer than anyone but you and the harper herself. Do I not deserve at least to look upon the end of it?"

Donovan sighed. "Stick with me, and don't get out of my sight."

Billy spread his hands. "Sahb! Where Billy-fella go?"

Méarana strode the ruined decks of the Vessel like the queen of High Tara. This was where Mother had meant to be, and she had come to walk those footsteps instead. She wondered if her footprints were big enough. When her mother's ship had been hulled, the air pressure had blown everything loose out into space, and that included Francine Thompson of Dangchao Waypoint, d.b.a. Bridget ban, Hound of the Kennel, R.Mh., S.hÓ., etc. There would be no funeral: no burial. Only a memorial service, with ancient words spoken over an empty box.

Their suit lamps cast a halo of soft, subtly tinted light about them. It created an eerie effect in the dark interior: broken and twisted walls and decks, cables and conduits, gaping chasms in which shadows seemed to move. Once, Méarana thought she saw another suit weirdly following them: perhaps an ancient crewman, wrapped in foil like a bonbon, drifting through the empty spaces of the Vessel until he should find his way accidentally to the void and freedom. But when she shone her spotlight on the apparition, she could not find it, and perhaps it had not been there at all.

Another time, they found a floating machine, tangled in cables like a skin-diver caught in seaweed. It had wheels and extensors that resembled arms and two lenses that gave the appearance of eyes; but the carapace was blackened and the unit dead.

Their lamps found an inscription on one of the bulkheads. It was in the Taņțamiž, and Donovan puzzled over it some before declaring that, if he guessed the sound-shifts correctly, it meant something like "Amphitheater" and the number five. Five decks from here? Amphitheater 5? Five paces this way? But the rest of the meaning had gone with the rest of the bulkhead.

Blankets and Beads tracked them and kept them informed of their position relative to the large pressurized sector. "When we find it," Donovan wondered, "how will we enter without losing the pressure?"

"Why worry?" said Billy. "You can't imagine there are people inside! Not after thousands of years."

Méarana entertained the sudden image of survivors of this ancient catastrophe; huddled in a redoubt, a civilization in a box. Would such a people commit mass suicide one day when the futility of it all came home to them, when they finally realized that they would never leave their box, that there was nowhere else they could possibly go? Or would they forget that they were even in a box and forget that universes might not have walls?

Méarana told herself it was absurd; but the notion of a spaceship the size of a small moon was just as absurd. So who could say where the line of fantasy ought to be drawn?

As they worked deeper into the Vessel, they found intact rooms and corridors, machines dead but undamaged. There was no air or power or gravity, but whatever had wrecked the Vessel's outer hull and torn up ordinary quarters and corridors had failed to penetrate this far into the ark.

Finally, they came to a door beside which small lights glimmered green and yellow and blue. What the colors meant was not clear. The Taṇṭamiž consisted of cryptic abbreviations. But that there were lights at all meant everything.

There was a button labeled ▶◀ and another labeled ◀▶. Beside them the symbol ௫ glowed green. Donovan studied all closely.

Billy coughed impatiently. "This means 'close' and that means 'open.' The symbols are universal."

"That does seem obvious," Donovan admitted. "I'm trying to decide if ௫ means 'pi.' *Pi*rāṇam means air, life, vitality, strength, power, so it might be the abbreviation for 'air.'"

Sofari said, "So the green light might mean there is air on the other side, or it may mean that the power for the door is on."

"Or there is life within," said Méarana with thumping heart.

Donovan shrugged. "Or all the above. They had words that cut crosswise through ours."

"One way to find out," suggested Sofwari.

"Maybe the rest of us should get out of the way," said Méarana. "In case pressing the button means something more serious than 'open.'"

"Umm."

"What, Debly? What!"

"If there is air under pressure in there, and the door opens, everyone standing in front of it gets blown away."

"It must be an airlock. What's the point of airtight doors with no way through them?"

"Aah," said Paulie, "enough o' this shit!" And he reached past everyone's shoulder and pressed the ◀▶ button.

Everyone flinched. The door split down its center— there had been no sign of a crack before—and they found themselves staring down a broad, brightly-lit corridor.

Donovan had a moment to register the sight. Then he braced himself.

But there was no hurricane of outpouring air.

"Magicians," he muttered. He stepped through the doorway and felt as if passing through a thick layer of gelatin. Then he was inside, and suit sensors activated. There was air around him. His helmet display read off temperature, pressure, and composition—well within the range of human atmospheres.

It occurred to him that, however long recycled, this was the atmosphere of Old Earth herself, that these very molecules had once blown in soft breezes on a free Earth.

His fingers fumbled at his helmet seals. By the time he had pulled the hood off, the others were around him and wondering at the tears that ran down his cheeks.

The ark was named *A. K. Prabhakaran*. It was the name of a person of such fabulous importance as to cause this enormous vessel to be named in his honor; but it was a name lost in an incalculable past. Warrior, politician, science-wallah, explorer . . . Even male or female. Whatever he had been, he was only the name of a ship now.

They learned the name from one of the crew.

Shortly after they had entered the pressurized sector, a multiwheeled cart with a raised front rolled down the aisle and stopped before them. The holostage flickered and the head and shoulders of a young woman appeared on the raised platform. The ymago did not have the ghost-like appearance of a normal projection, but seemed a solid body, so that the whole gave the impression of a mechanical centaur: half woman, half cart.

It spoke to them in the Taṇṭamiž, but with many words of the Murkans and the Zhōgwó and the Yurpans mixed in. Donovan learned that he could follow it, though he had to ask the thing to repeat itself several times.

"Why are ye awake at this time?" Donovan understood the thing to say. "Our planet is not yet ready."

"Who art thou, o machine, that thou mayest ask this of us?"

The ymago smiled. "I am Flight Attendant 8y493 pi-cha-ro, sri colonist; and such are my assigned duties."

"I will call you 'Peacharoo.'"

"As thou willst. This is not an alloted wake time. Hath there been a failure of thy pod?"

"And why should I not be awake?" He turned aside to tell his companions. "It says we're up past our bedtimes. I'm trying to stay outside its box."

"Be not foolish, sri colonist," the machine countered. "The planet will not be a world for another nine lakhs of hours. Thou willt be an old man before the landings begin."

"Nine lakh? Nine hundred thousand hours . . . Are those metric hours or dodeka hours?"

"Thy query signifieth naught. An hour is an hour. Which are your pods, and I will escort you to them. Do not waste your life-hours, for time spent is never to be regained."

"A Terran hour, then. Nine lakh would be, ah, about a hundred years."

Sofwari whistled. "Far less than a Gladiola ark requires to prep a planet."

"Well," Donovan told him, "a Gladiola ark is far smaller than this behemoth." He turned back to Peacharoo. "The planet Enjrun is already terraformed. We have come from there. It is time to wake the colonists and bring them down."

"I see no ecologist ratings on thy sleeve. Thou wearest not thy required bar code or insignia. Let me ask Ship's Sensors." The simulation hummed a bland ditty for a few moments. "The activation beam has been sent within the fortnight, but there is no return signal yet."

"Thou fool," said Donovan. "Thy sensors have been destroyed! The signals were sent more than a thousand years ago, but thine ears have gone deaf."

"It sorrows me to say so," said Peacharoo, "but such is not my department. If ye would please follow me?" The Attendant spun and rolled down the aisle at a walking pace.

"Tell it to take us to the control room," said Sofwari. "I'd love to know if their gravity grids are based on the same principle as ours. And the genetic data . . . Invaluable!"

Donovan gave it a try. "Peacharoo! We have an urgent message for the captain. Might thou summon him?"

The Attendant stopped. "Captain Salahuddin is no longer aboard *A. K. Prabhakaran*. He believed *End Run* successfully seeded and took many landers to the planet. But several weeks have now passed and they have neither returned nor contacted the ship. Clearly, the ecosystem is yet too immature to support life. I have exceeded my normal authority in telling thee, but may it persuade thee of thine error." The Attendant again started forward.

Several weeks . . . Donavan shrugged. "We may as well see where it's leading us." He caught up with the Attendant in a few strides. "What facility is this that we pass through? But speak slowly, that I may translate for my friends."

"This is Cold Sleep Dormitory Number 183, sri colonist. If thy friends speak neither the Taṇṭamiž nor the Murkangliš, they are in the wrong dormitory. This dormitory is reserved for Terrans. Colonists from the Lesser Worlds are housed elsewhere."

"The Lesser Worlds," said Billy Chins, confirming Donovan's suspicion that he, too, understood the Taṇṭamiž. "Would that include Dao Chetty?"

The Attendant fell silent for a moment, then the image of the girl said, "Tau Ceti is a valued and important member of the Commonwealth. They stand shoulder to shoulder with our comrades against the people of sand and iron." Peacharoo then added several more compliments in the Zhōgwó tongue.

Sofwari exclaimed over this. Like most, he believed the Commonwealth had fallen through the revolt of Dao Chetty, and that the prehumans were long vanished before humans ever went to the stars.

"I see no sleepers," said Donovan. "What section is this called that we walk through?"

"This, sri colonist, houses the local backup power and life support for this bank of dormitories. It has been activated, but I have not been informed of the reason. I am sure it is but a drill. There is no need for alarm among the colonists." The ymago actually managed to appear cheerful and reassuring. "If thou woudst return to thy pod, I will summon Attendants to escort thy friends also to theirs."

When Donovan had translated this, Méarana said, "Is *this* your artificial intelligence, Donovan? Artificial pighead, I say!"

"It's malfunctioning. What do you expect?"

"An ordinary automaton would not have disregarded a direct order," said Sofwari. "Or told you about the captain. Peacharoo passes the 'Enduring Test.' It *seems* as if we are talking to a person."

"Fash it. It seems as if we are talking to a bureaucrat! They only recite rules back at you, too. Seeming isn't being."

Donovan spoke to Peacharoo. "How long hath the emergency generator run?"

The ymago hesitated, and looked puzzled. "As much as an hour, or . . . longer. My clock synchronizeth not. Thank you for drawing my attention to this problem. I have sent a maintenance request to repair my clock. Please, do not be concerned, and follow me to your pods." Then, a moment later, "The Attendants for the other dormitories answereth not my summons. Until they arrive, I will house thy companions temporarily in this dormitory, as numerous pods are now empty."

As she said this, they passed through a portal into a vast open chamber within which floated evenly-spaced cubes in rows, columns, and layers. These vanished into the distance ahead, above, below, and to both sides. The Sleuth said, *This sector seems larger on the inside than it was on the outside.* That was impossible, of course; but here they were.

Each "cube" was a block of nested cylinders, twelve by twelve, and bore a holographic display with a letter and a number. Since Taṇṭamiž letters were themselves two-dimensional, this served to identify three-dimensional coordinates for each block. Between blocks, catwalks ran in every direction, including up and down. Sleuth estimated that the bay held as many as 50,000 cylinders.

And each cylinder held a sleeping colonist.

Donovan stared at the vast array and a great sadness overwhelmed him. The "great day" had come and gone, and they had slept through it. He wondered whether, had all the colonists made it down, there would have been enough to keep the planet from slipping into barbarism.

"And now," said Peacharoo, "ye must return to your sleep pods."

"No," said Méarana; and then using what she had picked up of the old speech, said "Panna matēn!" *I will not do it*.

A scowl of impatience crossed the ymago's face. "Must I summon the Proctors again?"

"Proctors." Paulie grunted. "If Teddy was here, I know what he'd say."

" 'That can't be good,' " said Sofwari. He turned and looked into the distance. Things moved in the shadows.

"Wait," said Donovan. "Peacharoo! *'Again'?* Was there another awakee?"

"The pods have been awakening people at random. There is no cause for alarm and maintenance is working on it. But the world is not ready for them, and they must be rehibernated. We are all anxious to establish the rear base, but 'Patience is the Watchword.' Terraformation cannot be rushed. You must trust us."

"Where did you take her—the most recent awakee?" said Donovan. "About a year ago. Red hair, golden skin; similar to my companion."

"I will access the record." Again, the ymago hummed a bland tune.

Mearana tugged at his sleeve. "My earwig is starting to pick up snatches."

"That's how neural nets learn. Careful. The Attendant is learning Gaelactic as well."

"You asked if it saw someone who looked like me."

"Yes."

Her grip tightened. "Did it? *Did it?*"

"Please board my extension," the Attendant said. "And I will take you to her."

A riding platform emerged from the Attendant's rear. It slid from no apparent opening and with no evident telescoping or unfolding. And there was no room within the Attendant to store it. Once they had boarded, Peacharoo sped off through the three-dimensional grid. Straight ahead, then left, then down. The catwalks had their own gravity grids. Whichever way they turned, they seemed to be on the level—and the whole vast chamber seemed to rotate ninety degrees. It was too much for Paulie, who lost his lunch over the side.

Bank after bank of pods flashed by. Almost faster than the eye could see.

Almost.

"Donovan. Father. They're empty. The pods are open, and they're empty."

"Peacharoo said there was room. I suppose the vacancies are where the ancestors of the Enjrunii came from."

Now and then, they passed other Attendants, some of them inactive hulks parked in special niches between pod banks or simply standing dead on the catwalks; others were active, like Peacharoo, and fussed over the equipment that fed and maintained the inhabitants of the pods.

Or used to feed and maintain them.

Not all the pods were empty. Donovan caught brief glimpses here and there into open pods and saw grinning skulls, mummified corpses, masses of corruption.

Other pods gave at least the seeming of functionality.

Lights gleamed on panels beside them, gauges displayed quantities and qualities. Peacharoo entered a sector where the pods seemed almost pristine. There, it slowed to a stop, and Donovan and the others slid gingerly off the platform. "Quite a ride," said Paulie, huffing.

Méarana found herself face-to-face with a viewing portal. Pressed against it from the inside was a woman's face, partly dissolved and stuck in a gluey mass to the glasslike material. Méarana bit down on a scream and buried her face in Sofwari's shoulder.

"An awakee," said Sofwari, "but the pod would not open. She suffocated . . . or she went mad and died in there."

She pulled away from him. "Is that supposed to comfort me? What if the same thing happened to Mother? That *artificial* intelligence stuffed her into a pod—and who knows if it was still working?"

"There is no need to be rude," said Peacharoo in Gaelactic.

Paulie grunted, but said nothing. Billy Chins was breathing hard and looking in all directions. "Sahbs," he said. "We have company."

"I guess this here's the Proctor," said Paulie.

The newcomer was taller, thinner, and boasted a multitude of arms. Its ymago wrapped wholly around it, so that—save for the wheels on which it rolled—it seemed almost human. Blue of skin, it resembled some ancient multiarmed deity. *Žiba the Destroyer,* Donovan thought.

"Here, here," it said in Gaelactic. "What's all this, now?"

Peacharoo said, "Officer, these colonists have refused to re-enter their stasis pods after I have repeatedly asked them to do so."

"We can't have that, now, can we? Sahbs, it is not safe for ye to be up and about. The planet will not be ready to sustain life for . . ." A pause. ". . . nine lakh of hours. That is one-third of a life span, and there is little for an awakee to do before Debarkation Day. Idle hands and all that, what?"

"I want to see my mother!" said Méarana. "Thousands of pods have failed. You must have noticed! I want to make certain that she is all right."

"The request seems reasonable, Attendant."

Peacharoo said, "I have brought her to her mother's pod. She can see all the lights are green."

Méarana cried, "Which is it? Show me!"

The Attendant projected a laser to highlight the next pod but two. Méarana shoved her way past Billy and Paulie and the Attendant and pressed her hands and face against the viewport of the indicated sleep-pod. Donovan stepped up behind.

"Is it her?" he asked.

"I can't see. I can't see. Peacharoo! Are there lights inside the pod so I can see if that is Mother?"

"Such filial devotion," said the Proctor, "is touching in these degenerate times."

The Attendant's laser interfaced with something in the controls. Lights inside the pod came to life, bathing the occupant in a yellowish gloom.

Méarana began to cry. Donovan wrapped an arm around her shoulder. "I never thought," he said. "I never thought we would actually find her."

"Donovan," the harper whispered in the thickest Dangchao Anglic she could muster, "wha' button wakes her oop?"

"How d'ye ken she be ainly in hyposleep?"

"An she waken oop when I press the button. If she's nae slaeping . . . An she's deid . . . She willnae wake oop."

"An she be ainly sleeping, the wrong button maun kill her."

"Aye, but I cannae lave 'er here. That would gae kill her.

Soon or efter, the pod will fail. She would dee wi'oot e'er waking . . . Or she mought wake and dee trapped like that . . . thing . . . back there."

Donovan turned to the Attendant and the Proctor. "There are certain prayers that we need to recite for her in our traditional language."

"Art thou then the sleeper's husband?" the Attendant asked in the Old Tongue.

Donovan hesitated a moment. "Yes," he said. "I am."

He had begun to bow with his arms crossed over his breast when he noticed that Méarana had touched her fingertips to her forehead, breast, and shoulders. He quickly imitated the gesture, lest he give Peacharoo an inconsistency to wonder about. "Father and Brother," he heard her say, "dinnae let the Fudir do anything glaikit."

It would take a stronger prayer than that, the Fudir thought. *Okay, Sleuth, Pedant, this is your show. There must be a manual override to wake up this one occupant. Pedant, what are the sound-shifts on those letters?*

It will be all right, said the girl in the chiton.

They will try to stop her, said the Brute, and his hand stole into a coverall pocket to grip his dazer. Inner Child watched and listened. He heard Paulie say to Billy, "They ain't gonna stuff *me* in one of those sausages."

But the part of his mind focused on the control panel found and translated what it wanted. He raised his eyes upward. "An' there be on your side of the door a blue button set in a well?" he asked in Méarana's dialect.

"Aye . . ."

"Ye maun press it whan I press this ain. On three."

"Ae. Twa. *Three*."

The Attendant cried out as they stabbed the emergency buttons, and the Proctor reached out with his arms to pull them away. "Please to be desisting, sahbs," it said. "That is a violation of Ship's Regulations. Assault against helpless sleeper."

The Proctor's three-dimensional shell flickered and broke up under Donovan's dazer, and the torso emitted a high-pitched whine. Behind him, he heard the pod door hiss as it unsealed.

The Proctor's arm knocked Méarana to the catwalk and pushed Donovan's gun aside. The image of the policeman recohered. "Assault on a Proctor is a termination offense. This is your first warning. Sahb, what are you thinking? Attendant, please restore the disturbed sleeper to her proper status."

Peacharoo tried to get past Donovan, but the Brute braced his back against the pod bank and shoved with both feet. Peacharoo skidded. He shifted his feet to the Attendant's superstructure—and his boots seemed to sink into the hologram's chest. The automaton tilted, her right wheels lifted from the catwalk.

Billy fired at the Proctor, and its image again broke up. Paulie swung his sword and clipped off the top of the projection core—and snapped his blade in two.

Donovan sidestepped as the pod door swung open behind him. The Proctor's arm let go and black smoke emerged from its casing. The Attendant toppled, wheels spinning. Somewhere, a klaxon began to hoot and a voice cried out in the Taṇṭamiž: "The Pod Bay is under assault. The Pod Bay is under assault."

Something shuddered deep within the ship. A dim, distant, low-pitched clank could be heard. And the catwalks shivered. The echoes reverberated into silence.

Paulie said in the silence, "That can't be . . ."

"Shut up," Donovan growled. He activated his comm. and called, "Franq, are you there? Speak to me." He heard nothing. "Hallahan? This is Donovan. Speak to me."

"There were no live systems in the engineering section," Méarana said nervously.

"Franq! Hallahan! *Blankets and Beads!* Anyone on the trade ship? This is urgent."

A rumble began in the depths of the Pod Bay, as of something massive rolling. There was a distant hiss.

Méarana said, "We should make our way back to where we left the shuttle."

"Right," said Sofwari. "Where was that . . ." The wallah's face was layered in despair. The Pod Bay looked the same in every direction. How far had they come? Which turns had they made? The Pedant remembered the way, but the Sleuth pointed out that they could not run as fast as Peacharoo had carried them. It might take hours to return to the entrance. *And I don't believe we have hours.*

"B-and-B, speak to me. We need guidance out of here. Lock onto our beacons and talk us to the nearest airlock or hangar deck. Speak."

A voice crackled through static. "Donovan, this is Franq. We got troubles. Almost at shuttle. Get outside. Anywhere. We'll locate you."

Donovan glanced at the now-dark Attendant. "Sorry, Peacharoo."

"How long was I asleep?"

Each of them jerked a bit at the new voice, though Donovan was startled least of all. A part of him—the Brute, he thought—had been aware of motion behind him. Méarana pushed past him, crying, "Mother! Oh, Mother!" Sofwari grinned. Billy looked at Paulie.

"I said, how long was I asleep?" She seemed remarkably alert for someone who had been but lately in a coma. By long tradition, the first words of such a one ought to be "Where am I?" But Bridget ban knew quite well where she was. She was still wearing the skinsuit in which she had been captured.

"About a year," Méarana said, "maybe a little longer." She was bouncing on the balls of her feet, suddenly looking years younger, crying, "We found you! I always knew it! I never gave up!"

Bridget ban said, "A year! What kept you?" Then she looked past her daughter, and the sardonic half-smile faded from her lips, and she said, "You!"

Donovan started to say, yeah, me; but *as swift as a black mamba striking*, Bridget ban had pulled a needler from a coverall pocket and fired.

Donovan ducked and the beam went wide.

Or it did not. Billy Chins snarled as the arm holding the dazer went numb. He ducked around the corner of the pod block. "Do it, Paulie!" he said as he disappeared. Paulie pulled his pellet gun and fired off four rapid shots.

He was a good shot, and four bullets would ordinarily have been sufficient to his purpose. But Debly Jean Sofwari had seen the hand move and had thrown himself in front of Méarana, and so the four bullets found one target.

The impact threw him backward onto his three companions. Donovan and Bridget ban leapt to either side, vaulting on the pod doors to the top of the stacks. Méarana jerked her arm forward and her knife flew from her sleeve and embedded itself in Paulie's throat.

The Wildman clawed at the knife, lost consciousness as the blood gushed out, and fell to the catwalk. His legs kicked twice, and then he was still.

Méarana knelt beside the science-wallah and bestowed the long-sought kiss on Debly's lips. His eyes stared at nothing. She thought she would miss the awkward little man with the strange enthusiasms.

Then she sprinted to where Paulie lay, pulled the knife from his throat without breaking stride, and clambered atop the pod rack, where she lay still.

She listened. She watched. Nothing moved. She might be alone in this vast abandoned ship.

"I see you've been keeping up your practice," Bridget ban said in a low voice beside her.

Méarana did not flinch. "I was coming to look for you."

"You . . . didn't have to come yourself."

"Who did you expect?"

"Little Hugh, to tell you the truth."

"Why him?"

"You liked him, back when he used to visit. I thought you would go to him for help. Not the old drunk."

"Did I guess right? I used to think it was Hugh; but it was Donovan, wasn't it?"

"Do you want it to have been him?" She peered down the aisle where Billy Chins had disappeared. "He better show himself soon."

"Why?"

"Don't you hear the rumbling down below? I hope you don't think one of those *Attendants* could stuff me in a tank."

Donovan was a little disappointed in Billy Chins, and more than a little angry with himself.

"Why didn't you see this coming?"

<I did,> said Inner Child.

I never did trust him.

"Not quite four to two . . . ," the Fudir muttered.

𝔗𝔥𝔯𝔢𝔢 𝔱𝔬 𝔬𝔫𝔢. 𝔒𝔲𝔯 𝔟𝔞𝔟𝔶 𝔱𝔬𝔬𝔨 𝔬𝔲𝔱 𝔓𝔞𝔲𝔩𝔦𝔢 𝔞𝔩𝔩 𝔟𝔶 𝔥𝔢𝔯𝔰𝔢𝔩𝔣, 𝔟𝔲𝔱 𝔖𝔬𝔣𝔴𝔞𝔯𝔦 𝔱𝔬𝔬𝔨 𝔣𝔬𝔲𝔯 𝔦𝔫 𝔱𝔥𝔢 𝔠𝔥𝔢𝔰𝔱.

"Two and a half to one," said Donovan. "Méarana doesn't have a chance against Billy."

Donovan didn't know if he had a chance, either. An old man, long out of practice. And a Hound just out of cold sleep. Separated so that they could not coordinate their moves. Billy might have the advantage.

"Brute," said Donovan, "you watch down that way with the left eye. Child, take the right eye. Sleuth, you and Pedant try to work out his strategy. Silky, you listen for anyone else coming up on top of these pods with us."

"What about me?" said the Fudir.

"Work with Sleuth. When they figure out what Billy is up to, figure out how to handle him."

"By the time the subcommittee reports are in, Bridget ban will have taken him out, packed up the harper, and abandoned us here."

"Check our chronometer, Fudir. It took us less than a beat to get ourselves organized."

"You know, yours is the persona that once worked as a Confederate courier. I was the masque, like that poor woman out at the Iron Cones."

"I know. I'm thinking, what would I be doing right now, if I were him."

"And?"

"He'll wait to ambush us," Donovan said, "from a direction we'd not expect."

From below.

When Billy had ducked around the corner, he had also ducked up or down. Donovan was as certain of this as if he had seen him do it.

𝔜𝔢𝔰. 𝔗𝔥𝔢 𝔥𝔲𝔪𝔞𝔫 𝔦𝔫𝔰𝔱𝔦𝔫𝔠𝔱 𝔦𝔰 𝔱𝔬 𝔩𝔬𝔬𝔨 𝔲𝔭 𝔣𝔬𝔯 𝔰𝔫𝔦𝔭𝔢𝔯𝔰. 𝔅𝔲𝔱 𝔱𝔥𝔢 𝔴𝔞𝔶 𝔱𝔥𝔢 𝔤𝔯𝔞𝔳𝔦𝔱𝔶 𝔤𝔯𝔦𝔡𝔰 𝔞𝔯𝔢 𝔰𝔢𝔱, 𝔥𝔢 𝔠𝔞𝔫 𝔰𝔱𝔞𝔫𝔡 𝔬𝔫 𝔱𝔥𝔢 𝔟𝔬𝔱𝔱𝔬𝔪 𝔬𝔣 𝔞 𝔠𝔞𝔱𝔴𝔞𝔩𝔨, 𝔞𝔫𝔡 𝔰𝔥𝔬𝔬𝔱 𝔲𝔭 𝔣𝔯𝔬𝔪 𝔲𝔫𝔡𝔢𝔯𝔫𝔢𝔞𝔱𝔥.

"I agree," said the Fudir, "but he'll be on one of the pod banks, like we are now."

Sleuth did some elementary calculations. *Unless he can move like the wind and climb like an Awzetchan grass monkey, Billy Chins cannot be any farther than . . .*

"There," agreed Donovan. "Brute? Fudir? This is your show."

He stood. The pod block possessed walkways, probably

for maintenance automata, that wrapped around the block like ribbons framing a gift. Gravity grids ensured that the pod block was "down," regardless which face one stood on. Commonwealth magic. Peripheral technology couldn't manage it. The gravity fields would overlap, create resonances, blow the generators.

He loped across the walkway to the other end of the block and, when he reached the end intending to leap to the next block over, the walkway stretched across the gap like Peacharoo's riding platform. He nearly stumbled in surprise.

Unless Billy has discovered this, he will expect any approach to be by the catwalks. That was some encouragement, anyway.

He crossed the next block the same way. Then he walked down the side for two levels, found the walkway running across the *underside* of the pod blocks, and hurried back the way he had come. Silky played gyroscope and maintained the original up/down orientation. To her, he was loping antipodally along the "bottom" of a block, whereas to the Brute, he was doing so across the "top."

He came at last to the block where he expected Billy to be waiting in ambush and spied him sitting cross-legged at the far end, looking down at the catwalk where he expected his quarry. From the point of view of anyone fleeing down the catwalk from Bridget ban's cocoon, he would be firing *up* from underneath.

When Donovan had crept closer, Billy spoke. "One direction, I could not constantly watch; and so from that direction you have come. Yet you did not slay me."

"I'm not a back shooter."

"One of your few weaknesses. Come sit beside me, brother."

Donovan crouched on Billy's left. "Brother? You and I are nothing alike."

Billy did not turn his head. "I did not mean bio-brother."

"Nor did I."

"No. We are sons of the same trainer—years apart, but the semen of his mind has generated us. You are the prodigal son, and I the faithful. You have gone off and lived among the pigs."

"It wasn't that bad. Really." After a moment, he said, "*You* killed the jawharry."

Billy tilted his head in thought; then resumed his watch of the catwalk. "After I overheard you and the harper in the restaurant on Harpaloon, curiosity sent me to question the woman. But she knew nothing. The effort was wasted."

Donovan heard a distant clatter, like a wheel rolling along jointed rails. It seemed louder than before. "Yes," he said. "Such a waste."

"Not so much of a such. In the eternity of the universe, what is a life but an eye-blink. What matter, then, a few years more or less?"

"Yet you saved Méarana on the endarooa."

"Am I a sociopath? Do I kill for no reason? The harper drove our quest, and I wished to see what lay at its end. And saving her caused you to trust me a little bit more. My duty is to report to Those what they need to know, not to slaughter unsuspecting Leaguesmen."

"Although you do that, too."

Billy shrugged. "Sometimes. When needful."

"When Bridget ban recognized you."

The Confederate nodded. "Yes. That was one of the times."

"You could have bluffed it out. Méarana would have vouched for you. You panicked. Listen."

Above them, from the depths of the ship, came the sounds of shingling metal, like a wind chime in a blustery gale.

"Something is coming," Donovan said. "You might make

it out of here if we all work together. You'll never make it alone."

Billy Chins sighed. "Brother Donovan, from the moment I saw this ship and learned of the *secret road*, was there ever a chance that I would return to my masters?"

"We could have arranged . . ."

"A comfortable prison? No, thank you. There are simpler ways to silence tongues. If you are too squeamish, others are not. I judged the moment my best opportunity, and seized it."

"And yet you fought by my side at Roaring Gorge and in the Pit atop Oorah Mesa."

The Confederate shrugged. "I thought then that I might yet warn the Lion's Mouth. Now, if I cannot inform my masters, at the very least I can prevent you from informing yours. If you and the Hound die, I count my life cheap."

"And the trade ship?"

"She must not take word back."

"And the harper?"

Billy hesitated. "It cannot be helped."

Donovan sighed. "I will not let that happen."

"I know. If only you had remained a loyal man."

"If only you had become a better one."

One does not chat with Naga the Cobra without a vigilant eye on his motion, for the words are but a screen to lull the attention. Inner Child had been keeping watch through the scarred man's right eye and saw Billy's hand move perhaps before Billy knew he had moved it. The Brute seized the gun arm and deflected the aim, although the umbra grazed him; and that gave Billy the opening to deflect Donovan's own return blast.

Locked in embrace like eager lovers, the two men toppled to the decking, and a swift sequence of moves and countermoves passed between them. Hands, knees, feet, a head butt. Then Billy smacked Donovan's hand on the maintenance walkway, and the scarred man's dazer skittered out of reach.

They fought in silence, only grunts and gasps escaping their lips, for only fools waste breath in taunts. They rolled, still embraced, over the edge of the pod block.

And they were "atop" the side of the tanks. Donovan glanced at the catwalk and barked, "Hurry!"

Billy turned his head, realized the trick immediately, but immediately was too late. Instead of holding off Billy's gun, Dononan yanked and tucked it between their two bodies, pressing the muzzle against the Confederate.

This close, the neural blast was overpowering. Billy spasmed. His legs splayed like two logs and his head threw back. Blood oozed from between his clenched teeth.

Donovan, caught in the umbra, went numb. He rolled to the side; but it was the gravity grid and not volition that moved him. Inner Child cried out soundlessly. Sleuth could not form a coherent thought. Random memories and imaginings flickered through his consciousness.

A young girl in a chiton squatted above him on her heels and with her arms wrapped around her knees. *The others,* she said, *will now have a chance.*

He saw the face of Bridget ban, and she smiled as she used to smile years ago. He blinked and it was Méarana, not Bridget. Then even the tingling in his limbs faded, and there was no sensation at all, and darkness had him.

Lucia Thompson, d.b.a. Méarana of Dangchao, mistress of the harp, turned to her mother, feeling once more a child, but also impossibly old, and buried her face in Bridget ban's hair and shoulders. "It wasn't supposed to end like this," she said. At her feet, Donovan and Billy lay like lovers.

The Hound pulled her away and shook her. "It isn't ended yet," she said.

The ship's AI had come awake, and had dispatched the

same monster that she had encountered once before. Slinky-Chinky, she had called it, for it moved fluidly with the sound of brass coins falling onto a plate.

"Lucy!" she said sharply to the weeping girl. "We must get to my ship. Time afterward for weeping, if there is time for anything at all. There's his dazer. Hand it to me."

"Your ship is wrecked, Mother. And how can we find our way to the shuttle I came in?"

"Fash it, girl! I can find my ship, whether she can fly or no. And you can have your shuttle meet us there. Nothing is lost until all is lost, and that time is not yet." The Hound unfastened a pocket and pulled out a flat instrument. "This way."

Méarana brushed her hand against the Fudir's cheek. "Good-bye, Father . . . ," she said.

Bridget ban scowled and slapped the slack face of the man on the deck. It rocked to the side, and the bright red of her palm glowed on his skin. "That is for all the years since!"

"Mother! Why did you do that?"

"Because he can't feel it now." She stared at the palm-print. "Come, take his left side. He's a used-up old man. He can't be all that heavy."

Méarana and Bridget ban lifted Donovan to his feet and wrapped his arms around their shoulders. The head lolled on Bridget ban's shoulder and she shrugged it off onto her daughter.

"Is he . . . ?"

"Enough to show red when he's slapped. That is a feat few dead men master. Run in step with me. Slinky-Chinky will come along the catwalks. If we stay atop the tanks, it cannae reach us. But when we cross the space from one block to another, it will have a shot. And remember, the catwalks run in three directions."

"I'm not afraid to die, Mother, if I'm at your side."

The Hound laughed. "And terrified at any other time? It's nae death ye risk, bairn. It will stun ye and stuff ye like sausage into one of yon pods. I will shoot you myself before I allow that to happen."

Méarana did not have her harp with her, but her voice was true and she sang a running song while she and her mother loped across the tops of the sleep tanks, holding Donovan between them. She maintained an easy gait, holding his arm around her neck with her left, and holding the belt of his coveralls with her right, lifting his feet slightly above the ground. She did not know how long she and Mother could carry him; but she did not know how long she could not carry him, either.

They stopped to rest and catch their breath, and listened to the metallic sounds of their pursuer draw ever closer. Bridget ban had set her beacon to respond with sharper pings as they drew nearer to where her field office lay. Méarana contacted Franq and told him where to rendezvous.

"Not a beat too soon," Number Two said. "Wrathrock is bad hurt, but we secured the shuttle and we are now outside the ship. What *are* those things?"

"Proctors," Méarana told him. "The ship is delusional. Her internal clock is disrupted; her sensors scrambled. She thinks we are wakened sleepers—and you are boarders."

"Can't gainsay her on that account," said the officer. "We *are* a boarding party."

As they resumed their flight, Donovan began to run on his own. It was a peculiar and intensely focused sort of running and when Méarana and Bridget ban let go, he jogged ahead for a few steps, then turned and awaited direction.

"Is that you, Brute?" the harper asked; and the man nodded dumbly.

"Did Silky revive you? She's got all the glands, right?" Again a nod.

"Are the others okay?"

The Brute placed his hand about three feet off the ground, palm flat and level to the ground. Then he spread his hands and shrugged.

"Inner Child is awake, but you don't know about the others?" Another nod.

"Another day," said Bridget ban just before leading them off again, "if there is another day, you will have to explain that, if there is an explanation."

They had reached the edge of yet another block when the Brute paused, crouched, and held his hand up. Bridget ban went to her knees in an instant; Méarana, a moment later. The metallic jingling had waxed and around the corner of the catwalk came a monster.

It was a machine, like the Attendant and the Proctor, but unlike any machine Méarana had seen before. A centipede of metal hoops, each self-powered, yet all marching forward in rough uniformity. The lead ring bore the seeming of a face. Partly that was the spotlight eyes and the grill where a mouth might be; partly too, the fringe of antennae and sensors that so resembled a bristling mane.

As it passed each intersection, rings scattered clattering and clinging down the four intersecting catwalks—left, right, up, and down. At the same time, other rings, scattered at the previous intersection, rejoined the main body. The whole seemed in a continual state of dissolution, on the verge always of breaking apart, and yet, despite the comings and goings of its constituent rings, maintaining its identity.

Bridget ban consulted her beacon. "This way," she whispered, pointing forward and to the right. "Yon beastie does nae yet stand 'tween us and my ship."

Méarana tugged the Brute on the sleeve, held a finger to her lips, and pointed. The Brute nodded and slipped off in silence.

"Will the rest of him e'er come back?" Bridget ban murmured.

"That may depend on how the umbra affected the cortex. Had the muzzle twisted the other way . . ." The harper shivered. "Did you see the way he looked at you?"

"I had a dog that used to look at me that way," Bridget ban answered.

"When did you ever have a dog? What happened to him?"

"He went rabid and I shot him."

It was a mad race in three dimensions. They stayed atop the pod blocks, but in places the extensible bridge connecting one block to the next failed, and they slipped down to the regular catwalks. Without Bridget ban's locator beacon they would quickly have gotten lost.

It was while on the catwalks that one of Slinky-Chinky's scouts found them. It rounded the corner just ahead of them and instantly, lights began to flash on its circumference and the sounds of activity came from below. Through the gaps in the catwalks they saw the main snake two levels below them turn abruptly and head up the next intersection.

The Brute meanwhile had taken his dazer, which Bridget ban had restored to him, and fired at anything that might have been a brain-case on the ring that had found them. The ring went dark, and the three of them retreated around the corner and scrambled like monkeys atop the tanks. There, they lay prone underneath the maintenance track, in the V where the cylinders nestled together.

In less than a minute the sound of clinking rings was all around them, as segments ran up and down the catwalks, joining and splitting and rejoining. *It's as if the tanks themselves are invisible to them,* Méarana thought. *A flaw in their instructions? A malfunction from age or from damage? Not my department?*

Finally, the sounds of pursuit faded into another sector, and they crawled from under the maintenance track and raced for the vestibule. There, they paused to activate their helmets before cycling through the air lock.

Orienting themselves on Bridget ban's locator, they quickly made their way through an open landing bay to the hull and Bridget ban's wrecked field office. There, they called for the *Blankets and Beads'* shuttle.

Wild Bill brought the boat in low, with the outer lock door already open and came to a hover only a few strides away. Méarana and Bridget ban hustled Donovan inside and Wild Bill was pulling away even before the lock had closed.

"Close call," said Méarana as they found seats in the cabin.

Wild Bill did not turn around. "Still is."

The shuttle bucked and twisted as the pilot used the gravity impellers to hopscotch across the *Prabhakaran's* hull. Franq sat in the copilot's seat and the two able spacers were in the back. One of them, badly injured, lay across a bench while the other treated him.

"Watch it, Bill," Franq said. "Those portals are opening."

"That can't be good," Donovan muttered. Then he shook himself and looked around.

Méarana noticed, and said, "Fudir? Are ye back wi' us?" And at the scarred man's uncertain nod, threw her arms around his neck. He winced.

"Silky must have put us in some sort of overdrive. I'm weak as a kitten." He looked around and saw Bridget ban and for a moment he did not speak. The red hair seemed lighter than when he had last known her, or the golden skin darker. "Billy?"

"Coagulated," the Hound said. "What did you do, push your dazer right up against him? That's a fool thing to try. The backlash of the umbra . . ."

"It seemed like a good idea at the time. That dazer was going to be pointed somewhere. I preferred him to me. We debated the issue some."

The shuttle swerved suddenly. The deckhand—De-Roche—cursed.

"Something behind those portals. Weapons, I think," Franq said. "I think we woke something up."

"The Artificial Intelligence," said Donovan.

"Father, if that Attendant was artificially intelligent, the concept has been quite oversold."

"No, Lucia," Donovan answered. "Peacharoo was no more intelligent than my little finger." The which he held up in illustration. "But you do have to ask what was wiggling it."

Lights in the craft flared and went dark. Wild Bill expressed his dissatisfaction with this and his hands danced in command. Emergency lighting returned. "Missed us," he said.

DeRoche, tending to his mate, muttered, "I'd hate to see a hit, then."

"Barnsey's bringing the BB to meet us," the pilot announced. "Hangar deck is open to vacuum. Locking in—mark."

"Is that wise?" Bridget ban wondered. "To bring a larger target into range?"

"*Prabhakaran*'s clock is malfing," Donovan said. "It thinks it's still activating the terraformation packages. When the clock resets, it loops around and does it all over again."

Wild Bill, having locked in on his landing target, turned

in his seat. "That's nice, Donovan. But how does that make her a poor shot?"

"Velocity is distance over time. If her timing is off, so is her estimate of velocity. Otherwise, she'd have hit us more than once by now."

"Which means," said Wild Bill, swinging back to his panel, "she could aim at our nose and hit our engines instead. Either way, we're soup."

"And if yon is the trade ship ye've spoken of," said Bridget ban pointing to the forward viewscreens, "even a miss would still hit something."

Donovan grunted. "I used to think the *B and B* was big."

As the shuttle entered the hangar, Wild Bill put her down hard to the deck. The gravity snaps engaged and held her fast, killing her forward momentum. The hangar doors closed and air dumped in—and with the air came the sound of klaxons. Alfven warnings. The *Blankets and Beads* was preparing to grab space to yank itself away from *Prabhakaran*.

Donovan pushed the others aside to reach the air lock. Bridget ban called after him, "There is no place to run to this time, Fudir." But the Terran popped the door, dropped to the deck, and ran to the intercom on the hangar wall, where he called the bridge.

Maggie B's face showed. "What is it, Fresh?" Then she scowled. "You! Get off my horn. You're not crew."

"No, I'm your charter. When you yank space, turn about and head for *Prabhakaran*'s dead side. If you pull forward, she can still shoot you out of the sky."

"Those little pop guns . . ."

"*That is Commonwealth tech!* You have not seen a tenth of what that ship can still do. The AI is awake now and thinks she's defending herself against attack! The apertures on the damaged side are fused shut. It can't fire from that quarter."

The captain's lips compressed into a thin line. "Every time you show up," she said, "I run into trouble."

"I've only shown up in your life twice."

"Let's not make it three." She turned from the screen. "D.Z., right about on the alfvens. Engage at fifty. Full power. Five tugs."

By then the others had joined him. Wrathrock was being carried aboard on a floater by the ship's medico. Franq, Hallahan, and DeRoche had rushed off to their emergency stations. Bridget ban nodded at the now-blank intercom. "Smart advice," she said. "I expect you are correct."

"Apology accepted. Come on, let's get to the control room."

Méarana led the way and Bridget ban followed. Donovan brought up the rear. Halfway through the tube that connected the shuttle module with the control module, the alfven klaxon hooted a second time—the short-long, short-long warning that engagement was immanent.

They grabbed railings and stanchions, and for an instant the ship seemed to stretch like taffy along a skewed axis. Most captains did not engage alfvens this far down a sun's gravity well. But *Blankets and Beads* carried survey-class alfvens and, against escape from the ship defense batteries of *A. K. Prabhakaran*, what did a few burnt-out capacitors matter?

Blankets and Beads skipped across the face of the Commonwealth ark in quantum jumps. Donovan entered the control room in time to see clusters of antennae on the derelict vessel twitch in unison, like grass flustered by a spring breeze.

And one of the cargo modules on the *B and B* exploded into vapor.

The ship lurched at the impact, her center of gravity suddenly relocated, her angular momentum abruptly changed.

Ripper Collins, in the pilot's saddle, cursed. D.Z. bellowed orders to damage control. "Was anyone in Cargo C? Was anyone in . . . ? Ma'am! Automatic vacuum doors closed on all connecting tubes. No one lost. Princess Wennawa reports her party is shaken but unhurt."

Wild Bill said, "Raising the dead side. Defensive batteries are falling below the ship's horizon."

A certain amount of tension drained out of the crew; but Bridget ban said, "We are only assuming that the defenses on this side were slagged."

Maggie B. turned to look at her. "I'll ask who the hell yuh are when I have time. Meanwhile, in my control room, yuh have the right to remain silent. Time for milk and cookies later. Full speed, Mister ad-Din, directly away from that adolescent fantasy."

"Full speed, aye, ma'am."

The captain settled back in her seat as D.Z. gave orders to DeRoche and Collins. Flint Rhem turned from his astrogation station. "Activity on the near side. I'm putting it on screen four"

Barnes leaned forward again. Missile port shutters and energy projector blisters, long fused shut, struggled to open. "Too close," Barnes muttered. She slapped her comm. "Duckie! How long before those alfvens are recharged? . . . Not good. I'll need a tug a mighty soon. I'll take thirty percent when yuh can give it to me. Out. D.Z., how's the helm?"

"We're a trade ship, Maggie. We don't turn on a dime."

"I'll take quarters. Give me what we have."

Moments passed, and none of the shutters snapped open. Maggie Barnes began to relax. "She can't fire."

There was a sudden flare deep within the derelict ship. Something buckled and part of the ship seemed to cave in on itself.

"She thinks the gun ports are open," whispered Bridget ban.

"Her sensors are slagged on this side," said D.Z. "How is she aiming?"

"She's not. She's firing blind. Expect a broadside."

A. K. Prabhakaran suddenly lit up like a candaleria. She glowed a serene and lovely orange. Radiances leaked from the edges of ports and from open hangar decks. Donovan thought of sunlight striking through gaps in the clouds.

And then *Prabhakaran* herself was a cloud—a bright, hot nebula of gasses that for a time held the shape of the ship she had been, and then began to disperse. The ark had been large enough that its own gravity would hold much of the debris together and someday it would congeal into a strange metaloceramic asteroid.

With traces of organic chemicals mixed throughout.

Good-bye, Billy, Donovan thought. *Sofwari. Paulie. Good-bye, nameless thousands of Terran colonists, dreaming of new lives on new worlds. Good-bye, Peacharoo.*

He sighed. "Damn," he said.

Méarana looked at him; took his hand. "What?"

Donovan nodded at the screen. "We broke it."

XVII WHERE HEARTS ARE

Praisegod Barebones looks up from the inventory that he is reconciling to see the scarred man enter the Bar of Jehovah and blink in the dimness. He raises his hand in salute.

"You came back," he says.

The scarred man grunts. "I could not bear our separation any longer."

"You were too wicked even for the paynim beyond our protected skies," the Bartender guesses.

"I saw wickedness even you might blanch to hear, brother Barebones."

"I am the Bartender. I hear so many confessions you might be surprised what I blanch to hear."

The scarred man sketches the ghost of a smile. "A bowl of uiscebeatha."

"I would hardly blanch at that, friend Fudir. My uisce sales suffered horribly in your absence."

The scarred man says nothing, and returns to his former niche in the wall. He wonders if anyone had sat here during his absence. He wonders if anyone knows he has returned.

The Bar is never empty, it is never at rest; but at midafternoon it approaches a pause. The sun casts a nimbus of white light through the front windows, giving those at the tables in the barroom an imprecision of outline, a faerie appearance. It reminds him of how the sun had dawned inside *A. K. Prabhakaran.*

Praisegod brings the bowl himself and sets it down. "You still owe a tab," he points out.

The scarred man pulls a chit from his blouse and shows it to him. It is a marvelous imitation of a Kennel chit. The Bartender has never seen a finer copy. But it does not glow when handled, as genuine chits do.

"Ah," mumbles the scarred man. "I had forgotten. The account is closed." He rummages in his scrip and pulls out Gladiola Bills.

"Friend," says Praisegod, placing himself discreetly between the money and curious eyes, "far be it from me to lecture the sons of this world on prudence, but don't flash a wad like that in here."

The scarred man presses a wad upon him.

"I almost hate to accept these," Praisegod says of the

Bills. "Your tab was your immortality. It bid fair to outlive you. If I close it out . . . Well," he continues after a bleak glance from his customer, "what happened to that harper you left with? Some of our patrons have asked after her."

"She has gone home to spend time with her mother."

"Has she now? Will you go visit her there?"

"She asked me to. Her mother was less certain."

The scarred man sits in the niche and drinks. He misses his inner voices. He knows that Inner Child is watching the door, is watching the barroom, is watching each of the other patrons. He knows the Pedant is mulling over lessons learned on this most recent scramble. But their voices are no longer those of strangers. They speak with his own voice, for they are now fully him as well as fully themselves.

Don't worry, Donovan. We're still here when you need us.

The scarred man smiles a little at that, and takes another drink.

I hear ye claimed to be my husband, Donovan buigh, Bridget ban had said on the way back to Gatmander.

It was one of those shipboard romances, he had answered. *You may have forgotten.*

I remember it too well, Donovan buigh. And I remember the aftermath.

Donovan had nodded toward Méarana, who had been playing her harp for the crew. *You could have treated her better, despite all that.*

Are ye the doting father now? I don't recall seeing ye much around Clanthompson Hall.

She doesn't recall seeing you there much, either.

It had been a long, silent transit back to Gatmander after that and, for Méarana, a bewildering one. She kept trying to build a bridge between them, to fulfill some fantasy that she had long entertained. But there is no bridge to span an ocean.

Greystroke and Little Hugh had been waiting on Gatmander, and Bridget ban and her daughter had passage back to High Tara.

Sorry, Donovan, Greystroke had lied, *but there's no more room in my ship.* He had approved Donovan's Kennel chit for passage back to Jehovah and for a generous consultation fee for protecting the harper. But he had sensed that there might still be a possibility for him and had moved quickly to seize it.

Don't feel too badly, Fudir, Little Hugh had told him. *You can't lose what you never had.*

Perhaps not, the scarred man tells his uisce. But in a peculiar sense, he had had it for a time, in the mind of Lucia Thompson, and that had been enough to make it real, for a dream strong enough may leak from one mind to another.

The sun has dimmed and the windows in the front of the Bar have darkened. The shutters have been closed against the creeping night. Into the bar steps Bikhram. There is no particular moment when one may say, "He has come," but there is a moment when one realizes, "He is here." It is the sort of skill that serves well a man whose profession is to enter places and to leave with sundry of its contents.

He represents the Committee of Seven, and sits himself at the table, positioning himself so that he, too, does not show his back to the room. A glass of masaala paal appears before him, spiced with clove and saffron. Bikhram tastes it and sprinkles some badaam powder into it from an envelope he carries in his blouse.

The scarred man watches him and, after a time, passes him a red envelope. "These are seeds," he says, "of the True Coriander, found only on the Wild World of Enjrun, and brought there by the Terrans of the Treasure Fleet itself.

Perhaps they will germinate in the soil of the Corner; perhaps they will not."

"You are a man of many humors, Fudir. Wild Worlds! The Treasure Fleet! Perhaps your grandmother's ancient recipe, passed on in secret?"

"Mock if you wish, Bikhram. It is not much of a such, but it is the coriander. Why not a fairy-tale origin for a fairy-tale spice?"

"Harimanan saw you earlier today. He said you sat down as if you had never left. But you have not yet come into the Corner."

"Everything that happens in the city is seen and heard in the Corner. I have only to wait and the Corner will come to me. What word do the Seven send?"

"Six of the Seven, at least. Denzel is in the wind. The Proctors wish to speak to him, but he does not wish to speak to them."

"He is a man of few words."

"One of those words concerns a shipment arriving in three days from Valency. Hizzoner, who governs wisely the Terran Corner of Valency, has noted several containers of drifting jewels, the sort from which moistened fingers may pull sweet music, are to be loaded and transshipped through Jehovah to Die Bold."

"Die Bold," says the scarred man.

"Yes, and Hizzoner says that among so many cartons, one or two may hardly be missed. Perhaps drizzle jewels, which precipitate in our own Arrat Mountains, cheap as glass here in the Tarako Sarai, but dearer on Die Bold and Friesing's World, may insinuate themselves in their place."

"Hardly to the loss of the Die Bolders," says the scarred man, "but much to the gain of the Corner. What is required?"

"Not so much of a such. The jewels must walk with the

gods, a few trifling documents must alter their appearance. A few records, hard and soft, must quiet the uneasiness that would otherwise disturb the peace of mind of others."

"It is something to think on," the scarred man tells him.

He thinks on it after Bikhram has gone. He is a man of some wealth now. The gratitude of the Kennel has been considerable, and once the parking stone jewelry becomes a regular item, the consortium on Dancing Vrouw will make him wealthier still.

He had stopped on High Tara on his way back, where he had tried to see Bridget ban, but had succeeded only in seeing Zorba de la Susa.

The Old Hound told him that Bridget ban and Méarana had already left for Dangchao Waypoint. But he had gifted him with a considerable fee, plus a bounty for the death of the one called Billy Chins. Donovan had accepted the fee, but for reasons he himself did not entirely understand, had declined the bounty. Zorba had told him that, the mission being accomplished, he no longer held his life as collateral against its failure. By then, it no longer seemed to matter to Donovan.

"You have but one more task in front of you," the aged man had said; but he would not say what it was. "If you need instruction on it, it is not the task for you." He had added only that failure this time would be its own punishment.

In three days, the Terrans of the Corner would highjack several containers of fabulous drifting jewels from Valency and substitute drizzle jewels from Jehovah, altering the invoices to suit. It was the sort of scramble that had once occupied his time. But he now sees very little point in it. It is not his newfound wealth that has changed him, although he does foresee a future highjacking in which he might divert the income from his parking stone imports from his own pocket into . . . his own pocket. There is an irony to that prospect that pleases him. If one is to steal, it is best to steal from those who deserve it.

On his left, seated at his table, sits a young girl in a chiton. She says nothing, but looks at him with head cocked and manages to shrug without moving a muscle.

In the end, the scarred man sighs and rises from his seat. Praisegod watches him go with sad bassett eyes.

Outside, the scarred man turns his footsteps to the Jehovah Spaceport and enters the Terminal building, where he finds the kiosk for the Hadley Lines. There, he notes that *Jezebel Hadley* will depart High Jehovah Orbit in two days, inbound to the Old Planets with stops at Die Bold, Old 'Saken, and Abyalon, but with a flyby drop-off at Dangchao Waypoint and other byworlds. The ship's name brings a smile to his face. An omen! He books a third-class ticket—he still has his pride—and arranges with the concierge to pick up his luggage from the Bar.

"Dangchao," the concierge says. "Looking to simplify your life, eh?"

"Complicate it, I think. Maybe, I'll herd Nolan's Beasts."

The concierge laughs at the mental image of the old, hook-chinned man astride a pony in the Out-in-back whirling a bola above his head while he chases after a maverick. But the scarred man does not laugh, and there is something in the not-laughing of the scarred man that smothers the laughter of others.

When he leaves the Terminal and turns onto Greaseline Street a shadow detaches itself from other shadows and falls into step beind him. How quickly wealth whispers its presence! But before he can act he feels against his spine the now familiar shape of a dazer muzzle.

"Watch out for the backflash on the umbra," he says aloud.

"Soo, Doonoovan, my friend," whispers a voice twenty years from his past. "It has been loong years between oos."

He turns, and it is Ravn Olafsdottr: still slim, ebony-black, blond-haired. Her dazer's aperture seems much wider than when seen from more benign angles.

"There is a struggle in the Lion's Mouth," she says in unaccented Confederal Manjrin. "The names that were never forgotten have been remembered. Your duty is to come with me."

She plucks the Dangchao ticket from his hand and flicks it to the ground. "Coome along Doonoovan. Dooty is a bitch, is she noot?"

TOR

Voted
#1 Science Fiction Publisher
20 Years in a Row

by the *Locus* Readers' Poll